3 FEB 98/18

D0933732

THE QUICK AND THE DEAD

Also by Alison Joseph

Sacred Hearts
The Hour of Our Death

THE QUICK
AND THE DEAD

Alison Joseph

HEADLINE

Copyright © 1996 Alison Joseph

The right of Alison Joseph to be identified as the Author of
the Work has been asserted by her in accordance with the
Copyright, Designs and Patents Act 1988.

First published in 1996
by HEADLINE BOOK PUBLISHING

10 9 8 7 6 5 4 3 2 1

All rights reserved. No part of this publication may be
reproduced, stored in a retrieval system, or transmitted,
in any form or by any means without the prior written
permission of the publisher, nor be otherwise circulated
in any form of binding or cover other than that in which
it is published and without a similar condition being
imposed on the subsequent purchaser.

All characters in this publication are fictitious
and any resemblance to real persons, living or dead,
is purely coincidental.

British Library Cataloguing in Publication Data

Joseph, Alison
The quick and the dead
1. English fiction – 20th century
I. Title
823.9'14 [F]

ISBN 0-7472-1627-4

Typeset by
CBS, Felixstowe, Suffolk

Printed and bound in Great Britain by
Mackays of Chatham PLC, Chatham, Kent

HEADLINE BOOK PUBLISHING
A division of Hodder Headline PLC
338 Euston Road
London NW1 3BH

For Tim, as ever,
and in memory of my father, to whom I owe so much.

ACKNOWLEDGEMENTS

I would like to thank Sarah Dobson IBVM and Ex-Detective Sergeant Bob Hinde, again. Also Detective Superintendent Ivan Dibley and Ian 'Chas' Charles. Thanks are also due to Tim, Becca and Phil at Road Alert, and everyone who was at the Fairmile camp on the A30 in June 1995. Thanks, too, to the people of Essex Record Office for allowing the fictional world to intrude on their normal life.

Chapter One

'What do you mean, she's gone? Gone where?'

The boy was perched on the kitchen unit, swinging his legs.

'Dunno, miss. She just said she was goin', din't she.'

'My name's Agnes.'

'Agniz then.'

With each swing of his legs the heels of his scruffy trainers made a heavy rubber thump against the cupboard door.

'You mean she went out for the evening?'

He shrugged, sniffed, thumped his heels again. Agnes noticed the marks his shoes were leaving on the white melamine. She grabbed him by the shoulders. 'Do you mean she's walked out of here? For good?'

'P'raps. She din't say. She 'ad a bag, though.'

'For God's sake, tell me. What were her last words?'

He screwed up his nose, sniffed again. 'She said she'd be safer out of 'ere. Somethin' like that. Can I go now?'

The boy slithered off the work surface and out of the door. Agnes heard shouting in the corridor as he joined the other hostel kids, the noise of the television being turned up in the beige and battered room they called the lounge. Safer out of here. Agnes took a cloth and started dabbing at the marks left by his shoes. We've let her down, she thought. I knew this would happen.

'I told you, Julius, I said she'd go. She didn't trust us any more. All this bloody prevaricating, those half-wit social workers—'

'All we know is that Sam has absconded. She may come back.' Julius sat in his favourite chair in the little office attached to the church of St Simeon's where he was priest. It was a humid July

1

evening, and the leaded windows behind him were dull with the last of the daylight.

'She won't, Julius, I know she won't. Would you stay here if you were her? She's found by the police, soliciting in the West End. She's brought to the hostel, and we tell her it's a safe house, where we can work with her to sort out what she's run away from, so that she doesn't have to go back there. So she calms down a bit, begins to trust us, finally discloses all that stuff about her god-awful family – and then, what do we do? We get pea-brained bloody social workers involved so that they can send her straight back there—'

'That's not true, Agnes. No one was going to send her back. The Social Services team—'

'What about that case meeting yesterday? She told me afterwards that she'd asked everyone, am I going back? And no one in that meeting could promise that she wouldn't.'

'That's not true, Agnes – if you'd been there you'd have realised—'

'If I'd been there I'd have given her my word there and then, that no one was going to send her back to that mother and that stepfather. No one. How could you schedule that meeting without me?'

'I didn't know you were going to be summonsed by your superiors all of a sudden.'

Agnes got up and began to pace the tiny office. Julius watched her, his eyes a piercing blue behind his half-lenses. Nearly twenty years, he thought, since those early days in France, when he was a curate and she was a young married woman locked into a life of terror and despair with her husband, Hugo Bourdillon. Julius shuddered as he remembered the night when Hugo's violence had almost cost Agnes her life. Nearly twenty years, he thought, watching her restless pacing, since he'd rescued her, since he'd arranged for her to come to London and join her first community. And in a way she'd hardly changed. No longer that cowed young woman, no longer shadowed by fear, of course; but he saw now the same passion, the same intensity, the same strength and faith, that he'd recognised in her then.

'I'm so angry, Julius.'

'I know.'

2

'Just because I had to see my Provincial that day—'

Julius sensed something in her tone. He wondered what had happened at the meeting. 'I'm sorry,' he began.

Agnes shook her head. 'It's not your fault. If it's anyone's fault, it's mine.'

Still the same compulsion to blame herself, thought Julius, whether justified or not. 'It's not your fault either,' he said, quietly.

'Oh God. She's only just sixteen.' Agnes sat down at the desk and leaned her head on her hands. Outside it began to rain, a warm drizzle, softly rattling the window panes. Julius touched her hand gently with his own. After a moment Agnes lifted her head, smiled briefly at him, ruffled his soft white hair and stood up.

'Where are you going?'

'Out.'

'Where?'

'To look for her, of course.'

'In this?'

Agnes picked up her coat.

'But where do you think—' Julius began.

'The obvious places. The West End. Kings Cross – she had friends down there.'

'She'd have more sense—'

'Look, Julius. Compared to her stepfather, Kings Cross is a lovely warm comfy place. And safer than here.'

She's glad it's raining, thought Julius, as the door closed behind her. The colder and wetter the night, the better she'll feel. Mortification of the flesh, he thought, taking off his little glasses and polishing them absently. Still the same old Agnes.

At three in the morning, Agnes was perched on a bar stool in a tiny cappuccino bar behind Leicester Square, warming her hands round a large cup of coffee. The rain had eased off, and there was a fragile stillness outside, fragmented from time to time by shouting revellers, passing taxis and the occasional police car siren. Two young women teetered pass the glass door with wide, mascara'd eyes. Agnes made as if to follow them to ask, yet again, Sam? Samantha? Sam Whittaker? She sighed and sipped her coffee. Needles in bloody haystacks, she thought. She could see in the mirror two hollow-eyed young men glancing nervously at the door, saw them stiffen as someone came through the door and approached their table. 'You seen 'im? Eh? You seen 'im?'

The two boys shook their heads, panic in their eyes.

'You diss me, someone roun' 'ere goin' ter get wasted, you hear me?'

The young men talked in low, pleading voices. Agnes felt suddenly weary. Behind her, the spiky nervous conversation; in her mind, still, the endless stream of faces as she'd searched for Sam. Bleached hair, black-circled eyes, dilated pupils, nervous, twitching mouths chewing chipped nails down to the quick.

'Nah, no one called Sam 'ere. Nah.'

And then the men, some scuttling for the shadows, the others pushy. 'You 'eard the gel. No one called Sam. Now fuck off.'

The conversation behind her had eased, and the man got up to leave. 'Respec', my man, respec'.'

The two young men were left sitting over their cans of Coke. Agnes passed a couple of coins to the jumpy Italian-looking man behind the bar and left, in time to see a sleek BMW with darkened windows drive off into the night. She headed down to Trafalgar Square in search of a cab. The pavements glistened; a dirty breeze twitched the litter into sodden heaps. At Charing Cross the cab-driver sighed heavily when given her address in Southwark.

Agnes let herself into her flat and switched on all the lights. She poured herself a whisky and sat on her bed. This was the tiny home, no more than a couple of rooms, that Julius had found for her two years ago. Dear Julius, she thought, rescuing her from Hugo all those years ago, rescuing her again when, in spiritual crisis, she found herself no longer able to fit in with the quiet discipline of her enclosed order. And now she was part of an open order, whose London base was a house in Hackney, but whose sisters lived and worked wherever the order thought fit.

She sipped her whisky and looked at the clean white walls, the antique French high-backed chair, the little wooden icon of St Francis, the rich embroidered bedspread. She breathed in the peace and harmony after the ragged chaos of the London night. She wondered whether Sam had survived so far – and for how long she'd continue to survive, living on her wits, out on the streets.

'OK, you lot, now listen.'

'But Agnes, I've ate me toast—'

'Sit down.'

The defiant young redhead, surprised at Agnes's forceful tone, sat down heavily and exchanged sulky glances with the spiky blonde girl sitting next to her.

'Sam's gone, and I – we – need to know where.'

'Gone? Where?' said one of the boys.

'She seems to have run away.'

'Din't wanna go back to her mam,' said the redhead.

Agnes sighed. 'No, she didn't.'

'She'll be back up West again, then, won't she,' said the boy.

'You don't know where, do you?' asked Agnes.

The boy shook his head and spooned cornflakes into his mouth. Milk dribbled down his chin.

'I spent half the night looking for her,' Agnes said.

'Nah, she'd've seen yer comin',' said the spiky girl.

The boy took another spoonful of cornflakes. 'There's them other lot, in't there,' he said with his mouth full. 'She might've gone there.'

'Which other lot?'

'He means Kings Cross, don't yer, Mick?'

'Nah, not there. Them road ones.'

'What road ones?'

'Yer mean like what Becks done?'

Mick nodded through another mouthful of cornflakes.

The blonde girl elaborated. 'Becky, right, after she left 'ere, she went out east somewhere, some forest. Where they're buildin' a road. She went to, you know, like, stop them.'

'Rainbow doobries,' Mick said, his mouth still full.

'Fuckin' stupid,' the red-haired girl said. 'Livin' up a bleedin' tree.'

'Nah, it ain't stupid. Pollution, all that, savin' the planet. It's OK.'

'Shelle, it's stupid. Get knocked off yer perch wiv bleedin' chainsaws and banged up and they still build the bleedin' road in the end, don't they. Can I go now?' The red-haired girl sauntered out of the kitchen.

'Yes, you can,' said Agnes, as all the others scraped back their chairs, cleared their plates noisily and left the room. The spiky blonde girl began to run water into the sink.

'Is it your turn on the chores rota, Michelle?' Agnes asked her.

'I don't mind,' she said.

'This road place – do you know where it is?'

'Becks said it was out near Epping, I think. Somethin' ter do wiv the M25.'

Plates dripping with foam appeared on the draining board and Agnes took a cloth and began to wipe them.

'She'll be OK,' Michelle said. 'S'better than goin' 'ome, anyway.'

'You look exhausted,' Julius said later that morning, when Agnes went over to the office. He put a cup of coffee down in front of her. 'And I suppose you didn't find her.'

Agnes shook her head.

Julius paused, his hand on her shoulder. 'There's not a lot we can do.'

'We owe it to her—'

'It's not prison, the hostel. The kids are free to go.'

'What sort of freedom's that? Of course I'm going to look for her.'

Julius sat down at his desk. 'Fine. It's only that we're short-staffed at the moment, as you know.'

'Just a day or two to find her.'

'I know all about your Just-A-Day-Or-Two. It had better not be like last time, that's all,' Julius smiled, then stopped as he saw Agnes's face.

'That was different,' she said.

'Yes. I know. Sorry.'

'And it's over.'

'Yes. Agnes?'

'What?'

'I've said this before, but don't be too hard on yourself about –

about all that.' He watched her carefully. 'What is it, Agnes? Something's worrying you. That meeting?'

Agnes sighed. 'The meeting was just Sister Christiane and her team being over-concerned about me.'

'What happened?'

'They suggested that I might be getting too involved with the hostel kids, at the expense of my religious life. How can you be too involved? There's no such thing.'

'If you were a secular person, then you'd be free to choose your involvement. But in this case, surely they have a point? I mean, look at last night, for example, walking the streets in search of Sam—'

'And isn't that the work of the Lord?'

Julius looked at her. 'That is not for me to judge.'

'They've even suggested I consider taking a year away from London. I told them there was no need.'

'Agnes – what did they say?'

'Oh, something about needing me to teach French at the order's school in Yorkshire. Someone's left or something. Of course, it's out of the question, as I told them.' She took a gulp of coffee. 'It's nothing to worry about, they'll have forgotten about it soon.' She drew a piece of paper towards her and began to write on it. 'I just need to know I've done what I can for her,' she said. 'Sam, I mean. There,' Agnes went on, handing him the paper. 'The rest of the week's rota. Without me. See, it works, and I'll start again next week.'

Julius took it and nodded. 'By the way, Sister Madeleine's popping in for a sandwich, she's back at the hostel for a while. Do you want to join us?'

'I'd love to, but I'm seeing Athena for lunch.'

'Right. So I'll expect you to roll in at about half past three clutching shopping bags and reeking of Chablis.'

'I'm so glad you understand, Julius, dear,' said Agnes from the doorway. 'So many men wouldn't,' she laughed, closing the door behind her.

'I've already ordered the Chablis,' Athena announced. 'What's so funny?'

7

They were sitting in an Italian brasserie just off Fulham Broadway. Athena was wearing her lilac linen suit, and her thick black hair was pinned into an untidy bun, from which long tresses escaped. She wore red lipstick and from her ears hung huge twists of silver.

'Oh, just something Julius said,' Agnes replied, hanging her raincoat on the back of her chair.

'He's never approved of me,' Athena said. 'From the very beginning—'

'You're quite wrong there,' Agnes replied. 'Julius is very fond of you.'

'But when we first met—'

'When we first met it was over Hugo. Julius hates Hugo, that's all.'

'Hmm.' Athena tasted the wine, paused for a carefully poised moment and then nodded graciously at the waitress.

'So, how are you?' Agnes smiled.

'Oh, OK.'

'As in, not OK.'

'Well . . .' Athena took a sip of wine. 'Bored, really, that's all.'

'How's the gallery?'

'Fine. Selling more and more. We've got some lovely watercolours in at the moment, sort of Oriental things, and then in the main room we've got this huge installation, it looks like a pile of broken old radios, those big chunky ones from the fifties, and they're draped in pink quilted dressing-gowns, and there's Henry Mancini music coming out of it. Anyway, everyone comes in to see the installation and goes out with a watercolour. Great, eh? That's art for you.'

'But it's not enough?'

Athena put down her glass. 'I think it's my age. Even me, decadent old hedonist that I am, even I'm starting to think, what's it all for? What does it all mean? And don't look at me with that gleam in your eye, I'm not about to convert.'

'I wouldn't dream of it, Athena. It's a broad church, I know, but there are limits.'

'Of course, the sad fact is,' Athena went on, 'that all this cosmic doubt would probably disappear if a gorgeous hunky geezer appeared on the horizon.'

Agnes sighed. 'So much for the yearnings of the soul,' she said, as their pasta arrived. 'So easily displaced by altogether different yearnings.'

'And talking of yearnings, that Jonathan wrote to me.'

'Oh.'

'Yes,' Athena went on, taking a forkful of tagliatelle. 'He wants to put up my rent. Bloody cheek.'

'How much was he charging?'

'Well, nothing at all – but it's the principle, isn't it?'

Agnes laughed. 'It must mean things are going well for them if he wants you to rent out his flat long-term.'

Athena nodded.

'So he's – they're – staying in New York?'

Athena nodded again.

Agnes fiddled with her fork. 'How's Alexander?'

'His paintings are doing really well, he said. Nothing more, really. You know what men are like. The whole letter was barely half a page long, and that was big writing too.' Athena looked at Agnes. 'You still miss him, then, Alexander?'

Agnes met her eyes. 'No.'

Athena grinned. 'As in, yes. There's no point waiting for these things to go away. What you need, poppet, is to chase it away. In fact, that's it. What we *both* need is some gorgeous hunky geezer to appear on the horizon—'

Agnes laughed. 'Speak for yourself, Athena. Spiritual yearning is enough for me these days.'

'As if you had the choice,' Athena giggled.

They walked back to South Kensington underground station together.

'Do you have access to the Internet?' Agnes asked suddenly.

'Whatever for?' Athena said.

'I'm trying to track down a road protest, that's all. I thought they might have an e-mail address.'

'I just can't keep up with you.'

'Well, do you?'

'Simon's got some screen thingie in the back office that whirrs and beeps at him from time to time. But I'm not sure it's any good on eco-warriors; it only knows about art.'

'Hmm. Would it be all right if I came back to your office and made a few phone calls, then?'

'See?' Agnes announced to Julius. 'It's only two forty-five. Not only that but I'm empty-handed.'

'It must be a record,' Julius laughed. 'Whereas Madeleine and I are still here. And the Chablis?'

'Only a glass – I'm driving.'

'Julius told me that Sam's gone,' Madeleine said.

'Yes. I think she's at an anti-road protest. I spoke to a couple of campaigning organisations on the phone, and there's one in Epping which sounds likely. They've even got a mobile phone number, but I couldn't get through, so I thought I may as well drive over and check it out.'

'Well, good luck,' Madeleine smiled.

'By the way,' Julius said as he got up to close the window against the traffic noise, 'talking of Sam, her social worker phoned again.'

'Great. Did she apologise for her stupid, heavy-handed—'

'If you'd just let me finish – she said they'd had a call from a man claiming to be her father. Not her stepfather, this is her birth father. He hasn't seen her since she was a few months old, when he left her mother, but he's tracked them down, and wants to renew contact with Sam.'

'How odd.' Agnes looked at the piece of paper he handed her. 'How very unusual. And what are we supposed to do about it?'

'Ask her what she feels about it. If we see her again. See, I wrote the name down. Michael Reynolds.'

'Not the same surname, then?' Agnes put the slip of paper in her pocket.

'He wasn't married to the mother.'

'Well,' Agnes said, getting up. 'I'll tell her. If I ever see her again.'

'What car are you hiring this time?' Julius grinned. 'The Jag again? The Rolls?'

'If only. No, these days I have to rely on the community's own horrible chuggy little Metro. If it goes over fifty-eight, bits start falling off it.'

The M25 snaked its way round London, flashing with mirages in the July heat. Agnes turned off towards Ongar, glad to leave the traffic jam behind. She passed leafy villages, golden arable fields ripe and swaying, flat pastures where elegant horses grazed. She reached the village of Broxted, then turned off up a dirt track as directed, and parked by a gate at the end. The field sloped upwards away from the village, and at the top she could see a clump of trees, interspersed with bright blue tarpaulins. She climbed the gate and set off up the hill to the camp. As she approached she saw the trees were festooned with streamers, the tarpaulin tents decorated with flowers, tinsel and old coat hangers.

A young woman was crouched by a smouldering fire, prodding at the embers, trying to balance a blackened kettle on the stones. She looked up, grinned at Agnes, then carried on. A boy was sitting further off, playing the guitar. He had long blond dreadlocks. He looked up. 'Hi,' he said.

'Hello,' Agnes said. 'I'm – um – looking for someone called Sam. She might have come here. She's a friend of a girl called Becky.'

'Yeah,' he said. 'Yeah, they're here. They went off to buy stuff in town.' A few notes trickled from his guitar.

'Sort of shoulder-length hair, mousy-brown—' Agnes asked.

'Yeah, that's the one. They shouldn't be long. Have a cup of tea if Jenn ever gets the kettle to boil.'

'Oh yeah, and you have a PhD in thermodynamics,' the girl by the fire said.

'Might do.'

Agnes sat down, screwing up her eyes against the smoke. There was a jangle from the nearest tree and a boy abseiled gracefully down. He threw some rope to the young man. 'Jeff – we've done the walkway between these two,' he said. 'Rona's up there now.'

Agnes looked up and saw a young woman suspended in mid-air. On each side of her the huge oaks reached out their ancient branches into the shimmering sky. Her long red curls danced as she began to move, and Agnes saw that her hands were on one rope, her feet on another. Against the blue sky she walked from one tree to the next. Agnes began to see why Sam would want to stay.

Jenn rinsed some mugs out and made tea, squeezing every last thick brown drop out of each teabag. Agnes watched a figure sauntering lazily up the hill from the village. As the girl came close

11

she saw Agnes and stopped in her tracks.

Agnes looked at her. 'No, I haven't come to take you back.'

Sam broke into a broad smile. 'Great. 'Cos you can't, I'm staying here, it's great, look these are my friends, this is Jeff and this is Jenn and there's Rona up there and there's Col, only he's away somewhere, and Paz, and Becky, she's still in town, and there's Zak and his dog called Dog and – and we're saving these trees from the diggers,' she finished. Jenn grinned and handed her a mug of tea. Agnes looked at Sam's tanned skin, her clear grey eyes, the laughter that bubbled from her. She remembered the nervous, huddled person that she'd last seen at the hostel.

'No,' Agnes said. 'Of course I haven't come to take you back.'

The day wore on. Paz arrived with bags of vegetables and started to cut them up for stew. People worked up in the trees, building platforms. The fire was stoked up, the sky turned pink. Sam took Agnes into the woods to show her where the road would go. Agnes saw a column of smoke rising some way away. 'What's that?' she asked Sam.

'Oh, that's Bill. He's lived here for years, I think. He eats rabbit and dandelions and things. Got a gun and everything.'

'He's not one of you, then?'

'Nah. He's quite friendly if you meet him, but he keeps himself to himself. Bit of a weirdo. Come on, let's get back, Becky might be there by now.'

They wandered back to the camp, and Agnes told Sam about Mike Reynolds.

'My dad, he says? Never 'eard of 'im.'

'He left when you were a baby, apparently.'

Sam shrugged. 'Nah. Bet me mum just made it up to get me back. Lyin' cow.'

They sat around the fire and ate stew, as the moon rose in the darkening sky. Someone wondered where Becky had got to. Someone else picked up a guitar and started a song, and other voices joined in. Sam was singing by the fire, her face radiant. Up in the trees, lights went on in a tree-house and there was laughter and shouting.

Then, a scream. A strangled cry from the woods. The music stopped. Another scream, a man's voice crying for help.

'Paz,' someone said. They scrambled to their feet, people slid down from the trees, grabbing torches, heading towards the sound, the voice which cried again, 'Help, help, come quickly.'

They ran into the trees, and their torchlight picked out the outline, the chalk-white face of Paz. He was speechless, pointing back the way he'd come, and he led them stumbling into the woods, then stopped.

They all converged at a point between the trees. Torch beams swayed across the rough ground, picking out a bundle. It wore a striped jumper, and thick locks of hair fell around its face.

Agnes heard Sam whisper, 'It's Becky.'

Chapter Two

Becky's eyes were wide and staring and bloodshot, and her face in the torchlight was white, twisted in horror. She was lying at an odd angle, one arm flung out stiffly to one side. Agnes noticed there were deep red marks around her neck.

Sam burst into tears, an escalation of shrieking sobs, and Paz put his arm round her and tried to lead her away, but she ran back, screaming Becky's name.

Rona caught her, restrained her. 'We'll call the police,' she said.

'Hang on,' Jeff said, above Sam's cries. 'Do we want to invite them in?'

'What else do we do?' Rona shouted. 'Bury her ourselves? Someone's done this.'

Jeff looked at Rona, looked at Becky, looked at Rona again. He nodded.

Rona took Sam's arm. 'Come with me,' she said, heading back to the camp. As Sam allowed herself to be led away, Agnes heard her say, between sobs, 'I didn't know she meant it.'

The others began to stumble back to the camp. Paz said to Agnes, 'We ought to sit with her, maybe?'

They crouched down next to the body. Paz kept shaking his head, his hand over his mouth, his eyes staring fixedly at Becky. 'Shouldn't we close her eyes?' he asked at one point.

'No, just leave her,' Agnes said. She, too, was staring at the body, at the bruising on the face and neck, at the dishevelled clothes, the face seared with the anguish of a soul wrenched to freedom. She tried to remember Becky alive, as she'd been for the few brief days she'd spent at the hostel, when Sam had first become friends with her. Agnes recalled spending an afternoon with her, sitting over mugs of tea and trying to find out from gentle questioning why

15

she'd run away. Agnes remembered her neat brown hair, her ordinary jeans and cheap trainers. She'd been quiet and well-behaved, and in her three days with them had given nothing away. It was the raucous ones who survived, Agnes always felt, the loud, rude ones who pierced their noses and tattooed their arms with safety pins and somehow managed to fight their way out of their hell. It was the Beckys of this world who would accept their lot, who would drift quietly away, unable to say what they'd run from in the first place; defeated by their belief that disclosing what had happened would just make everything much, much worse.

And now, here she was. How many others have we failed, Agnes thought, staring at the body. And of those we fail, how many end up like this?

The night was still pitch-black, and the warm air hung heavily over the trees. Agnes got up and stood over Becky, allowing every detail to imprint itself on her mind. She saw a rope slung across a nearby tree-stump, and wondered whether anyone would leave behind a murder weapon like that. Some spiky twigs were sprinkled across Becky's face and around the body. Very carefully Agnes picked one up and sniffed it. It was rosemary.

From the camp they could hear voices, sobbing, shouting. Agnes smelt woodsmoke nearby. Then there were sirens, the flash of blue lights from the lane below.

'Thank God,' Paz said.

After that came the slow invasion of the outside world. Policemen, floodlights, a photographer, people with sticky tape and plastic bags, at one point a police surgeon, the crackle of radios, the taking-down of statements.

Agnes stood at the edge, eavesdropping on the barked instructions, the snatches of speculation. At one point she was asked by someone to give a statement.

'Sister Agnes?' he repeated when she told him her name.

'Yes, I'm a nun,' she said.

'Hardly your cup of tea here,' he remarked.

'I knew Becky. She stayed in a hostel I work at.'

'Oh. Right. Charlie Woods,' he said, holding out his hand. 'Detective Sergeant.'

'She was strangled, wasn't she?' Agnes asked.

'Can't say anything at this stage.'

'But those marks—'

Charlie met her eyes. 'Not a nice way to go,' he said.

The outside world retreated, taking its photos and statements with it. The dawn was cold and grey, and everyone found themselves huddled around the tiny fire, tear-stained faces, fingers wrapped around mugs of tea. Agnes began to build the fire up into a blaze. Sam gazed into the flames, grey with exhaustion and shock.

Finally Jeff spoke. 'What shall we do now?'

'What is there to do?' Rona asked.

'I mean, now Becky's gone.'

'We carry on, don't we?'

'With her, I mean, not even buried or anything . . .'

'Are you saying we should give up now?'

Jenn said, 'We should think about what Becky would have wanted.'

'And Becky would have wanted us to stay and fight,' Rona said.

Jeff stared at the fire. 'Yeah,' he said at last.

'Maybe whoever killed her wanted us to go,' Paz said.

'You mean it was to scare us?'

'Oh, I dunno,' Paz said. 'It seems a bit fuckin' strong for the usual heavies, however much they hate us.'

'Might be a security guard?'

'On his own? In the woods at night? No,' Jeff shook his head. 'On an eviction, maybe, but one on his own—'

'What about the Press?' Zak said.

'What about them?'

'Oh God,' Rona said, 'that's all we need. "Anti-Road Girl Murdered on M11 Link Protest" . . .' She buried her head in her hands.

Agnes looked across at Sam. She was gazing blankly into the fire; but there was a terror behind her eyes.

Someone started a warning cry, a 'Yip, yip, yip,' as a figure approached the camp.

'It's only Col,' someone said.

'Col—' Sam shook herself, jumped up and ran to meet him, flinging her arms around him, talking at him. The others watched

17

as he stopped dead, hearing the terrible news, staring at Sam in disbelief, then breaking into a run.

'Is it true?' he said, stumbling to the fireside. He was a slight, dark-haired boy of about seventeen, with hollow eyes and a thin face. Sam sat next to him and they whispered for a while.

Now that Col was here, Sam was edgy, anxious, desperate. Agnes remembered her words when she'd first seen Becky's body – 'I didn't know she meant it.' She watched Sam for a while, then quietly went and sat with her and Col. They both fell abruptly silent.

'Sam,' Agnes said, 'you need to eat. And we need to talk. Do you fancy breakfast somewhere?' Sam looked at Col. 'Both of you, if you like?' Agnes added.

Col shook his head and wandered off towards the trees. Sam shrugged and followed Agnes rather aimlessly down the hill, away from the camp, back to the track where, a lifetime ago, Agnes had left her car.

'So, what do you want to do?' Agnes sat opposite Sam in the garish restaurant of a service station just off the M11. She took a mouthful of limp bacon. 'You can stay at the camp. You can come back with me – I can find room at the hostel. And you ought to have a think about Mike Reynolds too.'

Sam pushed a mushroom around her plate. 'I can't think straight, can I?' she mumbled. 'I've 'ad it wiv me mum, I've 'ad it wiv fuckin' do-gooders trying to send me back there, and now Becky's dead and me and Col—' She stopped herself, glanced at Agnes, took a huge mouthful of toast.

'You and Col what?' Agnes said gently.

Sam shook her head, her mouth full. After a moment, Agnes said, 'No one's going to force you to do anything. You're sixteen now, you have rights of your own. If you feel safe at the camp you have every right to stay there.'

'It's like, I feel I belong there, you know?' Sam said.

They drove back to the camp. A police car was parked by the gate, and two officers were standing by the kitchen bender, talking to Jeff.

'. . . advise you all to leave here,' Agnes heard one of them say.

'Is that all the protection you can offer us, then,' Jeff said angrily, 'that we have to go?'

'The choice is yours, sir,' the officer said. Jeff muttered something and wandered off towards the woods.

Agnes turned to the police. 'Those marks around her neck,' she began. 'Becky's, I mean. Was it that rope? Only I noticed, near the scene of the crime . . .' The policemen exchanged glances and Agnes felt suddenly foolish.

'The rope's being examined,' one said.

'But those marks—' Agnes tried again.

The policeman eyed her closely. 'We're still searching for the ligature,' he said.

'What do you mean?'

'A chain, we think. Like jewellery. That sort of chain. It might have broken in the process, hence the rope. Off the record, you understand.'

From the corner of her eye Agnes saw Col appear by the furthest benders. Sam ran to join him, and together they went off to the woods.

'I don't know, Julius,' Agnes said. 'I felt bad leaving her there. I'm not sure she's safe.'

'I'm surprised the police haven't just cleared them out. If there's some psychopath at large—'

'But I'm not sure there is. Sam seemed to know – to know something about it.'

'Aren't you being a bit—'

'Fanciful?'

'Well, you do have this tendency . . .'

Agnes yawned. The church clock chimed four, and Julius closed the file on his desk, raising a cloud of dust which sparkled in the sunlight. 'I don't suppose you've slept,' he said.

Agnes shook her head. 'By the way, I told Sam about Mike.'

'He's been on to us again.'

'What now?'

'Apparently he got quite heavy with Mary, her social worker. She asked whether you'd phone him, although in the circumstances—'

'No, that's fine. Maybe tomorrow? I'm having supper with Athena, if I can stay awake.'

Leaving Julius, Agnes was tempted to linger in the empty church for a while. But she thought of Becky lying dead in the woods, and the image was so strong, so overwhelming, she was frightened to allow it in.

'Well, frankly, poppet, if you must set up home in some filthy patch of trees, what can you expect? Oh these blasted cartons, the stuff inside's delicious, but you die of starvation before you can ever get to it. Thanks, sweetie,' she added, as Agnes came over and neatly opened a carton of fresh asparagus soup.

'So you think she deserved it then?'

'Oh, sweetie, no, of course not. But I mean, the rest of us manage to live our lives without having to swing from trees. Does that woodsmoke smell ever wash out?'

'I hope so. It's the fleas I'm worried about.' Agnes laughed as Athena recoiled in horror. 'Anyway,' she went on, breaking off a piece of bread, 'you seem happier than before. It must be that some lovely man has appeared on the horizon.'

'Not at all, darling,' Athena said, absently scratching her head, 'It's not as if I depend on having a man around to give me a purpose in life. I just decided to think positive, that's all. I enjoy my work, Simon's really pleased with how the gallery's going, I've got friends, a nice flat . . .'

'And?'

Athena poured the soup into bowls and brought them to the table. 'Well, there is this man, actually, not like that, I've hardly spoken to him, but he's been coming into the gallery a lot, and there is a sort of something between us, you know, a *frisson* . . . and yesterday he came in with these leaflets and asked if I'd display them. Some workshop thing he's doing.'

'What sort of workshop?'

'Oh, I don't know. Probably one of those drumming things for New Men when they all cry about their dads. And he's got a ponytail, I never trust that in a man, you know.'

'No, quite.'

'Nice eyes, though, sort of blue, intense. When he looks at you, it's kind of like he knows you – am I boring you?' she added, as Agnes yawned again.

'No, of course not, I'm just knackered, that's all.'

'Poor you. Finding that girl dead like that, it must have been awful. Mind you, there must be all sorts of people who'd want those kids out of the way.'

'What do you mean?'

'Well, there they are, trying to take on the Government, and big business, and people like bailiffs and security guards – in fact, it's amazing they survive at all.'

Next morning, Agnes sat in the chapel of her community, joining her voice to those of her fellow sisters in the Mass. She listened to the murmuring liturgy and felt cleansed by it, soothed, like sand at the tide's edge. Afterwards Madeleine joined her in the kitchen.

'So, you OK for the hostel rota this week, Agnes?'

'Oh. Um, yes. Except, not tomorrow. And maybe not the next day, I'm not sure yet.'

'Julius told me about Becky. But I don't see why—'

'I'm needed at the camp,' Agnes said, as if it was obvious.

They were alone in the kitchen now. Madeleine sat at the table. 'Why?' she asked.

'Well, Sam's there, and she's quite upset, and there's this business with this Michael, her father. In fact, that reminds me, I must phone him today, I promised Julius – and anyway, I think Sam's in danger too.'

Madeleine traced the rings of the pinewood with her finger. 'Aren't the police dealing with it?'

'Well, yes, of course, but—'

'It's just – well, I might be talking out of turn, but I gather that you had a meeting with Christiane . . .'

'Oh. That.'

'Did they mention Yorkshire?'

'How did you know?'

'They did the same to me, once,' Madeleine said.

'Did you go?'

'Yes, of course. It was years ago now. Did me the world of good.'

'What, really?'

'It turned out to be the right thing.'

'But how can it be right, to take me away from something I'm good at and put me somewhere where I'll be unhappy—'

'Agnes – why did you choose the religious life?'

Agnes looked up. 'Well, I don't – well, I suppose, it chose me.'

'That's just it, isn't it. Maybe it's time *you* chose *it*. Maybe that's what they want.'

Agnes met her eyes. 'Why did they send you to Yorkshire, then?'

Madeleine sighed. 'It was a long time ago. I had what was considered an inappropriate relationship. To me, it didn't feel inappropriate at all. It felt bloody brilliant. But they sent me away. And I was so angry with them all, for forcing us apart, for breaking up something so good, so right . . .' She sighed again. 'I thought it was the end of my religious life. And it looked like it would be, for a while.'

'What happened?'

'I spent a long time thinking about my priorities. Once I stopped feeling angry, I realised that life's too short to put yourself first, to put this illusory sense of self before the greater good.'

'My God, I'd have eloped. Of course you have to put your own needs first, you can't serve God seething with resentment.'

'But beyond the resentment?'

Agnes looked at Madeleine. 'Well, you're just a higher life form, then. If you can allow them to do that to you and still be serene . . . And what happened to your lover?'

'She left. She writes to me sometimes.'

Agnes considered her friend. Then she smiled. 'All the same,' she said, 'I'm not sure that teaching French to little girls is the fast track to eternal enlightenment.'

Before leaving to drive back to the camp, she phoned the number that Julius had given her.

Michael Reynolds's voice was warm and friendly.

'Hi, Agnes, great to hear from you. Just call me Mike, everyone else does. I'm sorry if I've seemed a little forceful, I just want to get this thing moving. I just want what's best for my little girl . . . Sure. No, of course we must respect Sam's wishes, sure, I understand that.' His warm tones modulated to deep regret when he told her how he'd come to try to trace Sam after all these years. 'I should have done more, I shouldn't have disappeared off the scene, but you know, I was young, it was very difficult for me . . . Still, water under the bridge, eh? I'll wait to hear from you, Agnes, great talking to you.'

All the way back to Epping, Mike's voice rang in Agnes's ears. She wondered whether it was a coincidence that he should appear on the scene so soon after Sam's sixteenth birthday, at the moment when she ceased to be the legal responsibility of the care agencies. It was very unusual, in fact almost unheard of, for a father to want to make contact again after so long. She'd never encountered such a thing before. Still, she thought, just because it was odd, it was still no reason to distrust him.

There was an electrical charge in the humid air, in the heavy clouds that hung over the motorway. As she turned off towards the camp, she heard the first thunder starting in the distance.

Chapter Three

Everyone at the camp seemed weighted down with a flat depression. Jeff was wandering about with a leaflet which he'd designed, but no one could find much enthusiasm to discuss it with him.

'We're bound to be evicted in the next month or so. We need to mobilise support from the locals. I thought if we printed off a few of these then they'd be ready . . .'

People nodded, went about their business, made more cups of tea. Of greater concern was the presence of the Press, who had already started to visit. Rona suggested a policy of saying nothing at all. Jenn was arguing that if it helped find Becky's killer perhaps they should cooperate. Jeff put down his leaflets and picked up his guitar. A few languid notes issued from his fingers.

Sam and Col appeared from the woods, arm in arm. Sam brightened on seeing Agnes and came and sat next to her.

'I spoke to Mike Reynolds,' Agnes said to her. 'You know, your – um – father.'

Sam shrugged.

'You might as well meet him,' Agnes went on.

'Where?'

'You can come back to London with me tomorrow, if you like.'

'And then will you bring me back here?'

'What do you want to do?'

Sam fidgeted. 'Dunno.' She looked up at Agnes, troubled. 'It's kind of changed, since Becky, all that.'

'Well, you can stay a few days at the hostel, if you'd prefer.'

Sam shook her head. 'Don't want that lot to come lookin' for me. Me mum, I mean.'

Agnes paused, then said, 'And you're not frightened of anyone coming for you here?'

Sam narrowed her eyes. 'Nah, I ain't scared of no one here. No one's gonna ruin this for me.'

'Fine,' Agnes said, watching her closely.

Later Agnes walked aimlessly in the woods, drawn towards the site of Becky's body, still cordoned off with police tape. She glimpsed a figure squatting by the edge of the tape.

'Col.'

He looked up, then looked down again. He was digging at the edge of the mud with a stick, and in one hand he was clutching a plant of some kind.

Agnes squatted next to him. 'It's very sad, isn't it.' She noticed that he had the same air of panic that she'd seen in Sam whenever Becky was mentioned. His fingers worked to deepen the hole in the mud.

'Col – if you're in danger – you and Sam – you can trust me, you know. If you need to escape—'

'There's no escape,' he murmured. He finished digging, then placed into the hole the ragged cutting with its withered blue flowers. He looked up at Agnes. 'Forget-me-not,' he said.

'Like Rosemary?' Agnes said quickly. 'Rosemary for remembrance?'

Col stared at her. 'How do you know that?'

'All I know,' Agnes said, 'was that there was rosemary sprinkled on the body.'

Col fixed her with his eyes. 'If she's sent you—' he began, then stopped.

'If who's sent me?'

He shook his head.

Agnes sighed. 'Col, no one's sent me. I don't know more than that.'

'Good,' he said, turning back to his flowers. 'Just leave it that way, OK?' He began to pat at the earth around the flowers.

'Col, if you're in danger,' she said again. 'If Sam's in danger—'

He ignored her, finished his planting, and stood up. He smiled down at Agnes, a smile that seemed ironic, even mocking, then sauntered away towards the camp. Agnes stared at the flowers, planted under the orange tape as if it was a graveside.

'Kids, eh?'

The voice made her jump. She looked round to see a man standing over her, chewing on a twig, eyeing her with his head on one side. The man grinned. 'You'll get no sense out of them.' He had neat grey hair, quite long at the back, and his eyes were dark, flecked like quartz. He was half-draped in a rough grey blanket looped through the belt of his jeans, which were clean and rather well-cut. Agnes noticed, as he sat down next to her and she braced herself for the customary smell of the tree-dwellers, that he smelt only of woodsmoke and the odd whiff of tobacco.

'You must be Bill,' she said.

He nodded, chewing on his twig, looking at the spot where Becky had been found. 'And you are . . .?'

'Agnes. Sister Agnes. I'm a friend of Sam's, at the camp, and I knew Becky too.'

'Ah.' He scratched his head. 'Sister, eh? Which goddess do you worship?'

'Same old God, I'm afraid. I'm just a traditional nun.'

'They still have them, then?'

Agnes looked at him. If you've been out of the world for so long, she wanted to say, how come you're so clean? 'Yes,' she said. 'They still have them.'

He produced a hip flask from under his blanket. He unscrewed the top and took a swig, then handed her the silver bottle like a challenge. She took it and drank from it. It was whisky. Decent whisky. Single malt. Agnes wondered how an ex-hippy forest-dweller could afford whisky like that. She imagined him slipping off to the bank in town to cash cheques from some family trust or other, keeping a suit hidden in a hollow tree specially for such occasions, nicely wrapped up in its plastic hanging bag from the dry cleaners.

She handed back the flask, smiled at him and said, 'So, what do you know about Becky and Sam and Col?'

He raised one eyebrow. 'You don't miss much, do you?'

'Well?'

'Very little. Apart from the fact that, like you, I've concluded there was some connection. They seem to know something. Once—' He stopped himself, then continued, 'Once, I heard them talking. Other lives, you know?'

'What do you mean?'

'Reincarnation. Karma, you know. Coming back in a new form.'

'I don't see . . .'

'They were saying something about someone coming back. I mean, it's OK finding out you used to be Trotsky or Jimmy Dean – but no one reckons on a bad trip, do they?' He took another swig from his flask.

'And you think the three of them were involved in something to do with their past lives?'

'It's just something they said, that's all.'

'What did they say?'

Bill produced papers and tobacco and began to roll a cigarette. 'Not much. It was all about who owned the land, this land, and people coming back from the past to claim it. Only, they seemed scared. Shit scared. Like, it wasn't just a laugh.'

Agnes looked at the mud where Becky had lain, and frowned. 'Do you think it's likely—?'

Bill grinned. 'Hell, Sister, how should I know? This is the New Age, man, people can believe whatever they like. You have your God-For-Grown-Ups, the hip daddy in the beard, Heaven, Hell, Queen and Country. But here, right, it's whatever turns you on.' He stood up to go, and Agnes got up too. They walked towards the camp. The quiet of the woodland was broken by voices, laughter, the smell of supper cooking.

'I'll leave you here,' Bill said. 'This is my patch.'

Agnes saw a little way away from them a bender of blankets and tarpaulins, a smouldering fire, a neat stack of wooden boxes on which were stored pans, mugs, candles. A coiled rope hung from a hook. Bunches of herbs were drying on overhanging branches.

Bill offered her his hand with ironic formality. 'It's been a pleasure to meet you, Sister,' he said.

Agnes shook his hand politely, then left him. At a distance she turned back to see him poking at the fire, burning something over it.

That night she woke suddenly in the bender she was sharing with Sam. She listened, hard, through the rhythm of Sam's breathing. She took her coat and shoes and crept out of the tent.

The storminess had passed. From time to time the moon appeared from behind a cloud. Agnes listened to the forest silence, the crack of twigs, the occasional hoot of an owl. She put on her coat and shoes over her clothes and, taking a torch, set off through the trees to the place of Becky's death. The thin moonlight washed through the branches. She thought she heard footsteps behind her and stopped dead, straining to hear. Nothing. She reached the site of the murder, and staring at the ground, saw once again the twisted face, the horror of untimely death frozen on those features. She wished she'd never left the safety of her bender.

Then there was a noise, an approaching footfall sound, but quick, quicker than footsteps, a thundering approach of – of hooves. Out of the darkness Agnes saw a horse, only a few feet away, and in the brief flash of moonlight she made out the rider, a woman in bonnet and long skirts, riding sidesaddle, cantering past in an instant, receding into the damp silence of the forest.

Agnes stood trembling in the darkness. She waited a few moments before she dared to switch on her torch, afraid she might catch some other phantasm in its beam. A bat whirred above her. She set off at a fast striding pace back to the camp, arriving with relief to see Jeff sitting with a candle by the smouldering embers of the fire.

'The delights of forest living,' he grinned at her. 'The call of nature in the middle of the fucking night.'

She sat down next to him 'I thought – I thought I saw someone. In the woods.'

He nodded. 'You get used to it. There'll be more now the eviction's coming up. Security heavies, detectives from the agency.'

'But – she was on horseback.'

Jeff looked at her. 'A rider – at this time of night? Are you sure?'

'Well, I—'

'Usually it's creeps with cameras. People sniffing around. I've never heard of 'em using horses before.' He laughed. 'Perhaps it was a ghost.'

Agnes brushed mud from the hem of her coat. 'I don't believe in ghosts,' she said.

Agnes's first thought on waking was that Bill had stage-managed the whole weird incident. She thought of him dressing as a Victorian lady on horseback just to add weight to his claim that Becky's death was all about people returning from the grave to claim their land.

'What you laughing at?' Sam muttered, sitting up, rubbing her eyes.

'Oh, nothing. Shall we see what's for breakfast?'

'Flippin' peanut butter sandwiches again,' Sam grumbled, wriggling out of her sleeping bag.

Agnes left her by the fire and wandered towards the forest, taking the same path as the night before. Again, she found herself standing near the site of Becky's death. The mud around the police tape was churned from endless investigation. She followed the path a few steps further into the woods, then stopped. A clear hoofprint, then another; a line of horseshoe crescents, stamped into the forest mulch, stretching away towards the fields beyond the trees.

'So,' Agnes began as the traffic thickened towards London, 'tell me what you know about Becky's death.'

Sam looked at her, her eyes wide. 'What 'bout it?'

'What do you and Col know about it that's so scary, then?'

Sam chewed her lip. 'Nothin'. I already said, din't I?'

'Sam, you and Col are both panic-stricken about it. You must tell me—'

'I can't.' There was a surprising force in her voice. 'Don't ask me, OK?'

'But Sam—'

Sam's hands were working in her lap. 'I'm saying this once, right? If I tell you, if I tell anyone, it'll just get worse. Much worse.'

Agnes glanced at her. 'Sam, if you're in danger, I need to know. You've wriggled out of everyone's grasp, your mum, your step-father . . . I'm all you've got.'

'That's your bleedin' choice, then, innit.'

Agnes put her foot down and pulled out into the fast lane, only to find herself braking suddenly behind a Mondeo. 'Oh for God's sake,' she shouted, 'if you want to tootle along at seventy-five get back into the bloody middle lane.'

That evening she settled Sam into the hostel, then went home. She put all her clothes into a bag ready for the launderette and ran a hot bath with Givenchy bath foam. She sank into the warm bubbles, feeling the dirt of the forest dissolving, the woodsmoke smell being washed away. She watched the white foam caress her skin and wondered, once again, how Bill stayed so clean.

30

Chapter Four

'I've brought you a bacon butty,' Agnes announced at nine thirty the next morning as she arrived in the office.

'Mustard?' Julius asked.

'Of course,' Agnes replied.

'All this forest air must be agreeing with you,' Julius said, unwrapping his sandwich. 'Usually you don't even speak until at least ten thirty.' He eyed her suspiciously. 'What are you doing with those files?'

'Oh, just checking something.'

'Becky Stanton's file, isn't it?'

'I was just curious—'

'Agnes – it's not as if there's anything you can do.'

'Coffee?' Agnes brought two mugs over and sat down at her desk. She began to flick through the file she'd taken from the cabinet. 'She was from Essex – the family live just outside Chelmsford,' she remarked to Julius. 'One brother. She'd left home once before, ran away last November. Then she did it again, not long ago, and ended up with us.'

'Agnes, I'm not that interested.'

Agnes began to scribble notes down with a very scratchy pencil.

'Agnes—' Julius looked across to her. 'I'm not sure it's any of our business.' The pencil scratched away. 'After all, she's dead now, and she wasn't even our responsibility, and I'm sure the police know what they're doing . . .' The pencil noise stopped short.

'Sam knows more than she's letting on. Which means she's in danger too.' There was more writing, then Agnes went on, 'And Col's in it with her. They're behaving like cornered animals at the moment. I've brought Sam back just to give her some breathing space. Don't you see, Julius? I've got to find out what happened to

31

Becky because it could happen to Sam too.'

Julius fingered the crucifix at his neck. 'You really are St Rose of Lima, aren't you,' he said.

'I'm not sure I carry quite the same scars,' Agnes said.

'Only in your mind. And while you're taking responsibility for the whole world, you'd better phone Michael Reynolds. There's a message from Mary, at Social Services, on your desk.'

Agnes searched her desk. 'This one?'

'Yes. Apparently, he was really pushy with them, quite unpleasant.'

'How odd. He was all sweetness and light with me. Well,' she added, 'Sam's got to meet him. I'll get on the case.'

Julius watched Agnes as she stood and gathered up her coat. 'It's not that I don't support you,' he said, as she paused by the door.

'Well, what is it, then?'

'Just – sometimes – give yourself some peace, that's all.'

Agnes opened the door. She looked at Julius, hesitated, then turned and went out. He heard her footfall on the wooden steps up to the church, heard the creak of the church door, the faint crunch of her feet on the drive as she went out into the street.

Mike Reynolds answered straight away.

'Hello, it's Sister Agnes.'

'Oh. Good. Good,' he said.

'I thought we might meet,' Agnes said.

'Yes. Fine. You haven't – um – those social workers . . .'

'Which social workers?'

'I wondered whether you'd been speaking to them.'

'We do liaise, yes. How else would I have this number?'

'It's just – I was rather hasty with them. Bit of a mistake, I thought afterwards.'

'Oh, I'm sure they've known worse. Are you free later on today?'

'Um, it's tricky. Hang on. I can do this evening, if you don't mind meeting me here at my office. Got a pen? I'll give you the address. Six-ish OK?'

'Fine,' Agnes said, writing down an address in Whitechapel as he dictated it. 'See you there.'

Agnes replaced the phone box receiver. 'Bit of a mistake,' she heard again. Why would he think that? If nothing else, she thought, he's a strategist. He must have a game plan. But then, she thought, looking at the address he'd given her, you would have a plan, if you'd gone to all the trouble to contact your long-lost daughter. She turned over the card she'd written on. 'New Naughty Miss,' it said, next to a sketch of a pouting young woman. 'All submissive services.' Agnes felt suddenly angry, suddenly filled with the impulse to dial the number and say, 'You don't have to do this, you know.' Only, of course, she thought, pocketing the card, leaning hard on the heavy phone box door to open it, that's just the point.

Popping into the newsagents to make some photocopies, she paused in front of the window. 'Body-to-body massage,' said a card. 'TV. All services,' said another. 'For sale, buggy with rainhood, £25.00,' said the next. Agnes found herself wondering whether buggies with rainhoods was a code for some bizarre sexual practice.

'I mean, is it just me?' she asked Athena later that afternoon over chocolate eclairs. 'Am I an innocent abroad, and is everyone else happily booking themselves in for sessions of bondage and massage and caning and – and whatever you care to name?'

Athena giggled. 'Neither, poppet. You are far from innocent, and most people aren't booking themselves in for anything because most of us are rather stupidly wandering around in the forlorn hope that our fantasy partner will simply turn up by sheer chance.'

'So who's going to visit these naughty young misses, or whatever they really are?'

'Oh, just men, darling, no one we know.'

Agnes went to her kitchen to refill the teapot. 'The thing is,' she said, returning, 'it's not OK at all, is it? It's not just that women freely offer these services and men freely take them up. It's not about freedom really, is it? It's about coercion, and corruption, and dependence and – and people's lives being ruined. Women's lives.'

'S'pose so,' Athena said, muffled with eclair. 'But what can you do?'

Agnes stood in the middle of the room, teapot in one hand. A burst of afternoon sunlight lit up the soft white of the walls, the muted green and blue of cushions and bedspread. She thought of

Shelle at the hostel, Col at the camp, Sam, any of the other young people she'd encountered over the years.

Athena wiped cream from the corner of her mouth. 'Sweetie, you can't worry about everyone.'

Agnes blinked, shook her head. She brought the teapot to the table. She balanced the tea-strainer on a cup, then said, 'There's this man at the camp. He told me that Becky, the one who was killed, and her friend Col, were involved in something to do with the past. You know, when you believe yourself to be someone else in a previous life?'

Athena's eyes widened. 'That's amazing—'

'It's not part of my tradition, it's not something I've thought about before . . .'

'No, really, that's amazing because—'

'But they seem to think it's true. Scared themselves silly, apparently, and now Sam's whispering to Col about it and won't tell me anything. And I thought I saw a horsewoman in the woods the other night—'

'If you'd just let me finish,' Athena broke in at last, 'it's amazing because Nic does that. I mean, exactly that. It's his thing.'

'Sorry – who – what?'

'The man in the gallery. The lovely one. I read his leaflet. His workshops aren't drumming at all, they're all about regression and memory.'

'I don't quite – who – which lovely – ?'

'I told you.'

'You mean Mr Ponytail? I thought you'd never spoken to him and you don't trust ponytails anyway?'

'Ah, well, there's always an exception.'

'So you have spoken to him?'

'No, but now I can. This is wonderful, sweetie. A perfect opportunity.'

'Perfect for what?'

'Well, to have a little chat with him.'

'Athena, we're talking about a murder.'

'Well, obviously, I'll leave out that bit. But, poppet, you need to know more about what your baby abseilers were up to, don't you?'

'Yes, but, surely, you can't just go bowling in and start up a conversation about some kids out in a forest.'

'Oh can't I? Just watch me.'

The office of Alborina Holdings was on the first floor of an old warehouse, large areas of which seemed to be empty. Agnes stepped through the dingy doorway and was almost mown down by a rail full of floral yellow dresses emerging from the lift, with two hurrying young Bengali men behind it.

She walked up the stairs to Mike's office. The door was ajar, and Agnes could hear a phone conversation going on. She sat on the edge of a worn pink sofa and picked up a trade magazine about paper products.

'That's not my problem, though, is it?' Mike was saying. 'If you ask me, the guys over at Majorwell need something up their jacksie before they'll see things our way.'

'Supermarkets to favour recyclables,' Agnes read.

'So he said I was heavy, did he? He hasn't travelled, mate. Any more of this arsing about and he'll find out what heavy is. Yeah, see ya.' Agnes put down the magazine and stood up as Mike came to meet her, one arm outstretched, the other smoothing his thin blond hair.

'Sorry about that,' he smiled, shaking her hand. 'Some people just aren't hungry enough these days. Now, where shall we go? There's a fairly decent pub on the corner, or we can venture towards the City in search of something posher if you like?'

'The pub'll be fine,' Agnes said, as Mike led the way down the stairs.

'So, are you a real nun?' he asked.

'Real enough,' Agnes said. 'We just don't tend to wear habit any more.'

'Shame,' Mike said, holding the front door open for her, and she felt suddenly irritated that he should presume to have a view on how she dressed. What a shame your suit is only polyester instead of linen, she felt like saying. What a shame you chose that cheap-looking pale blue shirt this morning. She tried to put these hostile thoughts to one side, thinking, as they approached the pub, that it must just be nerves, wondering, as she watched Mike fight his way to the bar, what Sam would make of him.

'So, how is Sam?' Mike asked, as he brought two drinks to their table.

'Oh, you know. OK,' Agnes said.

'Enjoying London?'

'Maybe.'

'Or isn't it London?'

Agnes smiled as warmly as she could. 'You know I can't tell you where she is,' she said.

He smiled back. 'No, of course. Sorry. It's just that when it's your only daughter . . .' His face clouded, and Agnes felt sorry she'd been so evasive.

'It must be tough,' she said. 'But now, you're here.'

He looked up. 'If she wants me, yes.'

'What made you decide now? And how did you track her down? And how did you lose contact with her in the first place?'

He smiled and nodded. 'Yes, it's a long story. Well, she'd been on my mind ever since, really. Since she was born. Forever, really. I've never regretted anything so much as losing her, although I have to say, it takes two. Her mother was pretty – feckless, in those days. Still is, stupid cow, letting Sam run off like that . . .'

'How did you get involved with her mother – Linda, isn't it?'

'I'd been around with her for a while . . . She was a bit of a tart, really, but I was young, and she was easy . . . I wanted out, but then she found she was pregnant. I thought I'd better stay. I was barely out of my teens. My mum said I'd regret it.' He swigged at his beer. ''Course, she was right, in the end. Linda was off with other men soon as she'd got her shape back. Hurt my pride, you know. After a few months I'd had it. Moved away for a bit to work out what to do. When I came back, they'd gone. Been rehoused.'

'She doesn't have your surname.'

'No, she thought of taking mine, Linda did, but after all those kids from different fathers—' He shrugged. 'Whittaker's her own name. Must be easier in the end.'

'And how did you get back in touch?'

'Oh, that was easy. Her sister lives near me in Harlow. I called on her one day. It must have been about eighteen months ago.'

'Linda's sister?'

'Yup. She's lived there for years. We kept in touch.'

'What made you decide – I mean, when did it occur to you to get in touch?'

Mike sighed. 'You see, Agnes, I'd never let go. I'd always thought of myself as Sam's dad. And one morning, I woke up and everything seemed really kind of simple. And I thought, that's it, then. You are her dad. Why wait any longer? And that's when I talked to Annie, Linda's sister, and then she told me about the new love of Linda's life. Some things never change, do they, Agnes? If the bleedin' Terminator himself was to walk through those doors, you can bet your last half-crown that Linda'd be simperin' along behind him in her best kit. And Annie told me that he'd been dishin' it out to Sam, and that kind of sorted it for me really. So I talked to some helpline thing, and they told me the procedure.'

'So you contacted Social Services?'

'Yeah. Annie told me what to do. Where they were, which area to get in touch with. I did all that. The rest you know.'

Mike picked up a beer mat and flipped it over. Agnes, sipping her drink, watched him. Something felt too easy about all this. Why now? she wondered. Why this easy belief in his right to be Sam's father? But then, she thought, people need their fathers. People need to know who they are. It must be better for Sam, she thought, that Mike wants to be back in her life. A real father.

Without warning, a memory flashed into her mind. Warmth and scratchiness; of being nestled up close, watching flames leaping in a huge fireplace. Long, pale fingers turning the pages of a book, a rare, leather-bound edition of Cuvier's *Natural History*. Papa. Reaching out to trace the raised blue veins on the back of his hand, allowing her own fingertips to touch the rich, yellowing paper with his.

'Of course,' Mike was saying, 'those social workers don't seem that bothered.'

Agnes gulped her drink. 'Social workers?' she mumbled. 'They're very over-worked, you know.'

My own father, she thought, wondering how she'd begin to describe him, the man who had wafted unpredictably in and out of her life, provoking unbearable feelings of love and loyalty only to abandon her when some new business project, or mistress, called him away. She blinked as Mike flipped the beer mat again.

'Another drink?' Mike was saying. The pub suddenly seemed unbearably noisy.

'I'd better go, thanks all the same.'

Outside the pub they shook hands.

'I'll tell Sam I met you,' Agnes said. 'I'm sure she'll want to see you soon.'

Mike held her gaze. 'I hope so,' he said. 'Oh, God, I hope so.'

Agnes walked briskly away from him towards the Tube, descending the station steps, breathing in the humid air with relief. She found a seat on the platform. Really, it was unfair of her, she thought, to allow her own confused memories to cloud her judgement now. Mike seemed a nice enough man, and compared to Sam's current set-up, might prove to be a very good thing for her. In the end, it was up to Sam; she was the one who had to decide. Agnes shivered in the sudden breeze of the approaching train.

'Well,' she said to Sam the next morning, 'I might as well take you back to the camp, if you want to go. It's going to be a day or two before we can arrange for you to meet Mike.'

'What was he like?' Sam said, crunching breakfast cereal. 'Is he rich, and is his house nice, and has he got cable telly?'

'He's very keen to meet you,' Agnes said. 'And I've no idea what his house is like.'

'And how old is he, and what does he look like?'

'He's about thirty-seven, he's got blue eyes—'

'Like mine?'

Agnes looked at Sam's eyes. They were a soft grey, not the sharp blue she remembered from her meeting with Mike Reynolds.

'Yes,' she said, 'like yours.'

The blackened kettle was steaming tepidly on its bed of warm ash. There was a jangle of abseil harness as Jeff descended from a tree and rubbed his eyes.

'Any tea?' he asked, giving Sam a hug.

'I can't get this fire going,' Paz replied.

Jeff knelt by the stones and prodded at the bits of wood under the kettle. Rona appeared from her bender and nodded at Agnes.

'How's it going?' Agnes asked.

Rona sighed. 'We're all still reeling. And the Press don't help. But, you know, we've got the eviction coming up.'

'Have you got a date?'

Jeff sat back on his haunches. 'Not officially. But one of the locals, Sheila, one of her daughter's mates was down the job centre and they're recruiting security guards round here. And that means they're gearing up to get us out, right? And it's like, we've got to get full on.'

'So who evicts you?' Agnes asked. 'I mean, who owns the land?'

'The Department of Transport,' Rona replied.

'And before them?'

'The farmer here. He still leases it from them, but they bought it off him some time ago, when they first decided to build the road here.'

'Has it always been in his family?'

'I wouldn't know. Oi, Jeff, don't use that treated wood, there's good stuff from the forest next to it.'

Paz said, 'The farmer? You mean, Nicholson? He told me his great-uncle got the land cheap.'

'Who from?' Agnes asked.

'I'm not sure. I think it was a local family. You'd better ask him if you're interested.'

Agnes noticed that Sam was standing silently. Her fists were clenched at her side, and she was staring down at the fire from which guttered a few small flames.

'So,' Agnes went on, 'this land. Is Nicholson happy about handing it over to the road?' She felt Sam tense next to her.

Rona shrugged. 'They're always compensated. Bought off. Half the time they don't care.'

There were shouts from the trees and Col and Jenn abseiled down.

'Just in time for you to make the tea,' Rona said.

'I'll do it,' Paz said, wandering to the kitchen bender in search of tea bags.

'Oh no, Paz's tea,' Jenn groaned, settling by the fire.

'It's either that or making it yourself,' Paz said, returning with some grimy mugs.

Col joined Sam and they hugged. 'You OK?' he asked.

She nodded, then shook her head and whispered to him. They wandered off a little way into the trees. Agnes helped Paz pour boiling water over cheap tea bags, then, taking two mugs, went to find Sam and Col. They were sitting on a log, side by side, their heads bowed, talking quickly.

'But how do we know where she's gone?' Col was saying.

Sam shrugged, then looked up to see Agnes there.

'I was just—' Agnes began, handing them a mug each. 'I wanted to check you could meet Mike Reynolds this week – I'll be going back to London soon.' Sam exchanged quick glances with Col, then nodded.

Agnes wandered back towards the fire. The others were some way away coiling rope. Paz was poking at the wood, one hand over his eyes. He looked up.

'Paz—' Agnes said. 'You were the one who found Becky.'

He sighed. 'Yeah.'

Agnes sat down next to him. 'Do you mind me asking you about it?'

'No. I don't mind. Nothing to tell, mind you. The pigs were keen on me being the last one to see her alive – like I'd done it or something.'

'Did you see anyone, anything?'

'Yeah. That's what they wanted to know.'

'Well, did you?'

''Course I fuckin' didn't. If I'd seen some mad strangler, I'd have gone for 'im, wouldn't I?' He shook his head. 'Nah. The pigs told me she'd been dead an hour or two before I found her anyway.' He shuddered.

'It must be awful for you all.'

Paz looked up. 'For some of us, yeah. Those of us who still have a soul.'

'What do you mean?'

'Everyone's throwing themselves into this eviction, like they don't have to think about Becks then.' His eyes were watering – from the smoke? Agnes couldn't tell. 'She hadn't been here long. I didn't know her that well. I did try and – well, once I tried it on with her. She weren't interested. Usual tat.'

40

'Did she see anyone? Family or anyone?'

Paz shook his head. 'Nah. No family. She hated them, she said. She was friends with Jenn, they were close. Then there was a girl she saw a lot of – she lived in the town, I think. Sometimes I thought they were a couple, you know, but then you think like that if someone turns you down, don't you.'

'What girl?'

Paz shrugged.

'Did she ride, this girl?'

'No idea. I met them once together, when I was out blagging stuff. They were laughing.'

'What did she look like?'

Paz screwed up his eyes. 'Couldn't tell you. Smart, maybe.'

'Becky spent a lot of time with Col.'

'Yeah. And Sam. Up to something.'

Agnes sighed. 'Well, the police are dealing with it now.'

Paz looked at her hard. 'Fuckin' pigs. What can they do? They'll lunch it, fuckin' babylon shit.'

Agnes smiled at him. 'Yes. Well, we'll see.' She stood up. 'Look, let me know if anything occurs to you.'

She fetched some water from the stream and began to wash up the mugs. She watched Rona climbing a tree, calling to Jeff, saw her reappear a long way up between the branches, throwing lengths of rope to him. They hung there, the two of them, spinning their web, building their magic fortress in the sky.

Chapter Five

'They're right, of course, these protesters,' Agnes said to Madeleine as she arrived in the office later that afternoon. 'Julius not here?'

'Julius is visiting the needy folk of Southwark. What do you mean, they're right?'

'I've just driven, or rather crawled, around the M25 from the camp to here in this heat, breathing in God knows what, passing houses where all the kids must be asthmatic . . . What I mean is, it's not sustainable, is it? Roads aren't the answer.'

'And how else would you have got here?'

Agnes frowned. 'Well, that's the problem, isn't it? But at least the people protesting are saying something's got to change.' Agnes filled the kettle with water and switched it on.

Madeleine said, 'You seem tired.'

'I'm OK.' Agnes fiddled with her bunch of keys. 'Madeleine?'

'What?'

'Nothing. Tea?'

'Camomile, please. The bags are in the blue tin there. So what's worrying you?'

'Me? Oh, it's silly really. I was driving around the M25 and I thought, God the Father.'

Madeleine laughed. 'You thought that?'

'Do you think of God as a father?'

Madeleine raised one eyebrow. 'You're serious, aren't you?'

'You see, these kids at the camp, the way they believe' – Agnes poured boiling water into the teapot – 'they're sort of pagan, and herbalists, and they have solstices, and astrology and tarot and – and they don't have to struggle with it, you know.'

'So what are you saying? That your faith is a struggle because God's male?'

'Is He?'

Madeleine took the mug Agnes handed her. 'Well, no, I'd say God is beyond gender, wouldn't you?'

Agnes signed. 'Yes, of course. Except, why do we choose a male God to pray to?' She shook her head. 'I mean, there's Becky's death, and then there's all this business with Sam's father, and it made me think . . . What I mean is, if our image of a loving God is based on fatherhood, you only have to look around you to see it isn't working.'

Madeleine watched her for a moment. 'Is all this about the order, then? About your meeting with Sister Christiane?'

'Why should it be?'

Madeleine sipped her tea. 'Dunno. It's just, you seem angry.'

Agnes looked at her. 'Angry? What with? The order? My father?'

'I was only asking.'

'I can't be angry with my father. He's been dead for years.' The phone rang and Agnes snatched it up. 'Hello?'

'Sweetie, are you free this evening?' Athena gushed.

'Um, yes, s'pose so.'

'There's an opening at the gallery, private view thing, quite decent wine, I chose it myself. I meant to ask you ages ago. Thing is, Nic is coming, almost definitely, and I thought you two should meet, he's so interesting about this reincarnation thing—'

'You do work fast,' Agnes said.

'Hardly, it was sheer luck, darling, he came in yesterday evening, the gallery was very quiet, I just seized the moment. He's gorgeous. Anyway, about six thirty?'

'Yes, OK. Thanks.'

Agnes put down the phone. 'What does one wear to private views?' she asked Madeleine.

'Heavens, don't expect me to know,' Madeleine said.

'I should have asked Athena. Mind you, she'd have just insisted I borrow her dalmatian fun-fur mini-dress, and I can't see it, can you?' Madeleine was looking at her blankly. 'What were we saying?'

'About fathers,' Madeleine replied.

'Oh yes, that. Maybe a glass of wine will cheer me up.'

'So where's the Bakelite radios?' Agnes said as she walked into the gallery just behind Bond Street where Athena worked.

44

'Gone, darling, all packed away to go on tour or something. No, it's these abstract landscapey things now, hence the bit of a do. Simon, darling, you know my friend Agnes, don't you?'

Agnes nodded vague greetings to a bustling man in angular tortoiseshell spectacles. 'Agnes, great you could be here,' he said, shaking her hand, looking beyond her towards the door. 'Feel free to buy as many as you like,' he added over his shoulder as he went away.

'He's a sweetie,' Athena said. 'And he knows so much about art, you know, not just these sort of things, but Titian and Botticelli and everyone . . . Oh my God, he's here! Oh heavens, really, I didn't expect him to turn up this early. Is my lipstick straight? I'm sure I smudged it earlier—'

'Athena, your lipstick's fine,' Agnes said, surveying the doorway, watching a lean, tall man pause by the entrance, his head slightly on one side as he looked around the room. He was relaxed, upright, his long greying hair tied back at his neck, his leather jacket accentuating the line of his shoulders. He noticed Athena and sauntered over.

'Hi,' he said.

'Oh, it's you,' Athena smiled up at him. 'Let me get you some wine,' she said. 'This is my friend Agnes: Agnes, Nic.'

'Hello,' Agnes said.

Nic was eyeing the paintings that surrounded them. 'She said these would be my type but I'm not so sure,' he said. 'Still, there's always the booze.'

'Perhaps everyone here is thinking the same thing,' Agnes said.

'Sad but true,' Nic smiled, as Athena appeared with three glasses of white wine. Agnes drifted away to study a painting, glass in hand. It was oil on canvas, a series of rough whorls in granite grey and ochre. 'Portland Beach' read the label, then Agnes's eye was caught by a little shelf of leaflets and she saw the heading 'Regression Workshops'. She picked one up and read it. 'Encounter your multiple selves' it said. 'The way we live our lives often excludes many facets of our personalities, leading to a sense of dislocation, and sometimes to depression and ill health . . .' At the bottom of the leaflet was: 'Workshops led by Nic Rosborough', with an address in Kilburn and a phone number.

45

'You've found my leaflet, then,' Agnes heard him say, and looked up to see him standing next to her.

'Yes.'

'Interested?'

'I'm not sure, I haven't really thought about it before.'

'It has astounding results,' he said.

'Why leaflet this place?' Agnes asked.

'I have a system. I target different bits of London each week. I'm on Soho at the moment.'

'And does it work?'

'I've had people come in on the edge of total despair and go out just glowing with energy.'

'I meant, does the leafletting work?'

'Oh. Yes. I'm doing pretty well at the moment.'

Agnes noticed his soft voice, his gentle manner. 'Don't you worry about being responsible for people, though?'

He smiled. 'I like helping people. They trust me, you see. A lot of it's just intuition, you know. That, and healing energy.' Agnes turned the leaflet over in her fingers. 'You should come along – with your friend.'

'Yes, um, I might. I mean, I think she'd like, I mean, we'd like – Athena, Nic's suggesting we go to one of his workshops.'

'Poppet, how lovely. Are you sure, Nic? We're mere novices at that kind of thing, aren't we, Agnes? And anyway, she's a nun, and Catholic – probably not the right kind of material at all, but I'd love to, how super.'

'What, really?' Nic said to Agnes. 'A nun?'

'Yes,' Agnes said. 'But don't worry, I'll probably find out I used to be Pope Joan in a previous life.'

Athena said, charmingly, 'Oh, she's always like that, take no notice. And why don't I give you my number – you can let me know when you're next doing one. I'd love to be there.'

Some time later Agnes found Athena in the crowd to say goodbye. Nic was nowhere to be seen.

'He's invited me to the workshop on Saturday – he gave me his home number and everything,' Athena said gleefully at the door.

'Are you really going to go?'

'On Saturday? Yes, absolutely. Wouldn't you?'

'Wouldn't I what?'

'If you really fancied someone?'

'I'm not like you, Athena. But I can't wait to find out who you used to be. Boadicea, maybe.'

Agnes walked towards Regent Street in search of a bus. It was only nine o'clock but it felt later, despite the warm evening, the sky still deep blue. Discover the power of your multiple selves, thought Agnes. Though, in my case, one is probably quite enough. She walked briskly, aware of the rhythm of her feet. Each of us, she thought, a bundle of history, a summation of our own past. But surely it wasn't right to get distracted with other pasts, and other stories – particularly if it led you to an ending like Becky's, so brutally cut short. She felt time passing with each click of her heels on the paving stones. The street lights had come on, turning the sky to indigo behind their yellow haze. It was time to act.

'Can I speak to Charlie Woods, please?'

'I'm afraid Sergeant Woods isn't on duty tonight. Can I help?'

'I'm inquiring about Becky Stanton, she was murdered on the twenty-first of July.'

'And who's speaking?'

'Sister Agnes. I was acquainted with her. I was there when she was found. Sergeant Woods took my statement. I simply wondered whether there's been any progress in your inquiries.'

'It's a bit late in the evening, madam. I'll see who's about if you'll just hang on.'

Eventually he returned. No, there'd been no progress. Nothing had come to light so far. She was welcome to phone again in a week or two.

Agnes replaced the receiver. 'Nothing had come to light.' She got up and walked to the window. Who had they asked? They'd had nearly a week. What had they been doing? If it was me, she thought . . . If it was me, I'd have asked the family, of course. Yes, I'd have started with the family.

Agnes went back to her desk and sat down. Unless it really was a random event. Unless it really was the case that Becky had only herself to blame, that the civilised world is surrounded by lurking psychopaths just waiting for someone to stray beyond the edges.

Or was it, as Rona and everyone believed, some kind of out-of-control security guard? But then, thought Agnes, was it right just to accept that Becky's killer might never be tracked down?

Agnes felt a slow anger rising. 'No,' she whispered, rummaging for the notes she'd made from Becky's file. 'If we accept that Becky's killer will never be found, then we are one step nearer chaos, one step further from the light. *No*,' Agnes said aloud, and her voice reverberated in the room.

At two o'clock the next afternoon, Agnes rang the bell of a neat semi in a nice suburb on the east side of Chelmsford. The door was opened by Shirley Stanton, a tall, thin woman with nut-brown hair and a very pale face. She wiped her hands nervously on her apron as she led Agnes into the front room. There was a worn turquoise sofa, a carpet of beige and rust swirls, a small old-fashioned television. Over the mantelpiece Agnes noticed a simple cross placed above a large framed photograph of a rather dashing man in a suit.

'Morris – Sister Agnes is here,' she called up the stairs, and a moment later Morris Stanton appeared. He was large and bearded, with black hair and a red complexion. He was wearing a white nylon shirt. 'Sister, eh?' he said, in a voice which was gruff but welcoming.

'Yes, I'm a nun.'

'Catholic?' Agnes nodded. 'Oh well, all equal in the eyes of the Lord. Shirley, pour the tea for our visitor.' He sank heavily on to the sofa.

Agnes chose the armchair opposite. 'I was very sorry to hear about your daughter,' she began. From the kitchen, she heard a cup fall and break.

Morris forced a smile. 'The police came and told us. Constable – what was his name, Shirley?' he called to the kitchen. 'That nice police officer?'

'Baxter,' Shirley Stanton said, coming back into the room with a tea tray. Her face was even paler, and her hands shook as she put the tray down on the low table.

'Though I don't know how you come into it,' Morris was saying.

'Well, as I said briefly on the phone, I'd met Becky when she spent a night in our hostel earlier this year.' Agnes took a deep breath. 'And for various other reasons not connected with this, I happened to be there when her – when she was found.'

Shirley threw a glance at her husband, then quickly looked down again.

'I see,' Morris said. There was a silence. The three cups of tea stood untouched on the tray.

'Yes, the hostel. Of course. When she ran away to London. Silly girl. She was never the same after that.' Agnes waited. He went on, 'When I was young, we didn't think in terms of problems. But these days, they're encouraged to think they can do what they like. They blab to anyone who'll ask – teachers, do-gooders like you—'

'Morris—' Shirley murmured, but he went on.

'You're supposed to rescue them, not make it worse.'

'I don't think we did make it worse.'

'You give them a taste for it, you people. Running wild in London . . .'

Shirley gave a choking sound. She was working her apron in her lap, scrunching the fabric into a ball between her fists.

Agnes spoke quietly. 'As I'm sure someone explained to you at the time, the hostel is a safe house. We work with the police and Social Services. You were contacted when she stayed with us, and after discussions with her social worker, she was returned to you.'

'Only to run away again,' Morris said. 'After all we did, too. Going off to join these hippies and travellers and what-have-you—'

'That's hardly what we—'

'In fact, I don't know why you bothered to come. The police told us all we need to know.'

There was a knock, and a boy put his head round the door. He looked about twelve, with his mother's brown hair and large, nervous eyes. He went and stood by his mother, and without taking her gaze from her lap she leaned slightly towards him. The tea had cooled in the cups, leaving a creamy scum on top of each.

Agnes stood up. 'I'm sorry. I thought you might want to talk about – about Rebecca. It was wrong of me to come.' She walked to the door. Shirley was suddenly on her feet, darting into the hallway ahead of her. Before her husband had pulled his weight out of the sofa, she grabbed Agnes's arm and whispered, 'How –

49

how did she die? How did she look? Was she – how did she – they thought it was best if I didn't – see her . . .'

Agnes took hold of Shirley's hand. She said softly, 'She was at peace. She looked peaceful.' Agnes hesitated, seeing in Shirley's eyes a burning urgency. 'If you'd like to—' she began, but Shirley shook her head as they heard Morris approach. As Morris came into the hall his wife opened the front door and showed Agnes out.

'No, you were right,' Agnes said, sitting with Julius in their favourite Indian restaurant that evening. 'I shouldn't have gone.' She broke a poppadum in half and took a bite.

'I said nothing,' Julius said.

'You didn't have to. As ever.' Agnes smiled at him. 'I just upset them. They've got a nice police officer dealing with them, and they blame us for getting Becky into bad ways, and they didn't want to talk about her. Well, he didn't.'

'Do you mean she did – his wife?'

Agnes nodded.

Julius took a sip of lager. 'Becky ran away again, didn't she? After she'd been with us, she went home, and then turned up at the road camp some time later.'

'You've been reading the file.'

'It caught my eye this afternoon. The thing is, we're supposed to be more successful than that. If someone passes through the hostel, we set in motion a process that should change their lives for the better so that they don't need to run away again. Right?'

'Well, yes, but we can't do it every time.'

'No.'

Agnes looked at him. 'You mean, there might be something she didn't disclose to us at the time?'

Julius nodded. 'It crossed my mind.'

'There's not much in the file.' Agnes spooned some pickle on to her plate. 'She hated her parents, apparently. The family are part of a house church group. And she might have been gay.'

'We really did fail her, then, didn't we,' Julius said.

'Mmm.'

'What will you do now?' he asked.

Agnes looked up. 'I thought I wasn't supposed to get too involved.'

'As I said, what will you do now?'

Agnes laughed. 'I can go in two different directions, it seems to me. One involves following the same trail as the police, forensic evidence, asking questions, returning to that family again, Heaven help me. The other way, I'll find myself dabbling in a load of mumbo-jumbo about past lives and reincarnation, and ghostly horsewomen in forests.' She smiled and shrugged.

Julius broke the last bit of poppadum into two small pieces and offered one to Agnes. 'It's just as well it's you, then,' he said. 'After all, you're used to believing several different things at the same time.'

Chapter Six

'Athena, it's me,' Agnes said on the phone at ten on Friday morning.

'Sweetie, how are you?'

'You sound very chipper.'

'Mmmm.'

'So what's happened?'

'I saw him last night.'

'Nic?'

'Uh-huh. He phoned to confirm the details for tomorrow, and we were talking and he just said, why don't we meet for a drink. So we did.'

'And?'

'He's lovely. A sweetie. And mature, you know? Like, not one of these silly boys, really thoughtful, like, he's been there, you know, he's got a son who's seventeen, and now he feels able to be clear about what he wants from life, and the workshop stuff is going really well and—'

'And you sat there and listened and didn't get a word in edgeways.'

'Deliberate strategy, darling, there's no need to be snide.'

'And are you going on Saturday?'

'Absolutely, sweetie. He said that I had enormous power, not just sexual but, you know, kind of life energy, and if I learned to direct it I could change things in a positive way. You're not *really* interested in coming along too, are you?'

'I – um, yes, actually, Athena, I think I should.'

'It's not your type of thing.'

'No, but—'

'To be honest, I'd love you to be there. It all sounds a bit scary from what he was saying.'

53

'Oh. Well, we can always nip out for a cup of tea if it gets too much, can't we.'

The young woman at the Inquiries Desk of Essex Record Office pushed her glasses back up her nose. 'The village of Broxted, did you say? And did you want the tithe maps, or the land tax records, or was it more recent than that?'

'Well, um—'

'Land ownership is quite a tricky one, you know. When was it for?'

'Um, as far back as possible—'

'I know, I'll get you the Ordnance Survey maps and the tithe rolls and we can start from there.'

Agnes pored over the maps, familiarising herself with the terrain. There was the church, and next to it Glebe Farm was marked. There was the stream, the same in 1950, and in 1879, and in 1841, as it was today. Although, not for much longer, if the road went ahead. There was the farmhouse – that must be the one belonging to – Nicholson, that was what Paz had said – before the Department of Transport took it over. In 1879 it was marked 'Harton's Lower Field'. In the earlier tithe maps, Agnes noticed, it was part of a larger farm, plots 43-45, which extended much further east. It must have been divided after that.

She took the tithe rolls and searched through them. Plots 2-16, Loamy Field, First Stubb Piece, Second Stubb Piece, owned by the Revd Philip Velley, occupied by Edward Gibson . . . plots 20, 30, here we are, plots 43-45, owned and occupied by Miss Emily Quislan. Checker Mead, Well Mead and the Homestead.

Agnes looked at the map again, at the old ink marks that outlined the patch of land, once an unassuming couple of fields, now the site of a controversial battle. She recalled Bill's suggestion about some past legacy returning. She checked the name again. Miss Emily Quislan. It meant nothing, she thought, this name, this Victorian lady long since dead. Just because some phoney forest-dwelling hippy had led her to believe that Becky and Sam and Col had dabbled in the past . . . Agnes sighed. It was twenty past three and she'd had no lunch.

* * *

That evening she went to St Simeon's. It was late and the church was locked. She let herself into the office, went to her desk and switched on the anglepoise lamp. The crucifix on her desk was illuminated in the bright pool of light, beyond it the shadows of the office, the door in darkness, still slightly ajar where she had left it. Above her head the old floorboards of the church creaked from time to time. She took out Becky's file from where Julius had tidied it away and read through it again. She felt as if she was searching – but for what? For some explanation, among the various testimonies, from teachers, social workers, GP – as if they might describe something of Becky that made it all make sense. But here it all was: good school work, a bit of truancy just recently; a supportive home environment; no apparent drug problem; just a normal girl.

The word normal began to stand out from the few thin pages as Agnes turned them. A normal teenage girl. She just happened to be a murder victim. And would it help, wondered Agnes, if I could find something *ab*normal, something to pin it on? In the end, she thought, it wouldn't change a thing. However Becky chose to live, she chose to live. It was someone else who decided differently.

On one of the pages of notes she found the address of Becky's house church group. 39 Fairfax Place, Chelmsford. She noted it down, switched off the lamp and left.

Athena appeared at Agnes's door at nine o'clock sharp on Saturday morning, clasping a large bag of warm croissants.

'You never know when they're going to let you eat on these things,' she said, breezing past the yawning Agnes and going to put the kettle on. 'Tea or coffee?'

'Tea,' mumbled Agnes, going into the shower.

Half an hour later they set off in Agnes's car for Kilburn, Athena in the passenger seat brushing the last few croissant crumbs from her short-sleeved mauve angora jumper. 'It's not too overdressed is it, sweetie? Only, I refuse to wear some ghastly track suit affair when I'm still at the making-an-impression stage.'

'I think we'll all be too busy breathing our way back through the cosmos to ancient bloody Egypt to worry about what anyone's wearing. Shall I do Westminster Bridge?'

'You're not keen, are you, poppet?'

Agnes's eyes were firmly on the road. 'Maybe Waterloo's as good, I can do Camden Town from there.'

Nic welcomed them all into a warm, light room, its pine flooring piled with large cushions. There was soothing, tinkly music playing, and a vague scent of jasmine. Everyone filed in rather uncertainly and then found a place and a cushion in a ragged circle. Nic sat in front of the window silhouetted against the bright sunlight.

'I want you to feel that this space is absolutely safe,' he said. Agnes was surveying the woman opposite her. She wore tight black leggings and heavy mascara, and now she produced from her chic patent leather handbag a large pack of tissues and laid them down neatly in front of her with the air of someone who knows what to expect.

'. . . so whatever you feel,' Nic was saying 'that's OK. There's nothing to be frightened of.' He smiled warmly at Athena, who gave him one of her best smiles back. 'And if something happens, that's fine – but have no expectations, OK? If nothing happens, that's fine too. We are just pinpoints in time, right? We're little flickers of consciousness. It's all about being aware when we've touched down. I'm going to start on some exercises where we can all get to know each other a bit, but first, is there anything anyone wants to share at this stage?'

A tanned, middle-aged man in a beautifully cut white shirt said, 'Nic, I wondered how you felt about someone having a place they want to get back to. Like, the self that I need to be at the moment is kind of locked away, and I need to return to it.'

Nic nodded for a moment. 'My feeling is, Patrick, that that's the self that will come.' Agnes wondered whether she had a self which was locked away, and how many workshops it would take to find out.

Half an hour later she had learned everyone's names and what they wanted from the workshop. There was Lynne and Andy and Patrick, and Phoebe with the chic handbag who rather tearfully explained that she had been talking to her dead mother a lot recently and it was important she find her own direction now; and Helga, who said that her husband had done a lot of regression therapy and now he felt she should too. When it came to Athena she said with studied thoughtfulness, 'I do think it's so important to accept the challenge of releasing one's own potential,' and allowed her gaze to alight, charmingly, on Nic. And then it was Agnes's turn and she muttered something about being interested in other spiritual paths whilst pulling at the sleeves of her worn grey shirt.

And then she wasn't really sure what happened. They all lay on the floor and did relaxation and breathing, and Agnes thought she must have dozed off for a while. She seemed to have a dream about a child sitting in the window seat of a large and beautiful house, gazing out at a car in the drive. She remembered the detail of the child's dress, made in layers and layers of fine cotton, with little violets embroidered at the hem. Something about the violets made her want to cry. Then Nic was talking to them gently, and Agnes came out from the dream with an overwhelming sense of relief. She noticed that he'd pulled down the blinds to block out the bright sunlight. Lynne told some kind of story, murmuring about carrying a large weight on her back, a basket, and she has to take it across a river, it has food in it, and the weather is cold, so cold, and the eggs will spoil. Nic was gently encouraging her, and Agnes, watching her, was struck by how happy she seemed, lying curled on her cushion, recounting bits of an altogether different life. When it was Patrick's turn, he simply said, 'So it *is* you. It *is* you,' in tones of radiant discovery, and Nic was talking to him, too, in a low voice.

Agnes noticed that Athena was lying artfully across a floor cushion, her eyes closed, her lips slightly parted. She opened her eyes briefly to check where Nic was in the room, then seeing he was next to Agnes, she closed them again.

Nic said to Agnes, 'How're you doing?'

Agnes looked up at him, and felt like bursting into tears. 'There was this girl, this child,' Agnes began, and then stopped.

'Go on,' Nic said gently.

'It was just a dream,' Agnes said.

Nic said, 'Has it upset you?'

'No,' Agnes said.

Nic considered this. 'It sounds like you're resisting this person.'

'It was only a dream,' Agnes said.

'Or a memory,' Nic said, watching her.

Agnes thought about the embroidered violets, so real she could taste them.

'I think I'll go home now,' she said. She stood up, found her bag, and without looking back left the room. As she went out through the reception area, she was amazed to find that the sun was still shining brightly. It was ten past one.

Agnes drove home, went straight into her tiny kitchen, put eggs on to boil, opened a tin of anchovies and a jar of olives and assembled something resembling a salad nicoise. As she laid out a fork and a plate, and poured herself a glass of mineral water, she realised she was angry. Very angry. She sipped at her glass and wondered whether she was cross with herself for leaving. Or with Nic, for allowing all those people to feel those disturbing, illusory things. Or with the others, for having so little sense that they were happy to be there, these Lynnes and Andys and Phoebes with nothing better to do than breathe themselves into a state and then witter on about their other selves instead of concentrating on the one they were stuck with.

Agnes put the salad out on a plate and began to eat. At least I've got my faith, she thought. At least I don't have to do that, experiment with other ways of being. At least as far as I'm concerned it's between me and God, and that's all, she thought. Yes, that's all.

She took an olive stone from her mouth. She knew what it felt like to wear that dress with the embroidered violets. She knew that when she looked out of the window of the large and beautiful house, on to the drive with the waiting car, it would be raining.

She washed up her dishes, changed into her scruffiest clothes that still smelt of woodsmoke, and set off for the camp. On the M25 she pulled into the fast lane as soon as she could and drove hard, her jaw clenched, flashing her lights at anyone who got in her way.

Sam ran to greet her. The fire smouldered as usual, but there was no one else about. 'Paz has hitched into Brentwood to sign on, Jeff's up in the chestnut there, the others are somewhere. Do you want some tea?'

Jeff descended from a tree and asked Sam if she wanted to climb. A few moments later, all rigged up in abseil harness, she disappeared after him into the branches. Agnes surveyed the deserted camp, the benders, their blanket coverings lifted to air in the sunshine, the makeshift clothes-line with one filthy pair of jeans swinging from it; beyond the camp the gentle slope away from the forest down to the village, the church spire just visible through the trees. To the right of the church Agnes could see Nicholson's farmhouse. The man whose family had acquired the land before passing it on to the DoT. Agnes picked up her bag and set off.

Half an hour later the farmhouse door was opened by a ginger-haired boy of about fourteen, who squinted up at Agnes, then turned and called, 'Dad – someone to see you.' A man appeared from an inside door, stooping under the lintel, his shirt-sleeves rolled up above his elbows.

'Sister Agnes,' Agnes said. 'I'm involved with the road protest camp, in particular with Becky, who – um, died. I wondered if you had a moment.'

He gestured with his head for her to come in, and she followed him into the dark hallway and then beyond to the kitchen. She sat at the wide oak table and he sat heavily opposite her, waiting. She looked beyond him to the peeling beige paint of the walls, the crumbling, dirty window frames. A black Labrador was sleeping in a basket on the old flagstone floor, and now it lifted its head, considered Agnes for a moment and then lay down again.

'They said you owned the land here,' Agnes began.

The farmer nodded. 'Nicholson,' he said. 'James Nicholson. My great-uncle bought it in the fifties, cheap.'

'Were you from round here, your family?'

'Lincolnshire, to start with. My great-uncle, called James like me, he moved away, settled here.' He paused, waiting.

'But now you've sold it.'

'For ten times what he paid for it, yes.'

'For the road.'

James Nicholson nodded again. 'It's been time for us to go for a long while now.' A shadow passed across his face. He slowly unrolled his shirt-sleeves over his arms. 'Sometimes I look across the land, early in the morning, when the sun touches the edges of the trees there . . . I loved this place once.'

Agnes hesitated. 'So – what went wrong?'

He looked up from fastening his cuffs. 'Are you with them, that lot up the hill, then?'

'I knew Becky, the one who was murdered. That's how I got involved.'

He shook his head. 'I know nothing about that. All I know is, this place is trouble. Them road-builders is welcome to it. Though them'll find they's tractors don't work any better'n mine.'

'Has it been difficult to farm?'

'Didn't question the price, you see, Old Jim. What I reckon is, they were desperate. Desperate to get rid, they were.'

'Why?'

James Nicholson shrugged. 'It's just never gone right. And since my wife died, it's got worse. Our kid there, you saw 'im – he needs a better life than this. I'm back to Suffolk come the spring, my brother's there, nice little school nearby.'

Agnes frowned. 'Do you think – if something had gone wrong in the past, for example—' She stopped.

'What do you mean?'

'Would it cause problems for the land? I mean, if something to do with the farm had gone awry?'

'What kind of awry?'

Agnes smiled at him. 'Oh, I don't know.'

'What've you heard?' he said.

'Me? Nothing.'

'There was some story, the old people used to talk of it from time to time – someone buried here or something. But I en't seen nothing in all these years.'

'What did they say, the old people?'

'Oh, someone came back. Something like that.'

'You mean, a ghost?'

For the first time, James Nicholson smiled. 'Ghost?' He shook his head. 'No, ma'am.' He smiled again. 'The only ghost you'll see here is the ghost of my younger self. Wasted away in ploughing land that won't give nothing back. That's all. We farmed it good enough, don't get me wrong, we made a living. But it's been uphill, that's all. And now with Mary gone, and them Brussels lot, and the money all haywire these days . . .' He stood up to show her out. 'Why, do you believe in ghosts?' His eyes twinkled.

Agnes thought of the horseshoe prints embedded in the mud. 'No,' she said, getting up to follow him. 'No, I don't.'

In the hallway he said suddenly, 'Harton. That's who they were.'

'Who?'

'My family bought this place from them. Hartons. Brother and sister, I think they were.'

'Harton? Do you know what became of them?'

'They sold up. Went abroad, I think.'

They shook hands. Agnes said, 'Thank you so much, Mr Nicholson. I hope the camp isn't bothering you.'

'Oh, it's not my fight any more,' he said. 'And them girls mended my fencing for me over by the east gate.'

On the drive back to London, Agnes thought about Athena, whom she had left artfully reclining in the quest to discover her former selves. It seemed like a long time ago. She wondered whether Athena's vigorous strategies for catching her man had succeeded by now. Almost certainly, knowing Athena, thought Agnes, resolving to go and see her after Mass the next day and pass on her apologies for her peremptory exit to Nic, who, after all, was entirely well-meaning. Agnes thought about the crumbling Essex farm she'd just left, the farmer so weary of tilling the land that he now welcomed the chance to have it shrouded in concrete instead. Agnes had an image of the people of England all turning away from their land, deserting it generation by generation, abandoning their fields to the encroaching cities only to find themselves some years later lying on floor cushions in jasmine-scented rooms trying to remember who they used to be. It made her smile, and she felt like a foreigner once more, until she remembered that her own father had been English too. Once upon a time.

Chapter Seven

'Don't tell me, you've been at your prayers since dawn,' Athena yawned, opening the door to Agnes.

'It's nearly eleven, it's late,' Agnes laughed. 'Come on, I'll fry you a huge breakfast – eggs, bacon, fried bread, tomatoes—'

'Ugh, how revolting,' Athena grimaced, loosely tying the belt on her white towelling dressing-gown and putting on the kettle. 'And anyway, we're very concerned about you.'

'Oh, we are, are we?'

'Walking out like that, just when we were all getting into it.'

Agnes sat down at the kitchen table. 'Athena, I couldn't – there was something . . . oh, I don't know. It's just not me.'

Athena spooned coffee grounds into a jug. 'I told Nic you always run away.'

'How loyal of you.'

'He said that you were really upset by something, and he felt really bad, but I said not to worry, you'd only have bitten off his head.'

'What a friend you are.'

'And it was only research, wasn't it?'

'Wha – oh, yes, Becky. Didn't help me there.' Agnes got up and opened cupboard doors. 'And how was it for you?'

'For me, poppet, it was wonderful.'

'I can imagine. Do you have any bread?'

Athena smiled radiantly. 'Nic says that I did really well and apparently I experienced an altered state of consciousness.'

'And when was this altered state of consciousness exactly?' Agnes smiled, putting sliced bread into Athena's toaster. 'During the workshop – or most of last night?'

'Well, now you come to mention it . . .' Athena giggled, sitting down at the table.

63

'You never fail, do you,' Agnes laughed.

'He's lovely. Mmmm.' Athena stretched, revealing tanned skin under white towelling. 'I only got home at five, no wonder I'm knackered.'

Agnes got up and poured the coffee. 'What's his flat like?'

'You mean, is he completely wonderful in bed?'

'No, I mean, what's his flat like?'

'You really want to know? Tidy. Smart. Masculine. And he is. Wonderful, I mean. Mmm.'

'Oh, shut up. Milk? Sugar?'

'Just milk. I suppose as your sex life's on hold, you don't want to hear about anyone else's.'

'On hold? Don't be so silly, I don't have a sex life.'

'You did.'

'Alexander?' Agnes brought two mugs of coffee to the table. 'You've never understood that.'

'I understand it better than you think.'

'Alexander and I met at a peculiar point in both our lives. He was in crisis, and I was – I was – well, for some reason, it was necessary. Perhaps. That's all.'

'Of course. You're completely over him, and he's forgotten you. End of story.'

'I'm not denying it was important. It exists as part of my life. But since then I've done a lot of spiritual work. Things are different now. And anyway, he'll have met someone else by now, probably loads of other women.'

'He sent you a Christmas card.'

'Yes. You saw it.'

'It said, "All my love, Alexander".'

Agnes sipped her coffee.

'And you wrote one back to him,' Athena went on. 'I saw that too.'

'I showed you, since you asked.'

'An engraving of the Madonna and Child, and all you wrote inside was the letter "A".'

'I couldn't think of anything else to say.'

'Poppet, if I could play it as cool as that I would have them at my feet.'

'I am not playing a game.'

'No. You're not. But you really think he's likely to have found someone else?' Athena shook her head and sighed. The doorbell suddenly chimed, loudly. 'Oh God, it's him. He said he'd come round this morning. Oh no.' Athena jumped up and ran to the mirror in the hallway, pulling at her cheeks, prodding the skin under her eyes. 'Oh God, I look terrible. I'm too old for this lark. Look, keep him talking while I try and lose twenty years off this face.'

Agnes sighed, and opened the door.

'Yes, it's me,' she said to a startled Nic. 'I'm sorry, firstly, for not being Athena, and secondly, for walking out of your workshop so inconsiderately. Would you like some coffee? Athena's in the shower.'

Nic smiled, hung his leather jacket on the bannister post and followed Agnes into the kitchen. 'It's OK,' he said. 'I just felt bad that you were upset.' He took the coffee that Agnes handed to him, and sat down.

'No, it wasn't your fault. It was some kind of memory. It's gone now,' Agnes said, buttering toast.

Nic watched her, then said, 'Athena says you know some people who got into trouble with regression stuff?'

'Sort of. They're quite young. I don't know much about it, but it might be that they think someone has come back to take revenge.'

Nic frowned. 'Where did they get ideas like that?'

'I've no idea. I get the impression it was all a bit *ad hoc*.'

'I certainly don't believe it works that way. People coming back for revenge? Sounds phoney to me.' He sipped at his coffee. 'But the problem is, in the wrong hands people can convince themselves of anything. Then you're in trouble.'

They heard the bathroom door open, and Athena wafted into the kitchen on a cloud of soapy peach fragrance. 'Darling.' She bent and kissed Nic, extravagantly.

He grinned up at her. 'I thought we might have lunch,' he said. 'All three of us, if you like.'

Agnes looked at her watch. 'I'm due at my community in half an hour. I'd better be going,' she said.

'So you really are a nun?' Nic said. 'Amazing, in this day and age.'

At the door Athena gave Agnes a huge wink as she showed her out.

Lunch at the community was busy and cheerful. Afterwards, the washing-up all done and the Sisters dispersed, Agnes went into the lounge. Madeleine was alone, reading. She looked up from her book, studied Agnes a moment, then closed the book.

'What's up?'

Agnes smiled and came to sit next to her. 'Just life, I think.'

'How's the spiritual crisis? Is God still male?'

'Yes and no.'

'I was going to ask you if you'd do a day shift this week at the hostel. We've got a gap with people being away.'

Agnes nodded. 'Yes. That's fine.'

Madeleine looked at her again. 'Is it that you're upset about Becky?'

'It's a terrible thing to have happened – although that wasn't—'

'What do the police say?'

'The police? Very little. They've questioned a few people. They seem to be treating it as a random killing.'

'And what do you think?'

'Well, they could be right. Or, it could be what the kids at the camp think, which is that it was a security person or a heavy from the DoT or someone.'

'Is that likely? From what I know those people only get murderous in a crowd.'

'That's what I thought. But I suppose it might have been some kind of warning that went wrong. And if it's not that, then—'

'Then what?'

'Well, her family life was quite unhappy, I think. Although, if family tensions always ended in murder, none of us would survive.' Madeleine very carefully placed a bookmark in her book. 'Are you reading Pascal?'

'Yes,' Madeleine replied, 'I am actually. So – what was making you so quiet over lunch?'

'Was it that obvious?'

'No, I just wondered.'

Agnes sighed. 'My past seems to be bearing heavily upon me at

66

the moment. And Athena was talking nonsense this morning. About Alexander. That's all.'

On Monday morning Sam's social worker phoned Agnes at the hostel and said that they'd like to arrange the meeting between Sam and Mike for Wednesday evening. Mike had agreed, and could Agnes check with Sam. Also, Agnes was welcome to attend. Agnes immediately phoned the camp.

'Hi, the Ark.'

'Rona? It's Agnes.'

'Oh, Agnes—'

'Since when have you lot been the Ark?'

Rona laughed. 'Since yesterday. We've had all these journalists sniffing around, and one of them said to Jenn, "What tribe are you, then?" You know, like the Dongas or something? And she said, completely straight-faced, "Oh, we call ourselves the Ark." Rona giggled. 'Anyway, everyone's adopted it now. Listen, I'm glad you phoned. We've been trying to get hold of you. Col's in a bit of a state.'

'What's the problem?'

'You'd better talk to Sam.'

'Hi.' Sam came on the line. 'It's Col, he's in a bad way, it's really scary. And with his asthma and everything . . .'

'What is it?'

'I can't tell you over the phone. What with them all listening.'

'Who all listening?'

'You know, them MI5 lot.'

'For God's sake, what's happening?'

'He's saying he's next, that's all.'

'Next?'

'And he can't breathe.'

'Yes, but he's asthmatic. Has he got an inhaler there?'

'It's not just that. He's seen someone or something, he won't tell me. He went to the office in town, and he came back in a bloody awful state.'

'If he won't tell you. I'm not sure that I'm—'

'He's lost the plot, Agnes. He's gasping for fucking breath. I'm really scared.'

'Look, I'll finish my shift at four and come straight over.'

At five o'clock the M25 was at a standstill. Cars inched along in uneven ranks under a metallic, drizzly sky. Agnes stared at the rhythmic swishing of the windscreen wipers and wondered if she was ever going to get out of first gear.

By the time she reached the camp the drizzle had turned to a steady rain. The campfire puffed and sputtered as Rona and Jeff struggled to fix a tarpaulin over it. Sam led Agnes to see Col where he was lying in his bender. His eyes were open and staring and seemed unnaturally huge against the pallor of his face. Agnes knelt beside him listening to the laboured, rasping breaths. She spoke to him urgently.

'Col, is this just the asthma?'

He shook his head.

'Have you taken anything – drugs, anything?'

He shook his head. Sam picked up a Ventolin inhaler. 'We've tried to get him to take this,' she said.

Agnes offered it to him, and he shook his head. 'Why ever not?' she said.

He closed his eyes.

'Right,' Agnes said, and he opened them again. 'You're coming with me. You and Sam.' Col began to wheeze in protest but Agnes interrupted, 'You need to feel safe, right? So you're staying at the hostel. There's people there all the time. No one can harm you there, OK?' She noticed the greeny-grey flecks of his eyes, the shadows around them. He blinked slowly, then nodded.

On the drive to London he lay across the back seat, swathed in his sleeping bag, still fighting for breath. Sam sat next to Agnes, and Agnes remembered to tell her as they drove about the meeting with Mike on Wednesday, and how they'd be going to the local Social Services offices so that it would be on neutral territory. Also, she thought, it's time you told me what you know, young lady.

'Agnes, how lovely to see you,' Julius said as she opened the hostel door and found him in the hallway. 'I was just going.'

'Julius, um – I wondered if I could – um – help Daniel with the night shift.'

Julius's gaze went from Agnes to Sam, who was just behind her, to the whey-faced boy standing on the front steps clutching a sleeping bag around him. 'Agnes,' he said, 'if you think we can afford to give priority to your friends just whenever it suits you—'

'Col can sleep on my floor in the teamworker's room and Sam can be in the lounge. And I need to borrow a sleeping bag as that one there needs fumigating, preferably with a small hydrogen bomb.'

'When people say you won't take no for an answer—'

'Dear, dear Julius,' Agnes said, kissing his cheek as she brushed past him.

Col's wheezing was already beginning to ease as she settled him on a makeshift bed in her room. When much later she came to bed herself he was sleeping peacefully, his breath a gentle whisper in the quiet of the room.

Agnes woke early the next morning. In the dim grey light she saw that Col's bed was empty. The digital alarm clock flashed six fifty-four. She pushed open her door and went downstairs. The kitchen door was ajar and Col was sitting at the table, staring into space.

'Col?' He looked up. 'Are you feeling better?'

'Yup.'

'What are you doing here? You'll get chilled.'

'I always wake up early.'

Agnes put on the kettle. 'Oh well, we can have a quiet cup of tea before the hordes descend.'

They sat over their tea in silence. Outside it was raining, a determined, steady drizzle. Agnes said, 'You can stay here if you like, for a while anyway.'

He looked at her through the steam rising from his mug. 'Thanks. But – you can't protect me for ever. No one can.'

'Col – who have you seen?' He shook his head. 'If you'd only tell someone, we could begin to—'

'It's impossible.' Agnes heard the wheezing at the edge of his voice again. She stood up, touching his shoulder briefly as she did so, and began to open cupboards, getting out cornflakes, sliced white bread and cheap margarine for the hostel residents.

In the relative quiet of the afternoon, Agnes left Sam and Col giggling over tattered old copies of *Hello* magazine and slipped into the empty office. She got out her notebook, and then dialled the number she'd copied down from Becky's file.

'Is that Roger Murphy?'

'Yes.'

'Hello, my name's Sister Agnes. I believe you host a church group.'

'That's right.'

'That the Stanton family attend?'

'Who did you say you were?'

'Sister Agnes. I knew Becky Stanton.'

There was a silence on the line. Then Roger Murphy said, 'I'm not sure – I'm not sure I can be of assistance.'

'I just wondered,' Agnes said, 'whether you'd be able to give me a few moments of your time. Later this week, maybe? It's such a tragic business.'

'I'm not sure why you—'

'Just a brief meeting?'

There was another momentary silence. Then he said, 'Can I take your number and get back to you?'

'Yes, of course,' Agnes said warmly. She was about to give him her home number, but something made her give the office number instead.

That evening she arranged with Daniel that Sam and Col could stay until Thursday. She'd enjoyed seeing them both grow more and more relaxed as the day had worn on. By suppertime they were whispering rude words to each other and giggling helplessly like five-year-olds. She wondered what would happen when they had to leave. Sam was at least meeting Mike tomorrow, and perhaps something would come of that. But Col? Did he have family? Wasn't there somewhere he could go, someone he could run to, to protect him from this terror that had frightened him into speechlessness?

Just before they went to bed Agnes caught Sam on her own. 'Sam – when Col went to the office in town – who was he with? We've got to find out what happened.'

'I've tried asking him but he won't say.'

'You've got to tell me what you know – what you've both been so frightened of.'

Sam chewed her lip. 'I told you, it'll make it worse. If Col knows

I've been going on to you about it—'

'Who is this person you're scared of?'

Sam sucked in her cheeks and stared out of the darkened window.

Agnes wanted to slap her. 'Does she ride a horse?'

Sam paled, looked at her, looked back to the window again.

'For God's sake, Sam, why does she frighten you both so much?'

Sam glanced at Agnes, then turned back to the window.

'OK,' Agnes went on, 'you win for now. Just tell me who's at this office where Col was working?'

Sam shrugged. 'It's the local road campaign. It's just someone's spare room with a phone and a fax machine.'

'Can I talk to them?'

'Sure, she's called Sheila. She's really nice, she lets us have baths and everything. They'll have the number at the camp.'

'That reminds me, I've washed everything you two were wearing, twice. It still smells of smoke but it'll have to do. And I'm sure something bit me when I was handling it all.'

Sam looked pointedly at Agnes and scratched at her head with both hands.

Early the next morning Agnes found Col alone in the kitchen again. Again she made them both some tea.

'Col,' she began, 'isn't there somewhere you could go – someone you could go to?'

He shook his head.

'Somewhere safe?'

'Safe?' He laughed, abruptly, and all the softness of yesterday was suddenly gone. Agnes looked at the harsh lines of his face which seemed suddenly old. 'Safe?' he said again. 'You'll be fucking lucky.'

'You mean wherever it was you came from, is worse than – whatever it is you're frightened of?'

Col smiled mirthlessly. 'Since when have I been fucking safe?' He drained his cup, got up from the table and left the room.

After breakfast, Agnes went straight to her flat. She showered, put on some clean clothes, made some coffee and sat down to open her mail and listen to her messages.

'Hi, it's Athena. Everything's wonderful. Isn't love just the thing? Catch you later, byeeee.'

'Agnes, it's Julius on Tuesday evening. Someone called Roger Murphy phoned for you. He said you'd got his number. I trust you're still enjoying playing mother hen.'

'Silly old Julius,' Agnes muttered.

'Hello, this is Mike Reynolds on Wednesday morning. Just wondering if we could have a briefing chat before this evening – feeling rather nervous and all that. I'm at my desk all day.'

There was another message, but the caller rang off before speaking. Agnes picked up the receiver and dialled Mike's number, and his secretary put her straight through.

'You phoned me.'

'God, Agnes, I'm nervous. So much depends on all this.'

'It'll be fine. Sam's very keen to meet you – there's nothing to worry about.'

'They have so much bloody power these social workers. If they hadn't interfered when Sam was a baby—'

'Listen, the best thing you can do is get all negative attitudes towards social workers out of your head before this evening. Go in smiling, positive—'

'God, I haven't set eyes on her since – I'm just frightened I'm going to burst into tears or something.'

'No one'll mind if you do. Just don't come in reeking of booze, and try not to smoke either.'

He laughed. 'You'll be there, won't you?'

'Absolutely. Don't worry.'

The next number she dialled was Roger Murphy's. She was surprised to hear a new warmth in his voice.

'Sister Agnes, wasn't it? Yes, of course, you wanted to meet us, about poor Becky.'

'That's right.'

'Well, we're here. I'm sorry I was so reluctant yesterday, only there's been a lot of local interest, people wanting to meet us, the police, of course. But it's only right that we make ourselves available to people who need to talk about the whole ghastly business. When would you like to come?'

'Well, um—'

'Saturday – during the day sometime? You can meet Ross Turner then, he's our Pastor. Eleven o'clock?'

'Fine. Thank you. Thank you very much.'

As she replaced the receiver, Agnes caught herself wondering whether Roger Murphy had secretly vetted her since their first phone conversation. The paranoia of the anti-road movement was obviously infectious.

Then she phoned Rona, to reassure her about Col's health and to get Sheila's number. Finally she phoned Sheila.

'The thing is,' Agnes said, having explained who she was, 'Col came back from the office very upset.'

'Yes, I know, I was worried,' Sheila said. 'He was on the machine at the time.'

'On the machine?'

'The Internet. He popped in to send an e-mail about the eviction or something. When he left he was white as a sheet. Wouldn't tell me why.'

'Look – would you mind if I visited you later this week and had a go on this machine myself?'

'By all means, help yourself. I'm around most days, though I've got my sixteen-year-old daughter on her summer holidays who thinks she knows best. If you can cope with the fragile atmosphere, you're welcome.'

That evening Agnes and Sam walked into a bright room newly painted in apricot-pink and sat rather stiffly on two cheap red armchairs. Mary, Sam's social worker, was with them.

'Mike's already here,' she smiled. 'Shall I show him in?'

Sam nodded, chewing on her lip, and a few moments later Mike appeared. Agnes watched him as he came into the room. He stared at Sam, his gaze transfixed, until she became uncomfortable and looked at the floor, fiddling with her nails.

'Won't you sit down,' Mary said, and he took a chair, still gazing at his daughter. Agnes noticed that he was completely dry-eyed.

'Well,' Mary said, brightly, 'we'll leave you two alone together for a while.'

Out in the office Mary went to get some tea. Agnes wandered over to the window and stared out across the grimy street to the huddle of shops; a bookies, a kebab take-away, a newsagent. Agnes gazed absently at the fingers-crossed lottery symbol in the newsagent's window and wondered why Mike's failure to cry should make her feel so uneasy. She turned from the window and went to sit at a desk. Just because he said he might, she thought. It means nothing. She glanced down at the desk and saw Sam's file lying there. She opened it, and flicked through the pages until she saw the name Michael Reynolds. She read through the various notes taken from meetings with him, then on a scrap of paper wrote down his address and the details from his photocopied birth certificate, and the phone numbers of Sam's mother, and Annie, her aunt, whom Mike had contacted. She closed the file just as Mary reappeared in the room with two polystyrene cups of tea.

In the car going back to the hostel, Sam chattered happily about the meeting. 'He's got a lovely house, he showed me a photo, and there's this school nearby that's got its own swimming pool, and I could go back and get some exams, and he likes loads of different kinds of music, and he even knew who Björk was, and don't you think he was wearing nice shoes? You wouldn't have to be embarrassed about a dad who wore shoes like that.'

Agnes checked that Sam and Col were comfortably ensconced at the hostel and then went home to bed. That night she dreamed of Mike Reynolds, only after a while she could tell by the scratchy tweed jacket that it wasn't Mike at all, it was her own father, and he was weeping, really sobbing, and she felt embarrassed at the tears, and then she heard herself say in the dream, only she seemed to have the voice of a little girl, 'Don't cry . . . don't cry, Papa, it makes no difference now.'

Chapter Eight

The next morning Agnes was woken early by the phone. She snatched it up, but immediately the line went dead. She replaced the receiver and stared at it, then lay down again. The rain had passed, and warm sunlight filtered through the curtains. Agnes closed her eyes against the light, and thought about Mike Reynolds. In a few weeks' time Sam would become his daughter. Agnes had an image of her, gift-wrapped like a parcel, delivered to the door of his nice semi by a party of smiling do-gooders, herself included. It was Sam's choice, she told herself. She's sixteen, it's up to her. And it solves everyone's problem. Social Services can sign her off, she doesn't have to go back to her abusive home . . . Agnes curled up in bed and pulled the covers around her. Was it jealousy, then, this feeling? Was it too much for her, the idea that your father might really come back, might really sweep you up and take you off to a new life and love you after all. And all those years of waiting, of suffering your mother's escalating bitterness, being palmed off with assorted staff and governesses and second-rate schools, waiting for your father to turn round and realise that his daughter needed him, *needed him*, for God's sake . . . Was it just too much for her to accept that in Sam's case the dream had come true?

She got out of bed and went into the shower. Then, washed and dressed, she knelt in prayer. 'Our Father,' she began, then stopped. Another image came to her, of herself, gift-wrapped, being handed over by her father to Hugo, her husband, whose reign of terror had lasted for the few years of their marriage and then for a long time afterwards.

She opened her eyes, and got up from her knees. She sat on her bed and stared into space for a while, frowning. Then she stood up, picked up her raincoat and left.

75

'There are other ways to understand divinity,' Julius said half an hour later. 'God the Father is just one. And shouldn't you be at the hostel by now?'

Agnes ran her fingers through her hair and sighed. 'Yes, I should go. It's just, I suddenly couldn't face the day. I'm glad you were here.'

'There's Mary, the mother of God. And Jesus, who shares our humanity, and I know he's male but at least he's not in the patriarchal tradition of the Old Testament—'

'I suddenly couldn't stand the idea of calling God "Father"—'

'You've never minded before.'

'No, it's odd. After all this time.' She stood up to leave, then said suddenly, 'Julius, I'm worried about Sam.'

'Sam?'

'She's about to sign her life away.'

'She's going to live with her father.'

'Julius – this sounds ridiculous – I think he's not her father.'

Julius blinked at Agnes against a sudden dazzle of sunlight. 'Agnes, sit down, sit down. Is that what all this is about?'

Agnes sat next to Julius and he took her hand. She stared at her fingers, at his own entwined with them. She shook her head. 'I don't know. I just don't know. These days when I pray it's – it's all confused. I mean, I've even caught myself thinking that I only ever became religious so that I'd have a proper father. An absolute, unconditional father. It's ridiculous, Julius.'

'Agnes, it's not ridiculous at all.'

She touched the nail of his forefinger which was blackened from a recent injury. 'What do I do about Sam?'

'Well, she won't go immediately, will she? If I were you, I'd use the time left to reassure myself that he is who he says he is.'

'But we've already established that he is.'

'All his papers are in order, and he has no criminal record. Everything that can be checked out has been. But if you're still feeling like this, then you must put your mind at rest.'

Agnes stood up. 'And in the meantime, who do I pray to?'

Julius walked to the door and opened it for her. 'What I do sometimes, is just listen. Just listen and see who's there.'

Agnes looked up at him. 'It's OK for you. You have a direct

line.' She kissed his cheek and left.

Julius went to his desk and sat down, his hand on the side of his face where she'd kissed it.

At eleven that morning Agnes sat down with Sam and Col.

'We've got to think about where you two are going to live after today.'

'I'm going to live with Mike,' Sam said.

'Not immediately,' Agnes said. 'Let's be realistic.' Sam set her face sullenly. 'Look,' Agnes went on, 'nobody's disputing that he's entitled to a relationship with you. But living with—'

'And does anyone care what I think?' Sam said. 'It's not about what he's fucking entitled to – it's about my bloody future, right? And anyway, those social workers can't wait to get me off their hands. Where else am I going to go?'

'Fine,' Agnes said wearily. 'But between now and whenever it's all settled, where are you going to go?'

'The Ark,' Sam said. 'Where else?'

'And you, Col?'

Col's eyes flickered nervously to Sam's face, then to Agnes's. 'Yup. The Ark,' he said quietly.

'Are you sure?'

'I've nowhere else to go.'

And the dangers? Agnes wanted to ask, but realised there was no point asking. He was right, there was nowhere else. She felt suddenly annoyed with herself for having no solutions. The bed she'd scavenged for them was entirely temporary. She was as incapable of providing long-term solutions as anyone else.

'Although—'Col began, looking at Sam. He went on, 'Sam says maybe when she gets to stay with Mike, I could go too.'

'I'm not sure—'

'It'll be my house then,' Sam said. 'I can have all my mates to stay.'

It occurred to Agnes that this whole scheme of Mike's might fall at the first hurdle; that once Mike had fully grasped the reality of having a teenage daughter, he might abandon the scheme at once. The idea of Mike being off the scene brought a feeling of relief; once again, Agnes wondered why.

★ ★ ★

That afternoon she drove Sam and Col back to the road camp, and decided to sleep there herself. As she turned off the main road up the dirt track, she was startled by a camera flash close to the windscreen. She just caught sight of a figure vanishing into the trees.

'It's starting, then,' Sam said.

'What's starting?'

'All that hassle they do. Jeff told me. Detectives, security people, harassment. It's the run up to the eviction.'

She parked at the end of the track and the three of them walked across the field to the camp. The air was heavy with the heat of early August. Agnes carried two shopping bags of food into the kitchen bender and unpacked them. Fruit, bread, cheese, vegetables, a tub of peanut butter and several packets of biscuits. Rona tucked her head round the tarpaulin.

'Get flashed at, did you?'

'Apparently so.'

'It's number plates. Or something. They record it somewhere, I suppose. Or maybe it's just for fun.'

'Anything else?'

'Bloody everything. The phone box down the road got vandalised. We're getting all sorts of clicks on the mobile phone. Oh, and also, Sheila thinks someone broke into her upstairs room at the weekend, where the computer is. She's not sure, but the window was left wide open although nothing was nicked. It's typical of them, you see, harassment just to make themselves feel better.'

'Do you know when the eviction is yet?'

Rona shook her head. 'Nah. We're expecting a month's notice. But you can never tell.' Agnes followed her out of the tent. Rona looked at the sky and twitched her nose. 'Rain in the air; we'll all get smoked out under the tarp again tonight.'

By the time Jeff had boiled several pounds of potatoes, and Agnes had sautéed aubergines, peppers and tomatoes in olive oil and garlic, the rain was pounding on to the tarpaulin above them, trickling off the sides, filtering around the edges of the benders. The fire barely lasted the time it took for everyone to eat, and no one felt like singing. Earlier than usual the climbers sought refuge in their cosy

78

tree-houses, and those staying on the ground crawled into their benders.

Agnes settled down in her sleeping bag next to Sam. Her feet felt cold and damp through her thick socks, and she lay awake for a while listening to the rain hammering out its varying rhythms around her. She was just settling down to sleep when she thought she heard footsteps and voices some way off in the forest. She listened hard, prepared to go out and investigate; but she heard nothing more, and eventually she drifted off to sleep.

The next morning the sky had cleared again. Agnes left Sam still fast asleep and emerged from her bender to find Jenn rolling back the tarpaulin to dry in the sun.

'Sleep OK?' Jenn said.

'I thought I heard people.'

'Yeah. They're out there.'

'Who are they?'

'The usual form is detectives hired from a private agency. Though they don't usually hang out for no reason like that. And nothing's been nicked so far. Otherwise, it's security people staking out the ground. Or the bailiffs.' She shrugged and laughed. 'They just can't take it, you see. They haven't the faintest idea what we're about. Tea?'

'Yes, please. And then I must go. I said I'd visit Sheila this morning.'

'Right.'

'Jenn – these lurking people – how long have they been around?'

'We've only noticed them since the weekend really.'

'So – when Becky—'

Jenn bent down to put the kettle on the fire, then straightened up. 'Who knows, eh?' She rubbed her back. 'The police are silent. The local view from those old Tories down in the village is that if you live as we do, you can expect to get bumped off by a passing nutcase.'

'So you don't expect the police to solve it, then, Jenn?'

Jenn rearranged the kettle on the fire, then looked up at Agnes, blinking through the smoke. 'I think these days, life is cheap. And according to the powers that be – ' she stood up again – 'some lives are cheaper than others.'

Agnes followed Sheila down the narrow hallway of her cottage aware of a warm smell of coffee and toast. The hall gave way suddenly into a wide, sunlit kitchen, the far end of which was entirely glass. There was a huge abstract painting in red and purple taking up one wall, and a jumble of house plants, some hanging from the ceiling in curly baskets, some trailing haphazardly along the polished wood of the floor and skirting boards.

Agnes sat on a stool at the table while Sheila poured coffee and buttered toast. Sheila was a thin, wiry woman, with untidy grey hair and high cheekbones. Her eyes were piercing blue and surrounded by laughter lines. She wore a large baggy jumper and a multicoloured skirt that fell in floating layers.

'So, are you really a nun?' she asked, depositing various jars of home-made jam onto the table. 'Oh, wait, you must try this,' she added, rummaging through her cupboards and eventually producing a sticky, unlabelled jar. 'I've started helping a neighbour with her bees, and this is my reward.'

'Yes, I am a nun,' Agnes replied, spreading her toast with honey, licking her fingers.

'Smelt the coffee, did you?' Sheila called suddenly towards the door. A slender young girl appeared in the doorway. She was wearing a huge white T-shirt and she peered out at Agnes from straight, jet-black hair which fell around her face. 'This is Lily,' Sheila was saying. 'My daughter.' Lily leaned against the doorframe and yawned.

Half an hour later Sheila sat Agnes down at the computer and switched it on. 'Do you know about these things, then?' she said.

'Only a bit.'

'If you want to send an e-mail you just have to – I'll show you when it's done all this bit.'

'I don't really want to send anything. What I really wanted to do was find out what Col was doing when he – when he got all upset the other day.'

'Right, well, let's get into GreenNet and start from there.'

Sheila moved the mouse around and clicked it. 'I got this for my business. Then I got involved in the campaign against that horrible old road, so I ended up on GreenNet and various other news group things. Here we are. What do you want to do now?'

Agnes scanned the index. 'What are these?'

'Just messages received. We can go through them if you like, that's probably what Col was doing.'

'OK.'

Sheila pulled up a chair next to Agnes and called up the first file. It said: 'Update on Twyford Down.'

'I'll download this. Hang on. Right, next one. Oh, this is boring, we've already had that.' Some clickings later, a new file filled the screen, just as the phone downstairs started to ring. 'Mum, it's for you,' Agnes heard Lily call. 'Some boring woman.'

Sheila sighed, got up. 'Back in a moment.'

Agnes read the screen. It was something about a European-wide network of anti-road groups based in Amsterdam. Suddenly, all the letters began to move and jumble themselves up. Agnes blinked and stared as the words collapsed in a heap at the bottom of the screen. Then a message flashed up in huge letters.

'Put your hands in the air. Go on, do it.'

Agnes hesitated, common sense telling her that no one could see her. Another message appeared.

'Or as they say, Stand and Deliver. You have just been cyberzapped by the SUPERHIGHWAYMAN!!!!'

The screen went blank. Agnes heard Sheila come up the stairs and open the door.

'What happened?' Sheila asked, seeing the blank screen.

'I – I've no idea. Someone calling themselves the Superhighwayman—'

'What? Did it clear the screen?'

'It seems so.'

Sheila clicked the mouse. Nothing happened. 'I don't understand it.'

'All the words sort of fell down the screen.'

'A virus? But that couldn't happen on the Net. How weird.' She reset the computer, and after a moment the screen showed the file index again. 'Phew.' She clicked on a file, which came up as normal.

'Would this Highwayman have left an address?' Agnes asked.

'I don't know. Let's see – where were you?' Sheila scrolled through the messages again. 'No. Nothing. That's the weirdest thing I've ever seen – to leave no trace like that . . .' She sighed. 'Well, I guess that's what scared Col.'

'Hmm,' Agnes said.

'And it explains the break-in too. Someone must have left the infected disk with the others. I bet it's just bloody harassment again, just because of the road campaign—'

'Did you report it?'

Sheila sat down next to Agnes, her eyes still on the screen. 'Actually, I didn't. For reasons of my own.' Agnes waited. Sheila looked at her, and said, 'My brother's a Detective Sergeant. A copper. In the local force. Charlie.'

'Charlie Woods? I met him. He's nice.'

Sheila smiled. 'Yeah, he's OK. We're quite close in a way. The thing is, with all this harassment – I couldn't face finding out—' She twisted a lock of hair around her finger. 'They must know, you see. The local police station. And I just can't be bothered to find out that my own brother is part of all that.'

'It may not be them. It might be some other—' Agnes's eye was caught by a name on the list of files. She blinked. 'What's that?' she asked Sheila. 'There. Where it says, "Emily Quislan"?'

'That – just a message. I'll call it up for you if you want.'

Sheila clicked the mouse, and a moment later the screen said, 'Emily Quislan rides again.'

'Don't know what that is,' Sheila laughed.

'No,' Agnes said, knowing that she was looking at the words that had caused Col nearly to die of asthma. She checked the sender's address. 'JEL @ Bosh.Co UK', it said.

'Oh well,' Agnes said, lightly. 'Who knows? What with security guards everywhere and Becky's death—'

'That hasn't helped the atmosphere in this house, either.'

'What do you mean?'

'Lily knew her, Becky.'

'How come?'

'They used to ride together. There's a lovely woman the other side of the village, runs a small stables, and Lily and Becky used to

82

ride there. And then they met up again when Lily got involved in this church thing.'

'Hang on – Lily?'

'Some ghastly evangelical thing.'

'Lily goes to Ross Turner's set-up?'

'You know him?'

'Only by name.'

'I don't trust them. Cults. When I was her age I was into free thinking and having fun, not all this right-wing claptrap about family values.'

'Surely that's just the point. She's not you.'

Sheila looked at Agnes. 'I know. If I say anything against it, it just makes it worse. But I'm worried. I hope next term when she starts at college she'll find other interests and move on.'

'I'm sure she will. And anyway, it might be perfectly wholesome, most of them are.'

'Mmm. Maybe.'

'Your friend with the stables,' Agnes began, feeling a sudden surge of yearning.

'Diane – what about her?'

'Does she still hire her horses out?'

'Sure, yeah. Why, do you ride?'

'I used to,' Agnes sighed, remembering long days in France hurtling across fields and fences.

'I'm sure she'd find you something,' Sheila said.

Agnes shrugged, smiled. 'Oh, I don't know. It's ages since I've been in the saddle. I'd probably be hopeless now. And anyway, I'm not sure I've got time at the moment.'

Driving back to the camp, Agnes was aware of an idea forming in her mind, a kind of hunch. She caught up with Sam and Col as they strapped on abseil harnesses ready to join Jeff up in the trees.

'I'll be going back to London soon,' she said. 'Will you be OK?'

They nodded, sullenly.

'You must phone me if anything happens to frighten you,' Agnes went on. They exchanged glances, nodded again. 'I just wish you could tell me more about what's going on,' Agnes added, exasperated. 'No, I know,' she said, as they looked at each other again, 'it'll just make things worse. But don't think I'm going to leave you alone in this – this situation, whatever it is.'

As she set off to the woods, she glanced back to see them shinning up the trees in their bright jumpers like two creatures of the rainforest. Once more she followed the column of smoke, once more she caught sight of the blanket-draped figure sitting over his fire, despite the growing heat of the August day. He looked up and smiled.

'Little Sister,' Bill said. She sat down next to him. 'How's it going?' he asked.

She took a deep breath. 'It would go better,' she said, 'if people told me everything they knew instead of just selected highlights.'

'Human nature, kid,' he said.

'For example,' she said, 'there's a Superhighwayman out there – but who's going to tell me where?' She watched him closely. Bill's eyes seemed to smile, but his face was composed. 'Or,' she went on, 'does virtual reality bear no relation to this one? Perhaps virtual morality is entirely topsy-turvy; perhaps it really is however you want it to be.'

'Brave new world, man, the virtual world,' Bill said, eyeing her. 'I wouldn't know.'

'No,' she said. 'I'm sure you wouldn't. Well,' she said, getting up, 'I must be going now. It's been nice talking to you.'

She walked away from his patch without looking back. I know I'm right, she thought, as her feet crunched through the leaves of the forest floor. He knew what I meant.

On the drive back to London, she imagined Bill breaking into Sheila's office, deliberately sabotaging the campaign with a computer disk – yet playfully, harmlessly even. It made no sense at all.

At home, she played back her phone messages. The first was from Athena.

'Sweetie. Nic's away this weekend, and I thought we could catch up with each other. There's a new French brasserie sort of thing on the Old Brompton Road – fancy trying it? We could meet there tomorrow night, eight-ish? Let me know.'

The next message started as a series of clicks, and then there was the sound of someone breathing for a couple of seconds. Then it cut off. Agnes stared at the receiver. Did word spread so fast? Was she now subject to the same interference as the road protesters? Or was it from some other source? Agnes shivered, despite the warmth of the evening.

The next morning she hesitated over her wardrobe. Should she dress up for this Pastor? Or should she deliberately dress down, she thought, considering the pale blue jeans that she'd been living in all summer. Maybe she should even dust off her habit? In the end she dug out her grey pleated skirt and a cream silk shirt.

At five to eleven Agnes rang the doorbell of 39 Fairfax Place. It was answered by a man with a smooth pink face and a shock of short grey hair. He smiled warmly.

'Sister Agnes? I'm Roger Murphy. Come in, Pastor Turner's already here.'

He led her into the front room. There was a spotless brick-look fireplace against a background of beige woodchip. Ross Turner rose from the sofa, his arm outstretched. The room seemed suddenly small. He was about forty, and had neat brown hair, greying at the temples. Agnes noticed his well-cut suit, his even features, his warm hazel eyes, as she shook his hand. His voice was deep and warm.

'It was good of you to come,' he said. A bustle of noise came from the kitchen. 'They go to so much trouble,' he shrugged, still smiling, 'there's really no need.'

Agnes was glad she'd chosen to dress with a sense of occasion. She took the chair opposite his, as a plump woman appeared from the kitchen with a tray of four cups and a plate of biscuits. Agnes smelled instant coffee. The woman handed the Pastor his cup, and he gave her the same warm smile as he said, 'Thank you, Elizabeth,' then turned to Agnes again.

'It's very kind of you to see me,' Agnes began.

'No, no, it's we who should be grateful,' he said. 'This community is grieving the loss of a lovely young woman, and we need to take every opportunity to speak of her.' Elizabeth finished handing out the cups and settled down on the sofa next to Roger.

'Yes, it must be awful for you all,' Agnes said.

Ross Turner nodded. 'The family have been part of our little community for some years. Both Morris and Shirley have contributed enormously.' Roger and Elizabeth nodded at this.

'How long has your group been going?'

'As we are now, about two and a half years. Before that we were part of another group, based out towards Sevenoaks, but we – we split from them.'

'Why – if you don't mind me asking?'

Ross Turner smiled. 'Partly on matters of doctrine. Also, mainly, that we wanted to concentrate on outreach here in our local community.'

'Do you have many young people?'

'We consider it the mainstay of our work,' Ross replied. 'They are, after all, the future. If the new generation can go forward with Christ in their hearts, then there is hope for the world.'

Roger and Elizabeth both nodded, and Elizabeth said, shyly, 'Our son Steven is one of the youth group leaders.'

'A gifted boy,' Ross said, and Elizabeth blushed and pulled at her skirt.

'And Becky?'

Agnes noticed Roger and his wife glance at each other, then both looked across to Ross. 'Well, you must know, from your work with young people—' he paused, and smiled at Agnes, and she felt caught up in that clear, frank gaze. 'You see, Agnes, not everyone does what's best for them, do they? Becky had so much going for her, her caring parents, her young brother – she was doing well at school. When she began to be – difficult – we all prayed for her, and waited for the Lord to move her to come back to us. And we knew she would. She would have come back, if Satan had not intervened.'

There was a flurry of noise from the hall, and then two young men came into the room.

'I heard you were here,' one said, a tall, muscular boy of about eighteen with thick, untidy brown hair.

'Steven,' Ross smiled, 'how nice to see you. And Jerry too, bless you.' Jerry stood awkwardly behind Steven. He looked about the same age as him, but seemed slight and pale next to Steven's jolly solidity. He wore square spectacles that were wrong for his thin, angular face. They both sat on the floor by Ross's chair. Steven exchanged a quick grin with Elizabeth.

'We were talking about Becky,' Ross said, gently. Steven stared at the carpet and began to pick at a loose thread. 'Sister Agnes here knew her out at that Epping place. It's particularly difficult for the young people, who counted her as a friend,' he said to Agnes.

'And with the awful circumstances of her death—' Agnes began.

'That's the worst thing,' Elizabeth blurted out, emboldened by the presence of her son. 'You just keep thinking about her last moments, over and over again. Shirley's half-mad with it all, and not only that but not having a funeral. I mean if the police could catch the person then at least we could bury her properly, but thinking of her lying in that – that place – and sometimes I have to physically hold on to Shirley to stop her driving up to the mortuary just to hold her daughter – "Let me hold her once more," she keeps saying, but Morris thinks she shouldn't see her . . .' She stopped, breathlessly, red-faced, staring across at Steven. Roger took her hand and patted it. Jerry shifted his long limbs into a different position.

'It's terrible for the parents,' Ross said. 'Terrible.'

'I met them,' Agnes said.

'I know,' Ross replied. 'You mustn't judge them by their present state.'

'I do think—' Agnes hesitated. 'I think Shirley ought to see the body. She can't even begin to grieve – I know it's none of my business, but—'

Ross was staring at her intently. 'I think you're right,' he said. 'Elizabeth, would you be able to take her?'

'We've asked, Pastor, we've both asked time and time again. But Morris is adamant.'

'I shall speak with him.'

Agnes broke the silence that followed. 'Does anyone in your church – does anyone have any idea who might have done it?'

Roger and Elizabeth shook their heads. Steven pulled at the carpet thread which was now quite long. Jerry changed position again. Ross held Agnes's gaze in his own. 'Do you consider it to be the will of God?' he asked her.

Agnes blinked. 'Um – what do you mean . . . ?'

'I mean what I say. If we meet our end, like that – a young, innocent person, a Christian girl – do we say that God has welcomed her to be with Him?'

Agnes met his eyes. 'Yes,' she said. 'I would say that.'

'So you don't see the work of Satan in this?' Ross's clear stare gave nothing away.

'Well,' Agnes said, 'it depends what you mean by Satan. If you mean the absence of God—'

'I mean Satan. A presence, not an absence.'

The room had grown suddenly cold.

'So,' Agnes said, and her voice seemed to echo in the silence, 'you're saying the Devil killed Becky?'

'Someone acting on the Devil's behalf, yes.'

'Where does that leave God, then? Picking up the pieces after the Devil has asserted his power? Gathering up the corpse to Heaven, even though He was powerless to prevent the death in the first place? The God I believe in is greater than that. Don't forget,' Agnes went on, suddenly angry, 'the Devil is a fallen angel. God created Satan too.'

Ross leaned back in his chair and smiled. It was as if the room itself had been holding its breath, and now smiled with him. Agnes waited.

Ross looked at her warmly. 'You have faith, don't you?'

'It's all there is.'

'And are you brave enough – brave enough to admit that there is room for Satan within you?'

'Oh, yes, I'm brave enough for that. Only, I won't call it Satan. I refuse,' Agnes said, 'to pass the responsibility on to any-one else. What there is of Satan in me – it's me. That's all. Just me. And if I pray to God to deliver me from evil, I don't mean that He should arm me in the holy battle with some external force.'

'But if you say Satan is part of you—'

'It's a distraction to call it Satan. I'd rather take responsibility for what I am, including the potential to do harm.'

'Then you make it acceptable.'

'So you mean calling it the Devil—'

'Calling it the Devil means that you can see it more clearly.'

Agnes considered this. 'Perhaps,' she said. 'And where does that leave Becky?'

Ross surveyed everyone in the room before answering. 'Becky

died at the hand of Satan. God's triumph is in taking her to Himself for eternity.'

'And the murderer?'

'What of the murderer?'

'If he or she is all Satan, then there's no room for forgiveness.' Agnes was aware that Elizabeth was staring at her. She glanced across but immediately Elizabeth looked away, smoothing the creases of her skirt.

'On the contrary,' Ross was saying, 'the murderer was possessed by Satan. If Christ can work within his heart, he, too, can be brought to the Truth.'

'And do you think he will be?'

'It's not for me to say,' Ross shrugged. 'Becky ran from us, you see. She left the safety of our fold. Out there . . .' he turned briefly to the window, to the sunlight falling on the neat front lawn. He shook his head at the perils of the world beyond.

Roger Murphy stood up; Agnes was relieved to take her cue to go.

'I've taken enough of your time,' she said. The two boys got up from the floor. Steven went over to his mother, and Jerry stood crookedly, shaking one foot to get the circulation back. Ross led the way into the hall and opened the front door for Agnes.

'I've enjoyed meeting you,' he said, taking her hand.

'It was kind of you to give up so much time,' Agnes said. 'And to put up with my Jesuitical rhetoric.'

Ross smiled at her. 'It makes a change, for me.'

Agnes started down the steps. 'Please try and get Shirley to see her daughter,' she said.

Ross nodded. 'I'll do what I can.'

As Agnes went down the drive past the hydrangea bushes, she was aware of Ross Turner being ushered back inside by his flock, anxious to press another wave of refreshments upon him. She thought about Ross's view of evil, as the black knight on the bloodstained battlefield where God and the Devil fought to the death for the human soul. She thought about what Julius would say when she told him; Julius, whose view of evil was that it was, on the whole, petty, everyday and utterly human. Good old Julius, she thought, walking to the station, feeling the presence of Ross Turner fading in the afternoon breeze.

Chapter Nine

'So was he gorgeous, then?' Athena asked that evening, raising her voice above the restaurant noise. 'I always imagine these preacher types to be really charismatic.'

'Gorgeous? You've seen those ghastly American ones on the telly.'

'Was he like that?'

'Well, no, he wasn't, but the point I'm making is—'

'Shall we have the salmon?' Athena perused the menu.

'I rather fancy steak tonight.'

'Actually so do I. I must be anaemic or something, I'm exhausted these days. So you mean, he was gorgeous.'

'I suppose he was quite good-looking. Nice eyes. The thing is, though, he's sincere. That's what surprised me. He obviously really cares about his community, and he obviously really – believes. Properly, you know.'

'He got to you, didn't he?'

'We had this discussion about evil.'

'He won?'

'It's not about winning and losing. Only—'

'Only, you didn't win.'

Agnes laughed. 'It's an uncomfortable feeling, Athena. For you the equivalent would be if you'd gone to all that trouble to catch Nic and he turned out to be married or gay or something.'

'In my experience, neither are insurmountable, poppet,' Athena replied, raising her glass. 'To true love.'

'That good, is it?' Agnes said, raising hers.

'Sweetie, it's bloody fantastic.'

Two hours later they walked back rather unsteadily towards Athena's flat, arm in arm and giggling.

91

'So you're going to get married and live happily ever after, you and Nic?' Agnes asked.

'You watch me, sweetie. I'm going to walk up that aisle in a white dress with you as my bridesmaid.'

'No, not bridesmaid,' Agnes giggled as they came to a lurching halt outside Athena's mansion block. 'I'm going to be the one to give you away. "Who giveth this woman," they'll say, and I'll say, "You can have her, mate."'

'I can just see it, can't you?'

'What, you getting married?'

They stood together under the streetlamp. Athena was suddenly serious, shadowed in the yellow light as she looked at Agnes. She shook her head. 'No. Not me getting married. Not really, poppet.' She kissed Agnes on both cheeks and teetered up the steps, then turned and waved. 'Super evening, darling, see you soon.' She kissed her hand to Agnes, then leaned rather heavily against the door, which opened and closed again behind her.

Agnes walked back to the main road, wondering whether to wait for a late bus or not. It was a warm night, and the street corners were dotted with idling loud young people. She set off towards the Embankment, finding herself heading east along the river towards home. At Westminster Bridge she paused by the stone wall and stared into the dark, silted waters. She thought about Ross Turner, his searching eyes, his belief in the empty, passive soul in which Good and Evil had to fight it out. She set off on her way, thinking about Col and his terror, and the Highwayman and Woodland Bill; and Sam, and Mike Reynolds; and the clicking on her telephone. And Becky, still lying in the morgue; still waiting for justice. She looked across the river, at the glittering decks of a restaurant boat. Was it all so fragile, she wondered, as Paz and Jenn claimed it was? Was justice something elusive, dependent on one's status? Was Satan now lurking just out of reach, jeering at us all? She looked down into the depths of the river, at the swirling blackness flecked with yellow splashes of light. Her fingers recalled the warmth of Ross's touch as he'd said goodbye. She envied him his certainty.

'You've never wanted certainties before,' Madeleine said, after Mass the next day.

'No. But wouldn't it be nice, to think God is our Father. Really really our father. And Jesus is the good guy, and Satan is the bad guy and it's all clear-cut. As if standing up and saying, "Yes, I allow God into my heart," does the trick. For ever. And if anything goes wrong after that it's just the Devil and you just have to get rid of him and—'

'And what?'

'Nothing. What was I saying?'

'You were saying you wanted to join the evangelical movement.'

Agnes laughed. 'No, not me. But Madeleine, it makes you wonder. Out there are great waves of faith passing us by, New Age stuff and anti-road protests and the evangelicals – how do we know we're right?'

'And all this because Sam wants to live with her father and there's nothing you can do?'

Agnes looked at Madeleine. 'And Becky's death, yes.'

'Maybe there's nothing mysterious about Becky's death. Maybe it was a heavy making a mistake, or a madman or something.'

'But her life—'

'The preacher was OK and very sincere, you said. And a family so lost in grief you can't tell what they're like . . .'

Agnes was aware of an idea just outside her reach, something about Becky, and the Devil being the source of all evil . . .

'Maybe you need to go to Yorkshire,' Madeleine was saying. 'Maybe you need quiet, to centre yourself.'

Getting rid of the Devil, that was it. If you were as certain as Ross about who Satan was, and you thought you recognised Satan in someone, then killing that person might come to seem . . .

'I mean, I know the kids at the hostel need you, but you still have to think about your own needs—'

. . . Might come to seem perfectly justifiable.

'You're not listening, are you?' Madeleine said, then laughed. 'As if you'd ever change your mind.'

'I'm sorry, Madeleine. I'm a bit distracted.'

'If a purer spiritual path is really what you're after, you could always join a nomadic order and travel from place to place with a begging bowl.'

'Do you know, when all this is over, I might just do that.'

* * *

On Sunday evening Agnes settled down at her desk with the notes she'd made from Sam's file. She had the phone number of Linda, Sam's birth mother, and all the details from Mike's birth certificate. She wondered where to start. Sam's Aunt Annie was probably the best bet. She checked the address. She was living in Harlow, married to a man called Brian Everett. Agnes got out the phone number, then wondered whether it wasn't too late in the evening to disturb her. She got up to make some tea, and while she was waiting for the kettle to boil gazed absently out of the window. The chestnut tree outside swayed lethargically in the summer night. In the phone box outside a man was making a call. Almost immediately, Agnes's phone rang. She picked up the receiver, and heard breathing. From where she stood she could see the phone box, and the man in it was holding the receiver, looking straight up at her. She remained there, frozen, staring down at him. Then he hung up, and Agnes heard her own line go dead. She stood there, holding the receiver, as she watched him leave the phone box and walk slowly away from her down the street, not looking back.

When he was out of sight Agnes replaced her phone receiver. She stared at it for a while. Just a coincidence? How could it be? She shivered, went to her drinks cupboard and poured herself a large whisky. She sipped her whisky, standing by the window, looking out – in search of what, she wondered.

It was too late to phone Annie now.

Later that night, before she went to bed, she pulled her phone out from the wall socket.

Annie Everett, née Whittaker, had a rough, harassed voice.

'That girl's nothing but trouble. She was trouble to 'er mum, and that father of 'ers is going to find she's nothing but trouble to him, neither.'

'Mrs Everett, I promise that after this visit, no one else will bother you about Sam. She's probably going to move in with her father now he's reappeared.'

'And there's 'im thinking you can just come back into people's lives when it suits you. They're welcome to each other. Well, I can't see you before four o'clock this afternoon, I'll be back from school with the kids then, make it four thirty, you might get a cup of tea. You got the address?'

'It's very kind of you.'

'She's family, ain't she.'

Agnes put down the phone.

It was not yet ten. She picked up her raincoat, looked outside at the glorious summer sky, and left her coat on the chair.

Half an hour later she was at St Catherine's House, scanning the shelves of the register of births, checking the dates against the notebook in her hand. She took down the book for June to September, 1979 and thumbed through it until she found the entry for Sam. Sam Whittaker, mother Linda Whittaker, place of birth Stepney, East London. There was no father listed. She made a note of the reference, then replaced the book. A thought struck her, and she pulled down the book for Mike's birth date. There it was, Michael Hugh Reynolds, born London 1958. She scribbled down his parents' names just in case, then went to order up the full birth certificate for Sam.

When it came, she found, again, there was no father listed. The mother's address was given as Flat 4, Kincaid Court, Atherton Estate, Stepney.

She emerged into the midday heat. The ozone smog of the Aldwych traffic caught the back of her throat. Ravenous, she decided to grab a sandwich before driving to Harlow.

Annie's house was on a shabby estate near the ring road. Her front lawn was a neat, shaved square, edged with immaculate rose bushes. On each window sill a box spilled forth colour, geraniums, verbena, pansies.

Annie showed Agnes into her kitchen. She was a large woman, with pink, sun-scorched skin and a blonde perm. Her T-shirt said 'Lanzarote' in bright orange letters across the front. The television was on in the front room, and in the kitchen a toddler sat at the table, sucking the jam out of the middle of a biscuit.

'S'cuse the mess,' Annie said. 'Kids everywhere. I've got four, though two's not back yet, and I mind me friend's two after school. Tea?' She bustled to put on the kettle. 'Nah, 'e's not a bad 'un, Mike,' she said, rinsing two mugs under the tap. 'We go back years.

Grew up together, Mike and his mate Bob, and my Brian too. I knew 'im way back as well.'

'When Sam was born,' Agnes said, sitting at the table, 'Linda didn't give her Mike's name.'

'Nah, I remember that. She wanted to, went down the Town 'All, 'opping mad she were, but they said unless he came too they couldn't do it fer 'er, not with them not being married. And 'e was out on the sites, weren't 'e, so she had to leave it at Whittaker. Then 'e pissed off so it was just as well.'

'Why did he go?'

Annie prodded at the tea bags in the mugs. She sighed. 'It's not fer me to say, really, but – Lin didn't really 'ave the makings of a wife. I know it takes two, and maybe he could have done more, but she was – she just weren't committed to 'im.' Annie removed the sticky remains of biscuit from the toddler at the table, and stuck a bottle of juice into his mouth. 'She took after our mum, I reckon. We 'ad so many uncles when we was kids, you could have had a bleedin' football team. I was older than Lin, I kind of watched and waited, and when our Brian asked me to marry him, I thought, that's it, I'm getting out, I'm not going to end up like her. But Lin, she was younger, she was there for longer, and it got worse, with the booze and everything. Biscuit?' She took a Bourbon biscuit and turned it over in her fingers. 'It's what you make it, innit, life. Lin never quite got out. She could have got married, settled down, she 'ad loads of boyfriends . . .'

'So when Mike says he's the father,' Agnes began, wondering how to put it.

Annie's eyes opened wide. 'Oh, 'e's the father all right. Ain't no doubt about that. There weren't one of them boys who'd have done that, fathered a kid and then denied it, not in them days.'

'Sam's really keen to live with him.'

'Good luck to them I say. I know I'm 'ard on her, we've had our ups and downs, and Linda's had it hard too, I can't say she's done right by the kid, and now that git of a boyfriend of 'ers is there all the time. Well, Sam's a handful but she don't deserve what he dishes out when all's said and done.'

'So you'd have no doubts about it?' Agnes heard the front door open, and a tall, blonde girl sauntered into the kitchen.

'Stacey, this is Agnes, we're talking about Sam,' Annie said. The girl made a face, opened the fridge, and took out a Diet Coke. 'Doubts?' Annie went on. 'I tell yer, the only doubts I 'ave is thinking about him in his nice house, which I bet 'e's got, having to cope with a bleedin' sixteen-year-old.' She laughed. 'Does he know what teenagers is like?' She jerked her head towards Stacey, who was leaning against the sink swigging from her can. 'Eat you out of house and 'ome one day, then live on thin air and fags for a week. And the washing – they change all their clothes every two minutes . . .' She laughed again, as Stacey grinned, sat down at the table and took the toddler on to her knees. 'He don't know what's coming to 'im, does he, eh, Stace?'

Stacey pulled a face at the toddler, who chuckled, and then all three of them laughed together.

Agnes drove back into London against the traffic and was home by seven. She put some pasta on to boil. The phone rang. She hesitated, then picked it up.

'Agnes, hi, it's Mike. Look, I wanted to thank you for everything.'

'It's a bit premature, isn't it?'

'Well, I know nothing's been signed, but we're up and running, aren't we?'

'We are?'

'Yeah, sure. Sam's so happy now and she loves her new room—'

Agnes sat down. 'Her new – new room . . . ?'

'I know, I know, I'm sorry, but neither of us could wait. I gave her my address, she hitched over with that boyfriend of hers, mind you he's got to go, a wimp if you ask me . . .'

'When was this?'

'Today. I took the day off, made them lunch. What do they eat, these young people? I swear she'd never seen fresh salmon in her life.'

'Mike, you know this is against all the rules.'

'Oh rules, rules – who are they for, eh? Sam's sixteen, she can do what she likes.'

'But the procedure—'

'The way I see it, the procedure is to protect vulnerable kids from trouble, right? Not to prevent a kid who's had a rough ride

finding some kind of stability with her real dad. Isn't that so, Agnes?'
Agnes swallowed hard. 'I mean,' he went on, 'it's just a formality in
our case. It's not as if anyone has grounds to oppose our plan, is it?'

Agnes bit her lip. 'No,' she said. 'No grounds at all.'

'Thanks for doing your bit,' he said. 'Must go now, see you
around. Keep in touch with us, won't you. Sam's really fond of
you.'

He hung up. Agnes replaced the receiver slowly. She could hear,
from her kitchen, the sound of a saucepan boiling over. She went
to the kitchen and snatched the lid off the frothing pan, then yelled
in pain as it clattered to the floor. She swore loudly, switched off
the heat, and flopped on to a chair. 'Bloody Mike bloody smoothy
Reynolds,' she said, out loud.

She noticed a pack of peanuts in the corner of a kitchen cupboard.
And if Sam gets fed up with him, or he with her, she thought,
wandering to the cupboard, tearing the corner off the packet, what
then? She put a large handful of nuts in her mouth. How dare he
think that he knows best? A skilled professional team has been
dealing with Sam for several months, and he just waltzes in and
makes off with her . . . She stood by the window, munching, as the
phone rang. She picked it up.

'Hello,' she said, through a mouthful of peanuts. Immediately, it
went dead. She glanced out of the window. The phone box was
empty. Right, she thought, and dialled 1471.

'Sorry, no telephone number has been stored,' the well-bred
electronic voice told her. Agnes slammed the phone down.

She found she'd finished the pack of nuts. She went to her kitchen
and poured herself a gin and tonic. She took a large gulp, then
checked a number and dialled it. Sheila answered.

'It's Agnes, I wonder if you could help me?'

'Sure, yes, how are you?'

'OK. Listen, Charlie, your brother – do you think he'd talk to
me about Becky if I asked nicely?'

'Mmmm – dunno. We have an understanding – we get on really
well as long as we don't try to do each other's work—'

'I can see that. It's just that I'm getting menacing phone
calls—'

'You too?'

98

'Are you?'

'Everyone here.'

'How's the computer?'

'Trouble-free again. No problems at all.'

'And Charlie?'

Sheila paused for a moment. 'Oh, go on, give it a go. He's OK. Just don't get heavy or he'll clam up. Let me warn him, and I'll phone you back with his number, OK?'

Agnes sat and waited for Sheila to phone back. She took another large gulp of gin. So this was life, once you got outside the confines of normality. Being photographed by men in bushes, being telephoned by silent callers . . . The phone rang again, and Agnes jumped.

'Sheila, again. Charlie says OK. I reminded him who you were, told him you knew Becky and that you're a nun, it seemed to help.'

Agnes took down the number, thanked Sheila and hung up. She still felt jumpy. It was not yet nine. She finished her gin and dialled Athena's number.

'Hello?' Athena answered.

'It's Agnes.'

'Oh, hi.'

'You're not alone?'

'I am.'

'What is it then?'

'Sorry?'

'You sound kind of odd.'

'Me, no I'm fine. Have you eaten?'

'A large gin and a packet of peanuts. Various things have made me lose my appetite this evening.'

'You too?'

'Athena, what is it?'

'Could I just pop over for a while?'

'I was hoping you'd say that.'

Athena was wearing a crumpled floral dress and no make-up and her black hair was uncombed. She flopped on to Agnes's sofa-bed.

'Did you say gin?' she said.

Agnes poured two large glasses, and splashed chunks of ice into them. She handed one to Athena.

'You look terrible.'

'Darling, I feel terrible. I don't know what's wrong with me.'

'Is it Nic?'

'No, he's great. No, this is physical. I can't eat, I'm totally exhausted and I feel sick.'

'Since when?'

'Since the weekend, really. It's got worse today.'

'Have you seen a doctor?'

'No. Don't want to.'

'Why ever not?'

Athena took a large gulp of gin, looked at the glass and laughed, emptily. 'Mother's ruin,' she said.

Agnes waited. Then Athena said, suddenly, 'Agnes, women of my age don't get pregnant, do they?' Agnes stared at Athena, then took a long swig of gin. 'I mean, honestly poppet,' Athena went on, 'I'm practically menopausal, I must be, my mother was barely forty-five when she stopped – and my cycle's all over the place and anyway we've been sensible, only condoms but they're supposed to work, aren't they – are you listening?'

Agnes got up and twisted another cube of ice into her glass. 'Yes, of course I'm listening. I just can't imagine – I mean, what you've described – you're ill, not – not . . .'

'The word's "pregnant".'

'Athena – you can't be. You just can't.'

Athena poured herself another gin. 'Sweetie, I just hope you're right.'

Chapter Ten

Agnes squinted at the bottle of gin. It was completely empty. The morning was humid and dull, she already had a headache and it wasn't yet eight o'clock. She put the bottle with the rubbish, then noticed a large pan full of congealed tagliatelle still on her cooker. She opened the bin and tipped the whole lot into it. She put on the kettle, and then went and sat at her desk, leaning on one hand, while she waited for it to boil. Her eye fell on the note she'd made of Charlie's phone number. She sighed, picked up the phone and dialled it.

'Our Sheila said you might call,' Charlie said, when she'd explained who she was. 'You want to grill me about the Stanton case?'

'Well, if you don't mind.'

'Hmm. Well, I shouldn't rightly be talking to you, but if it's off the record, like—'

'It's just to set my mind at rest, really.'

'Can you drive over this way, then – maybe later this evening? Nine-ish?'

'That would be great. I'm in Chelmsford today anyway, at the library. Thanks.'

Once again Agnes found herself in the bright reading room of the Essex Record Office.

'I'd like to see everything you have about the village of Broxted,' she said at the Inquiries Desk.

'Everything?' The young woman pushed her glasses up her nose. 'We've got quarter sessions and tithe rolls, we've got deeds and parish records, we've got the correspondence of Hall Manor, we've got miscellaneous documents . . .'

'Fine,' Agnes said. 'All that. Please,' she remembered to add.

'From the Deeds of Jessops Farm in the Parish of Broxted Juxta Ongar . . . The Mark of James Wytham, the ninth day of November, in the year of our Lord seventeen hundred and six . . .' Agnes raised her eyes from the pile of papers in front of her. The clock said quarter to two. She had read through all the quarter sessions from the mid-seventeenth century onwards, she had heard the plea of Anne Dockrell against William Hume, her employer, who had used her most cruelly, she had handled certificates signed by Oliver Cromwell for the safe passage and future financial security of his wounded soldiers, she had read the deeds of Hall Manor in which there was a dispute over a well on the land. Now, as she wearily thumbed through the tithe rolls it occurred to her that the Manor's well was positioned on the same plot as Emily Quislan's farm. She turned to the description of Emily's land. The Well Mead, of course. And there, clearly marked, was the well itself. But then, she thought, remembering the camp, the well could only be a few hundred yards away from the proposed road link. In which case, why didn't the camp use it, instead of walking to the rather filthy stream each time they needed water?

She turned to the next batch of documents, and found it was a local essay competition from the 1960s. 'My Essex Memories' was the title, and all the entrants had to be over the age of sixty. Agnes began to browse through them.

'When I was six I was taken to Scotland to visit my grandma for the first time. I remember she stood by the table in a black dress with a white lace collar, and she had a little black-and-white dog by her side . . .'

'There was a scarecrow we used to pass on the way to school. Once my sister told me he'd come to life if the wind ever changed from north to south, and to this day I check the old weather vane just in case . . .'

'In 1926 my Uncle Jim had an accident with a piece of farm machinery, and his hand was completely severed from the wrist . . . all us children simply stared and stared . . .'

'I remember the local Squire had a plan to reclaim the swamp land after Fyffes Well was filled in, and we were dead against it because we used to go blackberrying down those fields . . .'

'That was the summer we built our den out by Harton's field. We had to dare each other to go out there because of the witch who was buried there, and everyone said she'd come back and curse you if you walked on her grave . . .'

Agnes yawned, closed all the files carefully, returned them to the desk and left.

Charlie's house was cool after the humidity of the day. She found him sitting with Sheila on the patio, both with a glass of cold beer. A woman appeared and struggled to light a couple of large candles which were stuck in the edges of the flower-beds.

'Leave 'em, Sue,' Charlie said. 'They're more trouble than they're worth.' One candle flared briefly, guttered and went out. 'And they just attract moths,' he added. Sue came past him, made a face at him and went back into the kitchen.

'I thought I'd keep you company,' Sheila said. Agnes sat down next to her, and Sue reappeared with two more glasses of beer.

'Cheers,' Charlie said, raising his glass. Sue got up and tried a candle again. 'So, you want to discuss Becky Stanton?' Charlie said. 'You knew her, you told me, before the road protest?'

Agnes nodded. 'Briefly in the hostel I work in, and then at the road camp. Although she was dead really, as soon as I—'

'If you ask me,' Charlie said suddenly, 'and Sheila knows I think this, it's just some psycho. Not that I'm in the incident room much these days, but I'm around the lads at work, you know. They reckon it's a sticker.'

'A sticker?'

Charlie took a gulp of beer. 'How can they charge anyone? No motive, no family problems, no boyfriends – no sexual assault either.'

'So you think if you sleep out in a field . . .' Agnes said. Sue's candle was at last flaring steadily, throwing guttering shadows across the grass. She checked it was firmly bedded in, then came to sit down with them.

'Put it this way,' Charlie said, 'I wouldn't let my daughter out across that way at night.'

'Charlie's not known for his tolerance of an alternative lifestyle,' Sheila said gently.

'Nothing to do with it, Sheila. Alternative or whatever, that's not the point. All I'm saying is, too many nutters about these days. There was a murder last year, out over towards Epping, on the common there. Couldn't pin it on anyone. Might be the same bloke for all we know. Not to say we won't catch him in the end, mind. But we need witnesses. And who's going to have been out and about in them woods in the middle of the night, eh?'

'All sorts of people,' Sheila said, 'if all these reports of detectives and security people are to be believed.'

Charlie drained his glass. He glanced at his wife and she went into the kitchen. 'Wouldn't know about that,' he said. Sue appeared with some more bottles of beer, and Charlie took one and opened it.

'Wouldn't you, Charlie?' Sheila said.

He shook his head. 'You know my views, Sheila. The Government owns that land, in law, right? It's a democratic process, the majority of those local people want that road. Simple.'

'It's not democratic when the Government is totally skewed in favour of—' Sheila began.

'And,' Charlie interrupted, 'it's not as if those friends of yours at the camp are angels, is it?'

'What do you mean?' Agnes said.

'I mean, it would be OK if these environmentalists stuck to the normal channels for stating their point of view. But when they're all tied up with anarchists and terrorists and—'

'Oh, don't be ridiculous,' Sheila said.

Sue got up and went into the house.

'You just won't face facts, Sheila. You've never grown out of Sussex bloody University—'

'Here we go again.'

'Show her, Sue,' Charlie said, and Sue, coming back into the garden gave Sheila a piece of paper.

'You'll have seen these before, won't you?' Charlie said. Sheila read it, shook her head and handed the paper to Agnes. Printed on it in large uneven capitals were the words 'WITHAM'S WATER IS POISON. FYFFES WELL IS RUN BY FILTH AND THEIR FILTH IS POLLUTING THE WATER. DON'T DRINK IT.'

Sheila looked at Agnes and then at Charlie. 'I've never seen one of these before.'

Agnes took the piece of paper and stared at it.

'Not one of your friends, then?' Charlie said to his sister. 'Mind you, there's so many of these groups now. But I bet someone you know'll know this lot.'

'Are the police taking it seriously?' Agnes asked.

'We're waiting. Might be just a nutter, or a hoax. Might develop into something else.'

'Fyffes Well,' Agnes said. 'Can I keep this?' She pocketed the flyer. 'I thought the well was filled in?' she said, as phrases from her day's research dropped into her mind.

'It was unblocked just recently; a local businessman has turned it into a spring water company,' Sheila said.

'Good luck to him,' Charlie said. 'If your friends don't get to him first.'

Sheila bit her lip. 'It's not far from the Ark,' she said to Agnes. 'Just a bit further up the hill.' Sheila drained her glass.

'Well, we'll keep an eye out for you, won't we,' Agnes said brightly. 'And perhaps you could check out all the threatening behaviour that we've experienced recently.'

'Oh yes?' Charlie said.

'I've had several silent phone calls at home. And Sheila's had the computer tampered with.'

Charlie poured himself some more beer. 'As I said, I wouldn't know about all that. I can help you put your mind at rest about the Stanton girl, but beyond that . . .' He shook his head. 'Some decisions are made way above the heads of the likes of me.' He smiled at Sheila.

She smiled back, then turned to Agnes. 'We should be going,' she said.

'I'll drop you back.' Agnes stood up. 'Thanks for agreeing to see me,' she said to Charlie. 'And if we find any more threatening things about poisoned water, we'll let you know.'

Charlie smiled. 'I doubt if she will,' he said, getting up to see them out. 'Too much of a hippy, and at her age too.' He laughed, and ruffled Sheila's hair, and Agnes saw a look of real affection pass between them.

She dropped Sheila off at her house.

'I'm sorry about my brother,' Sheila smiled as she got out of the car.

'He's all right,' Agnes said.

'Yes,' Sheila said. 'Yes, he is actually. Despite everything.'

As Agnes joined the M25 she found herself wondering what it would be like to have a brother. Or a sister, for that matter. She blinked against the pulsing headlights of the other cars and thought about the convent, with its echoes of family life, its imitation mothers and sisters. Better that, she thought, for me, anyway, better a family I choose than one which just happens along, like husbands or children. She thought suddenly of Athena, Athena feeling sick and tired and talking about pregnancy. It wasn't a fantasy she'd ever had, Agnes thought, believing oneself to be pregnant when one wasn't. With Hugo she was terrified that she might bring a child into such a marriage, and since Hugo . . . well, it was out of the question. As it was, of course, for Athena too.

Early the next morning she went to Mass at St Simeon's Church. Afterwards, at the church door, Julius shook hands with the few faithful communicants. Agnes was the last and he shook her hand too, and then grinned at her. 'How are you then?'

'OK,' she said. 'I'm at the hostel for the next two days.'

'Nothing more exciting than that?'

'No. And anyway, I need to reflect a bit.'

'How's the matriarchal goddess religion?'

'The what?'

'I thought that's where you might be heading, after seeing through God's illusory maleness.'

'Ah, so it's a put-up job, this male God, a smokescreen maintained by a male priesthood?'

'What else did you think it might be?' Julius smiled.

'Do you know, I did think – and in fact, still do – that God might be a truth so large as to be beyond gender.'

'Now there's a thought,' Julius laughed. 'You get off to that hostel now and fry some eggs instead of worrying your pretty little head with theological niceties,' he added, then ducked as she aimed a blow to his right ear, to the surprise of the last departing parishioners.

The day passed peaceably enough, giving Agnes time to reflect on the connection, if there was one, between Fyffes Well and the Ark. The point is, Agnes thought, as the day drew on, they're both on Emily Quislan's land. And Emily Quislan, whoever she is, is talking to Col – and scaring him half to death. And that horse and rider in the woods were as real as the prints they left behind.

Checking on her phone that evening, she was surprised to find no messages on her machine, and no strange clicks. The next morning, as she sat over a cup of tea before leaving for work, the phone rang.

'Agnes—'

'Athena, is that you? You sound terrible.'

'Can I come over – now?'

'Y – yes, sure.'

Ten minutes later Athena walked into Agnes's tiny flat waving something small and white. Her face was puffy and Agnes noticed that her hair, which was usually shiny black, had grey showing at the roots.

'I took a cab. Oh God, it's awful – look—'

Agnes looked at the plastic stick that Athena was thrusting towards her.

'Should I know what that is?'

'Bloody pregnancy test. Bloody positive. Look, thin blue line, couldn't be bloody clearer. I did two, they're both like this.' Athena flung herself down on Agnes's bed and hugged a cushion to her. 'What the hell am I going to do?'

'Um – do you want some tea?'

'And it's horrible, abortion,' Athena went on, while Agnes clattered in her kitchen. 'I had one with Chris, we were too young, we thought.' Agnes handed her a mug of tea. 'And then when we wanted a baby, one never came. Funny how these things work out. But now? Oh God, it couldn't be worse.'

'What does Nic say?'

'Nic – haven't dared tell him. I worked it out, either he's going to scream and run away and I'll never see him again, or he's going to go all gooey about being a trendy dad like you see in all the ads these days. I can't face either prospect, frankly.' She slurped on her tea. 'Actually,' she said, 'I think it broke up me and Chris. I thought afterwards, if we'd just ended up parents, we weren't brilliant together, but we'd have been OK. Not that I regret it now, but I thought it at the time.'

Agnes sipped her tea.

'I suppose you've never been through all this. Although, with Hugo—'

Agnes shook her head. 'I ended up thinking I was infertile when I was with him. Maybe because he kept telling me I must be. Another reason to hate me, my failure to produce an heir.'

'He said that?'

'Among other things. But a baby never happened. Thank God.'

'Agnes – if it had . . . ?'

Agnes shivered. 'I'd have kept it. I had no choice.'

'What do you mean?'

Agnes looked at her friend. 'I – it's just – with my faith, I have to.'

'Have to what?'

'I believe all life is sacred.'

'Well, you're a great help, aren't you?'

'It doesn't mean I'd judge you—'

Athena looked up, then shook her head.

Agnes went on, 'It's not that I'd think the worst of you, really, it's just that my tradition does hold the view that the um, unborn, I mean – if one was to . . .'

'Kill it, you mean.' Athena's voice was flat. She stared into her mug, swilling the liquid around inside it.

'No, not kill it, it's just that we do believe that life is, well, life really—'

'Oh God.' Athena's lips were pinched and dark against her pale skin. 'You really are the worst bloody person I could have confided in. I might as well have tootled off to Rome to have a chat with *Il Papa* himself.'

'Athena, please—'

'And there's you and his Holiness, conveniently celibate, or infertile – it's easy for you, condemning other people for things you're never going to have to think about, like murdering babies.'

'Athena, I never said murder, you're my friend for God's sake!'

They looked at each other. Athena took a swig of tea, then said, quietly, 'It's got to go. I can't possibly raise a child at my age, and anyway, there'll probably be something wrong with it.' She looked at Agnes. 'I don't care what you think. You can tell me it's murder all you like but it won't change anything.'

'Athena—'

'OK then, if you're my friend, tell me it's OK. Tell me that when I go down that clinic and emerge no longer pregnant, thank God, that that's OK by you. Go on, then.'

Agnes looked at the floor, struggling to find the right words. Athena waited, then got up and threw her pregnancy test into the wastepaper basket. 'It's not OK at all, is it?' she said quietly. 'Not as far as you're concerned. I might have bloody known.' Agnes, still staring at the floor, heard the door slam as Athena left.

The day at the hostel seemed muffled. Agnes had a sense of being surrounded by a grey fog, distanced from real life. As soon as she could, she finished her shift and took a bus across the river to Hackney, to the community house. To her relief, Madeleine was in that evening.

'Come on, you can help me with supper,' she said, seeing Agnes's drawn face.

'What should I have said?' Agnes asked her, explaining the conversation with Athena as they chopped vegetables and peeled potatoes.

Madeleine tipped a large pile of courgette slices into a pan. 'I don't know,' she said.

'You see, I do believe that all life is sacred. I can't help but think that.'

'Well, you were honest, then.'

'Yes, but not helpful. And all day I've been thinking, say I got pregnant with Hugo, like Athena said – what would I have done? And would it have been the right thing, to let a child be born into that hell, instead of – of doing what Athena's thinking of doing . . .'

'What do you think?'

109

Agnes looked at Madeleine and sighed. 'I know what I think. I think it's wrong. To kill a baby.'

'Yes, but now you're talking generally. I mean, surely one has to take each individual human dilemma on its own terms, like in cases of rape or something. Or medical reasons.'

'Yes, I suppose so.'

'So, what are Athena's reasons?'

'Because she's never really thought of herself as a mother, apart from a brief flirtation with the idea when she was married, and she doesn't intend to start now.'

'Do you think she'd suffer from having an abortion?'

Agnes imagined Athena dressed in a scruffy sweatshirt, putting all her dry-clean-only clothes to the back of the wardrobe. She thought about Athena's flat, imagining the spotless radiators bedecked with tiny clothes, the chrome chairs sticky with forgotten porridge, the Persian rugs matted with biscuit. 'I don't know,' she said.

Then she thought of Athena. All the life about her, her capacity to give ten times more love than she received, her limitless passion, more often than not squandered on unreliable men. A baby, she thought. A baby for Athena. 'All I know is,' she said, 'we can't know what God intends for us, can we?'

'So you think she shouldn't kill it.'

Her voice was barely a whisper. 'Madeleine, I *know* she shouldn't kill it.'

Agnes had a restless night, and on Friday morning was woken at five by a noisy lorry delivering in the street outside. She couldn't get back to sleep. She lay awake thinking about Athena. Maybe God will sort it out, she thought. Maybe she *is* too old and this new life that's only just touched down will quietly float away again. But then that's hardly a solution, she thought. She mused on Sam, and Mike, and what happened to your life when your parents didn't want you. And me, she thought, for all the apparent privilege of my childhood, was I wanted any more than Sam?

It was five thirty, and light. She got up and made tea, and sat by the window in her pyjamas, staring out into the distinctive grey brightness of the new day. She looked at the phone box, standing alone, illuminated. Two tall young men with mobile phones strode down the deserted street, silent in huge trainers, and disappeared into the flats across the road. Agnes dressed, got into her car, and drove to the Ark.

At the camp, no one was about. Zak's dog Dog growled sleepily as he heard her approach. Zak poked his head out of his bender, saw it was Agnes and went straight back to sleep. Agnes sat by the embers of the fire, and after a moment Dog came and joined her. She wondered why she'd come out so early, why she felt such an urgency to be here.

She needed to clear her mind. If the Ark people were caught up in something to do with Emily Quislan's land, how was it that only Col and Sam seemed frightened by the return, in whatever form, of Emily Quislan? She got up and wandered towards the woods, and Dog followed, sniffing at tree-stumps. She walked for a while, hearing in the rustling of the leaves the murmured voices from the past. The scarecrow that might come to life, the blackberry bushes in the swampy fields, the witch's curse on Harton's field. Harton's field. She halted, and Dog stood, alert, watching her. What had Nicholson said? Something had gone wrong in the past, and the land was never quite right. Emily Quislan's land.

Agnes set off again. How could it be, she asked herself, that someone who'd owned land in the mid-nineteenth century could be exerting an influence now? It was against all reason. She realised that she was now at the edge of the woods, and facing towards open fields. From what she remembered of the tithe maps, Fyffes Well must be just over the next hill. Her eye was caught by movement in the fields beyond, and she saw two figures pass by the edge of the field and then stop, deep in conversation. Dog watched them too, and Agnes realised the animal's concern for her was unusual, to allow him to be taken this far from his master's side. She looked again at the distant figures. One of them was Col, she was sure, judging from his posture, which was hunched and nervous. The other person was of similar height, with chin-length blonde hair, standing upright, legs apart, head slightly back. Agnes looked at Dog, who was staring at them intently. 'What shall we do? she whispered to him, and he glanced at her, then back at the scene. 'What do you think?' she went on. 'Is that Emily Quislan?

And if Emily Quislan rides again, where's her horse?'

As they watched, the pair separated, the stranger turning to run back across the fields towards Fyffes Well, and Col walking, slowly, to the edge of the woods, his hands in his pockets, every so often glancing behind him.

Dog looked up at Agnes expectantly. She patted him on the head. 'I don't know why you're looking at me as if I know what's going on,' she said to him. 'I thought you were in charge.' They walked back slowly together through the woods, Dog stopping from time to time to sniff at interesting bits of twig. Agnes heard the rustle of leaves behind her, the soft tread of feet, then a voice.

'Up so early, Little Sister?'

Agnes was cross with herself for passing so close to Bill's bender. She wasn't in the mood.

'I could ask the same of you,' she said.

'Me, I keep nature's hours,' Bill said. 'None of that clustering round campfires into the night. I'm asleep at dusk and up at dawn.' Somehow, Agnes doubted the truth of this. There was so much she wanted to ask him; about ghostly horsewomen, about Fyffes Well – but then she realised that even if she did, there was no guarantee he'd tell her what he knew. She stood there, uncertainly.

'Any sightings of the cyberbandit?' he laughed.

Agnes sighed. 'Do you know something?' she said, sweetly.

'What?'

'You're a bit of a prat, really, aren't you?' She smiled up at him, then went on her way, back to the camp, Dog at her heels.

Zak was up and blowing half-heartedly at the smouldering fire. 'So it was you kidnapped my dog,' he said. 'Not that I missed you,' he added, as Dog ran to his arms and licked his face. 'Something up? He don't usually go off like that.'

Agnes sat by the fire. 'I don't know. We saw Col talking to someone. Dog seemed to take it seriously.'

Zak blew at a single feeble flame and it went out again. 'Arse.' He stood up. 'That's it, then. I'm going to hitch into town and blag a cup of tea there, it's quicker'n waiting for this fuckin' fire. Look after 'im, will you?'

Agnes got to work on the fire, and had the kettle boiling just as

Rona abseiled down from her tree-house. 'Hi Agnes, how's it going?'

'Fine.'

'You've missed Sam, I'm afraid. She was away last night.'

'Where?'

'With her dad, I suppose. It's all worked out really well.'

'Mmm.'

Rona eyed Agnes. 'You're not convinced?'

'No, I mean, no, it's fine, I'm really pleased she's happy.'

'No, I don't trust him either. Fathers don't just pitch up again after sixteen years.'

Agnes looked at Rona. 'I've done all I can, I'm afraid.'

Rona shrugged. 'People have to make their own mistakes, don't they? Anyway, she's coming back here today, she hasn't shipped out there altogether. You'll see her if you hang about.'

'Rona?' Agnes fished in her pocket for the leaflet that Charlie had given to her and showed it to Rona. 'Do you know anything about these?'

Rona took it and looked at it. 'Never seen it before. What is it? Isn't Fyffes Well that new spring water company?'

'Yes. It's just, I wondered if anyone here was involved in a campaign against it?'

Rona screwed up her nose. 'Why would we do that? I don't know of anything going wrong up there.' She shrugged, and went to the kitchen bender to get tea bags. Agnes saw Col appear at the edge of the camp, then walk over to a tree and begin to climb up it. She followed him.

'Col—' she called out from the base of the tree.

He continued to climb. 'Col,' she said again, putting one foot on a jutting edge, watching him recede ahead of her. She took hold of the abseil rope with both hands and pulled herself up, her legs swinging wildly until she found a niche between two branches for one foot. One huge step up, and she was on a sort of platform as the trunk divided in two. She looked up and saw Col was only a few feet away from her.

'Col,' she said.

'What?'

'It seems to me,' she said, trying to catch her breath, 'that there's quite a lot going on with you.'

'Nah, not really,' he said. She heard the wheezing at the edge of his voice, as he turned to climb again.

'Col, wait.'

He watched her as she struggled to find a way up to his branch, grasping the rope again, realising, as she caught sight of the ground, that it was a long way to fall. She wedged one foot hard against the branch and took all her weight on her hands until she could get one knee against the branch and pull herself up.

Col was sitting on the branch as if born to it. He grinned at her. 'You must think I've got loads to tell you, to go to all this trouble.'

'Only if you want to tell me.'

'And how are you going to get down without harness, eh?'

Col laughed and Agnes realised he was wearing abseiling gear slung between his legs. 'Anyway, ain't got nothing to say.'

Agnes tried again. 'What makes you think,' she said, calmer now that she'd caught her breath, 'that there's anything I need to know?'

He stared at her, and his eyes were suddenly huge and childlike again. He swung his legs to and fro, watching his feet. 'Dunno. Just thought, wiv Becky an' all—' Agnes waited. 'Just thought, wiv you following me to the woods an' all, you'd worked something out.'

So he'd seen her earlier. 'Dog was concerned about you,' Agnes said. Col stared at his feet. 'Who were you talking to?' Agnes tried again. He didn't even look at her.

'Look,' Agnes said, taking the crumpled leaflet from her pocket again and showing it to him. He snatched it from her and stuffed it in his pocket.

'Where d' you get that?'

'Never you mind.'

'You'll get me killed, you will.'

'Col,' Agnes said, gently. 'Whatever the danger you think you face, it can't be as bad as your fears.'

'Can't it?' His voice was hoarse.

'Col, hadn't you better get away from here?'

'Like Sam?' he said. 'We don't all have daddies who appear from nowhere.'

'I can help,' she said.

'What can you do?' He turned dark eyes to her. 'Where would I go? On the streets? Into a fuckin' hostel – and then what?'

114

Agnes was silent at the truth of what he said. She could offer him three nights of safety, and then – nothing. She couldn't think of anything to say.

'Maybe after the eviction,' Col was saying, 'I'll move on with this lot.' He stood up, balanced perfectly on the branch, and proceeded to unstrap the harness. 'Look, put this on, get down yourself, and then just swing it back up on the rope, OK?' She clung to the tree-trunk, feeling suddenly foolishly shaky, as he passed the straps between her legs and fastened the harness around her waist. 'There. Sorted. All you have to do, right, is loop the rope around here, like this, and put this hand here, right, then you sit back on the other side, like this, and hold it tight. This hand controls how fast you go, if you're scared just lock it off like this. The main thing to remember is to keep your legs horizontal, so you can control how far you are from the tree. Right, ready?'

Agnes felt her legs shake as she swung out from the tree, with only a piece of rope between herself and certain mutilation. 'The leap into faith,' she muttered, thinking that as a metaphor it was rather apt. She took her feet off the branch and hung there, foolishly. A small crowd had gathered at the foot of the tree.

'Let some rope out,' Col said, echoed by the people on the ground. She let go and slid fast about two feet down, then tightened the rope in terror and stopped again. She suddenly realised the question she had to ask Col.

'Col—' she called up to him, seeing him standing a couple of feet above her where she'd left him. 'Col – who is Emily Quislan?'

Col seemed to freeze. He swayed on the branch for a second, and Agnes was worried he'd fall. Suddenly he whipped a penknife out of his pocket, grabbed the rope from which she swung and held the knife to it.

'See this,' he hissed. 'Swear to me now – now, right – that you never say that name again. Or you hit the ground hard.'

Agnes watched him saw away at the rope with the blade for a moment. Common sense told her that she'd be safely down on the ground long before his knife had made any impact on the rope at all. But something about his hissing voice, his ashen face shook her. 'Col,' she persisted, her voice trembling, 'I saw it on the computer.'

'Come on,' Agnes heard Jeff shout from below. 'What's the problem?'

'Not another word,' Col said, his knife still working at the rope.

'Col, what's up?' Jeff shouted. 'Talk her down.'

'Swear it now,' Col hissed.

Agnes saw she had no choice. 'OK, I promise. Not another word,' she said.

Col straightened up and put his knife away, and Agnes let out another length of rope. She could see Col receding through the branches, his face a pinched mask of fear.

'Great, ace,' she heard Jeff call. 'And again.' This time she let out enough rope to slide gently, even elegantly downwards, pushing with her feet against the trunk to keep straight, landing with, she hoped, some style, trying to look as if she made a habit of learning the hard way. Which, of course, in a way, she did.

'You an' Col up a tree together, eh?' Sam giggled, later that evening.

Rona handed Sam a bowl of soup. 'Side by side on a branch, they were, like bloody budgies.'

'An' you really abseiled down?'

'Piece of cake,' Agnes laughed.

'Wish I'd been there to see it,' Sam said.

'Did you hitch back?' Rona asked her.

'Nah, Mike dropped me off down the lane and I just walked up.'

'How's it going with Mike?' Agnes asked carefully.

Sam turned to her with a radiant smile. 'It's like a dream come true, Agnes, really it is. I never have to see my mum again. And he's got all these satellite channels on his telly.'

Agnes smiled at Sam. She could see Dog pacing up and down outside Zak's bender. 'Zak not back, then?' she asked Rona.

'No,' Rona said. 'He got a call from his girlfriend, he's going to pick her up from the M11 junction. He shouldn't be long, poor old Dog.'

Jeff got up and helped himself to more soup. Dog suddenly came over to Agnes and nudged her arm, whining gently. She put down her empty bowl and patted him. Sam was showing Rona a bracelet that Mike had bought her in town earlier. Agnes stood up, and Dog was ready, watching her, waiting for her to follow. Together they wandered off towards the woods. Agnes heard Jeff pick up his guitar, caught a few bars of music before they disappeared out of earshot altogether.

'Well, Dog, I hope you know what you're doing,' she whispered to him as they took the path they'd followed that morning. There was no sign of Bill, to Agnes's relief. Dog seemed sure of his route, and once again they went towards the edge of the woodland. From time to time Dog paused and sniffed. It was dusk, and the shadowy reaches of the forest seemed full of menace in the fading light.

Dog suddenly froze. They waited, listening, then set off again. Agnes could hear the odd snap of twigs behind them, and felt sure they were being followed, but Dog had a new urgency in his pace. The path came out into a clearing. They paused, and listened, Dog's ears alert, nose twitching. Again a crack of twigs. Agnes scoured the bushes around her for a weapon, a broken branch, a stone . . . when Dog suddenly set up a low keening, a wail that seemed to echo around the swaying shadows of the trees. He darted across the undergrowth, and seemed to disappear. Agnes ran after him and saw him lying down in the undergrowth, barking and yelping, next to – next to a prostrate figure. Col.

Dog was licking his face, and Agnes ran to him, turned his head, feeling for a pulse. To her relief there was one, low and irregular. He took a breath, laboured, endless, then no more. 'Col – Col,' she called, gently slapping his face. He made no response. Another breath, rasping and slow. She riffled desperately through his pockets, hoping to find an inhaler. A penknife. Some bits of paper. No inhaler. The sound of approaching footsteps made her freeze.

'There you are,' she heard a male voice, and saw the tall, draped outline of Bill. 'I heard Dog.' He took in the scene. 'Christ, is he breathing?'

'Just.'

Bill crouched down by Col, and put one arm under his head. 'It's OK, mate, we've got you. It's going to be OK.' He lifted him gently to a sitting position, then slung him over one shoulder as if he were a mere child. Again the horrifying, rattling breath. 'Let's get you to the camp and phone for an ambulance.'

Bill stood up, the limp white body of Col hanging from his shoulder. Agnes saw a warm flash of smile, then he turned and set off, Agnes and Dog loping to keep up with him. As they reached the camp, faces turned towards them in the flickering firelight.

'He's still breathing,' Agnes said, as Dog ran to Zak.

Rona wordlessly handed Agnes the phone, and she dialled 999. Bill laid Col gently down away from the direction of the firesmoke and said, 'We need blankets. Where's his stuff – does he have an inhaler?'

People bustled to the benders, whilst Agnes was saying on the phone, 'Yes, it's an anti-road protest camp – oh for Heaven's sake, everyone round here's heard of it . . . just off the A414 – right, head for Broxted, turn up the track behind the church . . . for God's sake the kid is hardly breathing – right. Good. So I should think.' She rung off, shook her head.

'They know it when they need to,' Rona said, as people reappeared with blankets.

'Sam?' Jenn was calling. 'Does Col have an inhaler?'

Agnes looked up to see Sam standing at the edge of the fire, white-faced.

'An inhaler, Sam? Quick,' Jenn said.

Sam turned and fled up to her tree-house, and a few moments later dropped something down to Jenn.

Bill took it and held it to Col's mouth. 'Breathe, man,' he whispered. Jenn supported his head, and they watched as he took a breath, then another.

Agnes checked her watch. 'Six minutes,' she said, to no one in particular. 'Six minutes since I phoned.'

Rona was pacing up and down. 'One of us should go in the ambulance with him.' She looked around for Sam. 'I'll go,' she said, pacing again. 'If they ever get here.'

Zak yawned. Dog stood next to him, immobile, watching Col.

'That's great,' they heard Bill whisper, 'good work, man, keep it up.'

Blue flashing lights appeared in the lane, and Rona ran down to direct the ambulance up the track as far as it could go. Bill was taking the inhaler away, and Agnes saw Col had his eyes open. She went over to him and took his hand.

'Col—'

He turned to her, his eyes aged and staring. She heard his

breathing, still rasping, but now more regular. Two ambulancemen were coming up the hill.

'It's all right,' Agnes whispered. 'I promised.'

Col patted Dog stiffly. 'He saved your life, that dog,' Agnes smiled.

Col shook his head. 'Nnn—' he said. Then he turned to Agnes, his eyes dark with urgency, and opened his mouth to speak.

'It's OK lad, you're OK now,' one of the ambulancemen said. Agnes saw Col's pale face, behind him the stout legs of the men, the stretcher, oxygen cylinders, coarse red blankets. She tightened her grip on Col's hand. He took a breath, then said, 'Em—'

'Come on then, lad, you're going to be all right,' said one of the men, as they crouched down to lift him on to the stretcher.

Col grasped Agnes's hand tighter, breathed in a rasping, wheezing breath, looked into her eyes and said, 'Emily.' Then he was lifted on to the stretcher, bundled into blankets, carried away from her.

Agnes watched as they processed back down the hill, the white shapes of the attendants crisp against the moonlight, Rona bobbing next to them as they reached the ambulance, the flashing lights and siren pulsing, fading, merging with the rumble of the distant road.

Chapter Eleven

Agnes sat emptily in the encroaching silence of the camp. Jenn took a torch and wandered off to refill a water tank. Agnes looked around for Bill but he'd vanished again. Zak had gone into his bender, Paz was somewhere up in a tree-house. She felt absently in her pockets and touched the papers she'd found on Col; she must have pocketed them in panic when Bill had come upon them in the woods. She fished them out now, realising, at a glance, that they were the same as the flyer that Charlie had shown her.

'WITHAM'S WATER IS POISON. FYFFES WELL IS RUN BY FILTH AND THEIR FILTH IS POLLUTING THE WATER. DON'T DRINK IT.'

Col had three of these, all the same, plus the one he'd snatched from her. Agnes folded them up together and put them back in her pocket, as she heard Bill's light tread again. She was aware of him behind her and looked up to see him standing with a mug in each hand. He smiled and crouched down next to her by the fire.

'I brought you a drink.'

She took the mug and smiled at him.

'Just tea. Thought you might need it.'

Agnes sniffed the whisky steam rising from the mug. 'I hope you haven't used your best single malt.'

He smiled at her.

'Maybe one day you'll tell me how you come to have whisky like that in a place like this,' she said.

He considered her, his head on one side. 'Mmm. Maybe.'

Agnes felt the whisky warming her. 'It's lucky you were there. In the woods, I mean.'

'No, it's lucky you were. I just followed you.'

'I followed Dog.'

'Good for Dog, then.'

They grinned at each other.

'I hope Col's OK,' Agnes said.

'He will be. You saw him rally.'

'Where did Sam get to?'

'She stayed up in her twigloo, I think.'

'Hmm. Strange.'

'Why strange?'

'Because of her usual concern for Col—' Agnes looked up at Bill who was now gazing at her intently, and remembered that only a few hours ago she'd called him a prat. She also remembered the footsteps she'd heard behind her in the forest, furtive and deliberate, keeping in rhythm with her own. She looked at Bill, his weatherbeaten face a warm brown in the flickering firelight.

'Do you still distrust me?' he asked, holding her gaze with his own.

'Do I have cause to?' she asked.

With a clatter of water tank, Jenn reappeared, stoked up the fire and refilled the kettle, just as the mobile phone rang. She picked it up.

'Hi – oh, hi, Rona, yeah, great – what? He's . . .?' Jenn sat suddenly, heavily, on the ground. 'He can't be . . . He was breathing . . . OK. Do you want one of us there . . . ? Sure, right.' She rang off, then slowly looked up. 'It's Col. He – he died. About five minutes ago.'

Agnes tried to speak. 'But he was—'

'That's what I said,' Jenn said. 'He was breathing and everything, wasn't he, Bill?'

Agnes turned to Bill. His face was suddenly drained.

'He must have been worse than I realised,' he murmured.

'Rona said could you go down there, Agnes? You're kind of official – it'll help, she said.'

'Of course, but I'm not sure of the way . . .'

Bill got up. 'Come with me,' he ordered. 'Which hospital?'

'They're at Chelmsford. In Accident and Emergency.'

Bill strode off down the track, and Agnes got up to follow him. 'Jenn – look after Sam, won't you?' she said.

'Sure.'

'I'm worried she'll do something stupid. I mean, this might panic her, with Becky as well.'

'It had crossed my mind,' Jenn said. The sound of a motorbike engine broke across the quiet.

'Is that Bill?'

'Pretentious git. God-awful news like this and he wants to play Leader of the Pack.'

Through the dazzle of a single headlight Agnes could see Bill holding out a crash helmet to her. 'I thought I was going to follow you by car,' she said.

'This'll be quicker.'

She took the crash helmet and fastened it under her chin, then got on the bike behind him, her arms round his waist. They set off, fast, searing moonlit hedgerows, emerging into the yellow haze of the dual carriageway. Twelve minutes later they swerved into the Casualty entrance and Bill screeched to a halt. Agnes handed him back her crash helmet.

He took it from her. 'Ephedrine,' he said, his voice flat, his eyes shadowed with anguish.

'The inhaler?'

'I should have known.' He revved his engine and turned the bike round. His headlamp streaked a path across the tarmac as he roared off again into the night.

Agnes pulled her coat around her and walked towards the bright lights of the hospital.

'So what are they saying?' Agnes asked Rona. A nurse had led her to a corridor, where she'd found her sitting alone on a line of chairs, clutching a paper cup. Rona shook her head.

'Someone will be with you in a minute,' the nurse said, then left them alone, her footsteps fading into the echoing reaches of the hospital.

Rona looked at Agnes with blank, shocked eyes, and Agnes took her hand.

'Were you with him?' Agnes asked.

Rona nodded. 'We were waiting to be admitted, he was still on his trolley thing, he was awake and everything. Some doctor came and talked to him, then she went away, then Col just . . .' Rona's voice faltered. 'He kind of grabbed my hand and then his eyes turned up, like when someone's really had it . . . oh God it was bloody awful, and he was shaking and I was trying to find someone. I left him to find a nurse and when we came back . . .' Rona burst into tears and Agnes took her in her arms.

'Are you with Colin Hadley? Could you come this way?' A young man in a white coat had emerged from a doorway and was now waiting for them to follow him. They went into a small room with frosted windows. A woman, also in a white coat, was there, and she nodded at Rona. Agnes saw her badge said 'Dr S. Shannon'.

'I'm very sorry,' she said to Rona. 'We did all we could.'

Agnes passed Rona a paper handkerchief.

'Are you – um, relatives?' the young man asked.

'I'm Sister Agnes. I'm a nun, I work with the Safe House project at St Simeon's Church in London. This is Rona. We knew him from the anti-road camp out by Ongar. That's where he was living.'

Dr Shannon said, 'He seems to have no next of kin. The address on his DSS documents is of an aunt, but he hadn't been in touch with her for months.'

'What did he die of?' Agnes asked.

The two doctors exchanged glances, then Dr Shannon said, 'We can't say at this stage. Obviously, he was brought in with all the symptoms of an asthma attack, but the post-mortem might show something more. We've informed the Coroner, of course. Apart from that, there's not much we can do at this stage.'

'Ephedrine—' Agnes began.

'Yes?' the doctor said.

'Can it – can it be fatal, sometimes?'

'If someone has a weak heart, very occasionally. Obviously, that's something we'll be looking for.'

Agnes nodded. She thought about Bill speeding back to the forest, saw once again his expression of despair.

'Can we see him?' Rona asked in a small voice.

The little group proceeded down the corridor to another door. Dr Shannon opened it, showed Agnes and Rona in, then left them alone. Col was lying there, covered with a sheet. Agnes gently drew back the sheet. His eyes were closed, and his hands were crossed against his chest, which was naked. His skin was chalk-white.

'Which one of us next, eh?' Rona said, tearfully.

Agnes put an arm round her shoulders. 'No,' she said, 'there's no need to think that way. It's just coincidence.'

'You don't really believe that, do you?' Rona asked.

Agnes looked into the eyes that were welling with tears. She sighed. 'I don't know what to think.'

'He knew he was dying,' Rona said.

'What makes you say that?'

'When he was wheeled in through the doors, off the ambulance, right? He said, he'd been in hospital twice in his life, once when he was born and now to die. He kind of whispered it to me.'

'Do you think he wanted to die?' Agnes said.

Rona gently reached out and touched Col's hand with her fingertip. 'Maybe,' she said softly.

Agnes noticed that Col's fingernails were stained bright yellow. 'He was talking of going to Wales when you all get evicted.'

Rona turned and looked at Agnes. 'Yeah, he wanted to escape from something, didn't he?'

'Any idea what?'

Rona shook her head. Agnes noticed a neat pile of his clothes on the chair next to the bed. She took his jacket and started riffling through the pockets.

'Don't nick anything, will you?' Rona said. Her eyes filled with tears again. 'Although it's not as if there's anyone else to care.'

Agnes brought out a dog-eared benefit book, his penknife, a cigarette lighter, two doorkeys on a ring, a chewed pencil and a bus ticket. On the back of the ticket the name 'Tom Bevan' was scrawled in pencil, with a phone number. 'Just an old bus ticket,' she said quickly to Rona, slipping it into her pocket, carefully putting everything else back where she'd found it. She checked all his other pockets but found only a handful of loose change and a half-smoked roll-up. She replaced the jacket and glanced down at Col. There were some leaves matted into his hair and she picked a few out, knowing already what they were.

'Rosemary,' she said. 'For remembrance.'

Rona blinked up at her. 'Sorry?'

'Nothing,' Agnes said. 'Do you want to say goodbye on your own?'

Rona stood up to go. 'Done all that, really. I just hope they invite us to the funeral.'

They left their names and details with Dr Shannon, then, feeling awkward and useless, wandered out of the hospital. Dawn was breaking, softening the angular bright windows of the hospital against the pale sky. Agnes and Rona set off in a directionless way, eventually finding themselves on the edge of the shopping precinct where an all-night tea-bar trailer was just packing up. Agnes bought them both sweet tea, and they sat on a bench and watched the pigeons pecking at mangled bits of polystyrene.

'You know—' Rona said.

'What?'

'I don't think he wanted to die. I think he thought he was dying, but that doesn't mean he wanted to.'

'No.'

They sipped their tea. 'After Becky, and now Col . . .' Rona said. 'It's all very weird.'

Agnes nodded.

'Or it might just be asthma,' Rona said.

Agnes took a large mouthful of hot tea. 'I hope Sam's OK,' she said.

'Sam's gone,' Jeff said, when Rona and Agnes arrived back at the camp. Agnes paid the taxi-driver, marvelling at the warm morning sunlight so inappropriate to the events of the night.

'What do you mean?' Agnes asked, turning to Jeff as the cab bumped back down the track and Rona went over to the stream to wash.

'Soon as Jenn told her what'd happened, she cleared out her bender, packed her bag and walked.'

'Where?'

'Mike's. We tried to stop her, she was going to hitch, there and then. We asked her to wait for you, but she said she couldn't hang about, not after Becky and now Col, she said she had to go. In the end Zak said he'd hitch with her, that's where they've gone.'

'To Mike's?'

Jeff nodded.

'And where's everyone else?'

Jeff knelt and blew on the fire. 'Who else? Two down, six and a dog to go – this is going to change the fucking face of protest, when word gets out.'

'Wait a minute, Jeff, there's no evidence to link Col with—'

'If the pigs can tell me they're doing all they can to find out what happened to Becks, if that hospital can tell me that Col died of asthma – them maybe, just maybe, I'll listen. But otherwise – you tell me, Agnes – fucking spooks hanging around the bushes all night, crazy phone calls to the office, Becky's corpse in a fucking fridge while the pigs do nothing – I'm angry, Agnes, I'm fucking angry . . .' He rubbed ash from his eyes and got to his feet. 'But they won't stop us. They can pick us off one by fucking one, we'll just rise up somewhere else . . .' He turned and stomped off towards his tree.

Agnes sat by the fire, blinking back tears from the smoke. After a while she got up and wandered into the woods, following the same path she'd followed with Dog the night before. As she approached the point where the paths diverged, she saw a figure standing on the lower path, about where they'd found Col. It took her a second to realise it was Bill. He turned and saw her, as she scrambled down to join him. He stared at the ground.

'How was it?' he said at last.

'OK, I suppose,' she replied at last. 'Tough for Rona. We're superfluous, now the next of kin are on their way. Not that he's got anyone obvious.'

'Did they talk about the inhaler?'

'They said,' Agnes began, 'that if someone has a weak heart—'

Bill thumped a tree-trunk with his fist. 'Why did the kid have a bloody inhaler when it was quite clearly the wrong stuff for him?'

'We weren't to know.'

'And after what he'd been through, anyone would have a weak heart, and I just go and fill him up with fucking poison—'

'It's not your fault,' Agnes said firmly.

He looked at her. 'It's nice of you to say so,' he said flatly.

She returned his stare. 'And what had he been through? You just said, "after what he'd been through—"'

'I don't know what you mean.' There was a distance in his eyes.

'Oh come on, Bill—' He surveyed the surrounding trees. 'Last night,' she went on, 'it seems to me that you were close enough behind me to help with Col – almost as soon as I found him, you were there.'

'So?'

'So how come you appear not to have seen the person who was shadowing me?'

Bill eyed Agnes for a moment. 'I don't get you.'

'It's quite simple, Bill. Someone was walking behind me, making sure that their footsteps were in time with mine, almost as soon as I left the camp. Now either it was you – in which case, why so furtive? Or, it was someone else, someone known to Dog, too – in which case, why didn't you see them?'

Bill paused, then said, 'I thought we might be getting on better than this by now.'

'Or,' Agnes went on, 'you did see them, in which case the question is, why didn't you say anything? Now I'm sure you have your own reasons for lurking in the forest, and I'm not actually interested in what they might be. But when it comes to someone's life being in danger, a boy not yet out of his teens, and you lurk and lurk and know more than you bother to tell until it's too bloody late—'

Bill's voice was quiet. 'You're angry with me?'

'Of course I'm bloody angry with you. You and your silly hippy ego trip of Knowing the Ways of the Forest, when we all know that for every vole or fox you see, you see ten bloody detectives or bailiffs or security guards or whatever they are – it seems to me, you could have done more than you did.'

Bill was staring at the ground. His voice was quiet. 'Do you think I don't know that?'

There was silence between them. Bill said, 'You're right to be angry. I'm angry too. And yeah, I should have been quicker. I knew he was in danger, and I was too late.'

Agnes looked at his profile as he stared out towards the edge of the wood. He blinked and turned to her. 'And unlike you, I have no one to shout at.'

Agnes swallowed. 'Bill.' He was looking at her. 'Bill, I'm—' She took a deep breath. 'I didn't mean to sound as if I was accusing you.' He waited. 'I'm upset, I suppose.'

'We both are,' he said. He sat on the ground, and she sat down next to him, pulling her raincoat around her.

'OK,' he said, after a while. 'In answer to your questions. Firstly, yeah, sure, I see the odd geezer sizing the place up at odd hours of the night, usually at first light when all your crusties there are still asleep. But what's the big deal? It's Department of Transport land and they want it back. Secondly, there wasn't anyone else following you last night. It was me.'

'So why—?'

'Why creep along? Because, Little Sister, I wanted to know where you were going. It's simple. You interest me.'

Agnes fiddled with a loose button on her coat. 'But – but you must have seen Col come into the woods earlier?'

Bill shook his head. 'He must have come from the village, across the fields. He wouldn't have passed me.'

'But you knew he was in danger. You just said—'

'I know only what I told you,' Bill said sharply. 'I heard one conversation about their shared history, and that's all. And I knew they were scared. And, yeah, sure, I should have known more, but like I say, I live here. I have my meat to hunt for. My purpose is not to look out for the safety of that lot, although I do what I can. In this case, it wasn't enough.' He pulled at some bits of moss on a tree-stump next to him. 'Agnes?' he said, and she turned to him. 'Once you've decided that someone's a prat, do you ever change your mind?'

Agnes wound the loose thread around its button. 'I'm sorry about that.'

Bill stood up and stretched. 'Shall we go back?' Agnes got to her feet next to him, and he reached over and brushed a twig from her hair. 'I'm only a prat sometimes,' he said.

Agnes turned towards the camp, smoothing her coat where she'd been sitting on it. 'That makes two of us, then,' she said.

'I'm not sure women can be prats,' he said, as they walked back to the camp. 'Isn't it just a masculine noun?'

'Like priest, you mean?'

Bill stopped and looked at her. 'You're angry about an awful lot, aren't you, Little Sister?'

Agnes joined the M25 at the slip road and swerved fast into the middle lane, ignoring the flashing lights of the driver behind her. It had never occurred to her before to question the masculinity of the priesthood; let alone to be angry about it. In her calling she had met so many interesting, scholarly, maverick, intelligent women that it had never crossed her mind that being excluded from the priesthood was any kind of issue at all. She put her foot down and dodged into the fast lane to overtake a BMW, and wondered why she had let slip that remark to Bill. Why him, she asked herself, realising as his name crossed her mind that once again, he had eluded her; his slippery sympathy, his apparent concern being a screen behind which he could hide, opaque, invisible.

She stopped for bread and cheese on the way home. There was a message on her machine from Madeleine giving Agnes her hostel rota days for the next week. She picked up the phone and dialled Mike's number.

'Hi,' she heard Mike's voice on a recorded message. 'Mike and Sam aren't able to come to the phone right now, but please leave us a message after the tone.'

Agnes hung up. Mike and Sam. It was all too neat, too easy. This Us, this Father-and-Daughter Us after a mere few weeks of half-hearted administration on the part of over-stretched Social Services departments. Agnes picked up her London street map and looked up the estate in Stepney where Linda and Annie had spent their uneasy, chaotic childhood. She put the map in her pocket and went out, back down the stairs to her car, and drove, seeing the dilapidated blocks of post-war housing grow more grey, more shabby, until she reached the Atherton Estate. She parked in the main road opposite the estate, next to a high fence. There was a smell of burning plastic. She walked past the first block, called 'Aberdeen Court' and found herself in a courtyard surrounded on three sides by balconied, three-storey flats. Some were obviously still well-maintained, with window boxes of petunias and geraniums; others were derelict, their broken windows boarded up. The tarmac yard was covered in broken glass, crushed cans and graffiti. Amongst the scrawled, brightly coloured names someone had written 'Death, First and Last'. Agnes wandered further in, under an archway, emerging into another, similar courtyard. She surveyed the neat, optimistic architecture, the new hope of slum clearance, now dying in the embers of the welfare state. Somewhere in here, she thought with sudden conviction, lies the key to Sam's past. She looked up, at the nailed-up doors, at the straggling washing, signs of the struggle to maintain some kind of life amongst the debris. Where to begin, she wondered, walking back to the street. When she reached her car she saw two young men, their feet huge in roller blades, one lounging against the driver's door, the other sitting on the bonnet. She smiled at them and they stayed exactly where they were, eyeing her as she approached them. Then the boy on the bonnet suddenly smiled back, slid off the car and both glided away down the street.

Agnes drove back to Southwark, wondering whether Julius was free to go out to eat that evening; thinking that she must phone Athena; wondering where to start to trace Sam's early life. Back home she tried Mike's number again and he answered.

'Hi, Agnes, good of you to call. How's things?'

'I suppose you know about Sam's friend Col having died?'

There was the briefest pause. 'Yes. She told me he had asthma. I guess living rough doesn't help all that. Hey, she's here, do you want a word?'

Sam came on the line. 'I was going to ring you,' she said quietly. 'Running off and that, lunched it, you know.'

'It's OK,' Agnes said. 'It must have been a bit much for you after Becky too.'

'Yeah.'

'So you haven't told Mike the whole story?'

'What do you mean?'

'He said Col's death was asthma.' Agnes waited.

Eventually Sam said, 'It was.'

'And Becky?'

'What about her?'

'And the past lives? And Emily Quislan?'

Agnes heard Sam catch her breath, before she said, 'Oh, you know, all that tat—'

'Sam, I need a straight answer.'

'It weren't really me, it were Becky and Col, and now they're gone anyway, like she said—'

'Like who said?'

'I never met her, Col told me about her, and when Becky died

131

he got scared 'cos of what she'd said.'

'Sam – who'll be next?'

'No one. That's it now.'

'Not you?'

'She never knew about me. It was only what Col told me, that's all I knew. He said it was secret. I gotta go now.'

'Sam, you've got to tell me more. If Becky's murderer is out there—'

'Mike says it's me tea. Bye.'

'Sam—'

'I'll tell you what I think, Agnes. I think they made it up. I think they wanted to liven things up a bit. Anyway, it's over now. Gotta go. Bye.'

Agnes held the receiver in her hand, then slowly put it down. She remembered that Julius had said he was visiting friends that evening; anyway, she wasn't hungry. She poured herself a glass of Côtes du Rhone and sat at her desk, thinking. Emily Quislan was a mid-Victorian lady who owned a nice little patch of land in Essex. Col was a young homeless boy who had died in hospital the night before from a weak heart and an asthmatic attack. Agnes put down her glass and began to doodle on a notepad. And, she thought, Col and Emily were linked because Emily Quislan once had the rights to a water source called FyffesWell, which was on the land occupied by the Ark, and which was blocked up, only to be reopened 150 years later. And now someone was threatening to poison it. And Becky and Col were both found with rosemary.

Agnes sipped her wine. And Bill knows more than he's letting on, she thought, remembering the measured tread of cracking twigs behind her in the forest. And Sam is now rewriting her story so that all her terror has vanished, and it turns out that Becky and Col were just making things up.

She drained her glass, stretched, got up and looked absently out of the window. It had begun to drizzle, although the night was still warm. She felt as if everyone was drifting away from her, Bill with his rhetorical tricks, Sam with her new-found loyalty to Mike; Becky and Col, now beyond her reach altogether. Someone went into the call-box, hesitated, then picked out a card and left hurriedly. Agnes stared down into the street, thinking it was time to do her evening worship and go to bed. She drew the curtains. The truth about someone, she thought, is separate from them. Emily Quislan, long since dead, still has a truth about her that I can uncover: maybe several, conflicting truths. And Sam, whatever she tries to tell me now, still has a history that is accessible to me. And Becky and Col – yes, even Becky and Col, Agnes thought, lighting a candle and preparing to pray – even they have left behind a truth that can be uncovered – not only can be, but must be. She stared into the candle flame as it threw juddering shadows onto the plain white wall.

Chapter Twelve

On Sunday afternoon, Agnes was startled by a ring at her doorbell. She had attended Julius's Mass in the morning, and had had lunch at her community, and was now at home, not expecting visitors; so it was with some surprise that she opened the door to find Nic standing there. The rain of the night before had cleared, and he stood in the sunshine in denim jeans and a plain white T-shirt.

'I'm – um – I hope I'm not disturbing you,' he began.

'No. Well, come in.'

He looked uneasily around her bed-sitting-room, choosing eventually to sit on the chair by her desk.

'Can I get you a drink or something?' Agnes offered. Nic shook his head, so she sat opposite him on the bed. 'Is it about Athena?' she asked.

'Yes,' he replied, and she realised then that the reason he looked so different was that he no longer had a ponytail but had had his hair cut short. 'She's told you, presumably,' he went on.

'About the – the baby, yes.'

'I don't know what to do.' His hand went to the back of his neck where his hair used to be, then dropped to his lap again. 'I couldn't think of anyone else I could talk to about it.'

Agnes waited, then said, 'How is Athena?'

'Not brilliant. You've seen her, I guess?'

'On Thursday. Not – um, not since then.'

'She didn't say what happened. Only that you both—'

'She wouldn't listen,' Agnes said. 'I didn't want to judge her, really I didn't.'

'Anyway, she went to her house in Gloucestershire on Friday. You know it? It's just a little terrace apparently.'

'Yes,' Agnes said, remembering the beginning of their friendship,

135

the boozy evenings by Athena's fireside, the lopsided Grecian rug hanging on the wall, the chrome dolphins in the bathroom. 'Yes, I know that house. When's she due back?'

'This evening, supposedly. The thing is, Agnes, she's made an appointment. For a termination.'

'Oh. When?'

'Tuesday.'

'Right.'

Nic looked at her. 'I really want her to keep the baby.'

'Look, are you sure you don't want some tea or something?'

'And,' Nic went on, 'I thought perhaps you'd feel the same.'

'What I feel is hardly relevant.'

'But, about life – I mean, surely you believe, with your faith, that abortion is wrong. And in my work I've come to believe the same. You see, there are times when I'm really aware of this kind of legacy, this sense of lives that haven't formed, it's kind of karma and I think, who are we to know what's right? The problem with our society, now, is that we live in the short-term, with no regard for the consequences. It's all Me Me Me and—'

'And what do you think is right for Athena?' she interrupted.

Nic matched her direct gaze. 'That's what I'm trying to say,' he said. 'If she gets rid of that baby, no one knows what she'll have done to herself.'

'And if she doesn't get rid of it?'

'Then she'll be a mother. And I'll be . . .'

'You're already a father, aren't you?'

'That was a long time ago.'

He looked away and Agnes studied him for a moment. He turned to her again. 'I really like Athena,' he said. 'I'm surprised by her. She's so uncertain, and vulnerable, and she has all this passion and everything.' He smiled. 'She's so honest, you see. She pretends all this sophistication stuff, but she's so instinctively truthful she can't hide. She's an innocent. I never thought I'd feel like this about her.'

Agnes looked at the grey streaks in his newly-shorn hair, at his frank, clear eyes, at the long, tanned fingers which once again searched the back of his neck. 'To be honest,' she said, 'I'm not very happy about the idea of this termination either. But if she's sure it's right for her—'

'But you know her. She's not sure about anything really. It's like my ponytail, I knew she didn't like it but she wouldn't say. She never actually asked me to cut it off. She wasn't sure enough of what she thought to impose her views on me.'

'She seems sure about this, though.'

Nic sighed. 'Yes. Yes, she does.' He rubbed the back of his neck. 'Agnes, what do you think?'

Agnes looked at him. 'I think, like you, that life is sacred.'

After Nic had gone, Agnes was restless. It was still early in the afternoon, but the sunshine had given way to the same damp humidity of yesterday. She had promised Nic she would talk to Athena, although now it seemed unlikely that Athena would want to listen. She thought about Nic, his obvious affection for Athena, his attempt to explain his views. Did he believe the soul was eternal, she wondered. For that matter, did she?

She thought of Ross Turner and his faithful followers, and on a sudden impulse picked up the phone and dialled Roger's number. Elizabeth answered.

'Hello, it's Sister Agnes here, do you remember, you very kindly introduced me to Ross.'

'Pastor Turner isn't here at the moment,' Elizabeth replied.

'No, it's just a quick question for you or Roger, perhaps.'

'I'm not sure I've the authority to—'

'Did a boy called Colin Hadley, known as Col, did he ever attend your church?'

Elizabeth seemed to be whispering to someone in the background. 'It's that nun who visited,' Agnes heard, before she came back on the line. 'Sorry about that, Steven was talking to me.'

'Colin Hadley,' Agnes prompted.

'Colin Hadley?'

'He was a friend of Becky's.'

'Here?'

'That's what I'm asking you,' Agnes said.

There was more conferring, then Elizabeth said, 'No. We don't know anyone of that name.'

Agnes thanked her and hung up. As if, she thought, I could

expect anything to break through the wall of secrecy surrounding Ross Turner. She opened her notebook again and stared at the phone number of the Stanton household. She picked up the receiver, imagining the conversation with Shirley, probably still silent with grief, or worse, the call being taken by Morris, who would swear blind that Becky knew no one called Col; whether she did or not. She replaced the receiver and stared out of the window, and tried to imagine what it would be like to have a father like that, so desperate to be a part of one's life. She remembered how, aged eight, she had a best friend called Antoinette, and how, after that, her father would refer to any girl who came to the house as Antoinette. In the end, it was in part his negligence that had driven her, aged eighteen, into the arms of Hugo. She frowned and fiddled with a pen, and then thought, everyone has their reasons; Sam had, finally, had enough. Col, who knows? And Becky; what drove Becky to run away? All the papers in the file, all the conversations with the people at the Ark, even meeting her parents, nothing had quite answered that question. Whatever had triggered her decision to stay away from home had also driven her into circumstances that were to cause her death.

It was five thirty-five. Agnes picked up her coat and bag and went out.

The grey outlines of the Atherton Estate looked even more forbidding against the thunderous sky. Four kids were playing some kind of gambling game throwing coins in one corner by the staircase. They broke off to stare at her as she walked through the archway into Kincaid Court. Once again, she wondered why she'd come. She looked up to the first floor, imagining Linda Whittaker hanging out washing, shooing children back indoors. Her eye was caught by an elderly man making painstaking progress along the walkway. She heard him slowly descending the flights of stairs, heard the tap of his stick at each step, until eventually he emerged, breathlessly, into the courtyard. She went up to him.

'Excuse me, sir,' she began. He blinked at her nervously with opaque, watery eyes. 'I wonder if you could help me. Have you lived here long?'

'Since the sixties,' he said, eyeing her suspiciously.

'Did you know – did you know the Whittakers?'

He stared at her, then said, 'Aye. Those two girls, Anne and – Linda, weren't it?' He nodded. 'Proper tearaways. Drove their poor mother to drink.'

'I wonder if—'

'1962 I moved down here from Sheffield, me and the wife, Joan, God rest her soul. Yes, I remember the Whittakers.'

'But there were other young people, weren't there, who hung around with the girls?'

The man laughed suddenly, a wheezing laugh. 'If you mean lads, oh aye, there were lads what hung around those girls. And those girls give 'em reason to an' all.'

'Can you remember their names?'

There was a sudden shouting overhead, a stream of abuse, then a door slammed.

'The Wheeler boy, what was his name, Bob. And my boy would have done, only he were a bit young for all that, young Edward. He lives in Milton Keynes, you know.'

'Anyone else?'

'Those Reynolds, there were a girl and boy – Julie and Mike, that was them. Their dad worked for the Post Office and moved out Wembley way, I think.'

'Mike Reynolds.'

'Aye, that were 'im. In fact, now's I come to think of it, he 'ad a kid wi' one. That Linda, weren't it? Everyone said it were 'is kid. And those Yates boys, David and Alex, rough kids, they used to swap cigarettes for favours. And the Bevan boys, you've got me started now, aye, those Bevan boys—'

'Did you say Bevan?'

'Aye, Tom and Greg Bevan.'

'T – Tom Bevan?'

'Greg were the older one, he made good he did, had a chain of video shops in the end. Don't know what happened to Tom.'

The door above opened again, and there was more shouting and then the sound of glass breaking. The elderly man looked at Agnes and smiled vaguely. 'It's been very nice talking to you. Don't often get to hear the sound of my own voice these days. Goodbye.'

He tapped his way across the courtyard and Agnes followed at a distance. The kids stopped their game to watch him pass. A boy, smaller than the rest, spat in his direction, and was slapped by one of the older boys. As Agnes went out of the courtyard, she could still hear the sound of the small boy's crying.

Back at her flat, she put some pasta on to boil. Tom Bevan, she thought, going to her bag and fishing out Col's bus ticket. She laid it out on her desk, staring at the scribbled name, the phone number underneath. It was a London exchange. The same Tom Bevan, Agnes wondered. Or just a coincidence?

She felt suddenly tired, turned down the heat under the pasta and flopped on to her bed. Becky and Col, she thought, and Sam and – and Athena. She got up, picked up her phone and dialled Athena's number.

'Hi.' Athena's voice was tired.

'It's Agnes.'

'I thought it might be.'

'Do you want some supper?'

'What, now?'

'It's suppertime, isn't it?'

'Dunno, I feel so sick that food has just become some awful tyranny. Yes, I'll come over if you're sure that's OK.'

'Great. Athena?'

'Yes?'

'I've been thinking of you.'

'Oh. Right.' She rang off.

Athena looked terrible. There were more grey roots showing in her hair and she was wearing a pair of garish pink leggings with holes in the knees and a pilled grey jumper. She flopped on to the bed, while Agnes chopped onions and tomatoes for a sauce.

'How was Gloucestershire?' she shouted from her kitchen.

'It was nice to be home, actually,' Athena shouted, brightening a little.

'Didn't you have tenants there?'

'I did, they've left. I've got to work out whether to rent it out again, if I'm staying in London.'

'What do you mean, if?' Agnes said, coming into the room and pulling out the flaps on her table.

'Oh, you never know, do you,' Athena said. Agnes looked at her, then disappeared back into the kitchen. 'Guess who I saw?' Athena said, her voice lightening again.

'Don't tell me,' Agnes said. 'My horrible ex-husband. Back in Gloucestershire.'

'You don't think he's horrible. Ever since he remarried you've been quite well-disposed towards him. Anyway, I bumped into them in the High Street.'

'Them?'

'Hugo. And Gabrielle. The third Madame Bourdillon.'

'Oh.'

'You'd like her.'

'I doubt it.'

Athena laughed. 'Yes, you would. Anyway, they're thinking of buying property in England again.'

'How lovely for them. I hope they're not expecting me to visit.'

'Do you know, he never mentioned you. Not once.'

'He must have been on his best behaviour, then,' Agnes said, pouring Athena a glass of red wine.

'I'm not supposed to drink this,' Athena said, screwing up her nose and taking a huge swig of wine.

Agnes was about to speak, but instead she went quietly back to the kitchen to stir the sauce.

As they sat over plates of tagliatelle, Agnes said, 'Nic was here this afternoon.'

'Yes, he told me.'

'You've seen him?'

'Briefly. He dropped in, I sent him away.'

'He seems nice.'

Athena put down her fork, looked at Agnes, then picked it up again. Agnes took another mouthful, chewed a moment, then said, 'Athena, if we're not honest now, we're not going to survive this.'

Athena twirled pasta around her fork. 'Fine. What do you want to say?'

'Nic wants you to keep the baby.'

'I know.'

'For reasons that he calls karmic.'

'Yup.' Athena took a large gulp of wine.

'And – and because he cares about you.'

Athena put down her glass. 'Great. His karma, your God. I'm surrounded by people who really care, aren't I? Lucky old me.'

Agnes broke off a piece of bread. 'He's nice without the ponytail. It suits him.'

'Years and years of careful cultivation, that ponytail, all lopped off, apparently, for me. Such sacrifice. And yes, he's dying to be a dad because he made so much of a hash of it first time round and he's desperate to have a second chance so he can be like all those men in *GQ* or *Esquire* or whatever it is. So I have to ruin my body, and my life, in return – and to appease your God-The-Father who, let's face it, was quite happy to dump His only son on someone else when it came to it . . .'

'Athena – we care about you. That's all. This may be your last chance, you can't predict how you'll feel when it's too late.'

'If you both care about me, then you'll know that I've done the right thing. I've made an appointment, did he say?'

Agnes nodded.

'Good. Fine. People who care about me can bloody well accept my decision, then.'

Agnes hesitated a moment, then said, 'Athena – when I offered you wine, you said, "I'm not supposed to drink this".'

'Did I say that? Oh ho, silly me. Anyone would think I was going to have a baby.' Athena laughed hollowly, and Agnes saw her eyes fill with tears.

That night in her prayers Agnes was haunted by an image of a tiny, floating life, of a translucent foetal face and waving limbs. She tried to push it away, to concentrate instead on the familiar words of her evening worship, but even when she closed her eyes to sleep it was still there.

She woke late on Monday morning, aware of having spent half the night chasing dreams, and after a quick cup of tea got into her car and drove to the camp. She found a group of about twelve people sitting near the fire, most of whom she recognised, some she didn't. Rona nodded in greeting and went to pour her some tea. 'We've got the eviction order,' she said to Agnes. 'They've given us two weeks.'

'So,' Jeff was saying to the assembled group, 'the main thing we're going to need is people. People who can climb, obviously, but people on the ground too.'

Agnes noticed Sheila sitting by the fire. She also noticed Jenn some way away, wandering vaguely towards the forest. Sheila was saying something about producing leaflets for the local area, and Agnes got up and followed Jenn. She found her sitting on a log at the edge of the wood.

'Jenn?' Jenn looked up blankly, then seeing it was Agnes, smiled. 'You OK?'

Jenn nodded, then shook her head. 'I've never felt like this before.'

'Like what?'

Jenn raised her eyes to Agnes and said, 'Like I don't care. They can evict us for all I care at the moment.'

Agnes sat down next to her. 'Well, to be honest, they will, won't they? There'll be hundreds of them and a handful of you.'

'Yes, but – before, it's always felt worthwhile, the fight. It works, you see, it has a kind of snowballing effect for the future. But now I look at the camp, and I think, I've had it, I've been full-on for months now and Col's dead and Becky was killed here, and no one's going to find out why, ever, and . . . I dunno, I've lost it.'

'Do you have anywhere else to go?'

Jenn nodded. 'I'm having a year out from a university course, I can take that up again this autumn if I want. Sociology, at Manchester, though I might change to history.'

They sat on a log together in the August heat. There was a chirping of crickets around them. 'Jenn,' Agnes began, 'you know that inhaler?'

'Col's?'

'It was his, wasn't it?'

'It wasn't anyone else's.'

'He might have had a bad reaction to it.'

'He hadn't been well for weeks.'

Jenn watched the slow march of a line of ants at her feet. She stretched, and stood up. 'If you mean Bill, he's harmless. A lot of ego, and I know people here don't trust him, but he wouldn't . . .' She shook her head.

'Jenn – why do you think Becky died?'

Jenn glanced down at her. 'How do I know? I'm going for a walk, clear my head.'

Agnes watched her go. There was something not being said. Something, Agnes thought, as she went back to the fire, that Jenn knew.

The meeting had broken up. Sheila was sitting next to Jeff, who was strumming vaguely on a guitar. She smiled as Agnes came to join her.

'Will you be there on the day?' she asked.

'The eviction? I hadn't really thought—'

'Yeah,' Jeff said, 'she'll be there.'

'Isn't it rather dangerous?' Agnes asked, feeling old.

'Nah. Fluffy, it is,' Jeff said. 'You can bring your daughter.'

Sheila looked doubtful. 'The problem is, evangelical Christianity is all about wearing nice clothes and joining the establishment. And anyway, they'd be useless, all they do is smile inanely and bang their tambourines.'

'Tell them we've got all the angels on our side,' Jeff grinned. He got up and went off to climb a tree.

'How's Charlie?' Agnes said.

'The same,' Sheila grinned. 'He liked you, for some reason.'

'That's good. I could do with talking to him again.'

'He won't trade secrets, him. Copper through and through.'

'I don't think it's secrets I need.'

'I know, come back for lunch, now. You can phone him from my place.'

'Detective Sergeant Woods? Just putting you through,' the switchboard operator said. Agnes sat in Sheila's warm, bright kitchen, through which wafted the smell of pitta bread and coffee, and waited.

'Sister Agnes?' she heard Charlie ask.

'It's about this new sudden death. Col Hadley, from the road camp.'

'I'd heard a whisper from the Coroner's officers.'

'I just wondered—'

'You have the nose for it, don't you. What did you just wonder?'

'The post-mortem report?'

144

'Haven't seen it.'

'Charlie – there were bright yellow stains around his fingers.'

'Why should I find out more for you?' Charlie asked.

'Because I care. And because Col has no one else. I cared about him when he was alive, and I need to put my mind at rest now he's dead.'

There was a pause. 'You know,' Charlie said, 'there was a warehouse broken into last week sometime. Out by Southend. Chemical storage place. Various stuff gone missing.' Agnes heard him hesitate, then he said, 'Yellow, did you say?'

'Really bright. Weird.'

'Look, this post-mortem report,' Charlie said. 'I'll see what I can do.'

'Any return of the Superhighwayman?' Agnes asked Sheila over lunch.

Sheila shook her head. 'No. Though I haven't had much time on the machine recently. But something funny happened in town the other day. I bumped into a friend, an ex-colleague from my teaching days – and she's moved to Colchester. I was telling her about the Ark and the eviction and everything, and she said, had I met Forest Bill? Like it was a joke. And it turns out that she knew him, about six months ago. I think they had an affair or something, and he said he was going to live in the woods by Epping for a while.'

'But he behaves as if he's been there for years.'

'Yeah, but is anyone convinced?'

Agnes looked at Sheila. 'Go on.'

'Well, there's nothing more to tell. She obviously thought he was a bit of a joker, except I think she fancied him like hell. But the other thing she said, was that he was into computers and spent most of his time in Colchester on the Net.'

Agnes took an olive stone from her mouth. 'So your friend was cyberzapped by the Superhighwayman too?'

Sheila looked at Agnes, and they both giggled. Then Sheila said, serious again, 'Who knows? More coffee?'

Agnes absently scanned Sheila's chaotic notice-board while Sheila refilled their mugs. 'Are you worried about Lily?' she asked her.

'Should I be?' Sheila said, coming back to the table. 'You know more about religion than I do.'

Agnes shook her head. 'I know very little about that kind of religion. Does Lily seem distant, brainwashed? Is she turning against you?'

'No. Not brainwashed. Rather cheerful, most of the time. Happier than she's been for a while. Although she does keep going on about getting married.'

'Married?'

'This preacher of theirs is very keen on his flock marrying when they're barely out of school and then living happily ever after. With God on their side, of course.'

'Of course.'

'Still, there's no one specific, as far as I know. And at least he's not trying to make a harem of his own.'

'Well, that's something.'

'She gets cross with me, but then what child that age doesn't? Only in her case, it's because I won't welcome Jesus into my heart, and so I'm just going to burn in Hell, apparently.'

'Poor old you,' Agnes laughed. 'Still, you'll be in good company.' She finished her coffee and stood up. 'Mind if I check the computer before I go?'

She went up to the computer room and scanned the e-mail messages. One caught her eye, from JEL @ Bosh.Co UK, and she called it up.

It said, 'Two down. How many more before justice is done?' Then the name, 'Emily Quislan.'

Agnes erased the file, switched off the machine and went back downstairs.

Chapter Thirteen

At eleven o'clock on Tuesday morning, Agnes was sitting at a reader's desk at the Essex Record Office. The day was warm and still, and Agnes had a headache, brought on by the drive from London and now made worse by the hopelessness of the task before her. She looked at the documents she'd called up, maps, school rolls, the OAPs essay competition again, the land tax register . . . Needles in bloody haystacks, she thought. Emily Quislan, where the hell are you?

She turned once more to the competition and pulled out all the essays catalogued under Broxted. She flicked past the familiar ones, the witch buried in Harton's field, the blackberries on the swamp field. She found one about corn dollies. '. . . My grandmother used to weave a particular shape which she said originated in Broxted. She used to hang one over the lintel on the full moon, to protect her from the ghost, she said. Once I asked her which ghost, and she said the lady in the long dress who rides sidesaddle across Harton's field sprinkling sweet herbs . . .'

The sheaf of papers fell from Agnes's grasp in a rustling heap, causing the reader opposite her to look up. Her hands shaking, she gathered up the papers and read the words again, over and over. 'There is no ghost,' she said to herself, 'there is no ghost.' The man opposite her was staring again, and she realised she was muttering. She put the essays aside and turned to the next document. It was the school rolls for the parish school, founded 1837. She turned the yellowing pages, finding names and ages of children, their health, their misdeeds, the rather grim punishments meted out to them; wondering why she was bothering, knowing that Emily Quislan, a woman old enough to own land, was hardly going to be registered in the parish school. Quislan, she saw, in spidery black ink, as a page turned in her fingers. She turned it back. James Quislan, registered at the school, September 1840, aged six.

Agnes's headache had become a pounding in her ears. She stared at the name. She turned to September 1841. James Quislan, aged seven. September 1842, the same, aged eight. September 1843. The words swam before her eyes. James Quislan, it said, aged nine. But through this name there was a neat black line, and underneath, in the same ink, it said, James Hillier, aged nine.

Agnes looked up at the clock. It was twelve twenty-eight. Outside the heat was beating down from a metallic grey sky. There was no sense to be made of this at all. It's about the well, Agnes thought. Fyffes Well. Something happened in 1843 to do with the well. And, somehow, it's happening again now.

She read right through the school rolls to 1860. James Hillier attended for a couple more years after 1843. There was no more mention of a Quislan. She closed the book, and grabbed the essay competition again. The well, she thought, thumbing through the pages, someone here must have some memory of the well apart from it being blocked in.

Blocked in, she thought. In 1843 James Quislan became James Hillier, and Emily Quislan blocked in the well. In revenge, Agnes thought, her mind racing ahead. In revenge for her son becoming someone else's son. She put down the pages and gathered her thoughts. If he was her son. She might have had a younger brother. Or a cousin. Or some distant relative. And maybe it wasn't a change of name. Maybe James Quislan did leave the school, and another James took his place.

She picked up the land tax records from 1876, and turned to the plots listed for Emily's land. The Homestead at this point had someone called Widow Velley living in it, as a tenant. Checker Mead listed as its owner William Harton, who also owned the neighbouring farm. And Well Mead was owned by Edmund Wytham, along with much of the surrounding estate. So at some point Harton and Wytham carved up Emily's land between them. And the well? She turned to the Ordnance Survey map, made about forty years after Emily's time. There was no well marked.

All the same, Agnes thought, handing back the files, and going to find a cup of coffee, the well could have been blocked in any time from the 1840s to the 1870s. There was nothing to say it had anything to do with Emily Quislan.

The gate said, 'Fyffes Spring Water Company. No unauthorised visitors.' Agnes got out of her car, opened the gate, got back into her car, drove through, and got out to close the gate behind her. The perimeter fence glinted in the heat, the vertical steel lines slicing through the parched rolling curves of the stubble fields. Agnes turned to get back into her car. Ahead of her she saw the huge round tanks of Fyffes Spring shimmering in the heat, like an oil refinery in the Arabian desert. She drove up the drive, parked in the car park and looked around for an entrance. A series of sparse bungalows ended with a door marked 'Reception'. She approached it, and knocked, then opened the door. There was no one there. She closed the door again, and hesitated.

'Can I help you?'

The voice was gruff and male, and belonged to a man wearing a grey suit. He was short, with gingery hair and now he squinted at her in the glaring sunlight.

'Um, yes, I hope so,' Agnes began. 'I'm just visiting really. I'd heard a lot about your mineral water, and—'

'Purest stuff for miles around. Only no one'll believe us.'

'Um, yes—'

'Have you tasted it?'

'Not actually, but—'

'Come with me.' He led her past the bungalows to a huge windowless wall, in which there was a door. He opened it, and she followed him in. Inside there was a rumble of machinery, a gloomy darkness and a clean, wet smell like fresh earth. Agnes followed the man into a little office, which had a high window and a cheap Formica desk almost entirely covered with papers. There was a low plastic-covered armchair, also covered with papers. Strewn around the room were several blue plastic bottles of water. The man threw himself into the chair behind the desk, gestured vaguely to the unusable armchair and grabbed a bottle of water. He unscrewed the top and handed it to Agnes.

'There you are, then,' he said. He grabbed another bottle, opened it and began to swig from it. Agnes politely took a mouthful of hers.

'Only still at the moment. Pure spring water, bottled. We'll be going fizzy as soon as we can. Whaddya think?' He waited, his eyes bright with expectation.

'It's – it's very good,' Agnes said, truthfully.

'See?' he said. 'You try telling them, though. Those morons out there will knock back any amount of French bog water, could be recycled from the bidets of Paris for all they know, but do they care? If it has a fancy French name, then that's fine, they'll drink it by the bloody Froggy litre. But good stuff like this, pure, un-meddled-with crystal-clear H-Two-Bloody-Oh—' He sighed.

'I'm sure it's just a matter of time,' Agnes said. 'With something as good as this, word will spread, surely.'

'If we were bloody French, they'd be heaping Ecus on us just for the sake of it. Old Chirac would be lining my pockets even as we speak. But this country – this Government . . . I could be employing twice as many people if I had the money, I could be advertising, talking to supermarkets, getting this carbonation sorted . . . Richard Witham,' he said, abruptly. 'Managing Director, for what it's worth.'

Agnes took the hand he stretched out awkwardly across the desk. The name Witham resonated in her ears.

'Agnes – um – Bourdillon,' she mumbled, trying to pronounce her ex-husband's surname in the most English way she could manage.

'Come on, I'll show you round.'

Agnes followed him round pumping plant and bottling machinery, saying hello to the occasional member of his workforce, nodding over the plans for the carbonation plant – 'It's the future, in this business, if you can't do bubbles you might as well give up' – and being taken to the site of the spring itself which was imprisoned in clanking steel. 'People are always disappointed. They expect some bloody waterfall, mountain stream, that sort of caper,' he said.

Finally she followed him out of the factory and into the fields behind, listening to his plans for expansion. As she tramped across the bare earth, the plant humming in the background, she thought, This is Emily's land. This plot, with this spring, and probably that tree too, belonged in 1839 to Emily Quislan. She screwed up her eyes against the sun, staring towards the silhouette of a derelict building, a barn. Maybe even a farmhouse. Emily's house.

'. . . the bottling, you see, with fizzy, different bottles, new technology.'

'Yes,' Agnes nodded.

'And,' Richard went on, 'if no one's going to drink the bloody stuff I'm barking up the wrong bloody tree altogether.'

'What made you choose this?'

'Me?' He looked at her, taken aback. 'Oh, well, you know . . . well, actually – ' He stepped a little way in front of her, so she could no longer see his face – 'life fell apart a bit, rotten luck. New start.' He turned and faced her, blushing, then looked at the ground where his toe was prodding at a stone. 'My wife – well, not her. Not her fault, really. Business collapsed, last one, jewellery, salesman. Couldn't keep up, mortgage, you know, all that. Don't usually talk about it . . .' He raised his eyes and smiled, briefly. 'On my own again now, a bit of family money, we're local, go back years, started again.' He looked out over the soft curves of the hayfields.

'I'm sure it'll work for you,' Agnes said gently. 'People worry about water.'

'Yes.' He nodded. 'Only, this water . . . D'you know,' he turned to her, sharply, 'I've had a couple of the locals refuse to work here. Say it's unlucky. When you ask them why, they mumble into their beards about something their grandmothers told them. Which is crazy if you think about it, because I had the devil's own job convincing the borough surveyor and his cronies that there was anything here at all.'

'How did you find it?'

Richard Witham blushed again. 'Dowsing. I was looking for – um, well, treasure, actually. Bit desperate in those days. But I found water. Just as good,' he said, brightly. 'As long as it works.'

'When you unblocked it, was there any clue as to – as to how it had been blocked in the first place?'

Richard nodded. 'Now thereby hangs a tale. The council people were quite taken with it. A whole crowd of them came to pick over it. It had been packed with rocks. Thorough job, they said, difficult to keep it down, water like this. It explains the flooding in the valley down there, all the pasture there used to be swamp, nearly. They reckoned it had been blocked for about a hundred years, maybe more.'

'Deliberately?'

'That's what they said, yes. The records show various attempts to unblock it, various rumours about it being a spring, but I'm the first to make a go of it.'

They began to walk slowly back to the car park. Agnes sensed in his silence the hesitation of words about to form. As they reached her car he said, 'The problem is, it's still there.'

'What's still there?'

'The bad feeling. I've had threats, you know. Someone wants to poison the spring.' He stood, uncertainly, biting his lip, regretting having made his doubts take shape by speaking them aloud.

'Why should they want to do that?'

Richard shook his head. 'Grudge? Mad? How should I know? Wait here.' He ambled back to his office and emerged a minute later with a bottle of water and a piece of paper. 'Here. For you.'

'Thank you,' Agnes said, taking the bottle. 'I shall sing its praises wherever I go.' She unfolded the piece of paper, knowing in advance what it was.

'POISON BEGETS POISON. HE WHO SOWS ON STOLEN LAND WILL REAP A BITTER HARVEST.'

'You can keep that,' Richard said.

'You really have no idea who might have done it? Maybe someone you've sacked?'

He shook his head. 'I haven't upset anyone. You can ask them if you like: "what's old Witham like?"'

Again the name echoed around Agnes's aching head. 'How do you spell your name?' she heard herself ask.

'W-I-T-H-A-M,' he replied.

'Was it ever spelt differently?'

Richard looked puzzled. 'Well, maybe. We go back years around here.'

'With a "Y"?'

'Well, maybe. I'm more the Suffolk branch, but perhaps the Essex lot might have done that. Maybe.'

'So this land – you owned it once.'

'Me?'

'I've looked in the tithe maps, and—' Agnes realised she'd said too much. Richard Witham was now looking at her hard.

'You see,' Agnes faltered, 'I knew about this threat. I picked up some of these leaflets—'

'Where? Where did you happen to find leaflets like this?' Richard's voice had a new edge to it, his eyes narrowed as he waited for her answer.

Agnes took a deep breath. She met Richard's gaze and said, 'I've been spending time at the road camp. You know, the protesters, over in the woods there. No, wait, let me finish. Whoever is endangering your spring here is also threatening them. That's how I came to see the leaflets, that's what made me come to visit you.' She watched the steel of his eyes soften into grey again, and added, 'I wouldn't have mentioned the tithe maps if I didn't think I could trust you.'

'Trust me? It's not me who's—'

'I mean, trust you not to hassle the road-camp people. They're innocent. It's just that one or two of them might have got mixed up in something – um – sinister.'

Richard blinked in the bright sunlight and scratched his head. 'There was that girl killed down there.'

'Yes.'

'Do you think it's connected with – heavens! Do you think I'm in danger?' He smoothed gingery strands with his fingers, blinking down at Agnes.

'No.'

'Should I call the police? I've been thinking of it.'

Agnes smiled warmly. 'It's entirely up to you.'

'I'd rather not add to the rumours at the moment. As long as I'm not in danger. What do you think?'

'Perhaps wait and see.'

'Mmm.'

They shook hands by Agnes's car. 'We get all sorts dropping in. It's not for me to ask, but if you'd mentioned the leaflets first, well, saved a lot of time, that's all.'

Agnes smiled. 'Yes, I know. I'm sorry. There's one other thing. I'm a nun. Sister Agnes, it is. Look, here's my number in London,' she said, scribbling it on a page from her notepad. 'Just in case.'

'Quite,' he said, waving the scrap of paper at her as she got into her car. 'Y'never know.'

Emily Quislan, thought Agnes, pulling out into the middle lane, does not exist. The sun had bleached the sky to shimmering steel, and the traffic zipped and rumbled in a haze of smog. She did exist once, but she doesn't now. Emily Quislan is a person from the mid-nineteenth century. So how the heck does she think she can poison Fyffes Well? In all the Church's teachings on the subject of the after-life, and God knows there's enough said about it, there is nothing to say it is possible to come back and wreak revenge.

Revenge, thought Agnes. The bitter harvest from the stolen land. Emily Quislan lived on the land until Edmund Wytham took it over sometime in the 1840s. In 1843 something happened to James Quislan. And Emily – perhaps – Emily filled in the well. In revenge. And now the well is reopened – by a Witham. And Emily is back.

Agnes dropped her speed and slipped into the left-hand lane again. She found herself thinking about Nicholson, the farmer, wearily tilling the fields for the last summer before the road was built. And the land that had never quite gone right for him, been uphill all the way, he'd said. She pulled out to overtake a Volkswagen Beetle, remembering how Nicholson had said the Hartons were desperate to get rid of their land. A brother and a sister. Agnes saw in her mind once again the neat script of the essays, the words passing across her eyes so that the lights of the car in front rushed towards her and she only just braked in time, the Vauxhall behind hooting in rage and swerving to overtake her with a mouthing of silent invective. Agnes slipped back into the left-hand lane, still seeing, in somebody's best handwriting, someone long since dead, the words, 'That was the summer we made our den in Harton's field . . . where the witch was buried.'

She joined the endless lines of traffic into London, skirting the Thames, seeing beyond the bleak tower blocks the City's distant opulence, the jewelled prisms of sheer glass. The modern world, she thought. Whoever you are, Emily Quislan, you are neither ghost nor witch.

Agnes drew up outside her block and parked her car. It was a quarter to five. She caught the bus to Southwark Central Library, went straight to the telephone directories for Essex and flicked through their pages in search of anyone named Harton. Ongar and Epping proved fruitless, Chelmsford produced two names and Colchester one. She wrote down the numbers, then trawled through Suffolk too, finding one Harton in Lavenham. She wrote down that number too. Lastly she looked up Quislan and found none at all.

What do I hope to gain, she thought, leaving the library and heading for the bus stop, by phoning complete strangers and asking them whether their ancestors had ever buried a witch? It is hardly the action of a rational person, thought Agnes, boarding a number 21 bus and realising she was starving hungry.

'I've brought us buns,' she announced to Julius, walking into his office. 'And fruit cake. And bread for toast.'

Julius looked up from his desk, nodded vaguely over the top of his gold-rimmed spectacles, and turned back to a letter he was reading.

'Does this thing work?' Agnes said, fiddling with an ancient toaster.

'I believe Madeleine got a spark of life out of it last week sometime,' Julius said, not looking up.

'I suppose we could just be content with the buns but I really did fancy toast,' Agnes said, peering into the slots.

'I think in the end Madeleine had to stand there holding the thingie down,' Julius said, still reading.

'Ah. Right.' Agnes put two slices of bread into the machine, pushed down the switch, and stood there. After a while Julius finished his reading, looked up and grinned at her.

'I don't see what's so funny,' Agnes said, leaning against the table. 'I wanted some toast, that's all.'

'And I was the nearest source of a toaster, albeit an unreliable one.'

'It's perfectly rational.'

'Perfectly.'

'Julius – what do you think about revenge?'

'Well, this is turning out to be an exciting afternoon after all.'

'Do you think it could really make someone want to do something a hundred and fifty years after the event?'

'In that the human spirit carries great passion within it, yes. In that they'd be dead, no. Agnes, it won't pop up by itself, you know, with you leaning on it like that.'

'I know what I'm doing,' Agnes said, removing two beautifully golden slices of toast from the machine. She fetched plates and knives from a corner cupboard, and proceeded to butter the toast. Julius stood up and put on the kettle.

'Tea and toast,' he said. 'How surprisingly English of you.'

'It's Normandy butter,' Agnes replied.

'Of course,' Julius smiled to himself.

'It's just these two deaths, Becky and Col,' Agnes said, sitting at the other desk and taking a huge bite of toast, 'seem to be tied up with someone who lived in that area in the early 1840s, but who's leaving messages again. Now. From what I can gather she may have lived in Broxted with a boy, possibly her son, then left, maybe, probably not happily, and in revenge, perhaps, because the land was divided up, she blocked the well. And then it might have been this same woman who was known as a witch and was buried in the neighbouring field, which has never been successfully farmed ever since and is now going to be a road. Oh, and she might be a ghost too, sprinkling rosemary about the place.'

'And what about her husband?' Julius poured boiling water into the teapot.

'Her what?'

'The boy's father?'

'What about him?'

'If we're talking the 1840s, women didn't have children on their own. Apart from widows, of course.'

Agnes had finished her toast and was now dividing a large chunk of dark fruit cake into two. 'Do you know, it hadn't crossed my mind. But that might explain—'

'Single mothers would have been hounded from the village. And lone widows were never far from accusations of witchcraft. Although 1840 is a bit late for that, perhaps.' Julius took the cake Agnes was offering him, and a Chelsea bun, which he delicately divided in half, brushing sugar from his fingertips.

'You're right, Julius. The father. Again.'

Walking back home, Agnes saw an image in her mind of a woman in a long skirt and bonnet dismounting from her horse and walking through the fields towards Fyffes Well with a purpose in her stride, a purpose born of anguish and despair. How do you block a well? Agnes wondered, seeing the woman carrying stones, her fingers raw against the rock. An act of revenge; if she can't have the water, then no one will. In Agnes's mind the well was as she knew it, with its superstructure of steel tanks and the hum of bottling machinery. But the woman was the same, in the skirts and shawl and bonnet of 1843.

Agnes walked up the stairs to her flat. Emily Quislan, she thought. Once you might have dressed like that. But not now. She let herself in and stood in the middle of her room as the late-afternoon sunlight streamed in. Now you wear, what? Jeans? Leather jacket? Leggings and floaty layers, dreadlocked hair, earrings? For you see, Emily Quislan, Agnes said to herself, sitting down at her desk, I don't believe in ghosts. There is someone else. Someone following the same trail that I've been following. Someone who knows what made you block the well, who knows about your son and your leaving the land and the land being divided up, and the rosemary; and maybe they know, too, that you were buried as a witch in Harton's field. If you were. Someone who is angry on your behalf. Emily Quislan Junior is a very angry person.

Anger, thought Agnes; a dangerous emotion, remembering Col's fear at seeing the name on the screen. She got up and paced the few steps across her room, then sat down and leafed through her notebook until she came to the list of Hartons. She picked up the phone, hesitated, and replaced the receiver. Her eye fell on the other names and numbers listed in the notebook; Mike Reynolds, Roger and Elizabeth Murphy, Becky Stanton's parents, Nic. She felt suddenly weary. A phone call made to any one of these people would mean going down that path, intruding into that life, trying to make sense of any number of small chaoses that, in the end, were perhaps nothing to do with her. If Mike was lying to Sam, what good would it do to say so? If Sam was deluding herself about Mike, why bother to tell her? If the Murphys wanted to follow

Ross, if Ross wished to marry off his flock, who was Agnes to intervene? If Athena wanted to . . . It was today. Athena's appointment.

Agnes knelt down in front of her crucifix and her unlit candle. 'You, Lord,' she said. 'You know. You alone know the extent of Mike's deception. You alone know the anguish of Shirley Stanton as if it was Your own. You alone know whether Ross is speaking the truth, Your truth, when he talks of Christ entering the human soul. And I, Lord, I do not. You alone know whether Athena is right to . . .' Agnes opened her eyes and for a while watched the pattern on her rug made by the tree outside her window in the pink evening light, a feathered ripple across the plain chenille. And if You know everything, she thought, and I know nothing, what does that mean? Does that mean I should do nothing? And if I do nothing, if I have failed to convince Athena, then I, too, am responsible . . .

'Thy will be done,' she murmured, tracing the flickering light with her fingers. The phone rang, loudly, and she jumped.

'Agnes, it's Nic.'

'Hello.'

'Has Athena rung you?'

'No.'

'I thought she might. She didn't go. Today. She cancelled the appointment.'

'Oh,' Agnes said. There was a silence, then she said, 'How is she?'

'I – I don't know. I haven't seen her. She phoned me. She's at home. I said did she want company, but she said no.'

'Oh. You – you must be pleased.'

'I think so. Yes.'

'Right.'

'Agnes?'

'Yes?'

'Thanks.'

He rang off.

Thanks, he'd said. Nic had thanked her. She picked up the phone to dial Athena's number to say – to say what? To say, 'Well done, you must be very happy'? Agnes knew her friend too well for that.

It was just a postponement, probably, to give herself more time to think.

Agnes put down the phone again and sat motionless. It was hardly right of Nic to thank her. She couldn't claim to have had any influence. It wasn't as if she'd directly saved that baby's life. And yet she supposed, in some small way we all contain the potential to do harm or good. She stood up and walked to the window, then back to her desk. In which case, she thought, doing nothing is simply not an option.

She picked up the phone and dialled the Murphys' number. Roger answered.

'Hello,' she said, 'it's Sister Agnes again. I was just wondering . . . well, I was very interested in what Ross had to say when I met him, and I wondered whether I might come along to one of your more general meetings, if it's convenient, of course. I don't wish to intrude . . .'

There was a pause, and a brief sound like whispering. Then Roger said, 'There's a study group tomorrow night. Here. You'd be very welcome. There'll be a couple of new members, so you won't be on your own.'

'That would be lovely,' Agnes said.

'Eight o'clock.'

'I finish work at seven, so that should be fine.'

Agnes hung up and wondered what Madeleine would make of her bolting out of the hostel on the dot of seven instead of hanging around and drinking tea as usual. 'I've decided to attend a house church group,' she'd say; and Madeleine would just laugh.

Chapter Fourteen

'Satan loves our weaknesses, he feeds on our weaknesses,' Ross was saying. 'Satan is hungry for our sins.' His eyes shone with the urgency of his words, as he allowed his gaze to alight on each person in the group in turn. Agnes counted twelve people including herself, all squashed into the Murphys' front room.

'And it is we who feed Satan, by allowing him to feast on our sin,' Ross went on. 'Even in the face of the great sacrifice of our Lord Jesus Christ do we continue to nourish Satan in our hearts.'

Agnes shifted on her floor cushion, glad that she had arrived too late to take one of the chairs. At least here, sitting with her legs curled under her behind an armchair, she was half-hidden from Ross's view.

'People ask me, "Pastor, what can we do about this?" And I say to them, the answer is simple. In Jesus is our salvation. And however hard Satan tries, however much we in our frailty give him cause for triumph, the Lord Jesus is there. Because, and this is the great glorious message of the Gospel, Jesus died for us. Once and for all, in that great act of love, he cleansed us of our sins. And as long as we remember that, as long as we recall to mind every day, every moment of every day, that act of love, then Satan will never find a way to our hearts.'

Agnes glanced at the faces around the room. Morris Stanton was there, but not Shirley. Elizabeth, near the door, ready to greet latecomers. Roger by the window. Steven next to him, and Jerry at Ross's feet, as he was before. There were two young women sharing an armchair rather uncomfortably, both wearing jeans, both with long blonde-tinted, cheaply permed hair. There was a smartly dressed Afro-Caribbean man in his twenties, sitting straight-backed, gazing at Ross. Lastly, there was a shabby-looking grey-haired woman sitting with a stooped elderly man who appeared to be her husband.

'In the passage from the Bible that Steven chose to read to us earlier, St Paul clearly states to us what we must do. We must follow Christ. That is all we have to do. As long as you keep that idea firmly in your mind, that you are a follower of Jesus, then all else will come from that. In all your daily dealings with people, in your work, with your friends, you are above all else a follower of Christ. And this is the next piece of good news. Because the more you allow Jesus into your heart, the more empowered you will be. You will find Jesus living amongst you, as real as I am now; and you will see Satan recoil from you.'

Ross's eyes were bright, his tanned skin seemed to glow. Agnes studied the broad forehead, the straight nose. He really was very good at his job. She watched the two girls in the armchair, both concentrating very hard on staring at Ross to avoid having to catch each other's eye. Agnes had arrived too late for the reading, and now she wondered which epistle it was that Steven had chosen.

'Let us consider a minute how Satan works to distract us, to confuse us so that we serve him instead of our Lord. I have said to you all before, that we must beware the world. We must beware the gifts that the world appears to offer us, the rewards that it spreads before us for following its ways. And let us give thanks that St Paul chose to give us this message—'

'Amen,' the smart young man murmured.

'—for the Lord knows how best we may serve him, and we do well to obey him. And does it not say in Genesis – male and female created He them. And do we all not know this, brothers and sisters, that the Lord has called us to use our strengths as best as we may, and that he does forgive us our weaknesses. The Lord loves us as we are, man and woman. You know my thoughts on this subject, that it is laid down that men must be men and women must be women. And not only is it what the Lord wishes us to be, but, and hear this, brothers and sisters, it is the only way we can find true happiness in this world.'

Ross paused, produced a fine cotton handkerchief from his pocket and wiped his brow. He smiled around the room, then resumed. 'But what does the world tell us? The world tells us, we know better than that. We know that whatever men do, women can do as well. If not better, eh?' Ross smiled, and the room smiled with him, apart from the hunched elderly man. 'So, what do we do about these words? If they're telling us something we disagree with, do we ignore them, or do we think about them? What do you think, Janine?'

One of the girls in the armchair blinked at Ross, blushed, looked at her friend, grinned, looked at the arm of her chair and said very quietly, 'Dunno.' Both girls giggled.

'Anyone?' Ross said, looking at Agnes, before allowing his gaze to pass to Roger.

'I think first and foremost,' Roger said, taking off his glasses, 'we must accept the authority of St Paul.' Ross nodded. 'And then, after that, we must see how the teachings of the Gospel can have relevance to our lives. After all,' Roger smiled, 'we can change our lives to fit the teachings of Jesus, but we can't change the teachings of Jesus to suit the way we live our lives.'

'And that's just it,' Ross said. 'The Bible is the word of our Lord. It is clear for all to see. If we can't see what the Lord is trying to say to us, then it is because we are not allowing our view to be clear. So, what is St Paul saying here?'

Jerry shifted, crossed his legs over the other way, and said very quietly, 'Is it that the man is stronger in some ways, and the woman is stronger in other ways?'

'Good,' said Ross, and Agnes saw Jerry lower his eyes, a faint smile pass across his lips. 'Anyone else?'

Steven said, 'Men and women are different,' then smiled at his mother who fiddled with her apron on her lap, blushing.

'Precisely,' Ross said. 'But what are we told these days? We're told that men and women are the same. We're told that women can be brain surgeons, men can be nurses, women can work on building sites, men can stay at home and raise the children. And yet, what we are not told is the suffering this causes. People are forcing themselves to behave in ways that are not true to them. Women who want to stay with their children are being forced to go out and work; men who would gladly take a job and support their family are deprived of work, deprived of their true role.' Ross leaned forward and took a sip of water from the glass on the table in front of him. '"I will therefore that the younger women marry, bear children, guide the house, give none occasion to speak reproachfully. For some are already turned aside after Satan." So says St Paul to Timothy. Brothers and sisters, I tell you, it is only in the ways of the Lord can we find true happiness.'

Agnes saw Ross's fingers move as if to touch the top of Jerry's head, felt rather than saw Jerry shift at the movement as Ross checked himself. In her head suddenly she heard what Paz had said about Becky's mysterious friend; 'I thought maybe they were a couple, but then you do think that if someone turns you down, don't you . . .' And there was Jenn, hesitating, on the verge of telling her something. Something about Becky.

Agnes was staring at Steven, at Elizabeth Murphy in her neat feminine clothes, at Morris Stanton, nodding florid-faced at Ross's words, until he sensed Agnes's gaze and looked up with a flash of hostility. Agnes blinked and looked away. And Jerry, sitting at Ross's feet, leaning back imperceptibly until his soft blond hair brushed Ross's knees, his eyes half-closed as he listened to the Pastor's lilting voice; 'The Lord's path is the true path . . .' Agnes thought of Becky running away, being brought back, running again, fighting to keep her sense of self, to live as she needed to live; to survive. No wonder Morris could hardly bear to hear her name.

Afterwards, Elizabeth served cups of tea and plates of Bourbon biscuits. Ross had talked for well over an hour, fluently, persuasively. At the end they had bowed their heads in prayer. 'Lord Jesus Christ, grant us the strength to match Your supreme sacrifice with our own . . .' Agnes glanced towards Ross and saw once again that compulsive movement of his fingertips towards the blond softness of Jerry's head.

Now, having sipped a few mouthfuls of tea, she stood up to go.

'I hope you found our little evening helpful,' Elizabeth smiled as she led her into the hall. 'I thought Ross was in fine form, ready for Sunday.'

'What's Sunday?' Agnes said.

'Our first big public prayer meeting. We've hired the old Methodist Hall in town, put up posters, everything,' Elizabeth said with girlish enthusiasm, as Ross appeared in the hall.

'Going already?' he said. 'I was hoping to have a chat.'

Agnes smiled into the warm, bronze eyes. 'I have to catch a train,' she said.

'Do come again,' he said, taking her hand.

Agnes felt the warmth of his grip. 'You're a very good preacher,' she heard herself say.

He smiled down at her. 'But not good enough for you.'

'I would never presume to judge—'

'There is much of the Lord's work still to do.'

'Yes.' She glanced at him. 'Your views on marriage—' she began.

'Not mine, the Lord's. As written down in the Holy Bible.'

'You seem to feel it very strongly.'

'As strongly as St Paul.' His eyes darkened and Agnes saw the tension around his mouth.

'Is it part of your mission, then?' she persisted.

'It's part of my mission to protect our young people from Satan's desires,' he said, flashing her a glance. 'The world out there lays before them such filth, such works of evil as to turn the strongest heart from Jesus. On Sunday I hope to offer safety to anyone who will hear, to bring them into the fold—'

'But marriage?'

Ross's voice came unevenly. 'How else can we be safe?' he said, and it seemed to be a cry from the heart. '"The young women do turn aside after Satan."'

'And the young men?' Agnes ventured.

Ross stared down at her. His face was flushed, and he was breathing shallowly. 'What would you know of young men?' he said at last.

'I just meant—'

'"'Tis better to marry than to burn",' he said, hoarsely.

Agnes said quietly, 'St Paul's true meaning is obscure.'

Ross shook his head. 'No, not obscure,' he said, his voice so low he was speaking almost to himself. 'Not obscure at all. I know all too clearly what he meant. To burn with desire, with Satan's desire . . .' He turned back to her, his eyes hollow, his lips working. 'And you too, Sister, can you honestly say you have never known desire? Even to betray your calling, your vow of chastity?'

'No, but—'

'Satan touches us all,' Ross said. He looked beyond her, staring at the corner of front lawn visible through the glass in the door, and Agnes saw him grow calm again, as if the anguish she'd just witnessed had been a mere performance. He leaned across her and opened the front door. He looked out into the warm night, the darkness punctuated with the regular glow of lamplight. 'Satan's power is everywhere,' he said, his lilting voice restored.

'But if you concentrate on Satan,' Agnes said, 'aren't you denying the greater power of God?'

'Ah, but that's where you people are wrong,' Ross said, turning back to her with a hint of a smile. 'Satan's greatest triumph is in convincing so many of us that he no longer exists.'

He stepped back to let her pass, shook her hand with another warm smile, then turned and went back into the house. Agnes walked to the station through the tidy streets, imagining Lucifer jeering at her from the privet hedges and the crazy paving. 'So, Satan,' she addressed him. 'You know so much about evil – which of those people in that room is capable of murder?'

Agnes woke the next morning still reflecting on her conversation with Ross. She imagined him presiding over a mass wedding, great crowds of young people in dinner jackets and frilly white dresses, all holding hands in smiling couples. She made herself some coffee, feeling more and more uneasy. Still in her pyjamas, she dialled Sheila's number.

'I was wondering,' she said, 'whether Lily's mentioned this prayer meeting on Sunday?'

'Mentioned it? She doesn't stop talking about it. Anyone would think they were going to bring Peace in Our Time or something. Why?'

'Has she talked any more about getting married?'

'A bit, yes. Mostly to criticise me for not staying with her father.'

'She hasn't mentioned anyone's name?'

'No, too busy evangelising, I think. They're out in force by the shopping precinct most days at the moment, with their tambourines and things. I have to wear my Jackie Onassis dark glasses if I'm passing in case I'm recognised. Although—'

'What?'

'Come to think of it, she did say something the other night.

What did I think of her having a boyfriend, or something. I felt like saying I didn't mind as long as he was a hard-drinking, hard-swearing, chain-smoking biker, but luckily I managed not to. What's all this about?'

'I saw that preacher of theirs last night. He seems very interested in marrying people off. It's difficult to tell what's real with him, but it crossed my mind that he might be on that kind of power trip, you know, not to seduce anyone himself but to have control over people in some other way.'

'Great. How very reassuring. What should I do?'

'That's just the trouble. What can you do? Just let me know if anything more happens, I suppose.'

'And then what? We'll organise a mass kidnap?'

'I hope it won't come to that,' Agnes laughed.

Agnes was just coming out of the shower when the phone rang.

'It's Sam,' the voice said.

'Hello. How're you?'

'Oh. OK.'

'Great,' Agnes said, checking her watch, wondering how long this call was going to be. Her shift at the hostel was due to start in less than half an hour. 'Anything I can do?'

'No. Just thought I'd ring. Maybe, if you're passing, you could come and see me, um, us.'

'Yes,' Agnes said. 'When would you like me to?'

'Oh, you know, whenever. No rush. Better go,' she added hurriedly, as Agnes heard movement in the background.

'This evening,' Agnes said, firmly. 'I'll call on you this evening. Seven thirty OK?'

'Yeah, great, thanks, bye.' She'd hung up.

Agnes dried herself, pulled on underwear, T-shirt and jeans, brushed out her hair. The feeling of unease wouldn't go away. Lord, keep her safe, she thought. At least until I can get there this evening.

Before she left for the hostel she dialled Athena's number and heard Athena's giggly recorded message. 'Hi, it's Agnes,' she said, after the tone. 'I hope you're OK. I really hope you're OK. Look, I'm – I ought to have phoned you earlier. Please phone me. I really do—' A series of beeps indicated some technical fault, or the end of the tape or something. 'Damn,' Agnes said, hanging up. Oh God, she thought, please make sure she knows I've phoned.

Later that day, in between getting lunch for the five current residents, booking in a fourteen-year-old girl from Leicester caught shoplifting in Oxford Street, and spending a couple of hours trying to get sense out of a boy called Mick who claimed he had friends in Wembley and they could put him up, and he promised not to go back on the rent again, honest, Agnes managed to phone Athena again. Again she heard the answering machine, the jolly voice on the tape so much at odds with her empty silence, her unreturned messages.

'Hi, it's Agnes. Again. Listen, um – I'm here if you need to talk. I'm at home or at the hostel. Any time, really. Um, right then . . . bye.'

When she returned home that evening having picked up the car again, there were no messages left on her machine. She felt Athena withdrawing from her, from the world, turning inwards towards this strange new life still growing inside her. She changed, downed a quick cup of coffee, and set off in the car for Harlow.

The door was opened by Mike. 'Hi,' he said, stepping back to allow her in. 'Sam said you might drop by.'

'Is she here?' Agnes asked.

'Sure, yeah, up in her room, I expect, as usual. You know what teenagers are like,' he laughed, in exaggerated cheerfulness.

Agnes looked beyond Mike and saw Sam at the foot of the stairs, silent and pale. Sam came forward and smiled, briefly, at Agnes, then took her arm and made as if to lead her back up the stairs.

'Where do you think you're going?' Mike asked, his good humour ringing false.

Sam shrugged, changed direction, and led Agnes into the front room. The three sat down awkwardly.

'So, how's life, Agnes?' Mike asked. 'It's nice of you to drop by.'

'Life's fine, though I'd love a cup of tea,' Agnes smiled in reply. Mike looked at Sam, who ignored him, flicking instead through the pages of the *Radio Times*. After a long moment Mike got up and went to the kitchen, where they could hear him banging around, putting on the kettle, finding mugs.

'It's his bloody house,' Sam said, keeping her voice down. 'He can make the bleedin' tea.'

Agnes seized the few seconds of privacy. 'So, things aren't what they seemed?'

Sam looked at her, shrugged, then shook her head. 'I dunno what I expected. He's so bloody possessive. Like I'm a child.'

'In a way, he thinks you are. As your father . . .'

'If he is—'

'What makes you say that?'

Sam turned wide bewildered eyes to Agnes. 'I dunno,' she said. 'I just keep thinking, if he was my dad, really really my dad, we'd be mates. You know. As it is . . .'

'As it is what?'

'Oh, I dunno.' Sam shrugged and looked up as Mike entered the room again, clutching mugs of tea, two in one hand, one in the other. He put them down awkwardly, sloshing tea on to his glass coffee table, then grinned sheepishly and left the room again in search of a cloth.

'Sam – do you need help?' Agnes said in the few seconds left to them.

Sam looked at her. 'I'm not in danger, if that's what you mean. Just bored, really. I feel like a prisoner here. Col was right, you know.'

'Col? What did he say?'

Sam noticed a broken nail on one finger and started to fiddle with it. 'He said people like us don't ever find a home.'

'What did he mean?'

'He said he'd broken up his home, he reckoned his dad had done all he could after his mum went. Like it was his fault, you know? He said he'd worked out that there was no point him spending his life trying to find a replacement, right? He said it would be just the same wherever he went.'

Agnes looked at her, at her newly washed hair, her short skirt and ribbed jumper, her brand-new clumpy sandals, her eyes shining in the cosy warm light of Mike's front room. 'And is it the same for you?' she asked, as Mike came back into the room. He put down a plate of biscuits and then mopped up the spilt tea with a fistful of kitchen roll.

'You two catching up?' he asked, holding the dripping wet paper, his eyes searching the room for somewhere to put it.

'Sam was just telling me about – um—'

'About how it's boring round here,' Sam finished.

Mike looked at her hard, then turned to Agnes. 'Kids, eh?' He strode to the wastepaper basket, threw the wet kitchen roll into it, and then sat down heavily in an armchair.

Agnes smiled back. 'And how are you, Mike?'

'Me, oh fine.'

'And how's business?'

'Not bad. Not bad at all, for the time of year. Got a big order in for next week.'

He didn't look like someone who was rejoicing in the company of his long-lost daughter, Agnes thought. But then, what did she expect that to look like? Just different, she thought, from this edgy nervousness.

'How're they all at the camp?' Sam asked.

'Oh, you know. The same. Jeff's still swinging from tree to tree,' Agnes laughed. 'Jenn's talking about going back to college in the autumn. And Rona and the others are gearing up for the eviction.'

'Is it really happening, then?' Sam leaned forward on her seat.

'Apparently. End of next week.'

'I'll be there.'

'You won't,' Mike said sharply.

Sam looked at him. 'I will,' she said.

'If you think I'm going to let you risk your life like that . . .' he began.

Sam's face was set in defiance. 'Them bastards are goin' to kill our trees. We've bloody fought for them trees, we're not gonna give up without a fight. An' it's not just that, it's the world, right. I ain't goin' ter sit 'round watching them bastards ruin the planet—'

'You forget, Samantha—'

'I'm not bleedin' Samantha—'

'I'm responsible for you. And I won't have you endangering yourself climbing on to bulldozers and being hauled off by the police who, let's face it, are only doing their job.'

'You ain't responsible for me,' Sam said quietly. They sat, facing each other, outstaring each other with a peculiar intimacy, like

170

strangers on a long train journey. The phone rang and Mike went through to the hall to answer it.

'Sam,' Agnes said, her voice low, 'this isn't right.'

'You're telling me. Someone's got to get him to see that even if he is my bleedin' dad, he's still got to—'

'That's my order confirmed,' Mike said, breezing back into the room. 'Worth over twenty grand,' he said, sitting down again. 'And all thanks to old contacts,' he smiled, turning to Sam. 'Remember I mentioned Bob Wheeler? Well, he's pulled out all the stops and come up trumps. Just like the old days. Good old Bob.'

Sam barely looked up at Mike, working away at her broken nail with studied indifference. Bob Wheeler, thought Agnes, wondering why the name was familiar. Then she remembered the old man at the Stepney flats listing the names, the Bevan boys, Mike and Julie Reynolds, Bob Wheeler . . .

'He's an old friend?' she asked Mike.

'We go back years,' Mike grinned. 'Schooldays, you know. Always thought he'd go far. He's been doing nightclubs, branched out into catering, wants a whole range of paper products and marketing stuff. We stick together, the lads.'

'Is he near you?' Agnes asked casually.

'Over in Chingford, but his sandwich bars go right across to Enfield. Anyway, we were saying . . .'

'The eviction,' Sam said. 'And I'm going.'

Mike turned to Agnes. 'Agnes, tell her. Tell her it's no place for a girl like her . . .'

Agnes stood up. 'I'm afraid it's time I left.' Mike stood up too and she said to him, 'Sam's over sixteen. She has some rights. Also,' she added, 'with people like Sam, it's not a question of taming them. As I tried to explain at the time.' At the doorway she looked back to Sam and said, 'Don't forget, you made your choice. You can't rely on other people to settle your differences now.'

Mike got up and followed her into the hall. He hesitated, then said, 'I'm just frightened she'll run away again.'

'Well,' Agnes said, 'she's been running away for some time.'

'But she mustn't, she just mustn't,' Mike said, with an urgency that surprised her.

Agnes looked at him. 'In that case, you must let her feel she can be herself with you. Trust her.'

Mike nodded, and Agnes studied him for a moment. She touched his arm and said, 'You can always phone me.' Then she opened the front door and went out to her car.

Driving back to London, she thought about Mike. Something was not quite right. He seemed unable to cope with the responsibility of caring for Sam, but at the same time it was clear he couldn't bear the thought of her leaving him. And yet in his situation, Agnes felt, she'd be prepared to cut her losses if it didn't work out. He'd done what he could. As Sam's father, he'd tried. If he was Sam's father, she thought, wondering why that doubt was always there. And even Sam felt it now, although perhaps that was more teenage rebellion than any real assessment of the relationship. None of it made sense, Agnes thought. Why did he appear to need her to stay so desperately?

And now Sam wants to go back to the Ark for the eviction. Agnes remembered Sam's earlier fears at the camp, and wondered why they'd evaporated with Col's death. She wished Mike hadn't insisted on sitting there with them. At least she might have had the chance to ask Sam about her feelings about Col, about why she'd been so frightened; about Emily Quislan.

She turned off the motorway, resolving to phone Sam the next day. If Mike didn't intercept the call, she thought. She wound the window down to let some air into the car against the heat of the night. But then, she thought, perhaps that's what it is, to be a good father. Perhaps real fathers do prevent their daughters getting hauled off bulldozers by riot police. Perhaps it's only my history of parental neglect that prevents me recognising good fathering when I see it.

She drove through the deserted City and saw across the river the spire of St Simeon's piercing the dark sky. A few minutes later she was parking the car in the church driveway. The light was still shining in the window of Julius's office.

'I had this feeling I might see you tonight,' Julius said, looking up as she came into the room. 'And it's just as well, because there's a phone message. Two actually, but one was a heavy breather, or something. Hung up as soon as he heard my voice. The other was Sister Christiane, your Provincial.'

Agnes flopped into a chair. 'What did she want?'

'You were supposed to ring her. Last week.'

'Was I?'

Julius looked at her. 'You know you were. About Yorkshire. About the school. She needs your answer.'

'I've had lots to think about.'

'Agnes, you're not doing yourself any favours. This whole issue about Yorkshire is to do with you ignoring your spiritual needs. They're concerned for your own wellbeing, that's all.'

'Great. So Christiane and you had a grand old chinwag about me.'

'Of course not. But Agnes, there's no need to be so resistant. Just give her a ring, tell her what you think.'

'She knows what I think. I'm staying in London.'

'Fine.' Julius turned to the papers on his desk and began to fold them away.

'I'm not a child, after all.'

'No,' Julius said, 'of course you're not.'

'I mean, just because I made a vow of obedience, it doesn't mean they can dictate my life to me.' Julius put the last file back in his in-tray. 'Does it, Julius?'

Julius looked up. 'Do you want my honest answer?'

'Yes.'

'You know what I'm going to say. It's about faith. Becoming a religious isn't just a lifestyle decision. It's about finding a place in which your faith can grow. That's why you took a vow of obedience. Because as an individual, you don't always know what's best. You're in their hands, the way we're all in God's hands. Heavens, you know all this, Agnes. You aren't helping yourself by resisting it.'

'It's naïve, Julius. Do you think we're really in God's hands? And if so, why does He let such awful things happen to people?'

'We've discussed this before.'

'Yes, but I've never felt angry about it before.'

Julius took off his spectacles and laid them carefully on his desk. 'What's making you angry?'

'Oh, I don't know. Everything. Innocent people being killed. Stupid superiors trying to send me away. Men pretending to be fathers—'

Julius saw her bite back her tears. He stood up. 'Come on, I'll walk you home.' He took her arm and led her out of the church, locking the door behind him. 'Agnes,' he said, as they walked down the drive, 'don't phone Christiane tonight. Not while you're this angry.'

'Why not?'

'Because if you speak to her like this, you'll be lucky if it's just Yorkshire. They'll be sending you off to some left-over missionary posting in Lesotho or somewhere instead.'

Agnes smiled at him. 'At least it'll be warm there.'

It was after eleven when Agnes let herself into her flat. Her answering machine flashed one message, but when she tried to hear it back there was just a click. She dialled 1471 and the electronic voice gave her a number. She stared at it for a while, wondering why it was familiar, then remembered. She opened her desk drawer, and got out Col's bus ticket. On the back it said 'Tom Bevan' and a phone number – the same phone number that she'd just written down.

She glanced at it, picked up her phone to dial it, then stopped. She hung up the receiver again and, sitting at her desk, leaned her chin on her hands. Tom Bevan. If it was the same Tom Bevan from the Stepney estate . . . but why should he be phoning her, now? I could just call him, she thought, and ask him what the hell's going on, and what does he have to do with Col, and Sam, and – and he's got hold of my number, thought Agnes, suddenly chilled. Mike Reynolds and Tom Bevan and Bob Wheeler and Sam is right in the middle, caught up between them.

Agnes ran her hands through her hair. I'm a fool, she thought. I've sent Sam into some dubious network of men who've known each other since they were kids. Perhaps Ross is right, Agnes thought, Satan does walk the land, picking for himself the choicest flesh. And there's Lily . . . She got up and poured herself a large whisky. Now hang on, she thought, let's get a grip. Lily's a sensible girl. She'd get out if anything dodgy was going on. And Sam. She looked at her glass, shot through with glancing amber light. Sam chose, she thought. I am not responsible for Sam. She looked down at the scrap of paper, the phone number, the name Tom Bevan.

The room seemed cold. I am no more responsible for Sam than I am for Athena, she told herself, taking a large gulp of whisky. She went and sat on her bed. *Fiat voluntas tua*, she thought. Thy will be done. O Lord, our Father . . . Father, she thought. My father, Sam's father, Becky's father, she thought, remembering the silent hostility of Morris Stanton. And Emily Quislan, trying to do it on her own, and being punished in some awful way for not having a father for her child.

Agnes got up, suddenly angry, and paced her tiny flat. And what is God, then? she wondered. This benign omnipotent deity, who loves us unconditionally, like a father, we're told. Like a father? What do I know of fatherhood, but neglect? And what does Sam know, but her stepfather's abuse? And now Mike, her so-called father, following some power-crazed purpose of his own? And what did Becky know? Oh God, what did Becky know of fatherhood?

Agnes picked up her whisky glass and drained it. Our Father, Who art in Heaven . . . She went and poured another measure. Hallowed be Thy name . . . She sat on her bed and sipped at her glass. A flash of memory, a white dress embroidered with violets. A drizzly morning, more than thirty years ago. Looking out of the large drawing-room window of her parents' country house in Provence, on to the drive. Seeing a strange car parked there, a sleek black Citroën DX with a chic woman poised in the passenger seat, a flash of red lipstick and patent leather handbag. Feeling a sudden, sickening dread, knowing that her mother, lying in her room, had turned to face the wall. Watching her father bring his bags down to the drive, load them, smiling, into the back of the car. And then her father looking up, seeing the child's face at the window through the drizzle, the child seeing the moment of doubt pass across his face only to vanish at some coquetry from the unknown woman in the car. The child climbs down from the window, begins to run into the hallway, wrenching the huge front door open as the car starts up, runs down the front steps as the car pulls away, shouting 'Papa, Papa!' crunching on to the wet gravel, running after the car, shouting, screaming, crying, 'Papa, Papa, don't leave!' all the way down the long, long drive, long after the car has vanished out of sight . . .

And eventually, soaked with tears and rain, stomping back up the drive towards the house, towards the mother who had retreated into illness because there was nowhere else to go. 'Papa has gone,' the child would say, 'in a car with a woman. I tried to stop him, I tried, really I tried . . .' Her mother looked up from her couch, and told her off sharply for being out in the rain in her best shoes, and then fell back on to her pillows, sighing.

Agnes drained her glass for the second time. Tears welled in her eyes, but she dashed them away. How dare they, she thought. The mother who didn't give a damn, the father, receding in the rain-soaked car, the spinning black and silver wheels speeding away from the child running, crying down the drive . . . How dare they, thought Agnes, for the first time in her life. It was not Becky's fault, and it isn't Sam's fault, and it wasn't Emily Quislan's fault – and for God's sake it was not my fault. *It was not my fault.* How could one running, weeping child bring back that car? It was not my fault. Agnes stood up, burning with rage, and once the rage came there was no stopping it. Her child's voice rang in her ears. 'Papa, come back! Papa, don't leave!' and although she had grown up, that voice was still there, translated into yearning for a father that she'd never had. Our Father, she had prayed, for years and years. Please let me be good enough; please come back.

Agnes paced her room, white with fury. She wanted to phone Athena and tell her, do what the hell you like; she wanted to phone Ross Turner and say, who do you think you are, talking male and female roles, when the whole damn thing is based on a lie. God the Father, God the loving father, not the receding father, not the neglectful absent father. Agnes dashed more tears from her eyes. She had tried to forgive her father, now dead, her mother, still alive in her nursing home in Nice. But she had never forgiven herself. And now she was angry. Now it was time to say, it wasn't my fault. It was never my fault. I don't have to yearn for this absent male figure, I don't have to – I don't have to play the child to God the Father.

Agnes flopped on to her bed. She felt she was standing, dizzily, on the edge of a precipice. Still dressed, she lay down and pulled the covers around her. Her eyes were now dry, and she lay there, staring at the ceiling for a while, before rolling over and turning her face to the wall.

Chapter Fifteen

Seven sixteen the clock said. Plenty of time to get up, go to Julius's eight o'clock Mass and then on to the hostel. Agnes closed her eyes against the slanting early sunlight. She could hear birdsong, sporadic chirping in defiance of the traffic in the street. Her head ached. She opened her eyes again and looked around her room, her gaze coming to rest on the icon of St Francis which hung on the wall by her bed. Something had changed. Some part of her had gone, consumed in the burning whisky-fuelled anger of the night before. It was a puzzling sensation.

No, she thought, I will not go to Mass. She found clean underwear, pulled on her jeans, phoned the hostel to leave a message with the night shift that, no, she wouldn't be coming in today. 'Sorry if it messes up the rota,' Agnes said, feeling not sorry at all. She grabbed a cotton sweater and went out, down the stairs, into the morning sunlight. She felt light, liberated; cauterised.

She went straight to her favourite shabby café on Borough High Street and ordered Full English Breakfast, and ate her way through bacon, eggs, tomatoes, beans, sausages and fried bread, her headache lifting with each mouthful. She sipped a mug of hot, stewed tea, feeling the day stretching ahead of her like a blank page. She'd been awake for nearly an hour and she hadn't yet said a single prayer. She chewed on the novelty of this thought for a while.

It really was a most peculiar feeling. She paid and went out of the café, sauntering down the street in the August sunshine, looking at everything anew. Is this what it looks like, she thought, a world without God? Can that tree continue to exist without Him willing it to exist? That Fiat Tipo parked over there, is it still a Fiat Tipo without Him naming it such? These flats, this sunlight, that sky –

177

can they still be brought into being without a Creator to create them?

She sat on a wall in the sunshine and deliberately summoned up the memory of her parents' driveway, one drizzly morning more than thirty years ago. Once again she saw the car drawing sleekly away from her, only this time, in the London sunshine, thirty years later, she allowed it to go. She allowed her father to drive away; she allowed the wheels to scrunch on the wet gravel. In her mind the little girl stopped running, stopped crying and just stood still, a calm, upright figure in the misty rain. Now, across the road a very old, stooped woman emerged from the bookie's and furtively crossed herself. Agnes sat down and watched her, and in her mind, the little girl on the driveway faded into the drizzle and then vanished altogether.

'*Adieu*, Papa,' she murmured. She stood up, feeling lighter than air, and went back to her flat to pick up her notebook and pens.

She arrived at the library as it opened, and after ten minutes with the phone directories had written down the addresses and phone numbers of all the catering companies listed for the Chingford area, and numerous Enfield sandwich bars just in case. By ten o'clock she was back home, sitting at her desk with a mug of coffee, looking at her list of caterers. She decided against Jenny's Kitchen and WonderSnax, thinking that if Bob was anything like Mike this company would have an anonymous, off-the-shelf sort of name. She saw Blueline Catering Ltd., Chingford. She dialled and asked for Bob Wheeler.

'Mr Wheeler's not in yet,' the young, female voice said. 'Can I take a message?'

'I'll phone back later,' Agnes said, wanting to punch the air in triumph. Right first time. This new, lighter-than-air self certainly knew a thing or two.

Then she dialled Athena. Again, the machine. 'Listen,' Agnes said, after the tone, 'this sounds ridiculous, but if you want to, you know, change your mind about keeping the baby, don't worry about me judging you, or God, or whoever, because I've been thinking about this God-the-Father business and—'

A sleepy voice came on the line and the machine cut out with a beep. 'You've been what?'

'I've been thinking about this patriarchal God and—'

'A fine time to tell me. Hang on while I throw up.' The phone was put down, and eventually Athena came back on the line, sounding surprisingly normal. 'That's better. We've got about ten minutes till the next one, if past mornings are anything to go by. Sorry I didn't get back to you before.'

'That's OK. Sorry I didn't phone before.'

'That's OK.'

'Pregnancy sounds awful.'

'Bloody nightmare, darling. I am at war with my body. My only ammunition is dry biscuits and camomile tea, and even that doesn't work half the time.'

'You – you didn't go for your termination.'

'No.'

'Athena – if it's on my account . . . what I mean is, I've been thinking about all this—'

'So you keep saying.'

'It's all about my father, and I had this bizarre realisation last night . . .'

'Had you been drinking?'

'Yes. Don't laugh, that's really not the point. It's all about Sam and Becky and fathers and me and – anyway, at two o'clock this morning I was going to phone you and say, do what the hell you like.'

'Right.' There was a silence, then Athena said, 'And how do you know I'm not doing what I like?'

'You mean you really are going to keep it?'

'Frankly, I can't think further than the loo at the moment, but all I know is, it felt right not to go. To the clinic, I mean. And Nic's being really sweet, and – and I thought you'd be glad.'

'I am glad,' Agnes said, realising it was true. Sort of. They sat breathing for a moment, then Agnes said, 'I'd suggest dinner but I guess you're in no fit state.'

'Darling, it's so tedious. I don't even want to drink, can you believe it? But I'd love to see you. Why don't you come round here Sunday night. Nic can cook for you and I'll nibble on toast and we'll have a whale of a time. Eight-ish as usual?'

'Athena, that'll be lovely.'

Agnes sat by her phone, looking out of the window at picture-book white clouds scudding across a blue sky. Her head was spinning. She was tiring of this new Agnes. She missed her old certainties, she missed her usual constant dialogue with God that was now silent, cauterised by rage. She missed being able to share it with Julius, and her hand went to the phone, poised to pick it up and dial his number. And there was Athena trying to keep her baby, and although she felt glad, she wasn't entirely sure she was right to feel glad. It was all very confusing. She picked up the receiver, and dialled the first two digits of Julius's number. She hung up, and dialled Blueline again and got put through to Bob Wheeler.

'Hello, Mr Wheeler? My name's Sister Agnes, and I wondered whether you could help me. It's rather a long story. You see, it's about Mike Reynolds, and Sam – his, um, daughter.' Agnes waited for a response.

'Sam? Oh, right, yeah. Go on.'

'I heard your name mentioned by Mike. You see, it's all a bit complicated,' she said, putting as much warmth as she could into her voice. 'I'm a friend of hers, well not so much a friend, but I'm part of the team in the hostel where she stayed.'

'Right. And where do I come in?' His voice was rough but friendly, with the same Cockney edge as Mike's, faded by time.

'I wondered whether we could meet? I helped reintroduce Sam and Mike, and I'm still involved with their new life,' Agnes went on, wondering how much to say. 'And last time I was there, there was a lot of friction. The thing is,' she said, feeling her way, 'I'd really like to talk to someone who knows the background to it all. And your name came up. Although,' she added hurriedly, 'he doesn't know I'm phoning you.' She took a deep breath and waited.

The voice was still friendly. 'Yes, right, well, any friend of Mike's. I'd be happy to meet. Can you get over here?'

'Sure,' Agnes replied. 'Later today?'

'I'm free from three thirty,' Bob said. 'Any time round then, just call in.'

Agnes thanked him and rang off. It was lucky she still had the car, she thought. She was supposed to ring her community and check that it was still available to her. Stuff it, she thought. I need it. She got her sleeping bag down from her cupboard, wrinkling her nose at the woodsmoke smell. At least this new Agnes had the freedom to go and sleep at the Ark tonight. For a start, it was time to talk to Bill again.

Agnes walked up the hill toward the benders, aware of people, bustling movement, drumming, mobile phones. It all seemed very busy, and as she approached the camp she realised there wasn't a single face she recognised. A young woman at the campfire looked up and smiled at her.

'Hi,' Agnes said, 'is Rona around, or Jenn? Or Paz?'

'Um, sure, somewhere. Up the trees, probably.'

'Any news on the eviction?'

'Next week. Definitely. They've said Friday.'

There was a jangle of abseil harness, and Rona swung down from a tree, followed by a young man Agnes hadn't seen before.

'Hi, Agnes, how're you?'

'Fine. How's it going?'

Rona grinned. 'Great. We've got about thirty people ready to be up the trees now, and another few training. We've got people coming over from the Welsh Quarry protest over the weekend. And the locals are mobilised – it's amazing how strongly they feel. It's great.'

The girl by the fire handed Rona a mug of tea.

'Sam wants to come back for the eviction,' Agnes said.

'Great. We need people who can climb. What about you?'

'Me?' Agnes hesitated. 'Um, do you think I'll be any use?'

'Footsoldiers, man.' Jeff appeared behind Rona, grinning. 'Don't let her say no, Rone.'

'You heard him,' Rona laughed.

'I'll bring Sam over anyway,' Agnes said.

'Sorted,' Jeff said. 'Any tea?'

Agnes noticed Jenn sitting by her bender, staring into space. She went over to her. Jenn looked up and smiled faintly. Agnes sat next to her. Jenn was staring across to the camp. After a while, she said, 'Look at them all. It's like they've forgotten.'

'Becky, you mean?'

Jenn nodded. 'And Col.'

'Maybe it's their way of dealing with it,' Agnes said.

'Rona's going on about the local support, but she's kiddin' herself. Half the locals are staying away. Not 'cos they want the road, but 'cos they don't want to come up here where Becks got killed. Like, they just won't touch it. And I don't blame them.'

Agnes looked at Jenn, at her clear young skin and spiky blonde hair, the frayed holes at the knees of her jeans. 'Jenn – you were close to Becky, weren't you?'

Jenn turned to Agnes. 'What d'you think?'

Agnes took a deep breath. 'You see, it seems to me,' she said, 'that it's very likely that she'd made a lot of people angry.'

Jenn eyed her. 'Who do you mean?'

'Her church?'

'Maybe.' Jenn looked at the ground.

'They aren't very tolerant, are they?'

'No.'

'Jenn – isn't it time to tell me what you know?'

Jenn's eyes filled with tears.

'Were you together?' Agnes said.

Jenn nodded. 'When she first arrived. But she couldn't handle it.' She began to pull at the frayed threads of her jeans. 'It was just a few weeks. But they fuckin' got to her, they did.'

'Her church?'

'Those God Squad bastards. Going on about her marrying someone. She said she couldn't be with me.'

'But she'd escaped from them.'

Jenn shook her head. 'Putting space between herself and them didn't mean she'd got away from them. They were in her fucking head, man.'

'Why didn't you tell me this before?'

Jenn sighed. 'Dunno.'

'It might be relevant. If the church took her away from you—'

Jenn shook her head. 'No. It wasn't the church that took her away from me. Not in the end.' Jenn looked tearfully at Agnes. 'She had another lover.'

'Who?'

'She never told me who she was. But she was going off to the woods at night, secretly. She was lying to me. And she knew I still cared.'

'Did – did Col know about this too?'

'He used to hang around her, yeah.' Jenn thought for a moment. 'He used to go to the forest with her, yeah.'

'And now they're both dead.'

Jenn turned fierce eyes on Agnes. 'Listen, this is 'cos I trust you, right? The reason I didn't say anything before, was, like, how did I know you were OK? And I didn't want those Press hacks down here doing a dyke murder story.'

Agnes picked a tiny spider from Jenn's shoulder and watched it scuttle away across the mud. 'Jenn – do you have any idea why someone would want to kill Becky?'

Jenn shook her head.

'This other woman?'

'I don't know anything about her.'

'Or anyone else? Her dad?' Agnes heard herself ask.

'Becky said he'd never kill her.'

'You mean, you talked about it?'

'He used to beat her. And her brother. But she said he didn't scare her no more.'

Agnes swallowed. 'Jenn – this is important. Why shouldn't it be her father? He's a fundamentalist Christian, his daughter's gay, he's angry about it, and threatened, and no amount of menace is bringing her back. He comes here to – to what? To threaten her until she returns? And she refuses. And he flips.'

'Yeah. Except he didn't know she was here.'

'Are you sure?'

'When she ran away, the last time, she went to London for a day or two first. That's what she said. The trail had gone cold.'

Agnes frowned. 'Hmm. Maybe.'

'Anyway, the police questioned him, you said.'

'Yes.'

'And let him go.'

'Yes.'

'It's doing me in, Agnes. It just goes round and round my head. I want out of here, I've been full-on for months now, it's time to go. I can't be up for the eviction – you have to really care to carry that off, you know?' She wiped tears from her eyes. 'It's not enough to die for. I just wish she'd bloody confided in me. It's not knowing,

183

you see. Not knowing if she loved someone else. She could've told me before someone bloody strangled her.' Her voice faltered and she started to cry. Agnes put her arms round her and Jenn leaned against her, sobbing. Agnes held her for a while, until her crying abated. After a while she said, 'Jenn – will you go back to college?'

Jenn nodded, sniffing.

'When you get there, will you promise me that you'll see someone? A counsellor, or chaplain, someone you can trust. Your tutor, maybe. You need to tell someone all this, else you'll never be able to move on from it.'

Jenn nodded again, taking the paper handkerchief that Agnes passed to her. 'And in the meantime,' Agnes went on, getting up, 'there's someone else I must talk to.'

Half an hour later, Agnes was in the kitchen bender making a large mound of peanut butter sandwiches. People came by, some familiar, some she'd never seen before, and she handed them out. When she got to the last two rounds, she cut them in fours, wrapped them in a cleanish-looking plastic bag and set off for the forest.

There was a trail of smoke coming from Bill's encampment as Agnes approached, and a hunched, blanket-clad figure sitting with his back to her.

'I thought you might be tired of rabbit, so I brought you these,' Agnes said.

Bill turned. For a moment he looked pensive, hostile even, but his face cleared on seeing her. She sat down next to him and unwrapped the sandwiches. He laughed.

'How exquisite. Finger sandwiches. Where's the Darjeeling tea and the scones?'

'If only.' Agnes smiled.

'How's my Little Sister, then?'

'I am certainly not little, and neither am I your sister.'

'What's wrong?'

'Firstly, there's an awful lot you know about these deaths but aren't telling me. Secondly, I'm having a crisis of faith.'

Bill chewed on a sandwich, studying her. 'Yeah,' he said. 'You seem angry to me.'

'I am.' Agnes's eyes fell on a length of rope slung across a branch of his bender.

'What about?'

'It can wait. Shall we talk about Becky? And Col?'

'I'd rather talk about you. You're much more interesting.'

'Too bad. Firstly, do you have rosemary amongst your herbal collection?'

'Rosemary? No. These are just bits from the forest I'm drying off.'

'OK. Secondly, when Col died – what did you think?'

Bill eyed her closely. 'What do you mean?'

'You appeared, if I may say so, to feel responsible.'

'Only that blasted Ventolin stuff, I should have known.'

'Is that all?'

Bill sighed. 'I should have known, too, that he was likely just to curl up and die. I should have gone in the ambulance, kept talking to him, kept him wanting to live.' Bill stared into the distance, as if reliving the events of that night.

Agnes spoke quietly, watching Bill. 'Why – why did he not want to live?'

Bill turned back to her. 'You saw him. He'd been living in fear for weeks. He hadn't been breathing properly for ages. Then whatever happened that night—'

'Which you know about—'

Bill's eyes narrowed. 'Whatever happened that night sent him into crisis. He gave up. He wanted out.'

'Bill, a boy of seventeen with everything to live for doesn't just give up.'

Bill laughed, mirthlessly. 'Everything to live for, Princess? Which planet are you on, then? That kid had no home, no parents, no one who gave a toss. Then he comes here, and finds some kind of friendship with two girls – then one gets murdered and the other's about to start a whole new life away from him.' Bill smiled the same empty smile. 'So that's everything to live for, is it?'

Agnes felt a wave of rage, hearing Bill try to evade her questions yet again. She looked at him, her eyes flashing. 'And what about Emily Quislan?' she said.

Bill blinked, opened his mouth, checked himself. Slowly he said, 'What about her?'

'You tell me.'

He smiled, recovered, charming again. 'One day. I promise.'

'For Christ's sake, Bill, there's a murderer out there. You could be done for obstructing the Coroner, aiding and abetting, breaking and entering—'

'You credit me with more intelligence than I deserve. Listen, Princess, how about this: Becky had a run-in with a heavy, all fists no brains, you know the type, shell-shocked from Belfast or Goose Green or somewhere, up to here on steroids – kills her. Oops. How's anyone going to track him down unless he gibbers on about it over a few pints one day? And Col, like I said, asthma. End of story. You see, it seems to me, Princess, that there you are having a personal crisis of some kind, angry with your order or your parents or someone, some deep anger that's really knocked you sideways; and so, being the kind of person you are, you're off chasing murderers as a distraction from the real issues, the things you ought to be thinking about on a personal level.'

Agnes stood up, brushing leaves from her legs. 'One day, Forest Bill from Colchester, who's always so mysteriously clean, I'm going to walk up to you and punch you on the nose.'

Bill looked at her, screwing up his eyes against the sunlight. He laughed. 'You'll have to catch me first. Thanks for the sandwiches.'

Agnes strode back to the camp in fury, muttering to herself in rage. 'That Bill,' she said to Rona, as she unloaded her sleeping bag from her car, 'I could whack him in his superior bloody face.'

'It's time someone did,' Rona said. 'He's a creep. We think someone's paying him to keep an eye on us – not that he's very efficient, the nearer we get to the eviction the less interested he seems in us. Have you noticed he's moved his camp further away?'

Agnes unrolled her sleeping bag in Rona's bender, then went back to the car. It was three o'clock. That gave her half an hour to drive to Chingford.

Bob Wheeler showed her into his office. It was small but comfortable. The window was open, letting in afternoon sunlight and a slight breeze. The walls were lined with photographs, snaps of functions, of jolly people wearing dinner jackets or paper hats. On one wall there was a gallery of celebrities, black-and-white photographs, each signed 'To Bob, many thanks . . .' Agnes didn't recognise the names or the faces.

'It was nice of you to see me,' Agnes began, as Bob sat down at his desk opposite her. He was balding, with a broad, open face and large blue eyes.

'Would you like some coffee?' he asked. 'Or tea?'

'Tea would be lovely, thank you.'

Bob picked up his phone and ordered tea, then leaned back in his chair.

'So, you know Sam. I last saw her when she was about two. What's she like? Pretty like her mum, I bet. Well, like her mum was. In them days.'

'You grew up with them?'

'We all knocked around together. On the estate. It's not like it is now, all kids hanging about, no work, nothing to do. I'm not saying we was angels, mind,' he laughed. 'But it's different now. Downright evil, some of these kids. Like that boy that was killed, up in Liverpool. It'll happen again, you know.'

'And so Mike and Linda?'

'We envied him. She was a – well, let's just say, we knew it wasn't just talk when he told us what they got up to. And we were young, still in our teens. They both had dodgy reputations, those Whittaker girls.'

The door opened and a young woman brought in a tray with two cups of tea and a plate of biscuits.

'Sugar?' Bob said, taking one spoonful himself.

'And you kept in touch with Mike?' Agnes refused the sugar.

Bob nodded. 'Both in business, you know. Both starting from nothing, him on building sites, me on the markets. He's had his ups and downs, like. When his first marriage split up, over in Chelmsford, his business went under then too. He moved back this way, started again.' He stirred his tea. 'Has guts, that man. And getting in touch with Sam again, that takes guts too. Most men wouldn't have the nerve. So, how're they getting on?'

'Well,' Agnes took a deep breath. 'It's a difficult situation. Sam had no one else, so in my view, they've rather rushed it.'

'Sam fallen out with Linda, then?'

'I think Linda had to choose between her current boyfriend and Sam. And the boyfriend won.'

Bob shook his head. 'Some things don't change. I'm glad I left all that behind me. Me and the missus, coming up to eighteen years of marriage us, two kids. I've been lucky.'

'And did you know the Bevan boys?'

'The Bevan boys, eh?' Bob chuckled. 'Me and Greg Bevan, what we didn't do, eh? Good times.'

'And Tom?'

Bob's face clouded. He stirred his tea again. 'Those two, it's like the proverbial chalk and whatsit. One gets looks, brains, the lot. Clever geezer, Greg. The other—' He looked up from his tea. 'Tom was a loser before he even started. Sad thing is, he was a really nice kid. Big eyes, soft, you know, wouldn't hurt a fly. But hopeless. The kind of guy you pitch up at a club with, everyone else gets let in, the bouncer says to him, no way, mate. Just, you know, face never quite fits. And no luck, neither. Like if his car breaks down, it's going to break down on a parking meter, ain't it. Greg left school with all his exams and that, went to university, didn't he. Tom left school at sixteen, worked on sites. When he was eighteen, he fell from a crane, knocked his head. In hospital for weeks. Left him with a limp. But worse than that, it kind of changed him. Greg said he was moody, depressed. Took to drink. Then he was stealing too. Greg bailed him out a few times, but he'd had it, you know? Just about disowned him.' Bob drank some tea. 'We all lost touch with him in the end. It's like, we felt bad in some way.'

'Do you know what happened to him?' Bob shook his head. 'You don't think Mike still knows him?'

Bob shrugged. 'I don't see why he would. He was trouble, you know.'

Agnes sipped her tea. 'When I last saw Mike and Sam, she wasn't very happy. And Mike was . . . impatient with her. It made me think that if I was her father, I'd be more aware that she'd need time to adjust. It's as if he's just decorated a bedroom for her, bought her a whole new wardrobe, moved her into the house and everything's fine. And it hasn't occurred to him that life isn't like that.'

Bob laughed. 'That's Mike for you. He's always worked on the basis that money can buy anything. And what's really annoying is that, for Mike, it works. Any time he wants a new toy, he just goes out and buys it. Wife, mistress, business, different wife—'

'Daughter?'

Bob looked at Agnes, then picked up his empty cup and arranged it carefully on the tray. He sighed. 'When he told me about this plan to get Sam, I have to admit, I thought here we go again. Mike wants another train set. Don't get me wrong, he's a good bloke. Heart's in the right place, and all that. But, yes, I have to admit, he's not what you'd call reliable. Although, maybe now he's got her to consider, it might be the making of him.' Bob reached across and gathered up Agnes's cup. 'Let's just hope this is one new toy he doesn't get tired of, eh?'

That night in Rona's bender, Agnes couldn't sleep. She went over and over her conversation with Bob, trying to see the connection. Col had Tom Bevan's phone number. Tom and Mike must be in touch, they must. Unless . . . unless Col had some other connection, totally separate. But that would be too coincidental. Tom had worked on sites. Mike had started work on building sites too. Tom had had an accident. What if . . . but that was ridiculous.

Agnes heard Bill's words in her ears, his mocking, superior I-know-you-better-than-you-know-yourself words. Distracting herself from the real issues of her spiritual crisis by seeing evil where there was none. Mike might turn out to be a good enough father. Col might have died of asthma like everyone said. Becky might have been strangled by mistake . . . Agnes sat up, rummaged between sleeping bodies for her coat and shoes and crawled out of the bender.

It was a clear, balmy night. The moon was full, a perfect silver round, and a gentle breeze rustled through the trees. From the tree-houses came the flicker of torchlight, the sound of laughter. She laced up her shoes, wrapped her coat around her and stood, listening. The odd crack of twigs from the trees. The heavy snoring of Zak, or Dog, or both. Another crack of twigs. Agnes went and sat by the embers of the fire. People don't get murdered by mistake, she thought. Even the most unfortunate confrontation with a stray security man isn't going to end in that. Is it? A rustle from the trees made her look up, and she tensed as she saw a figure emerging from the woods, furtive and hurried, a flash of white smile as he saw her and she saw it was Bill.

'Come on,' he whispered. 'You're just in time.' He tried to take her hand, but she shook him off.

'What the hell do you mean?' she hissed.

'I decided I didn't want you to punch me on the nose,' he said.

'So?'

'Emily Quislan. You were asking me, I'm going to tell you what I know. Or rather, show you.'

'Emily Quislan?' Agnes stood up.

'If you'll let me.' He turned to go, taking her hand again. She shook him off, but followed him towards the forest. 'How come you were sitting there all ready?' he murmured. 'We must be telepathic.'

He hurried into the trees, Agnes having almost to run to keep up. She could smell him next to her, the warm musk of sweat and tobacco, mixed with an incongruous minty tang – toothpaste? 'Where are we going?' she said.

'Shh,' he whispered, as they emerged from the edge of the woodland and set out across one side of a field. He quickened his pace. They hurried along the edge of the field, over a stile, across another field, the moon rising higher in the sky, bleaching the corn stubble white, the surrounding trees into eerie shadows. At the next field they paused for breath, both panting.

'Wh-why,' Agnes whispered, between breaths, 'why the hurry?'

'I knew she'd be up there tonight. I sat and thought about whether to bring you, and making the decision delayed me,' he whispered back. He waited for his breathing to settle, then said to her, 'One thing you must promise me now. Not a word to a soul, OK? I'm breaking the rules for you.'

She nodded, and they set off again, their shortening shadows scudding at their feet. She realised, as the landscape became hillier and they began to climb, that they were near the spring, and straining her eyes she could see the glint of the factory over the next hill. Bill, following her gaze, smiled and nodded.

'Emily's land,' he said.

They hurried on, skirting the edge of the next field, keeping close to the woodland until the trees gave out and they were on open hillside, scrunching stubble underfoot. The tall steel fence of Richard Witham's bottling plant rose up ahead of them, its spikes sharpened by the moonlight. Bill led her past the fence and up the side of Richard's land, and after a while the hi-tech fencing stopped and was replaced by rusty old barbed wire hammered into a deep ditch. Panting, they walked along the side of this, until Bill stopped. Agnes saw that a huge hole had been cut in it. They didn't go through the hole, but instead Bill led her past the factory and up the hill behind it. His pace was slower now, and after a while he stopped and looked back.

The factory was laid out below them, beyond it the hills they had climbed, merging into the distant darkness of the forest. Bill surveyed the scene and smiled, then looked around.

'Are we in time?' Agnes asked.

He nodded, and then walked a few feet away towards the tumbledown relic which Agnes had seen before, with Richard Witham. 'Emily's house?' she whispered, and Bill nodded. They crouched down behind the wall. Between the fragments of stone, they could see the field sloping away from them.

'What are we looking for?' Agnes breathed.

Bill held her gaze. 'I'm taking a big risk here. If it wasn't you I wouldn't bother. So, no questions, now or later. Promise?'

Agnes chewed her lip. Reluctantly she nodded. She had no choice. She felt a surge of anger at his ridiculous sense of drama. Presumably he knew what to expect, which meant that all along he'd known more about Emily Quislan than he'd ever told her. And there he was pretending the murders were just unfortunate random incidents. Her thoughts stopped dead at the sound of someone approaching from lower down the hill, the footsteps clear in the still, warm night. Bill tensed next to her and settled lower behind the wall. The approaching tread was quick-paced, the rhythm of four feet rather than two. Down below them, a figure appeared from the trees; a woman on horseback. She was wearing a long dress, with a shawl tied at her neck, her hair was pinned up into a bonnet but long tendrils escaped and floated at her cheeks. The woman rode at a walk, straight-backed. Agnes saw that she was riding sidesaddle.

Horse and rider crossed the field at a stately pace. They seemed insubstantial in the moonlight, almost translucent. Eventually they disappeared behind the bottling plant, at the point, Agnes realised, where the hole had been cut in the fence.

She turned to Bill, so amazed at what she'd just seen that she needed to ask him, needed him to say, 'Yes, I saw it too.'

Bill had gone.

Chapter Sixteen

Agnes waited, still crouched behind the makeshift shelter. She listened, and waited. He'll be back soon, she thought. She strained her eyes towards the spring, looking for movement, for the woman on horseback again, for Bill returning. There was nothing. Just the silence of the night, silence so penetrating that after a while it was peopled with noise, owls calling, bats whirring, distant footfalls. A horse's whinny. She began to move towards the noise, her feet treading much too loudly through the field. The thought occurred to her, as she approached the bottling plant, that Bill was around somewhere, probably watching her. It'll be more than a punch on the bloody nose, Agnes thought, when I next set eyes on him.

Again, the horse's whinny. Agnes dropped down to the level of the fence and followed it round, back to the hole in the barbed wire. She could hear the horse's breathing now, and as she came round the corner she saw it there, a handsome chestnut mare, reins looped loosely through the fence. Agnes and the horse looked at each other, and then Agnes approached, calmly, her head slightly bowed. The horse didn't move. At least, Agnes thought, this is no ghost. She began to feel calmer, reassured by the animal's warm breathing. The horse raised her head suddenly, shifted, pawed the ground and whinnied again, and Agnes, realising her owner was approaching, looked around for a hiding-place. She ran back a few paces and jumped down into the ditch, pulling some branches of the hedge down over her head. She heard a woman's voice.

'Lady? You all right?' The horse whinnied. 'Was there someone there? Come on, it's done, we're going.' Agnes peered through the branches and saw the young woman in nineteenth-century dress jump up lightly on to the horse's back and, this time riding astride,

193

set off in a canter, down the slope, away from the spring, the hooves fading away into the night.

Silence again. A thin cloud passed across the moon. Agnes climbed out of the ditch and went to the hole in the fence. What was it she said was 'done'? she wondered. And how safe was it to go and see? And where the hell was Bill?

Agnes stooped down and looked at the hole in the barbed wire. The rough edges where it had been cut looked new. She stepped through it on to the tarmac. She walked quickly to the door that Richard had taken her through last Tuesday, and tried the handle. It was locked. She looked around, crept round the back of the building, checking all the time for signs of a break-in. At the back of the building she stopped. A plain wall, no windows, no doors. There was nothing useful she could do here. She hurried back to the fence, through the hole, retracing the path along the side of the field that she'd taken with Bill earlier that night.

The moon had clouded over and was now beginning to sink in the sky. She entered the edge of the wood in virtual darkness. The anger that had kept her going, kept her striding through the fields, now began to fade, overwhelmed instead by fear. She walked hesitantly, feeling her way, wondering was this the path, or this . . . She stopped still, blinking, waiting for her eyes to get used to this new darkness. A rustle next to her made her jump and she found she was looking down into the golden eyes of – a fox, she thought, seeing the bushy outline of his tail as he turned and fled. Agnes's heart was racing. Oh God, she thought . . . Help me. She realised she could see the path ahead of her, so tentatively began to follow it, hoping it was the one that would lead her to the camp. She summoned up an image of Bill in an attempt to renew her rage, because anything was better than this fear, this irrational, gut-chilling fear. Lord keep me safe this night, she began, the first lines of a prayer she'd learned as a child, and now like a child lost in a fairytale forest she imagined witches and ghosts and wolves . . . But also, she remembered, forcing herself to walk on, in the picture-books of her childhood there was always Our Lord, a clear-eyed young man in flowing robe and sandals, with pre-Raphaelite blond hair. And it was He, she'd been taught, Who is with us in our darkest hour, Who will lead us to safety if only we ask Him. Agnes stopped walking. She stood still in the forest, in the darkness.

She swallowed her fear, cleared her throat and murmured, 'Our Father,' hearing the words out loud against the rustle of the trees. 'Our Father,' she said again, reaching out for her God, her Saviour; this Jesus with the blond curls. The words whispered in the silence and then were gone. There is no fairytale, she thought. There are no witches, no ghosts, no wolves; and there sure as hell is no angel to gather me up into his arms. There is only fear.

Agnes stood stock-still in the middle of the woods. I am afraid, she thought. That's all. I refuse, she thought, setting off again along the path she dimly recalled, I refuse to be distracted by sentimental claptrap. I claim my fear as my own.

She walked quickly, twitching her nose at the smell of woodsmoke. Above her, through the branches, the sky was no longer dark. She turned her face towards the camp as the birds began to stir.

Agnes's first sensation on waking in Rona's bender much later that Saturday morning was rage. The very thought of Bill made her want to scream, shout, spit. That he'd abandoned her in a field in the middle of the night was bad enough. But worse than that was the thought that he'd known. He'd known about Emily Quislan all along, and he hadn't bothered to tell her. Agnes's second sensation, as she sat up, was a creaky aching in her legs, no doubt from the miles she'd covered. She yawned, looked around. The bender was empty, and there was bustle and shouting outside. At least she'd slept well. She thought about the woman on horseback up at the spring. It seemed to have happened a long time ago – but for Richard Witham it would only just have started. She grabbed her bag, emerged from the bender, waved at the assorted people busying themselves around the fire and under the trees and set off down the hill to the phone box in the village. Using Rona's mobile would raise too many questions. She stuffed coins into the slot and dialled Fyffes Spring.

'Hello, Richard?' she said, hearing him answer.

'Agnes? I've been trying to get hold of you.'

'I'm at the road camp.'

'Even better. Can you come here now?'

'Of course. What's happened?'

'The water's yellow. Dyed yellow. I don't understand it. And the leaflets, bloody everywhere.'

The piece of paper said 'I have returned to claim what is mine.' It was in neat capitals, photocopied.

'Have you called the police?'

'They were here earlier, they're coming back. Criminal damage and trespass, they say.'

'How did it happen?'

'There's a hole in the fence, down by the ditch side. And someone's dug into the well itself and planted something down there, the water's still coming out yellow. They must have been working on it over several days, without anyone noticing, to dig that deep. It'll fade eventually, the dye'll wash out . . . but that's not the point.'

Richard was pale, his hair dishevelled. He sat down heavily in his chair. 'I just keep thinking, if it wasn't just dye, if it was . . . Agnes, why have they got it in for me? The nearest bottled water company is in Norfolk. I can't see I'm treading on their toes . . .'

Agnes said gently, 'It's not your competitors. It's a person with a grudge. It's not about you. It's about this land. And can I use your loo?'

Agnes stared at her reflection in the mirror. Her hair stood up comically, her face was filthy, one cheek was scratched and bloody, presumably from the barbed-wire ditch. She splashed cold water over herself, patted down her hair as best she could and then went back to Richard's office. He was leaning forward awkwardly, staring into space.

'I'm going to make you some strong, sweet tea. And then we'll talk about a strategy,' Agnes said.

'It's those anti-road people, it must be.'

'No,' Agnes said, 'it isn't.'

'Try telling that to this lot.' Richard indicated with his head the driveway, the police car which was pulling up in the car park. Agnes saw, to her relief, Charlie emerge from the car with another officer. She and Richard went out to meet them.

'Don't say "I told you so",' she said to Charlie.

'Wouldn't dream of it. Keeping an open mind at the moment. Could be anyone.'

'What's the dye?'

'It seems to be fluorescein.'

'Charlie—'

'I know what you're going to say. Your friends over the way there—'

'They don't know anything about it.'

'You can say that. But Agnes—'

'I'm going to tell you this before you start to put two and two together. Col, Col Hadley, the boy who died of asthma—'

'The one with the yellow fingernails?'

'Exactly. But he was separate from the Ark, really he was. You'll learn nothing from them.'

'Doesn't stop us asking them, does it?'

Sheila opened the door with an air of suspicion, which lifted slightly on seeing Agnes.

'Sure,' she said, when Agnes asked if she could use the computer. 'Come in. Help yourself. I'll make some coffee.'

Agnes scrolled through the recent messages. There was nothing. If Emily was responsible for the damage at Fyffes Well, she hadn't bothered to announce it to the world at large, or at least, to the world as it existed on the Net. Agnes switched off the machine and went back downstairs. Sheila was rather absently setting out mugs on the table.

'Sheila – you OK?'

'What – oh, yes. Fine.'

'What is it? Is it Lily?'

Sheila sat at the table. 'I don't know. After our talk on the phone – well, I think you're right. She is talking about getting married.'

'How old is she?'

'Sixteen. Just.'

'Who does she want to marry?'

'She hasn't said yet. But I think there is someone.'

'Doesn't she need your permission?'

'Yes. Unless she elopes.'

'She wouldn't do that.'

'She keeps going on at me, "Mum, lots of people get married at my age. And it's what God wants from me."'

'By which she means it's what Ross Turner wants. Where is she now?'

'Upstairs. I think I heard her getting up. Darling?' Sheila shouted. 'Would you like some coffee?' A moment later Lily appeared in the kitchen. She looked tired and pale. She took the mug her mother offered her and sat listlessly at the table.

'How are you?' Agnes asked her.

'OK.' She didn't look up.

'How's Ross?'

Lily raised her eyes from the table. 'Do you know him?'

'I've met him, twice now. Nice man.'

'He is. Yeah.'

Agnes had a sudden idea. 'And how's Steven Murphy?'

Lily was looking at her with interest. 'Do you know him too?'

'I've visited there. We religious people, we often mix between different faiths,' Agnes said. 'I gather you have a thriving youth group.' She was aware of Sheila, hovering, listening.

'It's great,' Lily said. 'And new people are joining every day.'

'It must be nice for you to meet like-minded people.'

Lily nodded, brightening.

'Better than having to go to pubs with your schoolfriends, and clubs, things like that.'

'When people haven't heard the Good News, it makes things difficult,' Lily said. 'It just doesn't work if people don't respect the fact that I'm a Christian.'

'No,' Agnes said, wondering where to go from here. Sheila noisily put down her mug and left the room. Agnes could have hugged her.

'And,' Agnes tried, 'with your mother not being—'

'Oh, it's so difficult,' Lily blurted out. 'I hate not being able to tell her things, and I envy Steven because his parents are part of the group, and—'

'Is there anything I can do?'

Lily looked at Agnes, wide-eyed. Slowly, she nodded. 'Maybe – I mean, if you could just talk to her. There's someone I want her to meet, but there's no point if she's just going to be hostile to him.'

'Who?'

'He's called Jerry.'

'I've met him too,' Agnes said. How surprising, she thought. How strange that Ross should . . .

'Have you?' Lily was animated now, smiling. 'When did you meet him?'

'Oh, um, around, you know.'

'Ross thinks we should get married. Poor Jerry, he's suffered so much.'

'S-sorry?'

'He was going to marry Becky, but then, you know, she joined those people and Satan found her.'

'Becky?'

'And I just so wish Mum would come round and not harden her heart before the Lord, and it would just be brilliant if you could talk to her, as you believe and everything, maybe you could bring her along with you to our big meeting tomorrow in town, it's going to be wonderful . . .'

'Um, I think it might be better in a smaller group, don't you, then she can really get to know everyone properly.'

'Maybe, yes. Monday then, oh, no, that's no good, they're going to the police.'

'The police? Who are?'

'Jerry and Steven. They'll be out all day. They're taking Shirley to the police station.'

'Becky's mother?'

'Yes. I'm probably not supposed to tell anyone, but she's been so upset, and Steven's mum, Elizabeth, they've got this plan because Becky's dad is away on business for the day and Jerry's going to borrow his cousin's car. So that Shirley can, you know, see her. Maybe another day?'

Agnes's mind was racing. 'Yes,' she said, 'another day. I'm sure it's best,' she went on, collecting her thoughts, 'if you don't exclude your mother. Even if she seems hostile. Sometimes people take a while—'

'For the Lord to work with their hearts. I know. I pray for her every day, you know.'

★ ★ ★

Driving back to London that evening, Agnes was aware of uneasy thoughts eddying around her. But one idea emerged with clarity. She must phone Elizabeth before Monday; and she must make sure to catch her on her own.

On Sunday Agnes stayed at home. She got up late, hearing the chimes from St Simeon's calling the faithful to Mass, and resolutely ignoring them. She made coffee, and for a while sat at her desk in front of her notebook, staring at the scribbles she had made in it. Jerry, she thought. It didn't make sense.

At lunchtime she heard the phone ring, heard Julius leave a message.

'Agnes, I will soon be forced to conclude that you've left us altogether and have gone with the Raggle-Taggle Gypsies, O. I will therefore have no choice but to emigrate in despair. If you'd like to stop me, you only have to give me a ring.' Agnes smiled at the phone but did not pick it up.

Sitting in her flat as the day passed, as she opened windows against the heat and watched her curtains sway from time to time in the occasional breeze, she could hear church bells marking time. Julius's own, and then, more distantly, Southwark Cathedral; and across the river, the peals from the City, echoing through the hot afternoon, reminding her of what she'd given up. She wondered how long all this would last. This is my choice, she thought. If only I could convince myself that it's the right one.

At seven o'clock she phoned Sheila.

'How's Lily?' she asked her. 'Not married off yet?'

'No, thank goodness. Came back from her meeting high as a kite. If I could feel that good just from bashing a tambourine for hours, think of the money I could save on booze. She was a bit vague about how many attended, it was probably the same old crowd. But no, nothing untoward.'

'Good. I'll keep in touch.'

At five past eight Athena opened the door with a broad grin. Agnes could smell garlic and oregano wafting along the corridor.

'How do you do it?' she said, as Athena led her into the front room.

'How do I do what?' Athena picked up a corkscrew and began to do battle with the Muscadet that Agnes had brought. Agnes looked at her friend. The grey roots were shiny black again, and she wore a crisp silk shirt and leggings.

'I meant, how do you find these men who can rustle up exquisite three-courses dinners without being TV chefs at the same time?'

Athena giggled. 'It's only some pasta thing. But, yeah, it's nice. If only I could eat some of it.'

'How is all that?' Agnes asked, taking the wine bottle from Athena and pulling out the cork with one swift wrist action.

'Oh, you know. Still sick. But only in the mornings now. It's OK.' Athena lowered her eyes.

Agnes saw the tension in her face. 'Athena—'

'No, really sweetie, it's fine. We're really happy. Come on, let's go and join Nic in the kitchen. It's all ready.'

Nic greeted Agnes warmly and they settled down to fusilli with smoked ham and a spinach salad. Nic handed Athena a bowl of plain pasta.

'Won't you have some sauce?' he asked.

'I'll only regret it later,' Athena sighed. 'Have we got any pickled cucumbers?'

Nic brought a large jar to the table, and Athena helped herself to several. 'Poor love.' She smiled at Nic. 'Last week it was taramasalata, and Nic had just bought a large pot when I went right off it. He had to eat the lot, didn't you, sweetie. Poor baby, you'll be living off these next week.'

'Never mind,' Nic said. 'In a few more weeks you'll have stopped feeling sick, and then you'll be all radiant and we can start to look forward to having a baby.'

'That'll be nice,' Athena said, staring at her plate. Agnes glanced at her. She was twisting a large spiral of pasta on her fork, round and round.

'Cheers,' Nic said, raising his glass to Agnes.

'Cheers,' said Agnes. Athena did not look up.

At the end of the evening, Athena took Agnes downstairs. Agnes hesitated by the big glass doors that led out to the street.

'Athena – are you OK?'

Athena's eyes filled with tears. She shrugged. 'S'pose so.'

'What are you going to do?'

'What can I do? There's only one other course of action open to me. We've been through all that.' She shook her head. 'No, I'm on my own in this.'

'But Nic—'

'Oh Nic, I can't – you see, he's so into it. His son Ben's at college now, and so for Nic it's the chance to do it properly, to have another go. When it's Ben's birthday we're all going to go out to dinner, apparently, with his ex-wife and her partner, vegan or macrobiotic or something equally dull – and there's all this "Won't it be lovely for Ben to have a half-brother or -sister . . . ?"'

'Is Nic the problem, then?'

Athena shook her head. 'No, not Nic. He's sweet. And he really seems to care. About me. Amazing, really. Maybe when our child's left home we'll find out that we get on really well. Only I'll be about ninety-three by then.' Her eyes filled with tears. 'No, Nic's not the problem.' Her hand went to her abdomen, still firm and flat, still betraying no outward sign of the life within it. She shook her head. 'Oh, I shouldn't be talking like this. I expect all mums-to-be feel like this sometimes.' She tried to smile. 'Me, a mum-to-be, eh? Just fancy.'

Agnes gave her a hug. It'll be all right, she wanted to say, but no words came.

Back home that night Agnes's hand hesitated over the phone. She flicked through her notebook and found the Murphys' number. Then she checked her watch. It was too late to try now. And anyway, she thought, it would be much better to try in the morning, when there'd be more chance of catching Elizabeth alone.

Chapter Seventeen

'Hello, it's Sister Agnes,' Agnes said to Elizabeth Murphy on the phone next morning.

'Oh. What can I do for you?'

Agnes took a deep breath. 'This – this might sound strange, but I was praying yesterday, and the image of Shirley Stanton was sent to me by the Lord.' Agnes was aware that she had broken at least two of the Ten Commandments in one short sentence. 'And I felt that her suffering was great, and I felt the Lord tell me that I could help her. And this morning, I decided I had to phone you.'

There was a silence from Elizabeth. Her voice when she spoke was almost a whisper. 'Her suffering is terrible. She didn't see the body, you see, because Morris said . . . anyway, she's in the grip of terrible imaginings of her daughter's last hours, it's really awful, you can't begin to know – really, she's half-mad with it, and that little boy, their son, I do worry so for him.' Elizabeth took a breath, then said, 'This morning we were going to drive her to Chelmsford, only Steven was going to come with us in his friend's car, and now that's fallen through. And it's got to be today because Morris simply mustn't find out.'

'It's just as well I phoned,' Agnes said. 'I know someone at the police station. And we could go in my car.'

'I think you have been truly moved by the Lord. Can you meet us at the clock tower by the Victoria Shopping Centre? Do you know it, it's an ugly modern thing, all the numbers are crooked. Just next to Debenhams. We'll be there at twelve.'

Agnes said goodbye and hung up. Moved by the Lord, she wondered – but then, who was she to question His ways? She dialled the police station and got put through to Charlie.

'It's Sister Agnes,' she said. 'Thank God you're there. Listen, you know the Stanton murder? The mother has decided to see the body after all.'

'Blimey. It's not always such a good idea.'

'I think in her case it's better than not seeing it at all.'

'No, well, maybe.'

'I was just checking that if we turned up this lunchtime, there wouldn't be a problem?'

'I'll put you through to the Coroner's Officer, he can help you. By the way, I've sorted out a copy of the post-mortem report on the Hadley boy. Fluorescein. Like you said.'

'What now?'

'What now, is that you've got some work to do if you don't want your tree-dwelling mates being hauled off their perches.'

'I'll see what I can do, Charlie.'

Agnes had only a couple of minutes to admire the clock tower, which she found witty and appealing with its spindly numerals against a faded copper-green background, before Elizabeth and Shirley appeared, Elizabeth pink-faced from hurrying, Shirley pale with tired, sad eyes. They allowed Agnes to lead them to her car, and got into the back where they sat in silence. Once Agnes thought she heard Shirley mutter, 'Am I really going to see her?'

Agnes told the officer at the security gate that they were expected, and soon they were in the clean, bright mortuary building. An officer appeared and greeted Shirley, and Agnes concluded from her response that she already knew him; perhaps this was the PC Baxter they'd mentioned before. He spoke to her in a low voice, then was joined by another man in civilian dress. Shirley was looking towards Elizabeth, and then nodding.

'Agnes.'

She looked up to see Charlie. He gestured towards the two women. 'They OK?'

'No, not really. The one with the brown hair is the mother. Her husband wouldn't let her see the body at first. This is a secret visit.'

'We had him in, didn't we?'

'Yes, I think so.'

The two women were standing up now. Agnes went over to them. She hesitated, then said to Elizabeth, 'Look after her.' The door was opened for them by one of the police officers. Agnes watched them go, leaving the mother to her awful, private grief.

Charlie reappeared with two cups of coffee and a sheaf of papers. 'Here you are,' he said. 'Seems to me you know more'n you're letting on.'

Agnes saw the name Colin Hadley. 'What makes you say that?'

'There it is, look. Yellow dye under his fingernails, traces of it on his jacket. Fluorescein.'

Agnes felt a rush of excitement.

'And there's our Sheila trying to tell me—'

'Charlie, please believe me. Col was involved in something separate from the anti-road protest.'

Charlie looked at Agnes. 'If you know so much,' he began, but was interrupted by a weird sound coming from the mortuary, a high keening. The door opened and Shirley and Elizabeth came out. Shirley was sobbing hysterically, almost screaming, and Elizabeth was pulling helplessly at her sleeve. Agnes jumped up and went to her, holding her by the shoulders, feeling the shaking sobs wrenching at the woman so that it took all Agnes's strength to support her. Agnes led her gently to the door and out into the air, Elizabeth following.

Charlie murmured to Agnes, 'There's a patch of green out the back, nothing special.'

Agnes led Shirley to a bench in the little garden and sat her down, still holding her firmly. Shirley had her hands clasped across her mouth, her fingers gouging her cheeks, still engulfed by sobbing.

Elizabeth said, barely audibly, 'She is at rest now.'

Shirley turned staring eyes to her. Her voice was almost a shout. 'Satan has triumphed.'

'No, no,' Elizabeth murmured, 'you mustn't think that.'

'Satan has taken her at last.' The sobbing had given way to fury.

Agnes said gently, 'When they find who did it—'

'They haven't far to look,' Shirley cried.

'What do you mean?' Agnes began.

A police car started up its siren and Shirley twitched at the noise as it streaked across the compound and then out of the gates. Shirley stared after it and murmured, 'He killed her, my Becky, Becky, Becky . . . I knew he'd do it in the end. The Devil himself, his own daughter . . .' The hand clamped itself across her mouth again.

Elizabeth looked at Agnes, then at Shirley, then at Agnes again. Her eyes blinked in her pink, bewildered face.

'Perhaps we'd better take her home,' she said.

Agnes drove them back, following Elizabeth's occasional directions. Shirley was murmuring to herself, but Agnes couldn't catch anything coherent. Her mind was racing. What did Shirley say? The Devil himself. Does she mean her own husband?

'First left after the lights,' Elizabeth said.

On the other hand, perhaps she really does mean that Satan killed her, Agnes thought. Becky who loved women – the Devil's own daughter. In which case, we're no further on.

'He had it,' Shirley was murmuring, 'her crucifix, he had it in his hands . . .'

'Turn right here,' Elizabeth said, and Agnes recognised the Stantons' street. She parked outside Shirley's house and followed the two women in. Elizabeth put on a kettle. Shirley hesitated in her own hallway, staring around her. Then she tentatively began to go upstairs, darting glances from side to side as if frightened of being seen. Agnes followed her at a distance.

Shirley went along the landing and into the last bedroom. She left the door open, and Agnes, approaching, saw it was Becky's room. Shirley was kneeling in front of the mantelpiece, on which stood several photos of Becky, two candles and a tiny bowl of flowers. The rest of the room was plain and ordinary, a pile of schoolbooks on the desk, a cross hanging on the wall above the yellow candlewick bedspread.

'My baby,' Shirley was murmuring. 'My own baby . . . I won't let him do it, I promise, I won't, he can kill me first . . .' Her words dissolved into choking sobs. One of the photos was of a chubby baby in a flowered bonnet. A crucifix was draped over the corner of the frame.

'My baby,' Shirley sobbed. 'They've closed your eyes . . .'

Becky's crucifix – but hadn't the police said – wasn't Becky strangled with a – weren't the police looking for – a chain. 'Like jewellery,' they'd said. 'That sort of chain . . .' Agnes took a deep breath. She remembered the gouged red marks on Becky's neck.

She stared at the silver cross in front of Shirley. The chain would have broken with the force of it, the police had said. Behind the photo frame the silver chain hung in two short lengths.

Becky would have had more than one crucifix. Of course she would. It's just coincidence – coincidence that this one, too, was broken.

Shirley stirred. Agnes said softly, 'Shirley, it's all right, it's only me.' She went to her and helped her up, and Shirley leaned against her, a dead weight of anguish and exhaustion, as Agnes helped her down the stairs.

Elizabeth had poured three cups of tea. Agnes helped Shirley to a chair, then crept back up to Becky's room. She went to the crucifix, touched it, half expecting to see blood encrusted in the tiny links. It was clean. Near the break, several links of the chain were stretched and bent.

Agnes's hand went to her neck and touched the crucifix that hung there. She unfastened it and held it in her hand. It was very similar, a simple cross, a thin silver chain. A present from Julius years ago when she'd joined her first order here in England. It had replaced another, the one she'd worn as a child. She remembered a birthday party in Provence, a gaggle of tall aunts clucking, a frilled dress. And her father placing around the neck of his daughter a silver crucifix, and everyone nodding and smiling and clapping, and the child Agnes curtsying, pulling at the lace of her new white dress until her fingers ached.

Agnes reached out and carefully took the broken silver crucifix from the photo frame, then replaced it with her own. She studied it a moment, then took it again and wrenched it hard in an attempt to break it in two. She was surprised at how it refused to break, however hard she pulled at it. She heard Elizabeth calling her from the hallway, starting up the stairs. She quickly draped her own chain over the photo, arranging the cross hanging down just as Becky's had, put Becky's in her pocket and went downstairs.

Elizabeth was hovering nervously on the staircase. 'Agnes, the thing is,' she said, descending with her, 'he'll be back soon. You must go. If he finds you here—'

'Yes, of course,' Agnes said.

Shirley was sitting at the kitchen table, staring into space, a cup of tea untouched beside her. At the front door Elizabeth said, 'Do you think we did the right thing?'

Agnes sighed. 'I hope so. Yes, I think we did.'

Elizabeth hesitated, then lowered her voice. 'He beats her. He used to beat Becky. He beats poor David. We pray for him.' Agnes nodded. Elizabeth said, whispering, 'We heard what she said. You and me. We heard.' Agnes waited. 'What will you do?' Elizabeth asked, her eyes pleading.

Agnes felt a sudden terrible pity for her. 'What about you?'

Elizabeth stared down at the front steps, her hands wringing her apron. 'There is nothing I can do,' she said at last. 'Roger says we owe it to Ross . . .' Her face trembled with conflicting thoughts, of her husband, of Ross; of young David still living in this house.

'For the moment,' Agnes said, 'I'll do nothing.'

'The police—'

'The police have already questioned Morris. It's up to them,' Agnes said and saw relief pass across Elizabeth's face. 'As for the rest—'

'We must pray,' Elizabeth said. 'That's all we can do.'

Agnes nodded and held out her hand. Elizabeth was fighting tears. She blinked, took Agnes's hand and held it tightly in her fingers for a moment. As Agnes descended the steps she heard the front door shut softly behind her, enclosing the house once more in misery.

'I'm afraid you won't get into the fiche room for half an hour,' the helpful young woman at the library desk said.

'I'll come back,' Agnes said.

At a quarter to four, one smoked salmon sandwich later, Agnes settled down to the census of 1881, the fullest record of the county that she could find. James Quislan had been just a boy when his mother had blocked in the well. Perhaps he'd moved away – although, Agnes reflected, she'd been buried locally, if the rumour about Harton's field was based on truth. So maybe he hadn't gone far.

Agnes trawled through the parishes, Ongar, Epping, Greensted, Brentwood, Harlow . . . in 1881 James would have been in his forties. He might have gone to London. He might have emigrated, joined the army, settled in India . . . The parishes of Harlow, Loughton, Saffron Walden – *Quislan*. The name seemed to jump off the screen at her. 'James Quislan.' Then in brackets it said 'Hillier'. Then it said 'And wife, Anne. One adult daughter, unmarried, Jessica.' So James Quislan did become someone else.

Agnes ran to ask for the previous years' census, and waited by her screen for them to be brought to her. 1871 arrived, and she turned to Saffron Walden, scanning the screen for Quislan. There it was again, the same address. A settled person, this James Quislan-Hillier. Wife Anne, two daughters, Jessica and Charlotte. Agnes stared at the screen. So, Charlotte Quislan, she thought, looking at the name staring back at her, it is you. You have the answer.

She left the library and walked to her car, picking up a local evening newspaper on the way. Why did James Quislan change his name at the age of nine? Perhaps Emily remarried, she thought. That would be the obvious answer. But then, why would she block in the well? And why was her land removed from her?

Agnes wished it was earlier in the day. She could hardly bear to wait until tomorrow to continue her pursuit of Charlotte Quislan. Still, she thought, there was another trail to follow in the meantime.

At home she dialled Mike Reynolds.

Sam answered. 'Thank God he's out,' she said. 'At last we can talk now.'

'What's happening?'

'I can't bear it,' Sam said. 'He thinks I'm about eight or something. I went out last night and I got back long before twelve but he hit the roof. He's threatening to lock me in on Friday morning, and we've 'ad such rows. I've told him, I'm going to this eviction, he can't stop me. I've worked it out, if you pick me up in the car he'll never know till I've gone.'

'Sam, wait a minute. Has he mentioned someone called Tom Bevan?'

There was a pause. Then Sam said, 'No, but Col did.'

'Col? What did Col say about him?'

'When Col came to see me here, not long before he died, he said he'd met someone called Tom Bevan.'

'Where had he met him?'

'In London, somewhere, I think. And he said he knew my dad.'

'What – Mike? He knew Mike?'

'Yes. No. Oh, I dunno. Col was always going on about how Mike wasn't my dad.'

'How did he meet Tom Bevan?'

'Dunno. Maybe just hanging out, you know.'

'Hanging out where?'

'You know, where people go.'

'What was Col doing in London?'

'He'd go there sometimes to get money. Begging, you know.'

'But why should Tom Bevan be there when Col . . . it doesn't make sense,' Agnes said. 'And Mike hasn't mentioned him, Tom, I mean?'

'Mike? No, why should he? Ain't nothin' to do with him.' Sam yawned. 'Agnes, you will be there Friday, won't you? 'Cos I'm going, right? And if he tries to lock me in I'll just escape anyway, and never come back.'

Agnes sighed. 'OK. I'll be outside, in the car, at five thirty. You'd better be awake.'

''Course I'll be awake. Special occasion, innit.'

Friday, then, Agnes thought, replacing the receiver. On Friday, Sam will be in my car. And she'll have no choice but to tell me what she knows about Emily Quislan.

It was eight o'clock. Agnes opened a tin of soup and stirred it over the heat with one hand. Her other hand felt in her pocket for the broken crucifix. And what of Morris Stanton? she thought. There must have been insufficient evidence to bring charges. Agnes poured the soup into a bowl. And what am I to do about Tom Bevan?

She sat down to eat and flicked through the local paper. There it was:

DYE MENACE TO FYFFES WELL

Police are investigating an attempt to sabotage the water bottling factory at Fyffes Well near Broxted. Intruders introduced fluorescein, a yellow dye, into the source of the spring, rendering several thousand litres of the water unsaleable. Managing Director Richard Witham said he was unaware of anyone with a grievance towards him. Police have not ruled out a connection with the New Age Travellers living on the nearby site of the new M11 road link.

Agnes sighed. What was Col doing, getting involved in some re-enactment of a past drama? And meeting Tom Bevan, apparently by chance? She shuddered, and her hand went to the gap at her neck where for years there had been a crucifix. The phone rang.

'Agnes—'

'Julius—'

'Are you OK?'

'Yes. Got a lot on.'

'Agnes, answer me. Christiane's desperate to talk to you, Madeleine is really worried, the hostel's very short-staffed and they've had no word from you—'

'Julius—'

'It's sure as can be a stupid childish way you're behaving.'

'I'm not ready to talk about it.'

Julius was quiet. At last he said, 'Fine. When you are in the mood, maybe I'll still be here.'

Agnes felt a heavy silence descend as she put the phone down. When, much later that night, she settled down to sleep, the silence was still there, still enclosing her in numbness.

Charlotte Quislan, thought Agnes waking the next morning. She walked to the bus stop, thinking about how old James might have been when he married, how old when his daughters were born.

1860, she thought, arriving at St Catherine's House and pulling down the volume for the first quarter of that year. Quislan. Thank God it's not Smith, she thought, going to the next quarter, and the next. Finally, in December 1861 she found Jessica Quislan. And then, in July, 1864 she found Charlotte Quislan, registered in Brentwood, Essex.

The search through the marriage volumes took longer. Agnes heard the bells of the City chiming noon as she took down yet another volume for 1884 and saw the name Quislan, Charlotte, married Robert Kemble, in London.

London, Agnes thought, as the last note of noon chimed in the distance. They could have lived anywhere; they could have had six children, or none. She went back to the birth volumes, and starting in 1885 she leafed rather half-heartedly through the Kembles, finding two registered for that year, William and Emily, four for the following year, and a James and a Sarah in 1888. She thumped the book closed and replaced it on the shelf. She had lost the trail.

She emerged into the heat of the afternoon with a headache and walked down towards the Embankment, then east along the Thames for a while, until at Blackfriars she picked up a number 44 bus.

At home she went to her bookshelves and took down a copy of Pascal's *Pensées*. She sat by the window, gazing at his words of faith and passion, trying to put on one side the numbness which was like a fog around her, blurring her vision.

That evening, Sheila phoned her. 'Agnes, it's about Fyffes Well. I was up at the Ark this afternoon, and this woman came to see us. She was very elderly, and she said she'd come to tell us that she knew it wasn't us who'd put dye in the spring, because she knew who did it. And she didn't want to tell the police, but she would if it would help us.'

'Who was she?'

'She said she was called Joyce Langdon. And she didn't want to tell us any more, but we could count on her support.'

'How odd. What did she mean?'

'I've no idea. Then she went, and no one really gave it any thought. They're so preoccupied with the eviction.'

'How's Lily?'

'What, since your little chat with her?' Sheila said. 'Actually, she's a bit strange too. She's coming to the eviction, she said. I was very surprised. I thought it might be thanks to you.' Sheila laughed.

'I didn't really do much,' Agnes said.

'She said she was bringing her boyfriend, and I was to be nice to him.'

'Ah, that's it then. A kind of truce; she'll support you if you support her.'

'Maybe. I hope he's OK, this boyfriend.'

'Well, at least you'll get to meet him. Although making polite conversation whilst being hauled off a tree by an army of security guards might be tricky.'

Sheila laughed. 'Well, we'll find out soon enough. See you.'

Agnes rang off, then dialled Fyffes Well, and Richard Witham picked up the phone.

'You're working late,' she said.

'I'm not taking any risks.'

'How's it going?'

'The police are keeping an eye. I've hired a private security firm as well.'

'Good.'

'Agnes – as soon as you find anything out, can you tell me?'

'I promise. If I find anything out.'

She hung up, her fingers poised over the phone to dial Julius's number. She got up and went to the window. In the lighted telephone box in the street outside she could see the shape of a man. He was dialling a number. Her phone rang. She jumped.

'Hello?' she said.

There was silence, then breathing. Still holding the receiver she glanced out of the window again. The man hung up. She heard the line go dead. The man appeared to glance up at her window, then set off down the street. She watched him as he limped to the corner, watched him turn and disappear out of sight.

Chapter Eighteen

Joyce Langdon sounded doubtful.

'Where did you get my number?' She spoke in quavery tones of perfect English.

'From the Essex phone directory,' Agnes said. 'After you went to speak to the anti-road camp.'

'I did so want them to know that I was on their side. Such marvellous young people. But I've done all I can. I don't want to talk to the police about it. And I'm afraid I don't particularly want to talk to anybody else either.'

'But Miss Langdon,' Agnes said, 'you must. You see, you and I are the only people who know that Emily Quislan is at large; and that Fyffes Well is once again her target.'

'I've put the kettle on,' Joyce said, as she answered the door to Agnes later that morning. 'It's not too near lunchtime for coffee, is it?' She led Agnes through the flagstoned hallway of her cottage to the living-room. 'Do take a seat, I'll just sort out the cups,' she said.

Agnes sat on a wide, old sofa, recently re-covered in fresh chintz. On the little Victorian table at her elbow there were two issues of *Country Life*, and on top of them a leather-bound notebook. Agnes picked it up and opened it. The pages were yellowed with age. On the first page someone had written in curly letters, PHYLLIS LANGDON, HER JOURNAL, 1839.

Agnes heard the whistle of a kettle coming from the kitchen. She turned a page.

'With the new year have I resolved to keep a journal, and this time I am determined to keep my resolve. Emily may tease me all she likes, but my journal shall be kept religiously, not like all the other poor abandoned neglected dear old notebooks that I have locked away from prying eyes, poor half-formed nothings that they are. But now should the world choose to look upon these pages, it shall find me made bold by the happiness we three have found at last . . .'

There was a clatter of a serving trolley, and Joyce came into the room. Agnes put down the book uncertainly, but Joyce smiled at her. 'I put that out for you. I decided, after our phone conversation, that I must count you as a friend to Emily and me.'

'This must be – this is what I've needed – I tried St Catherine's House, you see, but after Charlotte married Robert Kemble I lost the thread, any of those Kembles could have been theirs, any of those Sarahs or Williams—'

'It was Anna Kemble, born in 1889, she was one of Charlotte's three children. Anna married Joshua Lees in 1921. She had four children, Peter, Matilda, George and Edward.' Joyce counted out the names on tapering fingers. 'In 1947 this George produced a boy called John, and in 1973 John married a Victoria Campbell. They have two children, Joshua and Emma. Emma's just nineteen, Joshua is seventeen.' Joyce finished with a restrained smile and clasped her hands together.

Agnes found her voice. 'How did you find out – and how did you come to have this?'

'Phyllis Langdon's brother was my great-great-grandfather.' Agnes took a large gulp of coffee from the bone china cup that Joyce had handed to her. 'It was upstairs for years, just one of those things that families hang on to, you know how it is. I first read it in my teens.'

'And Phyllis and Emily Quislan?'

'They were eccentric, to say the least. They'd formed this very close friendship at some point in their childhood, and then Emily had a baby boy in her twenties, apparently in secret from her family, and in 1837 they bought the cottage over by Fyffes Well. There seems to have been some kind of trust of which she was the beneficiary, although it was all very odd for those days. She pretended she was raising the child for her brother – she couldn't have said it was her own. And Phyllis lived with her here, for five or six marvellously happy years, according to the journal.

James was enrolled with the local school.'

'And then what happened?'

'From what I can gather a family called the Wythams, a big local landowning family, had their eye on the well, for some kind of farming project. And it seems that they got Emily's brother to testify that the child wasn't his, but Emily's own. And the Wythams stirred up local feeling against the two women—'

'And James became a Hillier?'

'That's right, yes, he was taken away from Emily and adopted by the curate here. But at some point he took back his former name, perhaps out of loyalty. The parish register of his marriage is signed Quislan.'

'And Emily?'

Joyce sighed and folded her hands tightly together in her lap. 'Phyllis wanted to flee with her and find their happiness elsewhere. Emily wouldn't leave because of James. In the end Phyllis moved away, not far, but leaving Emily to her fate. And Emily poisoned the well.'

'Poisoned it?'

'Yes. Phyllis mentions it much later on, she goes back to writing fragmentary bits. There's a cryptic entry for that year about wormwood and vengeance.'

'And did it kill anyone?'

'Well, no, apparently not.'

'I'd assumed she blocked it in.'

'No, that was later. It may be that the whole episode got exaggerated, as she was already out of favour – the witch who rides across moonlit fields to wreak revenge. But whatever the truth of it, the local worthies had the well filled in a couple of years later. Which is why those lower fields have been a swamp for as long as anyone can remember. Until now.'

'And the witch in Harton's field?'

'You're quite a historian, aren't you? Emily finally ended her days as an outcast, one of those half-mad muttering women I shouldn't wonder, and not surprising with her son being taken from her like that, although there's some evidence they kept in touch. And the Church wouldn't bury her, so I suppose Harton agreed to have the body or something. After all, he'd benefited from

Wytham's action, he might have felt guilty.'

Agnes sipped her now tepid coffee. 'Poor Emily.'

Joyce nodded. 'Poor Emily. And when I met Emma . . .'

'You know Emma well?'

'Yes. I suppose it's not so odd that John would have chosen me as her tutor, I am rather well thought of—'

'Hang on, you tutored Emma Lees?'

'Yes. Last year, when she failed her "A" levels. I'm often called upon in that way, since I retired from the Girls' School.'

'And you made the connection, between her and Emily?'

'Oh yes. Not immediately, I have to say, but when I realised who she was I showed her Phyllis's diary. She was very taken with it all. Not that it helped her with her studies, she failed again. But then she was so distressed, I wasn't surprised.'

'What about?'

'She wouldn't tell me. At first she was very rude to me, and said I was "on their side", whatever that meant. After we talked about Phyllis and Emily, she was more friendly. But still wary. I think she was very angry about something.'

Agnes looked at Joyce. 'Why,' she began, as her thoughts suddenly came sharply into focus. 'Why should Emma Lees want to poison Fyffes Well?'

Joyce leant back in her chair. 'As to that, my dear – I was rather hoping that you might tell me.'

'It's an extraordinary tale,' Agnes said, two hours later, sitting in Sheila's kitchen.

'It's amazing that those two women managed to live with their child like that at all—'

'Well, except they didn't. Not for long, anyway.'

'No.'

'And is she still in touch with Emma Lees?'

Agnes shook her head. 'The parents split up last year, and both moved nearer to London. All we know is that Emma is lurking around Fyffes Well.'

'Shall we tell Charlie?'

Agnes frowned. 'I promised Joyce that I wouldn't. She feels responsible, in a way. For showing Emma the journal. Although, like her, I'm worried that Emma's going to do something really dangerous. If she hasn't already.' A thought occurred to her. 'Can we check the computer?'

Upstairs they scrolled through the messages. There was nothing from Emily Quislan.

'Shall we send her one?' Sheila asked.

'Like what? "Emma, don't do it?" It might panic her into action.'

'Have you got an e-mail address for her?'

'Yes.' Agnes produced her notebook. 'JEL @ Bosh.Co UK.'

'That's a company, then. JEL—'

'Of course. John Lees. Her father. Either he's in on this scheme too – or,' Agnes went on, remembering the lone rider, 'or little Emma is using Daddy's home computer when he's not looking. And probably stabling her horse and hiding full Victorian costume somewhere in the grounds of his house too. In fact, if we wanted to track her down now, all we'd have to do is find out where this e mail address is based.'

'If we wanted to,' Sheila said. The two women looked at each other.

'But we don't have to,' Agnes said. 'After all, the police are already on the case, aren't they? I mean, even if we did tell Charlie, we'd just be betraying a confidence for no good reason. Wouldn't we?'

'Suppose so. Do you think this Joyce Langdon wants to protect Emma?'

'Yes. I think she does. I think her hunch is that something's going to resolve itself through all this.'

'Hmm. I hope it's worth the risk. I know, how about if we address an e-mail to him? To Daddy, I mean?'

'And risk her intercepting it? No,' Agnes said, as an idea occurred to her. 'I've just thought of something better. If there's time before the eviction.'

'You'll be there tomorrow, then?'

'It seems so. I promised I'd drive Sam up there. Although I have to say, armed combat is not my usual style.'

That evening Agnes opened her door after a persistent ringing to find Julius standing there.

'I tried phoning you, but you were engaged all afternoon,

and then after that you were out,' he said, walking past her into her room. 'And you'd probably have refused to let me see you anyway.'

'Julius, I'd never do that.'

'You're behaving pretty badly in all other respects. What was it this afternoon? Chasing more homeless youth just in case someone bumps them off? Doing battle with bailiffs out in Essex somewhere?'

'That's for tomorrow,' Agnes said shortly. 'No, this afternoon I was having tea in Fortnum's.'

'Athena again?'

'Not this time. A woman called Victoria Lees, née Campbell. It's amazing who you can track down from talking to estate agents—'

'I'm sure it is.' Julius sat down on her sofa-bed. 'But I came to discuss more serious issues,' he began.

'—because I knew they'd divorced, you see, so I reckoned the old phone book address was the marital home, so I started there, and the new people mentioned the estate agents who'd organised the sale, and I knew she'd moved towards London—'

'Anyway, Agnes,' Julius said, 'the point is—'

'—and sure enough, with sufficient fishing, talking about property values, didn't give anything away—'

'—the point is I refuse to sit back and watch you ruin your life. Again.'

'—I managed to work out which area she'd moved to – Blackheath, it turns out – and then I rang round the estate agents in the Yellow Pages for that area, and then once I'd narrowed it down I got Directory Enquiries—'

'Agnes – are you going to listen to me?'

'Anyway, to cut a long story short, once I'd got her on the phone she agreed to see me at once, so we met in Piccadilly. And she was so smart, lovely blonde hair and a Hermes scarf just like that one I had once – she doesn't look her age at all. I felt quite dowdy in comparison. And such a nice woman, although what she had to tell me was—'

'Bye then.' Julius stood up and went to the door.

Agnes stopped talking. 'Julius?'

'Well what's the point?' His hand was on the door handle.

She felt suddenly exhausted, and leaned her head on one hand. 'Please believe me, Julius, I'm not ruining my life.'

'But you are. Your anger is destructive,' Julius said. 'It's dragging you down with it.'

'It's not just my anger. There's all sorts of things that aren't right, and there's a young woman on the loose who's downright dangerous, and Sam is living in very dodgy circumstances . . .' Agnes got up, went to the kitchen and poured two glasses of whisky. She held one out to him.

He hesitated, took the glass and sat down on her bed again. 'But relinquishing your faith, your order—'

'I'm not. Not really.'

'They seem to think you are.'

'Well, that's up to them. When I can make sense of the whole damn thing I'll talk to them.'

'And what doesn't make sense? Apart from all these tales of dangerous young people, what in your own life doesn't make sense?'

Agnes sighed and took a sip of whisky. 'It's about Yorkshire.'

'I'm sure if you really insisted—'

'That's not the point. If I was truly obedient to my order, I'd go, wouldn't I? But the reason I can't be, is that – you see Julius, it's all a lie. My whole faith is built on a lie. Which is, that if I was good enough, my father would come back.' She gulped her drink, then said, 'But of course he won't. I've realised that now. And I don't know what I'm left with.'

Julius watched her as she paced the floor. She stopped again, and spoke. 'When I was in the forest – it's a long story, but a few days ago I found myself in a forest in the middle of the night on my own – and I was scared. It's a long time since I've been so scared. And I saw that it was all fairytales, Julius. All this God on Whom we can call in our hour of need – however hard I'd prayed, no one would have come, would they? However strong my faith, in the end I was just on my own. Just me and my fear. And as soon as I'd realised that, it was OK. I just thought, there it is then. My fear. It can't get worse than that.' She sat down next to him on the bed.

Julius thought for a moment, then said, 'But is it worth attacking our faith for something it isn't?'

'That's not what I'm doing.'

'You don't need to have the fairytales. You can have all the twentieth century existentialist stuff instead, you can have Pascal at times, or St Ignatius himself.' He gently leaned over and brushed a stray lock of hair away from her eyes. 'After all, Agnes, what are you without your faith?'

'But Julius, that's just the point. I don't know any more.'

'Maybe Yorkshire will help.'

'That's what Madeleine said.' Agnes got up to make some tea.

Later, as he was going, Julius said, 'What your order asks of you, and what God asks of you, might not be the same thing. We can't know the mind of God. What I mean is,' he said, as they stood in the middle of her room and he took both her hands, 'that you might as well accept all this for what it is.'

'So if I fling myself under a bulldozer tomorrow and get six months in prison, you won't blame me?' she smiled.

'No. But I'll miss you.' He kissed her on both cheeks and then was gone.

Agnes's alarm woke her at four thirty in the morning. It was still just dark, a lingering charcoal blue. She set off along empty roads, driving fast, and at five twenty was parked outside Mike Reynolds's house in Harlow, her lights still on, wondering whether to use her horn. Before she had to, the front door opened noiselessly, and Sam was running down the drive and piling, giggling, into the car.

'He won't forgive you,' she laughed.

'No,' Agnes said, starting the engine and pulling away fast. Once they'd cleared Mike's street, Agnes said, 'So – this Emily Quislan?'

She saw Sam tense at the name. 'Who?' Sam muttered.

'You know.'

'No, I don't.'

'Sam, why aren't you scared to go back to the camp now? After Becky and now Col, and at the time you were terrified of someone—'

'It's over now, OK? I don't want to talk about it.'

Agnes braked hard. The car squealed to a halt. 'I've had enough, OK?' she said. 'Tell me.'

Sam sucked in her cheeks and looked out of the window.

'I can turn right round and hand you back to Mike.' Sam turned from the window, fiddled with her bracelet. 'Sam – what do you know about Emily Quislan?'

She looked up. 'She was just a girl they knew. I never met her.'

'So why were you so scared?'

'She'd threatened Col, he said. And Becks. They were scared of her.'

'But not you.'

'No. Can we go now? I don't want to miss nothin'.'

'And so you have every reason to think this girl you never met killed both your friends?'

'Nah, not really. I don't know nothin' no more.'

'Sam, what did they say about her?'

Sam sighed. 'It was all about some plan or somethin', and when they wanted out she was really angry, they said. And Col had to get this stuff for 'er, which he did, but he was still scared of her.'

'What stuff?'

'Dunno, chemicals an' that. There's no point lookin' at me like I'm lyin'. That's all I know, OK?'

'Sam, why the hell didn't you say all this before?'

''Cos I thought she might get me too. And anyway, that's all I know. It's nothin', is it?'

'Do you think she killed them?'

Sam stared at her lap, her fingers working the bracelet round and round her wrist. At last she looked up, and her eyes were full of tears. 'Even if she did – there's nothing I can do, is there? I can tell the pigs what I just told you, but it won't fuckin' bring them two back, will it?'

'But—' Agnes began, but could think of no answer. She started the car again, and they drove to Sheila's. Sheila and Lily were subdued, and the four drove in silence to the camp.

At ten past six, Agnes parked her car well out of the way behind the church, and they all set off up the hill to the Ark. There was a taut stillness in the air. Huge banners fluttered from the trees, magical webs of brightly coloured rags made star shapes between the branches in the early sunshine. Zak emerged from his bender, nodded sleepily at the four and wandered towards the trees, Dog at his heels. A jangling from the trees above them signalled the descent of Rona, Jeff and Paz.

'Oh, well, no dawn raid so far,' Jeff said.

'They'll be mustering, though,' Rona said. Below them, two black cars snaked along the lane towards the woods, then parked. People were emerging from benders now, rubbing their eyes. Jenn was stoking up the fire. Everyone paused as a bright orange van bumped its way up the track, parking right by the first bender.

'Declan,' Jeff said.

'Done the music,' said a young man, getting out of the van. 'Leccy should be on now.'

Jeff and Declan ran to the woods, and a few moments later music pounded from beyond the trees, a rhythmic beat that brought the few remaining sleepers from their benders.

People were busy now, some up in the trees, some carrying equipment into strategic places in the woods.

'By tonight,' Rona sighed, surveying the camp, 'who knows.'

'I'll be back in a while,' Agnes said, checking her watch.

She strode back down the hill to her car and drove up to Richard Witham's spring. She was met at the gate by a security guard with an Alsatian dog.

'Is Mr Witham here, by any chance?' she asked, smiling sweetly.

''E's asleep in the office. Who shall I say?'

'Sister Agnes,' she said.

'S'cuse the informality,' Richard said, two minutes later, gesturing to the bedclothes piled around his desk. 'At least I'm not in pyjamas,' he grinned.

'Any news?'

'All's quiet. Nothing. Not since the fluorescein. And that's washing out now. Beginning to think I can get rid of these boys.'

'I wouldn't just yet. I think something might happen soon. Are you still checking the fence?'

'Yes, every day. That's been the same too.'

'Well, let me know if anything changes. I must go now.'

She parked by the church again, and walked back up the hill. She could see a group of policemen standing by the kitchen bender. Rona came up to her.

'It's getting heavy. A rumour's gone round that we've been nicking explosives.'

'Why do they think that?'

'Dunno, some raid on a quarry near Colchester, loads of stuff gone missing.'

'Great,' Jeff said, joining them. 'They can search the place if they want, they won't find anything.'

'It'll mean a heavy presence when they do arrive.'

Jeff frowned and wandered back to the fire. The police went back to their cars and drove away.

People began to arrive from the village, a video team, a couple of journalists, local supporters, until about forty or fifty people were gathered on the ground. Gradually the tree-dwellers disappeared upwards, and Paz, Jenn, Rona, Jeff were joined by crowds of others, all taking up their places in the tree-houses and platforms. On the ground people ran to positions, locked themselves to concrete stumps, chained themselves to tree-trunks. Agnes watched the battle lines form, the numbers swell as people continued to arrive. The tension was palpable, as all activity slowed and then ceased, reduced to a silence, a collective waiting. The music started up again, but its pulsing seemed to add to the sense of dislocation.

'They're here,' Sam breathed, standing close to Agnes. Everyone was staring down the hill towards the village. From the shadows of the trees in the valley a phalanx of vehicles took shape, a row of police riot vans, followed by a bulldozer and a cherry picker crane, and then a line of lorries loaded with fencing equipment, windscreens glinting, creeping anonymously up the hill. Agnes was aware of her heart racing. She looked across to Sheila. Lily was standing next to her with another girl, and some way behind them she saw, to her surprise, Steven and Jerry. Lily turned and caught their eye, then looked back at the approaching convoy. From the trees someone started up a shout, and this was echoed across the camp, in time with the music's beat, until the riot vans shuddered to a halt and spilt out their cargo of police, all wearing dark jackets and white hard hats, all advancing on foot to the benders.

And then, very quickly, the advancing army was upon them, grabbing people where they stood, moving them away from the benders. 'I'm asking you to leave,' someone said to Agnes as she felt her arm gripped and she was propelled with some force away from the camp. She turned back to look for Sam, but was threatened with arrest and once more removed. She could see the bulldozer sliding across the camp now, the crane juddering against a tree; bailiffs appeared with fencing and began to make a cordon, and Agnes found herself outside, surrounded by shouting, abuse, people running, no longer able to see Sheila, or Sam or Lily.

'Damn,' she shouted, above the pumping music, the engine noise. She ran round the fence, to see Jenn being carried out and dumped on the ground, only to jump up and run back through, heading for the trees. A group of people had climbed on to the bulldozer. Above them, Agnes could see Jeff climbing higher and higher into the branches, away from the cherry picker platform that was clumsily attempting to follow him. Rona scuttled across a walkway, pursued by a climber. And there was Jenn, back up in the trees.

Another shout, and Paz seemed to swoop out of the sky, attached to the abseil rope against his will by a climber. He landed badly, swore, tried to get up but was carried out by three policemen. Agnes caught sight of Sam, running towards the bulldozer, climbing on to it, only to be thrown off forcibly by a heavily-built security guard. Agnes cried out as Sam lay in the mud, and began to run towards her, trying to dodge through the fence, only to meet a line of police in her way, her face brushed by the fabric of their jackets.

'Sam,' she yelled, then lost sight of her again as she was forced to retreat. And now the atmosphere grew uglier. There was the constant buzz of saws as protesters were cut away from their lockons, there were screams, someone was dragged from a tree and dropped heavily on the ground. Some of the people standing watching were crying, some were shouting angrily, trying to get back through the fence to help the injured. A young man sat dazed by the fence, blood dripping from a head wound, until someone helped him up and moved him away to safety. Agnes could see security guards grabbing people with bone-crunching force, there were yells and shouts and sobbing. More people were climbing on to the bulldozer, but now the battle was for real. The bulldozer started up, inching towards the benders, throwing its attackers off as it crawled forward like some primordial beast. People slid down and fell into the mud under its wheels, and then someone was there pulling them out, dragging them to safety, going back to rescue someone else. Agnes saw, with a shock, that it was Bill.

Sheila appeared at her side, breathless. 'Have you seen Lily?' she asked.

'No, have you seen Sam?'

Both women stood, nervous and frightened, staring helplessly at the scene before them.

'Oh, God, they've got Rona,' Agnes gasped, seeing, on the highest walkway, a climber grab her and somehow attach her harness to his own, and then she was whirled off the walkway and down the abseil rope. Bill was there as she hit the ground, but she shook herself off and scaled the next tree. Then Bill was surrounded by three police officers and thrown out of the cordoned area.

'Bill,' she shouted. 'Sam – have you seen her . . . ?' Her voice was lost in the music and the shouting and the constant grinding engine noise, and now there was a new noise, the sound of chainsaws, and everyone's attention went to the furthest tree. At first nothing happened, just a trembling in its topmost branches, then a quaking down to the roots, echoing the onlookers' terror as they heard the wrenching crack and the tree toppled, falling with a resounding crash away from the camp towards the woods.

Agnes felt sick with fear. All she could hear was abuse, swearing, screams of rage and terror, and now the police were beginning to arrest anyone they found inside the cordon, and Agnes could see people being thrown into vans. A boy staggered across the mud, clutching at his arm, crying, and then he, too, was grabbed and forced into a van. She could bear it no longer, and ran, instinctively, into the woods, away from the battle. The noise grew more distant, but the quiet that surrounded her as she ventured further into the woods seemed temporary, a moment's peace before the final onslaught.

Through the trees she saw movement. She watched. It was Steven, slipping silently away from the battle. She followed at a distance, hoping that Lily was with him. At least she'd be safer here, Agnes thought. She watched him pause by a tree-stump, then pace three careful steps to a line of chequered tape, all that was left of the site where Becky was found. He knelt in the middle of the patch of mud. Agnes could hear his voice, and realised he was praying. After a while he got up, and stood, his face raised to the sky, his cheeks wet with tears. Agnes retreated further away. The sun was beating down now, but she felt suddenly cold. Freezing cold. There was nothing to say that Lily was safe at all.

She sat, waiting until Steven was out of sight. She knew she should go back to the battle, but her legs were shaking at the thought. After a while she got up, and walked slowly back toward the camp. The first thing she saw was Sam, standing next to Bill. She ran to her.

'What happened? I saw you fall from the bulldozer . . .'

'Oh that,' Sam said. 'Bill picked me up.'

'She ran straight back and tried to attack the cherry picker,' Bill smiled. 'I pulled her out before anyone could arrest her.'

'I don't think your dad would forgive us that one,' Agnes said, ignoring him.

'Mike? Oh he can get stuffed,' Sam said. 'Oh God, look at it,' she added, and burst into tears. Around them was strewn the wreckage of the camp, tarpaulins ripped and churned into the mud, sodden rags of clothes and bedding, the kitchen bender upended, broken china everywhere. The last few bits of fencing were being put into place, the bulldozer had already started to flatten the land. People were standing in a crowd outside the fence, some tearful, some shouting. There were television cameras, helicopters overhead, the angry buzz of chainsaws. In the trees the battle raged, and above the music Agnes could still hear the shouts of laughter from the walkways. Planks of wood dangled from the branches, all that was left of the platforms that had been home to the Ark people for weeks, for months. Sam's face suddenly lit up. 'There – look – Jeff – he's still up there.' Far away on the highest branches, Jeff sat. The crane was nudging against the tree, and a climber was struggling with the walkway ropes to reach him. Sam ran to the edge of the fence, to join the crowd, shouting encouragement, laughing to see him still free as a bird.

Bill turned to Agnes. 'Go on then,' he said, 'punch me on the nose.'

Agnes looked at him. 'I might just do that.'

'I'll turn the other cheek or something, following your good example.' She didn't smile. 'I don't know what you must think of me,' he went on.

'I'll tell you what I think of you. People like you go walking on quicksand, telling the rest of us it's solid ground.' The climber was gaining ground on Jeff, who still sat peacefully. Agnes turned back to Bill. 'If you won't stop Emily Quislan, then at least stop protecting her. Tell the police, tell someone. There's explosives at large now, though I'm sure you know that already, like you know why you've been allowed to dip in and out of this protest without the police harming a hair of your head. Whose side are you on, Bill?'

Bill looked at her with something like sadness in his eyes. 'I envy you,' he said. 'One day I'll tell you why.' He touched her arm, then looked up to where Jeff was now cornered by the climber. In one leap Jeff abseiled away from the climber, scuttled along a walkway to the next tree, grabbed the rope and whooshed down it to the ground. He grinned at Sam, as a group of policemen closed in on him. Agnes darted to the fence, grabbed Sam by the arm and walked her firmly away as Jeff was bundled forcefully into a van. When she looked back, Bill had gone.

Later, sitting at Sheila's kitchen table, Agnes found she couldn't stop shaking.

'It's the adrenaline,' Sheila said. 'Takes ages to wear off.'

'Where did Lily go, then?' Agnes asked her, surveying her trembling fingers with interest.

'I found her with Amy, an old friend of hers. They left together, they went to Amy's to lick their wounds and swap tales of their bravery.'

Sam sat sipping tea from a mug. 'What's going to happen to the others, the ones that got taken away?' she asked in a small voice.

'They'll be OK, love,' Sheila said. 'They'll be down at the police station getting processed, and then they'll be let out. They'll probably end up here,' she laughed.

'Won't they go to prison?' Sam asked.

Sheila sighed. 'It depends. Maybe.'

'Didn't see Charlie anywhere,' Agnes remarked.

Sheila smiled. 'No,' she said. 'Not Charlie.'

* * *

It was dark when they left Sheila's. Sam had had a shower and borrowed some of Lily's clothes, and had eaten some toast, and then everyone waited for news of the others, and at nine thirty Rona, Jeff and Paz turned up and couldn't stop talking and Sheila made more toast. At last Agnes had persuaded Sam it was time to get back.

Now, sitting in the car outside Mike's house, Sam looked at Agnes. 'Here goes,' she said. 'You coming too?'

Agnes unfastened her seat belt. 'I might as well be the one to take the rap for this. After all, I haven't got to live with him.'

'Who says I have?' Sam slammed the car door hard.

As her key chinked in the lock, Mike opened the door. He was white-faced, his features pinched with rage. He grabbed Sam by the arm and pulled her into the house, then turned to Agnes. 'Get out,' he said.

'Mike—'

'I said out. *Out!* I will not be disobeyed.' The door slammed in Agnes's face.

Agnes put her mouth to the letterbox. 'Mike, you carry on like that,' she shouted, 'you're going to lose her.' She peered in and saw Sam running up the stairs to her bedroom, Mike standing in the hallway, his arms hanging at his sides.

And if you were her father, Agnes thought, straightening up, walking back to her car, you'd know better than to expect obedience.

She drove home, let herself into her darkened flat and sat at her desk. Her clock flashed eleven fifty-four. She leaned her chin on her hands, deep in thought. When a minute later her phone rang, she didn't even jump. She picked it up, glanced out of the window. She saw once again the man standing in the phone box, holding the receiver, looking up at her window. Only this time he spoke.

'I wasn't sure – your lights weren't on.' His voice was deep and hoarse.

'I'm here,' Agnes said softly.

'It's Tom Bevan,' he said.

'At last. You'd better come up.'

Chapter Nineteen

At nine o'clock on Saturday morning, Agnes rang the bell of Mike Reynolds's house. Eventually it was answered by Sam in a huge crumpled T-shirt, rubbing her eyes.

'He won't let you in,' Sam said.

'He's got to.'

Sam leaned wearily against the door frame. 'I've 'ad enough. Come back when he's calmed down . . .'

'No, listen, he's—'

'What the hell is she doing back again?' Mike shouted, appearing in the doorway next to Sam. 'I thought I told you to fuck off—' His voice faltered as he looked beyond Agnes.

A man was limping the few steps up to the house. He was tall and upright, with rough brown hair and a tanned, weathered face. He was dressed in a clean white shirt, suit and tie, and his beard was trimmed. Agnes was gratified to see him looking so good in Julius's clothes.

His eyes, soft, grey, childlike, were fixed on Sam, and as he came near her he stretched his arms out awkwardly towards her, as if in that moment his whole being was drawn to her, consumed by her.

As he approached, Sam shrank from him, from the hunger in his eyes. He blinked, stopped short. He glanced at Agnes, then at Mike.

Mike sighed. He stepped to one side to make way for them. 'Tom,' he said wearily, leading them into the house.

Sam went to put some clothes on. She seemed to take a long time. When she came into the living-room they were all sitting there, Agnes looking tired but determined, Mike perched uneasily on the edge of his chair, and the bearded man sitting calmly, his hands on his knees. He looked up as she came in, and again there was that expression of burning need. She avoided his gaze, choosing to sit on the chair nearest to Mike.

'So?' she said. 'Here we go again.'

Agnes spoke first. 'Sam, it hasn't been easy for anyone.'

'What you want now, sympathy?'

'This is Tom Bevan. He's your father.'

Sam looked at the floor.

'Mike agreed to help him by pretending to be your father.'

Sam glanced up, her eyes flashing. 'Great.'

Agnes went on, 'Tom was dating your mother when they were in their teens, briefly. Then she finished with him and started going out with Mike. But she was already pregnant. With you. Only no one knew.'

'Stupid cow,' Sam said.

'As she thought her future lay with Mike, she decided it was easier to pretend you were his. And she got away with it. Meanwhile, Mike was making money, working on building sites and doing rather well. In fact, he was the foreman when Tom, his mate, had an accident.'

Tom looked across to Mike. Mike got up and left the room.

Agnes went on, 'Tom was in hospital for ages, with head and leg injuries. When he at last emerged, the recession had begun and he found it difficult to get work. He didn't get compensation or anything. After a while it was easier just to drink. Just to forget. And then one day in a pub, he met a mate of your mother's, one of the girls who'd hung around with them all on the estate. And she said that he ought to have got money for his accident, and it was Mike's fault, and anyway, didn't he know about the rumours about Linda's baby girl, and he said, what rumours, and she said, that it was yours, Tom. Your baby.'

Sam lifted her head briefly and glanced across at Tom. Tom was smoothing the velvety fabric of the arm of his chair, slowly, methodically.

'But in a way,' Agnes was saying, 'this made matters worse. He'd gone too far, into drink and petty crime and the odd burglary. And then a prison sentence, and by the time he was out, Linda had moved away. So he tried to forget you, but he couldn't. When you were about ten he tracked Linda down and confronted her with it, but she said he'd never be able to prove it. After that he went abroad, got by on casual work, and managed to dry out. A year ago he came back to this country, determined to find you. He knew that no one was going to take his claim seriously – no proof, no home, a dried-out alcoholic with a criminal record, living on the streets. So he sought out Mike and asked him to help. It was a crazy scheme, that Mike should pretend to be your father wanting you back – but it was the only one that was going to work. And Mike felt guilty about Tom, about the accident all those years ago, and he agreed to help.'

Agnes looked at the two of them, Sam curled into the armchair, facing away from Tom, Tom staring at her as if his eyes would burn through her. In the silence, Sam slowly turned to meet his gaze. He smiled at her, and she looked away again.

Mike came into the room carrying four mugs of tea which he distributed. As he offered one to Sam she said, 'You lied to me. I knew all along. I knew you were never my dad, and you lied. You fucking lied.'

Mike put her mug down on the table. 'Sam, I was going to tell you. But it was difficult, we'd gone so far, me and Tom, I kept waiting for the right moment.'

Tom's voice was a bass rumble, and seemed to come from the depths of his being. 'You were never going to tell her.'

They all turned to him. Mike said, 'I was.'

'You wanted to keep her for yourself.' It was like the stirrings of a long-dormant volcano.

'I didn't,' Mike said. 'I had no intention of keeping her.'

'Thanks a bunch,' Sam said.

Mike turned to her, grey and weary. 'The thing is, love, he is your father. It's the truth.'

Sam looked at Mike. She looked at Agnes. Then she turned and looked at Tom. She saw his face, lined with pain and loss, she saw the pleading in his eyes; and a flash of recognition passed between them. He whispered, 'Sam.'

She stood up and walked out of the room. Her footsteps thumped up the stairs.

'This was just what I was trying to prevent,' Mike said.

'But you didn't try to tell her, did you? You didn't even try,' Tom said.

'I knew if it was sprung on her like this she'd take it badly.'

'But if you'd at least tried to explain to her – that's why I tracked down Sister Agnes here.'

'And Col?' Agnes said.

Tom sucked on his teeth. 'That was wrong of me. I was desperate about Sam then. I could see her settling into life with Mike, him buying her all she could ever want. I thought, how can I compete. And I followed them, and I arranged to meet Col, and I befriended him, tried to get him to understand that Mike was bad for her. But poor boy, he was the wrong person to choose. He had something else on his mind, running scared from some girl or other—'

There was the sound of footsteps dashing down the stairs, the front door opening, then a slam, and footsteps running down the drive, receding into the street, into the silence.

Tom said, 'Fuck.'

'You see,' Mike said, angrily. 'I told you it would backfire this way. You just can't trust me, can you, not even after all this time, not even when I'm trying to help. Dammit, Tom, I gave you my word. What more could I do? If I'd been left to choose my moment—'

Tom got to his feet, and gazed at Mike, and his eyes were dark as he tried to find words, tried to convey all the years spent searching, hoping against hope; a hope now betrayed. His lips moved, and at last he spoke.

'My God,' he said, hoarsely, as the rage smouldering within him found voice. 'I did trust you, Mike. I let go of the past and I gave you my trust. And where has it got me? I've lost my little girl. Again.' He lumbered towards the door.

'There's no point—' Agnes began.

'Going after her? Because of my leg, you mean? Because she's got three minutes' start and by now she could be on a bus, or a train? Sure, she could be anywhere. But I've spent my whole life looking for her. What difference is another few years going to make?'

Mike and Agnes sat helpless as he limped from the room and the front door closed behind him. At last Agnes murmured to Mike, 'I'm sorry.' He shook his head, began to speak, but she said, 'No, it's my fault. Both of them back on the streets now. How clever of me.'

'We could drive out looking for them,' Mike said.

'And then what? Just repeat the scene again?'

Mike sighed. 'I should have brought him in sooner. But what the hell was I supposed to do? The kid's an out-and-out consumer, everything was measured in terms of what I spent on her. He'd have been lost with no cable telly to give her, no new clothes and Blur CDs and disco tickets, no cruising Tesco's for the slimline passion fruit yoghurt . . .' Mike looked up at Agnes. 'I always knew she wasn't mine. Those early months with Linda, with the baby on the way, it felt wrong. And I thought, I'll be OK when it's born, but I remember the first time I looked at Sam, I knew – I knew . . . I suppose it's easy to say in retrospect. But I think that's why I ended up drifting away from them. When Tom came to me last year, when he told me, I was relieved. It was like this burden lifted that had been there for fifteen years.'

Agnes looked across at Mike. She took a sip of cold tea and realised that something in him had changed.

'What now?' he said.

'Firstly, you don't have to feel responsible. Tom's met Sam again, and Sam knows who he is.' She shrugged. 'No one was asking you to guarantee a happy ending. You've done all you could.'

'What'll you do?'

'I suppose I'll go and look for them. One day. But right at this moment, I've got rather a lot on.'

In Mike's hallway she paused, and offered him her hand. 'I misjudged you,' she said. 'I knew you were lying, but I didn't know why. I'm sorry.'

He shook her hand. 'I thought it must be something like that. Listen, you tell me if there's anything I can do – let me know what happens, eh?'

Agnes smiled. 'Yes. Though, like you, I can't guarantee any happy endings either. You see, I've stopped believing in fairytales – particularly where fathers and daughters are concerned.'

Back at home she made herself a tuna fish sandwich and listened to her answering machine. There was a message from Madeleine, saying, please get in touch. Then Richard Witham, wanting her to ring him back. The next message was a nervous, female voice. 'Hello, it's Elizabeth Murphy here. Oh, I hate talking on these things. I just thought you should know, Morris has confessed. About, you know, um, Becky. Roger told me. Apparently, Ross is, um, working with him now. I just wanted you to know. Goodbye.'

Agnes stopped the machine. She stared at it. Morris. Yes. Although . . . She switched the machine back on. The last message was from Sheila.

'Agnes, have you heard from Lily? She's vanished. I'm worried sick, she's never just gone off before. Phone me, please.'

Agnes dialled her number.

'Sheila,' she said, her mouth full of tuna fish.

'Oh, God, Agnes, thank God. Any news?'

'None at all. What happened?'

'She left the eviction with Amy, you know, like I said. But it turns out, Amy was caught up with the crowd, trying to get out through the police cordon, and she thought Lily was with her. When she got to the village she waited, but Lily didn't show up. I thought she was with Amy. I only heard this morning that she wasn't. I'd arranged for them to stay there, so that I could be here for the others—'

'Oh my God. Have you asked the police?'

'Yes, that was my first thought, that they'd pulled her in too, but no sign. Charlie's worried sick, he's checked all the notifications, nothing. I went back to the woods. I thought she'd got some romantic notion of staying there, but zilch. No sign. Agnes, what shall I do?'

Agnes stared at her sandwich, at the soggy white bread and the greasy flakes of fish inside. She recalled Steven praying loudly in the woods, tears pouring down his face while the distant battle raged. She felt suddenly sick.

'Sheila,' she whispered. 'I'll be right there.'

Sheila seemed to have aged ten years. She grabbed hold of Agnes at the door, and pushed her towards the phone.

'There. Phone them. Charlie, anyone. They've got to find her.'

'But you've already—'

'But you know them, this so-called church. Tell them. Tell the police they've got her.'

236

'You think—'

'What else?'

Agnes was put through to two other officers before she reached Charlie.

'Sheila's already told me,' he said, shortly. 'Here's what I know so far. No one's happy about this Ross Turner bloke, we're going to be calling on him. Hang on—' There was muttering in the background, then Charlie came back on. 'There's a shout, gotta go.'

'And now that Morris—' Agnes began. She heard more radio noise, then Charlie said, 'What were you saying?'

'Hasn't Morris Stanton . . . ?' Agnes stopped herself.

'Nothing new on the Stanton case for weeks,' Charlie said. 'Anyway, must go, tell Sheila to try not to worry, we'll be calling on the church lot.'

'Oh. Good.'

Agnes turned to Sheila. 'They're going to visit Ross Turner. Eventually.'

'I bet they've no idea where he is,' Sheila snapped.

'No,' Agnes said, as a thought crystallised in her mind. 'But I do. Come on.'

'Why are we going back to the forest?' Sheila asked, as Agnes screeched up the track where the camp had been and parked by the gate.

'I've just got to get something. Wait in the car.'

The landscape that greeted Agnes as she reached the top of the hill was completely alien, a desolate wasteland of churned mud, felled trees, scrubby grassland scarred by tyres. It was like crossing a battlefield, the dead still unburied.

She went into the woods and followed the smell of woodsmoke. Bill's camp was further away now, nearer the existing road. When she saw he was there, crouched over his fire, she felt an overwhelming sense of relief. He looked up, startled, then smiled.

'I thought I'd never see you again.'

'I've come to do a deal,' Agnes said.

'Yes?'

'You owe me an explanation.'

'Yes.'

'You also have a gun. A pistol.'

He grinned. 'I admit it. For rabbits.'

'Crap. You've never killed a rabbit with it. The point is, I need it. Now.'

'Why?'

'That's the deal. I don't ask you for an explanation. You don't ask me.'

He stood up, smiled, came towards her. He took her hand in his. 'I'd hate you to come to harm.'

'I'm in a hurry.'

He turned her hand palm upwards, then placed in it a .38 Smith and Wesson. 'It's loaded,' he said. 'Do you know how to use it?'

'I hope I won't have to,' Agnes said.

'Have this as well.' She looked down to see he was offering her a mobile phone. She took it. 'I haven't killed any rabbits with that, either,' he said, scribbling his number down. 'Just in case,' he said, slipping the scrap of paper into her pocket.

She turned to go.

'Be careful,' Bill said.

'Where are we going now?' Sheila asked, as they sped along suburban roads outside Chelmsford.

'To Lily, I hope,' Agnes murmured. It all depended on her hunch being right, she thought. Elizabeth is convinced that Morris has confessed. But the police know nothing about it. Which means, she thought, that Ross is still holding the whole thing together.

The dashboard clock said three minutes past two.

She pulled into the Murphys' neat cul-de-sac, ran up the drive and rang the bell. The door was opened a crack by Elizabeth, then, as she saw it was Agnes, a little wider.

'Where's Lily?' Agnes said.

'They're all with Morris. Shirley's here, with David,' Elizabeth murmured.

'Why Lily?'

'I don't know. Steven said it was Jerry's idea. Ross must need her to help in the work with Morris.'

'When you say "work" . . . ?'

'Sometimes people need help. Sometimes people are reluctant to confess the power that Satan has over them.'

'Elizabeth—' Agnes looked at the petite, nervous woman standing in front of her. She took a deep breath. 'Elizabeth, I need you with me.'

'They said to stay here. Just in case.'

'I need you,' Agnes said firmly, her foot in the doorway.

'I can't disobey—'

'Elizabeth. Think for yourself. For once.' Agnes tried to keep her voice firm, level, keeping Elizabeth's gaze locked with her own. 'I've got Lily's mother in the car. Think. Think if it was your son.'

'L-Lily . . .?' Elizabeth looked blank.

'Lily. Jerry's girlfriend. Think.'

'But it's Morris—'

'Elizabeth. I need you. She's in terrible danger. The same danger that Becky knew.'

'But her father – the Lord has told us—'

Agnes felt time slipping away. 'You know. Elizabeth, you know what the Lord tells you. In your heart of hearts. Be true to that, Elizabeth. You know what Steven knows.'

Elizabeth stared at the floor. 'I can't . . . I don't think . . .'

'I saw him, Steven. I saw him in the woods. Yesterday. At the place where Becky was found. He was praying. And crying.'

Elizabeth looked at Agnes. 'Steven . . . crying . . . ?'

'You know why, Elizabeth. Come with us. Please.'

Agnes watched the tiny pulse at Elizabeth's temple. Her eyes were full of bewilderment. Then she frowned, blinked. 'I'll – I'll just change my shoes,' she said.

As Agnes helped Elizabeth into the back seat of the car, she caught Sheila's glance. Not a word, she willed to her. Don't say a thing.

She drove slowly from the Murphys' house to the Stanton house, collecting her thoughts, aware of the pistol in her pocket.

She parked outside the house. It looked normal, orderly. Sheila grabbed at the door handle. 'Is this it? Is she here?' she said, opening the car door.

'Sheila, don't,' Agnes seized her arm. 'If you go in now—'

'What the hell are you saying? My daughter's in there, against her will. Of course I'm going to—'

'Sheila, please. If you go in now it'll get more dangerous for Lily.'

'I don't care, I'm going to—'

Elizabeth's voice rang clear as she broke her silence. 'If you care for Lily, do what she says. Do what Agnes says. She's right. I know.'

Something about her tone made Sheila hesitate. She sat back in her seat. Elizabeth turned to Agnes. 'We'll stay here,' she said.

Agnes handed Sheila the mobile phone. 'My hope is that I can send Lily out to you. When you see her coming out, dial 999. But not before. Please. It's important. Elizabeth will tell you how important.'

Elizabeth grasped Agnes's hand. She looked like someone who had awakened from a dream. 'And Steven,' she said. 'Send him out too. Here,' she said, handing Agnes a key. 'Shirley's spare key. Use it.'

Agnes went up the drive and let herself silently into the house. It was quiet. For a moment Agnes wondered if she'd been completely wrong. Perhaps there's no one here at all, she thought, but then she caught a sound from upstairs, a strange, deep sobbing. Then voices, raised in unison. Agnes started up the stairs. The sounds were coming from Becky's room. Of course, Agnes thought. Her hand went to her pocket. Becky's broken crucifix. In the other pocket, Bill's gun. Oh God, Agnes thought, I hope I don't have to use it.

She stood outside Becky's room. The sobbing had become louder, a choking sound that made Agnes's blood run cold. Then she heard Ross's voice, raised in prayer. 'Oh God, our Father,' she heard. 'Save this Thy child . . . Oh God, our Father . . .' It was a kind of chant. Agnes heard the words father, child, reverberating in the room; echoing in her head. She felt a steely calm descend on her. She put her hand on the door handle. 'Save this Thy child,' she heard. Like hell, she thought, flinging the door open.

The room was in darkness, flickering with candlelight. The curtains were drawn. The first thing Agnes saw was Morris, his eyes wide, his mouth open. His face was wet with tears. He was sitting on a chair surrounded by the others, all standing. Steven on one side, Jerry on the other, Roger next to Jerry, Ross standing right in front of the chair. Lily was the other side of Steven, and Agnes noticed her bright eyes, her look of blank calm as she glanced at Agnes and then back to Morris. Morris gripped the sides of the chair, white-knuckled.

'Sister Agnes,' Ross said, stepping back from Morris. 'Well, well. Though I'd expect you to know better than to interrupt people in communion with the Lord.'

Don't you mean Satan, Agnes wanted to say, but kept silent, as Ross took her hand firmly in his own and led her into the room. He shut the door behind her and stood by it.

'Won't you sit down?'

Agnes hesitated. She looked at Morris. He was pale, red-eyed, shocked, looking blankly at Ross, as if waiting for a cue, his fingers still locked around the edges of the chair.

Agnes sat on Becky's bed, on the yellow candlewick bedspread. 'I thought I heard someone crying,' she said, conversationally.

Ross smiled warmly at her, then touched Lily's shoulder. 'Perhaps our sister here will explain what we're doing.'

Lily looked up at Ross, then smiled at Agnes. 'We're praying to the Lord to help Morris.'

'So you see,' Ross said, 'you interrupted something very special, fragile even. Perhaps we have a right to know why? Why you decided to creep into our private space, breaking into this house like a common thief?' He walked across the room and half opened the curtains, letting in the sunlight. He blew out the candles, then pulled up a chair and sat down opposite Agnes, waiting for an answer. Agnes was glad the room was at the back of the house. The car parked outside was still safe from Ross's view. She noticed that Roger had moved to the door, as if standing guard.

'Well?' Ross said. 'How can we help?'

I've come to take Lily home, Agnes wanted to say, but looking at her as she stood next to Ross, her eyes shining with enthusiasm, she realised there was no point. She imagined herself shooting her way out, gripping Lily by the arm. But then, if I did produce the gun, Agnes thought, they'd get it off me in two seconds. It was time to try a different tack.

'May I ask why Morris needs the Lord's help?'

A chill passed across Ross's face. 'You seem to be taking a very keen interest in us, Sister,' he said. His voice sounded harsh and metallic.

'Only where the murder of a young woman is concerned,' Agnes said. The room seemed to have grown colder. Agnes was aware of Roger at the door, of Steven and Jerry, all somehow poised to do Ross's biding, of Morris, shifting uncertainly on the chair. She glanced across at the crucifix, her crucifix, hanging from the photo of Becky.

Ross stood up, and his face became warm again, his cheeks suffused with pink. 'Let us offer a prayer of thanksgiving to the Lord that Sister Agnes has come amongst us today.' They all turned to him, Roger, Steven and Jerry, and Lily, smiling at Ross's voice. 'For our brother Morris here is able to give witness to the power of Satan, to the evil Satan worked within him. And not just to us, his friends, but to our Sister Agnes here.'

'Amen,' came a thin, reedy voice, and Agnes realised it was Jerry.

'Morris,' Ross prompted, 'would you like to tell our sister here what happened?'

Morris's lips were working. After a moment he said, 'It's true. Satan possessed me, and I killed – I killed . . .'

Agnes looked at Ross, who was gazing at Morris with his open, gentle smile. She glanced at Lily again, whose smile was an almost exact replica of Ross's. There was no way she'd agree to leave now. There was no point trying to get her out by force. There was nothing for it. Agnes took a deep breath.

'It must be difficult,' she said to Morris, 'admitting to it, when you can't remember anything about it.' She felt the room hold its breath.

'That's the problem,' he said. Little beads of spittle appeared on his lips with each word. 'But Satan possessed me. I know now that he did. They've helped me to see that he did.'

'Of course, you were angry with her,' she said.

He nodded. 'She ran from us. She ran away. I only wanted what was best for her. It was wrong, what she did. I – I – wanted to make her better.'

'What did she do that was wrong?'

Morris chewed his lip, and bright red spots appeared on his

cheeks. 'I can't say. It's better that she's dead now, she's pure now, she can't do . . . do those things now.'

'What things?' There was silence. 'Becky loved women.' Agnes's words hung in the stillness of the room. 'Is that why you killed her, Morris?'

Morris darted glances to Ross. 'It's – it's better that she's dead,' he mumbled.

'And the police, Morris – they'll tell you, Morris, over and over again, they'll say – you killed Becky, Morris. That's what they'll tell you, time after time. You killed your daughter.'

Morris was red-faced now, his fists were clenched at his sides. At last he said, 'But I did. I was possessed by Satan and I – I did it. Her cross,' he said, 'her silver chain – I remember I had it, I brought it here, I hung it up.'

'All right, then,' Agnes said, 'let's go over the events of that night in the forest. They will, of course, be familiar to you. Becky is with her friend, a girl, in the woods that evening. They have a row. You've followed them there, you've been lurking in the woods all day, determined to fight with Satan for the soul of your daughter. Is that so?'

Ross was looking intently at Morris. Morris nodded.

'You see them in the distance. It's clear that they've had some kind of disagreement, because the girl storms off to the village, and your daughter, Becky, is left alone in the forest. She doesn't go back to the camp, even though it's late and they're all wondering where she is. She stays, to think things over, perhaps. And that's your chance. You come upon her. And what do you do?'

Morris looked at Ross. His lips were dry, and he moistened them. 'I – I—'

'Do you pray with her?' Morris nodded. 'So, you ask her to kneel. And you stand over her, and call upon Satan to leave the body of your daughter.'

'Amen,' came the same light voice.

'And then what, Morris?' Agnes said. 'Then what?' She wondered how long she had before Ross intervened. 'Perhaps the presence of Satan, of Satan himself, in the forest in the dark like that, perhaps it was all too much for you. And perhaps Becky began to object, and tried to get up and go back to her friends, to her life – and something snapped in you. Because Becky was at ease with herself, with the life she'd chosen to lead, the women she'd chosen to love – and you weren't. You aren't, are you?' Agnes felt Ross's eyes burning through her. She continued to address Morris, aiming her words at someone else in the room. 'You can't accept your desires for what they are – even though they, too, are gifts from God.'

'No,' someone whispered.

'And so you found yourself grabbing the crucifix that she still wore around her neck, and twisting it, and twisting and twisting until it broke, and then you grabbed some rope and carried on, pulling and wrenching until – well, you know the rest, don't you, Morris?'

Morris was openly weeping, staring at the floor, shaking his head.

'Except,' Agnes went on, 'you don't. Because you weren't there. Were you?'

Morris began to mutter, between sobs, 'No, no, no . . .' Ross exchanged glances with Roger. Agnes noticed that Steven and Lily were both pale, staring intently at Morris. Lily had lost her vacant smile. She was alert, now, frowning, as she looked from Morris to Ross. Thank God, Agnes thought.

'You see, Ross,' Agnes said, 'it's not going to work. There are some truths you can't make happen simply by repeating them enough times. Morris will never know what it was like that night with Becky, however many times you try and tell him. Even though the police are closing in, even though the only way you can save your church is to make Becky's murder a domestic affair, caused by her father's violence, so that the police take him away instead of—'

Suddenly Ross shouted, 'That's enough. That's enough.' There was a flash of metal as Agnes saw that Ross had a gun and was aiming it at her. He grabbed Jerry by the arm. 'We're going,' he said, inching towards the door.

Hell, thought Agnes. Here we go. She drew her gun too, and found she was yelling, 'Stop, stop right there,' as Ross yelled, 'Drop it, drop the gun,' and Agnes shouted, 'Steven, Lily, get out. Now. Get out, for God's sake. Wake up. Go—' She and Ross circled, yelling. Roger was calling out, 'Ross, *Ross*.' Steven and Lily dashed for the door, wrenched it open while Roger stood mouthing helplessly, and hurtled out of the house.

'I'm not afraid to use it,' Ross was yelling.

'What, and burn in hell?' Agnes shouted, thinking Oh God, dial that number, Sheila, now.

'You'll reach hell before I do,' Ross cried.

'Why marriage, Ross?' Agnes was shouting. 'Why try and marry off Jerry, first to Becky, then to Lily, when you feel for him—'

'No, *no*,' Ross interrupted, 'I must fight the desires that Satan puts before me—'

'But they're good desires—'

'O Satan's honeyed words,' Ross yelled. 'How can such things be good? "'Tis better to marry than to burn—"'

'Ross, if you love Jerry, why can't such love be God-given?'

'Daughter of Satan,' Ross cried, and for a moment Agnes thought he was about to shoot her. In the chaos, Jerry had wandered over to the mantelpiece and picked up the crucifix. He held it in his hands, allowing the cross to hang from the chain, dangling from his fingers. Now, like someone in a trance, he came and stood in front of Ross, so close that his body was almost touching the barrel of the gun.

'Look,' he breathed, smiling, 'a miracle. It's whole. It was broken in two, but now it's whole.'

The room fell silent. Morris and Roger were standing by the door. Ross stared at Jerry.

'Satan was strong that night,' Jerry said. 'I had to fight him on my own, he was like a – a serpent, his long neck, long neck, so strong, but so white and pure, like a woman's, but I knew, I knew who it was, I could see the evil within, I knew I had to win. It was for Becky, you see. I knew if I lost my fight with Evil she would die. I had to save her.' He was facing Agnes now. 'We prayed together, like you said, we knelt together, but then she said . . . and I knew that Satan was with her, she said she loved . . . and while she was kneeling there I . . . I saw Satan. I saw him. And I had to save Becky. I had to make her pure again.' Jerry stood in front of Agnes, holding the crucifix between his hands, smiling down at it.

Agnes felt in her pocket with her other hand and produced the other crucifix. 'No, Jerry,' she said, gently, still keeping her gun levelled at Ross. 'This is Becky's. That one's mine. I swapped them.'

It felt to Agnes like an act of terrible cruelty. Jerry took the broken chain, and held it, pinching the twisted links between his thumb and forefinger, staring at them. His eyes were hollow with anguish.

'How did it end up here?' Agnes asked him.

'I – I – looked for her. Afterwards . . .' Jerry said. 'I'd won . . . lay dead, it lay dead . . . I knew I'd won, but . . .' He didn't take his eyes from Becky's crucifix. 'So I went to look for her. I kept . . . I kept this . . . to give it back to her. I walked all night . . .' His voice faltered.

Morris cleared his throat. 'He gave it to me. Some time later he gave it to me. I put it there. I knew . . .'

And then outside there was a burst of noise, shouting, car engines, doors slamming, an eruption of chaos. 'Police,' loudhailers cried, 'the house is surrounded.' Roger darted forward and brought his hand down hard on Agnes's. Her pistol fell to the floor. Agnes cried out, more in rage than pain, as she saw Ross kick her gun out of the way. Morris was out in the hall, shouting. 'There's hundreds, guns, cars—' and Roger ran to the window and cried, 'We've got a hostage—' and all the time Ross stood immobile, holding Agnes at gunpoint.

'We're armed,' Agnes heard Roger call out, then there was another burst of noise from outside, sirens blazing, tinny amplified voices. Jerry sat down heavily on Becky's bed, behind Ross. Agnes saw him lean forward to pick something up off the floor. He held it in his hand. The gun. Bill's gun. No, she tried to say, above the noise. Ross, she tried to say, look. Jerry rhythmically stroked the barrel, wrapped his fingers round the trigger, raised it to his head. An oddly peaceful expression settled on his face, as she found her voice, shouted, 'No, Jerry. No—' but he put it to his temple and fired.

Then there was silence. Blood drenched, brain-spattered silence. Ross whirled, slowed by horror, his mouth open for several seconds before a roar of grief erupted from him. The whole room seemed to be frozen in shock, and Agnes ran. She bolted down the stairs, hearing noise on all sides – were those footsteps behind her, or gunfire? She dragged the front door open and staggered out into a haze of police, felt herself somehow lifted up, carried away on a sea of questions. Yes, they're armed, one pistol, no two, but someone's

246

just shot himself, yes, dead. Is Lily all right, where's Sheila, and Steven? Sorry? Yes, Ross, Ross Turner, he's in there. Yes. The dead boy is the one who killed Becky, yes, Becky Stanton, are you listening to me . . .

A burst of noise, a flurry of voices. Then a single gunshot.

'Ross,' Agnes said.

There was a sudden, terrible silence. Then, out of the stillness, three police marksmen approached the front door, cautiously, silently. Two figures appeared in the doorway, and then slowly raised their hands in the air. Agnes watched as Roger and Morris stumbled down the drive into the waiting cars. She watched as a team of police swarmed into the house. She knew the awful horror they would find there, the scene of devastation that was about to meet their eyes.

Two bodies.

Satan had triumphed.

Chapter Twenty

It was pitch-dark. Agnes tethered her horse, brought out her torch and flashed it across the fence, looking for the new hole that Richard had described. Last time she was here the bottling plant had been bathed in moonlight. Now, it was a shadowy outline in the darkness. Her torch beam flashed across a line of newly cut barbed wire, and she climbed through. She listened. The wind rustled the trees. Then, a horse's whinny in the distance, answered by her own, close by. Agnes crept towards the factory, listening hard. Once by the outside wall, she dropped down behind it and waited.

The events of the day, which had culminated in such horror, seemed to have happened in some other time. It was now three in the morning, still only a few hours since Jerry had taken his own life with such violence, since Ross had chosen to join him. Crouching in the darkness, Agnes found herself living it again, the long, long moment in which Jerry seemed to topple sideways as his head exploded; the silence before Ross's reverberating cry, the bedlam, her escape.

Agnes sat on the damp earth in darkness, her mind invaded by the crimson-soaked candlewick bedspread. The stench of death. The way Jerry had smiled as he'd raised the gun to his head. She shivered, wondering if the memory would ever leave her, that smile that had twisted so horribly across Jerry's face as the life burst out of him.

The horse whinnied again, and she heard a woman's voice murmur to it. She crept closer, hugging the wall. She waited, straining to hear. Silence. Then the woman's voice. 'Let's just hope the dogs appreciate our little presents.' Agnes heard faint footsteps, and then in the distance a growl, another growl, then sudden stillness which seemed to last for several minutes. Then there was the sound of running, the shout of a security guard, and a sudden flare of torches criss-crossing the tarmac. Agnes peered through the darkness, hearing dogs barking, running footsteps, men shouting to each other, and – and wasn't that a woman's laughter? Then there she was, running back across the field to her horse, and Agnes followed. She saw a streak of shadow across the field below her, heard Lady's hooves pounding the earth. Agnes reached her horse, mounted and set off in a canter after her, the dogs snapping at her heels.

Her horse was eager, with a long, easy stride, and she realised that Emma wasn't far away. They turned into the edge of the woodland and Emma disappeared over a hedge, which Agnes jumped, too, a moment later. Agnes felt her muscles stretch, felt herself settle into the saddle, a surge of joy as she flew over another hedge, gaining on Emma with each stride. They were in the thick of the woods now, impossible to see anything at all, but she trusted to her horse to sense Lady up ahead, to enter the race with her. She could hear the rhythm of the hooves ahead, and she slowed a little, settling into a steady canter as the trees cleared and she could see a curving sweep of yellow lights ahead of them as they reached the road. She brought her horse back to a trot. She could see Emma clearly now, hear her clip-clopping on to the tarmac. Agnes halted, baffled at Emma riding so openly on to the main road. She dismounted, tethered her horse and made the last few yards on foot, keeping to the grass verge to silence her footsteps. At the top of the hill they came out on to the junction with the M25. Lady was walking in the middle of the road, floodlit by the lamplight, the motorway below them streaked with the sparse traffic. Agnes hesitated. To follow her now meant losing her cover altogether. She slipped back to the grass verge and hid herself behind the last few trees.

Emma halted, looked around, then dismounted. She whispered to Lady, took the reins over her head and led her down the slip road towards the junction itself. Agnes realised that the little lane they had just come up was the beginning of the planned motorway link, due to be part of the same four-lane road that the protesters had been trying to prevent. In that case, she realised, they were standing on the edge of Emily Quislan's land.

Emma had now got to the bottom of the junction and was clambering down a slope by the M25, her horse picking her way behind her. There was a van abandoned on the mud slope, and Emma went to it, unlocked the back and took out a heavy bundle. Agnes watched as she dodged across the six lanes of the motorway to the slip road on the other side, then climbed down to the edge of the road and positioned the explosives by a concrete pillar. Agnes could hear a car approaching along the lane behind her, as she thought, that's what Emma's doing. If Emily can't have her land, then no one else can either. She's going to blow up the road.

The approaching car came up behind her and stopped in a blaze of headlights. The lights went off. She heard the car door open and shut, heard footsteps, turned to see a towering shape, heard a voice whisper, 'You've got my pistol.'

'Bloody hell, Bill—'

'Did I frighten you?'

'No.'

'Is that your horse I passed?'

'Yes.'

'He's eating dockleaves. Not a good idea.'

'What you mean is, aren't I clever getting here before you. And no, I haven't got your pistol any more.'

'Typical. Come on,' he said.

They walked out on to the slip road, then down to the junction. Emma had come back to her horse, and was now squatting on the ground. She took off her gloves and began to dig with a trowel by the edge of the hard shoulder. As they got near her, Bill called out conversationally, 'Hello, Emma.'

She looked up, startled. She was remarkably pretty, with short, blonde-streaked hair and a neat, straight nose. Agnes and Bill jumped down to join her.

'There you are then, Emily Quislan,' Bill said.

'So it's you,' Emma said, eyeing him. 'I sussed ages ago that you were following me. Pretending to live in the forest . . .'

'Are you really going to blow up this road?' Bill said.

She smiled at him. 'Yes. And you're too late to stop me.'

Bill looked down at the hole she was digging, at the detonator she now unearthed. 'Will it do any good?'

'Of course it will. That's what I tried to tell the others but they wouldn't listen. Direct action, that's what you need.'

'Including murder? You've tipped half a chemical works into Richard Witham's spring water, and now you're aiming to blow a crater across this lot, just because you don't believe they should build the bypass?'

'It's not just that, is it,' Emma replied. 'They stole from Emily, they took her child, they took her land, they stole from me . . .' She swallowed, then carried on. 'Now they're stealing from us again, with their bulldozers ripping up the land, suffocating it, killing the planet. But I won't let them do it again.'

Bill sighed. 'This won't stop them. They'll just repair what you do—'

'And we'll do it again. It's a warning.'

'Like poisoning the water too?'

'Yeah.'

Bill said, 'Hasn't it occurred to you, it has the opposite effect? It makes those in power more determined, not less, if they think that someone's waging war on them.'

'They'll soon find out, then, won't they? We are the spirit. We have the earth on our side.'

'When you say "we",' Agnes said, 'really, there's just one of you, isn't there? Becky dropped out, Col dropped out—'

'I didn't need them anyway.'

Agnes looked at her hands, her nails lined with earth, bitten to the quick, at the lethal tube lying on the ground. She looked at Emma's determined young face. 'For a while,' Agnes said, 'I thought maybe you'd killed Becky.'

Emma picked up her trowel and continued to dig at the scrubby earth by the road.

'Emma,' Bill said, 'it won't work, will it? The damage you do can be repaired, and then they'll build the road, same as before. And by then you'll be in prison.'

Emma muttered something. Agnes heard the word, 'Emily.'

'What did you say?' Bill asked.

'I said, I'm Emily, not Emma.'

Agnes crouched down beside her. 'When did you become Emily?'

'I didn't become her, did I? I *am* her.'

252

Agnes hesitated, looked at Emma, at her hair swinging against her cheek with the movement of her trowel. Gently she said, 'When did they take your son away?'

Emma stared wide-eyed at Agnes, then returned to her digging.

'James, wasn't he? Like the other Emily's son.'

Emma stabbed at the earth.

'Emily had her James for nine years before they took him away. I don't suppose you got that long. Maybe a few hours?'

Emma's eyes flashed blue rage at Agnes. 'Bitch. That bitch. She said she wouldn't tell.'

'What, his name? The secret name you gave him before they took him away?'

'Only my mum knew. Bitch.'

'Why did you agree to have him adopted?'

Emma's eyes flickered. 'They made me. They convinced me it was for the best – "Think of your future, darling!" – when what they really meant was it was best for them, not for me, not for the baby . . .' She swallowed, then looked levelly at Agnes. She stood up, defiant again. 'And you think you're so fucking clever, don't you. Well, listen, whoever you are, you don't know the first thing about it.'

Agnes stood up too. 'When you found Becky dead, you did nothing. Jerry had followed you both, listened to your row, waited until you left her, and then he'd killed her. It was another couple of hours before her friends from the camp found her. And before that, you'd been there. You were first at the scene – and you told no one.'

'She was dead. What was there to do?'

'So, you weren't upset. She'd been your lover, but you weren't upset. You just sprinkled rosemary and left.'

Emma stared at the ground.

'You wanted her dead,' Agnes went on. It was more a statement than a question. Emma looked at Agnes with eyes that were blue like flint, and nodded.

'Would you have killed her?' Agnes asked.

Emma took a strand of hair into her mouth and chewed on it. Eventually she said, 'I didn't have to.'

'But Col was more of a problem,' Agnes said.

'Yes,' Emma agreed. 'I thought I'd have to get rid of him.'

'He was very helpful to you.'

'He knew too much. He bottled out.'

'Before you dyed Richard's spring?'

'Emily's well, you mean—'

'Emily's well, then. Before it got that far?'

'He helped me nick the stuff, from the RAF base. We hid it in the woods. Then when it came to it, he got scared.'

'So what happened?' Agnes was aware of Bill, standing near her, waiting for Emma to speak.

Emma sucked on her hair for a moment, then said, 'I told him I'd killed Becky. I told him he was going to die. And I was right, wasn't I?'

'You killed him,' Agnes said.

Emma looked at her. 'No,' she said, mildly.

'He had a weak heart. It was his fear that carried him off. Fear of you.'

At Agnes's shoulder, Bill murmured, 'Col died from asthma—'

'He'd have survived, wouldn't he, if he hadn't already been frightened half to death, if you, Emma, with all your silly games, hadn't convinced him his time was up.' Agnes's voice was tight with rage. 'All I know is, I'd hate to see what you see when you close your eyes to sleep.'

For a second, Emma faltered. Her eyes clouded. She looked suddenly vulnerable. She shifted on her feet. Then the moment passed. She looked back at Agnes and smiled.

Bill took a step towards her. 'We should be going.'

'I'm not going anywhere.' Emma was holding a kitchen timer. 'I can turn this back to zero.'

Agnes saw her fingers move on the dial, heard the clicking of the switch. She felt her stomach clench, looked at Bill, surprised by his calm.

'I wouldn't bother,' Bill said. 'I made it safe, earlier today. That's a dummy detonator.'

The dial clicked to zero. Agnes was unable to breathe. Nothing happened. Emma dropped to the ground, pulled at the wires of the detonator, her face expressionless. Slowly she stood up, her head bowed, her hands hanging at her sides. Behind her the yellow haze of the motorway was blurred with the dawn. In the silence they heard the whine of police cars. Emma looked up at Bill, smiled, and raised her hands. 'Go on, then, arrest me.' She walked towards Bill, her arms above her head. Then, as he was about to take hold of her, she bolted away from him, ran to her horse and mounted, as the sirens were upon them and cars screeched to a halt on the slip road above them. Bill was by the horse's legs, but she turned Lady towards the lane and cantered off. Agnes saw Bill draw a gun, saw him aim at the horse. He glanced at Agnes, looked back to Emma, then shrugged. He slipped the gun into his pocket and ambled back to where she stood.

'I've done my bit,' he said. He walked past Agnes to meet the police officers emerging from their cars, and after a moment two cars raced off down the lane, while other men began to cordon off the area.

Bill took Agnes's arm and they walked back to his car.

'Your friends keep you in armaments, then,' Agnes said.

Bill shrugged. 'How did you know she was coming here?'

'I didn't,' Agnes said. 'Richard tipped me off earlier today that someone had fiddled with the fence again; I knew I might find her at the spring, and then I thought, if I wanted to follow her I'd have to do it on horseback. So I hired a horse.'

'That easy, eh?'

'My friend Sheila helped me. Earlier this evening we called on a friend of hers, who keeps horses, and we explained everything to her.'

'And she lent you a horse in the middle of the night?'

'She could see it was urgent.'

'And how come you can ride?'

'Oh, that. Just a misspent youth.'

'You are a mystery, Little Sister.'

'And now it's your turn. How did you know she was coming here?'

Bill looked at her. 'That would be telling.'

'Yes.'

He looked beyond her, to the grey concrete, the flashing lights of the roadblock. 'It was my job. That's all. It's finished now.' He smiled. 'Fancy a drink?'

'What, whisky at this time of day?' Agnes said. 'Anyway, I've got my horse to see to.'

'If it's still alive,' laughed Bill.

At his car he paused, his head on one side. 'One day I'd really like to hear your story.'

'Maybe. One day. On condition you tell me yours – if MI5 let you.'

He smiled. 'We could meet for a drink some time?'

'Sure. Give me a ring.'

Agnes walked over to her horse and patted his neck. Bill called to her, 'I haven't got your phone number.'

Agnes put one foot in the stirrup. 'I can't imagine you'd let that get in your way.' She swung herself up into the saddle and set off up the lane at a trot, breaking into a canter as she turned along the bridle-path, as the sun flooded the fields around her with golden light.

Chapter Twenty-one

'So that was Saturday? And it's only Tuesday now. You have been busy, poppet,' Athena giggled. 'Hasn't she, Nic?'

Nic appeared in the doorway of Athena's living-room with two glasses of white wine. 'So it seems,' he said. 'Are you sure you won't have a glass, love?'

Athena shook her head. 'There's no point me pretending I'd enjoy it.' She raised her glass of mineral water and pulled a face.

'So it wasn't past lives at all,' Nic said, settling into an armchair next to Agnes.

'Not in that way, no,' Agnes said. 'Only in the way that the past imprints itself on the present.'

'Yes,' Nic said. 'But we all have to deal with that up to a point.'

'Emma's was an extreme case. There was a peculiar resonance between her own life and this ancestor of hers.'

'Mmm.' Nic nodded. 'And I guess finding out that stuff on top of being pretty unstable in the first place . . .'

Athena sipped her water. 'Those church people have a lot to answer for, don't they? That boy, the one who killed himself – terrible.'

'Yes. Terrible.' Agnes tried to block out the image that flashed into her mind.

'You'd think they'd be more tolerant. I bet Jesus wouldn't mind people being gay if He came back now, would He?'

'It's often disputed—'

'And they just pick and choose bits of the Bible to back up the most preposterous views on women having to be second-class citizens and it being wrong to be gay and . . . and that you can't even go shopping on Sundays, can you? Ridiculous.'

Agnes looked across at Athena. She looked well-groomed, and

was wearing a deceptively simple loose shirt in rust-coloured linen. But there was a pallor about her, a shadow around her eyes.

'And what happened to that girl, Lily, was it?' Athena was saying.

'I spoke to her mother yesterday. She seems OK. She's glad to be home, and she seems to be clear about what happened. But you can't unthink things you've thought, not overnight.'

'I suppose if something has seemed right but then you realise it's wrong—' Athena began, then glanced across at Nic.

Nic stood up. 'Anyone hungry? Lunch was hours ago. I'll see what's in the fridge.'

'Well, I'd lock them all away. For life,' Athena went on, as Nic left the room.

'Lock who away?'

'People like that Ross chappie.'

'But Athena—'

'Telling lies, trying to get everyone to follow him—'

'He might not have thought it was lies.'

'Nonsense.'

'He might have thought he'd discovered a wonderful truth and wanted to share it with as many people as possible.'

Athena stared at her friend. 'You can't really think that.'

'It happens.'

'But him? After all he did, trying to change people, making them hate the way they were, even trying to marry off his own lover—'

'Maybe he didn't see it that way.'

'Do you really have to forgive everyone?'

'It's not for me to forgive.'

'There must be some actions that you'd say were beyond forgiveness.'

'It's not for me to judge. It's for—'

'God?'

'Yes.'

'But killing someone else . . .'

Agnes sensed a haunting uncertainty about her friend, an undertow of anguish. 'You see,' she said, 'Jerry hated himself. For whatever reasons. And I think, while he could believe that Satan was everything bad, he was OK. And then when he did kill, he thought that would make it all better, because it really was Satan he was killing.' Agnes sighed. 'In the end, killing himself or killing someone else – it was all the same.'

Athena muttered something. Agnes caught the words, 'someone else'. 'Did you say something?' she asked.

'No, sweetie,' Athena said brightly, as Nic appeared in the doorway. 'Nic, dear, do you know, I think I might have a teensy-weensy drop of wine after all.'

Some time later, after a supper of cheese omelette, Agnes set off for home. It was barely ten o'clock. Perhaps it will be all right, she thought, walking along the Fulham Road, watching the chic crowds jostling outside the cafés, the lithe T-shirted young people. Perhaps everything really does turn out for the best. Perhaps God meant Jerry to shoot himself. Perhaps it was part of His plan that Emma should be driven mad by having her baby adopted. Perhaps it was part of an ongoing process of redemption that Becky should be killed, that Sam should end up back on the streets, that Tom should spend the rest of his life looking for his daughter. And that Athena should . . . Agnes allowed herself to be distracted by a group of large teenage girls singing 'Dancing in the Street', linking arms and trying not to fall over as they crossed the road.

Since the events of Saturday, Agnes had stayed in her flat, alone, only venturing out for the odd pint of milk. On Sunday she was expected at her community, but she'd spoken to Madeleine and explained that she simply wasn't up to it. Instead she'd sat at home by the phone, waiting for it to ring, wondering whether she'd ever see Tom, or Sam, again. Once she'd tried the hostel number scrawled on Col's bus ticket, but a voice had said, 'Nah, mate. Not 'ere. 'E left 'ere last week sometime. Nah, can't 'elp ya.'

On Monday morning, Julius had phoned.

'Tell me, Agnes,' he'd said, 'did it involve the firing of pistols this time?'

'No. Yes. Well, sort of.'

'Sort of? How very reassuring. And how are you?'

'Julius, you remember how this all began? How Sam ran away from us, and I was so preoccupied in looking for her that my Provincial suggested I move somewhere else?'

'Yes.'

'Well, nothing's changed. Sam's back on the streets, again because of me, and I'm determined to find her, and my fellow Sisters, according to Madeleine, are far from happy. I'm a terrible person, Julius. Becky's dead, Col's dead, Jerry's dead, Ross is dead, and I've learned absolutely nothing.'

'Agnes, at the beginning of all this you were angry. You were burning up with anger, and scorching most of us who got in your way. You were hostile, inflexible, dogmatic and it was a tribute to my spiritual training that I was able to feel any affection for you at all.' Agnes heard the chuckle in his voice, then he was serious again. 'And are you still angry, Agnes?' Julius asked. 'Are you still blaming God for your own folly in making Him in an image of your own?'

Agnes had hesitated. Her mind unfolded a dance before her, of Jerry toppling sideways, bathed in blood; of Emma's hair swinging at her cheek by the side of the M25; of Tom Bevan limping down Mike's drive.

'No,' she'd said to Julius. 'No, I'm not angry any more.'

Now she walked along the Embankment, feeling the evening breeze against her face, scenting the stirrings of autumn in the air. She thought of her father. Methodically, she recalled him; fingering the yellow pages of his first editions; pouring thick black coffee in the morning; turning away as her mother complained of something, some failing, some untidiness; frowning as he opened a stack of bills; laughing as his daughter danced for him. Driving on the gravel in the rain.

No, she thought. No, I'm not angry any more.

It was nearly midnight when she got home. She was just brushing her teeth when the phone rang. She picked it up, glancing out of the window, seeing the familiar bearded figure in the call box.

'Tom – thank God!'

'I'm down here again.'

'Come up—'

'No, come down, I need you. I've found her, but I need you.'

They set off into the night, Agnes tying her raincoat belt around her waist as Tom took her arm, his eyes shining with the urgency of his mission.

'She doesn't know I've seen her. I tried on Sunday. I found her down Leicester Square. She was with them girls. She pretended she hadn't seen me.' His eyes were moist.

'Where is she now?' Agnes asked.

'Kings Cross. Her friend said she'd gone up there.'

Agnes was walking fast to keep up with him. 'Tom – are you sure this'll work?'

He turned his face to her. 'You're here, see? She trusts you.'

Tom, Agnes wanted to say – I can't make her something she doesn't want to be. She saw a cab turning into London Bridge Station and hailed it.

They walked up York Way, Agnes glad of Tom's tight grip on her arm. The huge gasometers made ornate skeletal curves against the sky. Under the railway arches Agnes could see the smoke and flames of bonfires, cars slowing, braking, thin legs silhouetted in the glare of headlights. As they approached, a couple of young men emerged from the shadows, nodded at Tom, walked by. Tom led the way into the smoky darkness. His leg touched a bottle and someone looked up at the noise, a pale young face, eyes briefly flickering with interest before looking down again as Tom and Agnes passed.

Suddenly he froze. 'There,' he whispered. A group of three girls in tiny skirts and high heels clustered together by the side of the road. Agnes could just make out someone who might be Sam amongst them. Tom was staring fixedly at her, then slowly he approached the group.

'Oh my God,' Agnes heard Sam say. She was arm in arm with another girl, both tottering on their shoes. 'Oh Christ.' Then seeing Agnes, she said accusingly, 'What are you doing here?'

'You've got to listen,' Tom said, his deep voice almost a whisper.

Sam rolled her eyes, shifted on her shoes.

Agnes said, 'We've got a deal, Sam. He's to say his piece now, and then he'll go, OK? He'll leave you alone.' She felt Tom next to her, but persisted, 'After tonight, you can forget you ever had a father.'

Sam shrugged, waited. Her friends melted away towards the cars.

Tom took a step towards her. 'Sam – I'm your dad.' Sam looked at the ground. 'I always have been. When Linda had you . . . all I

know is, when Nicky told me you were my baby girl, it was like I'd
known all along. And from then on, there wasn't a waking moment
when you weren't in my thoughts. I'm not like the others, Sam,
I'm not like your stepdad. I'm your dad, Sam.'

Sam glanced at Tom, and for a second recognition flashed
between them, the same clear grey eyes, the same dark eyelashes.
Then she looked away. Tom went on, 'I'll care for you, Sam.'

Sam chewed her lip. The breeze wafted smoke around them.
'Can I go now?' she said at last.

'Sam, I'll look after you.'

'I don't fuckin' need it,' she said.

'But Sam—' Tom's voice cracked.

'S'too late,' she said.

'And what if I need you?' he whispered, hoarsely.

'You ain't got nothing, though,' she said. 'You ain't even got a
home.'

'And you have?' he replied.

She shrugged, scuffed one pointed shoe against the pavement.

Tom looked beyond her. He saw the filthy street, the pale young
faces, the mini-skirted legs against the dazzle of headlamps. His
face glowed with anger. 'This, you mean?'

Sam looked at him, shrugged, turned away. 'Can I go now?' she
said.

'Sure,' he said. 'It's your life.' Sam glanced back at him. He
gestured to the scene before them. 'There you are, then,' he said.
'Yours for the taking. I know all about it, because, you see, it's
mine too. Look,' he said. 'See the woman there, the old one,
flaunting herself to that john, nothing to lose? Give yourself another
few years, Sam. One day, kid, all this will be yours.' She hesitated,
looked at him. 'You're right,' he went on, 'you want to get back to
work. No doubt there's some boy ready to slap you if you don't.
Who am I to argue, eh? These are your people, Sam. These are my
people too. We belong here. Tomorrow I'll blag my first drink for
five years, and after that, I'll be singing and swaying by the fire like
that geezer over there. I'll be happy like him. Won't I?'

Sam blinked against the smoke. 'I ain't stuck here, right? This is
just for now.'

'Oh, I see. And then what?'

Sam faced him. 'There's just me, right? I ain't relyin' on no one no more.'

Tom reached out his hand towards her. 'Try me,' he said. She took a step back. Tom spoke again, and his deep bass voice seemed to echo with the rumble of the distant trains. 'The thing is, kid, you and me, we know these streets. No one else is going to understand, not like we do. You see – I know your demons, girl, 'cos they're the same as mine. I know what it's like to scrape a razor-blade across your wrist just to find out if you can still feel. You watch the blood and you think, I'm still here, then.' Sam shifted her feet, pulled her little denim jacket around her. 'These streets – we've made ourselves at home here, ain't we? Cosy, innit?' He stepped towards her, and this time she didn't move. 'Without you, kid, this is my home. Without me, this is where you'll stay. But together . . . together we stand a chance. That's all it is, a fighting chance. But it's better than nothing.' He turned to her, his face alight with love, and Agnes, watching, saw Sam recognise in the lines of his face and the passion in his eyes something she'd been yearning for all her life without even knowing. Sam looked at Tom, scanning his face, taking in every line, every scar, every hair. Then she shook her head.

'It ain't gonna work, is it?' Her eyes filled with tears, and she moved away from him.

'Sam – please—' He took her hand but she shook him off.

'I don't know you,' she said.

'I'm better than nothing.'

'You ain't got nothin'.' She took a few steps from him, towards the waiting cars. Agnes saw her go, saw the harsh realism of her youth next to the innocence that Tom had learned with age. She cleared her throat, said to Sam, to Tom, 'I'll find you somewhere.'

Tom looked at her with his childlike eyes. Sam glanced back to her. 'Another bleedin' hostel—'

'A flat.'

Sam looked at Agnes. 'You're just sayin' it, ain't ya, just so's you don't have to feel responsible for me bein' back 'ere. I've 'ad it, right? Can't you see? I'm done wiv all that.' She turned away from them both and went back to her friends, her heels scraping the pavement. Tom watched her go, his fists clenched at his sides, as a car drew up beside her.

'If that fuckin' scum so much as speaks to her,' he snarled. Sam glanced back, hesitated, then walked away from the road, away from the cars, disappearing into the shadows of the crumbling brickwork. Tom wandered over to the fire. Agnes joined him. They sat in silence, watching people come and go, a fight flare up, two men squaring up, fists and abuse flying before someone intervened and the night grew calm again. Agnes wasn't sure how long they'd sat there, but she knew she was feeling chilled and stiff, despite the warmth of the night, the heat from the fire. Some time later, she was aware of someone watching them. Sam was standing on the other side of the fire. She came and sat down next to Tom. No one spoke. After a while Tom took Sam's hand. Sam didn't move. He pushed the cuff of her jacket up her wrist and looked at the scars she'd left there, rough red lines criss-crossing the skin. He traced the marks with his finger. Sam sat, immobile, looking beyond to where the railway lines stretched away into the fading night.

'What do you mean, Kathleen's flat?' Madeleine said to Agnes on the phone later that morning. 'It's nothing to do with us.'

'We paid a retainer on it, right? The order did?'

'Yes, but—'

'And now she's moving into sheltered housing before it expires?'

'Yes, but we'll just reclaim the money—'

'We bloody won't. I've got two very deserving causes who need that flat.' Agnes looked across at Tom and Sam who were sitting on her rug giggling over a rather haphazard game of chess.

'But that means the order must—'

'Fine, that's settled then. Bless you, Madeleine. I'll pop into the office later to sort out the details.'

Agnes hung up. 'That's sorted then. A two-bedroomed flat not far from here, over in Bermondsey. Ground floor, access to garden, riverside views.'

'Checkmate,' Tom said, and Sam laughed.

'Well, you are a fairy-godmother,' Bill said that evening. 'Can you rustle me up a Porsche out of this ash-tray?'

They were sitting in a bistro in Clerkenwell, surrounded by high white walls with touches of matt black. Agnes was wearing her black silk jacket and trousers and a crisp white shirt. She smiled. 'I reckon that ash-tray probably cost more than a Porsche in the first place.'

'Shall we nick it, then?'

'It's against my religion, I'm afraid.'

'It must be nice to have rules,' Bill said, suddenly thoughtful. 'I used to have all that, but—'

A milky-skinned waitress with bright red lips arrived to take their order.

'But what?' Agnes said, once they'd chosen goat's cheese salad with roasted red peppers, followed by Thai fish parcels.

'Sorry?' Bill took his eyes from the departing form of their waitress, her starched mini-apron and long black leggings.

'You said you used to have rules.'

'Oh. Yes.'

'So, what happened?'

'It wasn't so much rules, as knowing what you believed. Love, peace, sex, drugs and rock and roll. We had such optimism, you know? The world was going our way.'

Agnes looked at him. His hair was trimmed, he was wearing a well-cut shirt, and the stubble on his chin had gone.

'What are you thinking?' he said.

She took a sip of Australian Chardonnay. 'I was rather missing your beard.'

He rubbed his chin. 'It'll grow again.'

Their food arrived. Agnes tasted a mouthful of cheese, then said, 'So if you're so into love and peace, how come you're allowing someone to employ you to spy on anti-road protesters?'

'It's a long story. And boring. Yours is much more interesting.'

'That's for me to judge. Something must have disillusioned you at some point?'

'You find anyone of my generation who hasn't suffered some kind of cosmic disappointment.'

'Yes, but, specifically—'

Bill broke a piece of bread in two. 'I suppose it all went wrong after Melanie. I was crazy about her, we had a kid, though we didn't live together. She fell in love with someone else when Simon was fourteen. They live in Melbourne now.'

'That's the problem with women, isn't it? You chaps organise a groovy sexual revolution, they all go on the pill – and then they let you down by wanting to have kids and join the bourgeoisie.'

'So the sexual revolution passed you by?'

'I spent most of it incarcerated in a French château being abused by my then husband.'

Bill blinked. 'No wonder you're a nun.'

Agnes smiled. 'Yes. In the end, I have that to thank Hugo for.'

Bill speared a black olive. 'When I met you, you didn't appear to be someone who'd found their true path.'

'And now?'

Bill considered her, his head on one side. 'Mmm. Better, maybe. I wouldn't say cured.'

'No. Neither would I.'

'What are you going to do?'

'What do you mean?'

'When we met, you seemed so angry with everything. I couldn't imagine you staying in your order for much longer.'

Agnes took another sip of wine. She wondered how he'd managed to steer the conversation back to her. 'Do they train you to do that, in MI5? How to avoid giving anything away, by asking your interrogators searching questions about themselves?'

Bill shook his head. 'No. I'm asking you because I want to know.' His eyes darkened as he looked at her. Agnes was glad they were interrupted by the main course arriving.

'OK,' Bill said suddenly. 'Seeing as you asked. But it is boring. My dad was a military chap, quite high up. Sent me to the best schools, was outraged when I dropped out. We didn't speak for years. Then there was the eighties. I needed dough, got into the warehouse party scene, raves, that stuff. It was great. And he fell ill, and I felt bad about him, and we got to kind of talking again. And now we're not bad. In some ways, we're quite alike. And someone he knew was worried about this Emily Quislan scene. So I agreed to help. God knows why. I was intrigued, I suppose.'

'And the Superhighwayman?'

Bill rubbed his chin again. 'I'm afraid—' He stopped, then said, 'It took me a while to work out who the enemy was.'

'Did all that tuning in and dropping out wipe out all morality with it, or were you born that way?'

'Don't be too hard on me, Princess. When I first picked Emily up on the Net I couldn't believe she was on her own. We thought she was part of something bigger.'

'We did, did we? So what's the next assignment, 007?'

Bill shook his head. 'My father thinks it's all cut and dried. Us and Them. I shan't be doing this kind of thing again.' He took a mouthful of food. 'You don't believe me,' he said.

Agnes studied him. 'I'm not sure,' she replied. 'It's roughly what I thought.'

'Complete with military father?'

'I hadn't got that bit, no. But then, don't ask me about fathers.' Agnes yawned.

Bill was looking at her. 'Do you remember, I once said I envied you.'

'Probably just before you dumped me in a field in the middle of the night with an eco-terrorist on the loose—'

'I've already said I'm sorry for that.'

'Why did you vanish?'

'Am I always going to be in the wrong?'

'Until you've redeemed yourself in my eyes, yes.'

'It might take years, that.'

'I'm waiting.'

He smiled, then said, 'I felt a fool, to be honest. You were following the same trail as me, asking the same questions, and it seemed stupid not to involve you. And then there we were in that field, with Emily doing her bit, and I suddenly realised I couldn't possibly explain. I couldn't tell you what I was doing there. And then I thought, Emma might have done something really dangerous too. I had to go and see without dragging you into it. So I went.' He grinned at her, then said, 'And anyway, I knew you could look after yourself. Am I redeemed yet?'

Agnes studied him. 'Hmm. Not sure. And what's going to happen to Emma Lees?'

Bill sighed. 'They caught her. She'll be sent down.'

'What for?'

'Explosives, trespass, conspiracy—'

'How did she get the stuff?'

'Her father runs an engineering company involved in quarrying. He was working on a site over towards Colchester, she was "helping" him one day. With her van. Made off with several pounds of Gelamex.'

'Maybe she wants to be sent down. Maybe that's what she needs, some time out of life, to take stock, stop fighting.'

Bill took a sip of wine, and then looked at her. 'You sound envious.'

'Me?'

'Maybe we should both do some kind of criminal damage and end up inside.'

'Your life's OK—'

'Oh yeah? No kid, no family, no job, and anyway, none of that would matter if I had your – your faith, really. That's what I envy you.'

Agnes shook her head. 'We're not that different. It's just being human. If God was to send an angel now to tell us what to do, how simple life would be. Old Gabriel could tell me that a Yorkshire boarding school would be just fine, he could tell you to retrain as a management consultant and join a dating agency for glamorous forty-something executives, and we'd just do it. As it is, we're all floundering around in the dark, faith or no faith.'

'We wouldn't even believe him anyway, we'd think it was some kind of performance art stunt laid on by the management here.'

Agnes laughed. 'Speak for yourself. Angels are big in my tradition.'

Bill wiped his plate clean with a piece of bread. 'Maybe management consultancy isn't a bad idea.' He drained his wine glass. 'And Agnes – do you think my kind of woman would join an executive forty-something dating agency?'

Later they walked towards Holborn in search of a cab.

'Will I see you again?' Bill asked her.

'I hope so,' Agnes replied. 'If Gabriel visits, remember to ask him what I should do too.'

'No,' Bill laughed, waving madly at a distant taxi. 'You're OK, you are. If you know you're floundering in the darkness, then you aren't. It's those of us who mistake darkness for light that you have to worry about.'

The cab drew up and she opened the door, then hesitated.

'Actually,' he said, 'all Gabriel's going to say to me is, throw away your razor.' He bent and kissed her on the cheek.

'So angels are into designer stubble too?' Agnes laughed, getting into the cab.

'Absolutely,' Bill said. 'That's all the theology I know.' As the cab pulled away, Agnes looked back to see him wave, then he turned and sauntered away towards Farringdon Road.

Chapter Twenty-two

When Agnes appeared in Julius's office two days later, he got up from his desk and hugged her.

'I've been worried about you,' he said. 'Coffee?'

'Yes, please.'

'If I can find anything drinkable amongst Madeleine's camomile nonsense,' he grumbled, rummaging along the shelf by the kettle.

'You know,' Agnes said, 'there's no need to worry about me.'

'Don't be silly,' Julius replied, peering at the label on a tin. 'Who else is going to?'

Agnes sat at her desk. 'Anyway, I've been fine.'

'Cornering dangerous young people, challenging crazy teenagers armed with explosives, and then walking the streets of Kings Cross until you can find someone worthy of your assistance, and not just spiritual but financial too—'

'What's Madeleine been saying?'

'She thought it was hilarious, you insisting that the order keep that flat. No, not Madeleine.'

'Who, then?'

Julius sighed. 'You don't do yourself any favours, Agnes.'

'How come you know all about it? I spent all yesterday in meetings with my provincial team, and you're the first to hear. Perhaps you can tell me what they've decided?'

'I've no idea. Really, Agnes, all I know is from interrogating Madeleine because I hadn't heard from you and I was worried and—'

'They're adamant that I'd be better off away from the hostel for a while.'

'And what do you think?'

Agnes stirred a spoon round and round in her coffee. 'I'm tired, you see. I'm getting to the point where I'm too tired to argue.'

'Does that mean you'll go? To Yorkshire, I mean?'

'You're as keen to get rid of me as the rest of them.'

Julius smiled. 'You know I'll miss you. But it is only for a year or two. And it is more peaceful than all this—'

'And why does everyone think I want peace? I had peace for fifteen years in my enclosed order, it drove me mad. I like it here.'

'That's just the point.'

Agnes ran her fingers through her hair. 'I know, I know, it's not about what I want. It's about what God wants. But if He knew me at all, He'd know that I simply can't survive in temperatures below twenty degrees. And that anyone under ten years old brings out the absolute worst in me.'

Julius smiled. 'Perhaps they'll give you the sixth form.'

Agnes stared into her coffee. 'Julius – what do you think I should do?'

'Pray.'

Agnes sighed. 'I knew you'd say that.'

The following evening, Agnes was sitting quietly at home. It was Saturday, 2 September, and the summer had retreated in the face of a chilly autumn drizzle which now pattered against her window as night fell. She had a book open in front of her, but the words swam unread before her. Her mind roved restlessly over the events of the last few days. She wondered whether she'd always created conflict around her; perhaps there was a clear path from the horror that she'd witnessed at the Stanton house a week ago right back through the violence of her marriage to the silent battleground she'd inhabited as a child. She tried to think of a time in her life when she hadn't been at the centre of conflict. Perhaps when she'd first joined her enclosed order, when, shell-shocked by her married years, she had meekly succumbed to the routine and restraint of convent life. Until she'd emerged again.

She picked up her book, and was just finding her place when there was a buzzing at her intercom, followed by an insistent knocking on her front door. She opened the door, wondering what the hell was going on. Athena fell into the flat. She looked terrible, rain-soaked, her face a ghastly pallor, her eyes circled with dark shadows.

Agnes held her. 'Athena?' But she knew what had happened.

'I couldn't go on with it,' Athena sobbed. 'I couldn't pretend a moment longer. I've – I went to the . . . Oh God . . .'

Agnes held her in her arms, feeling her wet hair against her face, while Athena sobbed as if she might die. Agnes helped her to her bed and Athena fell on to it face down, still weeping. 'And it was horrible,' she cried into the bedspread, 'horrible white coats, and the floor was . . . and all I could think was that it was a baby and I was going to do this thing, and then I had an injection and I went all woozy . . .' She burst into renewed sobs.

Agnes sat next to her. After a while she took hold of Athena's hand. Her throat felt restricted. Her eyes were dry. She cleared her throat. 'Do you want anything?' she said. 'Tea? Whisky?'

Athena shook her head. 'I just want the pain to stop . . .'

Agnes felt irritated. At least if she wanted a drink it would give me something to do, she thought. I knew this would happen. I knew she'd feel like this. I was right all along.

Athena went quiet. Slowly, she sat up, fingering damp locks of hair. She looked at Agnes. 'You think I've done the wrong thing,' she said. She took a tissue and wiped the tears from her cheeks. 'Because you can see what I've done. You can see that I've . . .' She swallowed. 'But what you can't see – what you can't see, is that despite the pain and the bleeding and the horrible white coat I had to wear and the filthy floor . . .' She took another tissue and blew her nose. She found her bag and rummaged inside it looking for a comb. Then she looked up. 'What you can't see is – I've done the right thing.'

A strange calm descended upon the room. Agnes stared at her friend. She could think of nothing to say.

At seven o'clock on Sunday morning, Agnes woke up. The sun was pouring through her window. Agnes lay in bed, wondering why she felt so alert after only three or four hours' sleep. She pulled the covers over her head, hoping vaguely to go back to sleep. But the thought of Athena was too intense, too real, to shut out.

She thought about how they'd sat in silence, sipping whisky. Then, tentatively she'd asked about Nic, and they'd talked a bit about whether he'd mind, and how Athena was going to tell him, and Agnes felt angry for Nic then, at having his child removed from the world with no consultation, but, finding herself lost for words in the face of Athena's quiet resolve, she'd just drunk more whisky instead. At last she'd asked Athena why she'd come; why did you choose me to tell first, she'd said; and Athena said, because you're my best friend. Because there was nowhere else to go.

Lying in bed, Agnes thought about this. Athena had come to her, knowing that she, Agnes, would have no choice but to judge her harshly. But she'd come to her anyway in the certainty that she'd done the right thing. You're my best friend, she'd said.

Later, after several cups of tea, Agnes had called her a mini-cab. They'd stood in the street saying goodbye, and Agnes had suddenly hugged Athena, holding her for long minutes while the cab-driver sat bewildered with the car door open. And only then did Agnes feel her eyes, which had been dry all evening, well with tears.

'Who are you crying for?' Athena had whispered.

Agnes had shaken her head, unsure whether it was the baby, or Athena, or herself.

'For me or the baby?' Athena asked. Agnes shook her head again. 'Cry for the baby, not for me,' Athena had murmured. 'Someone must mourn for the baby.'

At a quarter to eight, Agnes appeared in Julius's church for the early Mass. She sat in the Lady Chapel, the first to arrive. She felt as if she was about to weep, but feared that once she started she might wail in great howls of grief. She looked at the representation of Mary in the stained-glass window, dressed in sun-filled blue, her arms spread out as if to embrace the world below her. 'And would you judge Athena?' Agnes asked her. 'You who were brave enough to carry your child to term in extraordinary circumstances, would you judge a woman harshly for being less than you?'

She heard Julius's footsteps cross the church. Agnes knelt on the prayer cushion, her head bowed. She thought of Mary the Madonna, holding aloft her precious new baby; then, years later, at the foot of the Cross when the body of Jesus was brought down, carrying her dead son. You whose destiny it was, Agnes thought, to bear that life, yet also to bear the ending of that life, to hold your own child in your arms, to share all the pity of human experience in your own. Someone must mourn for the baby, Agnes heard again, as tears came to her eyes. Mary, Mother of God, pray for Athena's baby. And for Athena; and for the whole damn lot of us, for Becky and Col, for Jerry, for Ross, for Morris and Shirley living with their terrible grief. And for all those lives that, like Athena's baby, briefly graced the world with their presence before moving on, for all lives cut short by violence, by war or famine, for the whole bloody, misguided, crazy, passionate, beautiful mess that is humanity itself – have mercy on us all.

Julius, about to ring the bell, glanced at Agnes. She was kneeling three rows back. A shaft of sunlight touched the edge of her hair, flecked the tears on her cheeks with blue. He gazed at her, joining her reverie with his own, until the beeping of his watch reminded him it was time to start the Mass.

Chapter Twenty-three

Agnes was glad of her Wellington boots. Tramping up a mud-washed windswept hill somewhere in Suffolk, in search of a celebration of the September equinox, she wished she'd worn two pairs of socks. It occurred to her she should have warned Athena about socks. And, she thought, she should have given Nic more detailed directions about the route they should take. Still, they'd probably found some charming little restaurant on the way instead. Agnes wrapped her raincoat tighter around her and strode on towards distant shouts and snatches of music.

Arriving at the top she was cheered by the sight of a huge bonfire, a crowd of people. She could pick out several familiar faces. Rona appeared and hugged her, and Jenn, and Jeff, who was playing the guitar, nodded. Paz waved at her from a tree where he was trying to rig up a makeshift tent with a couple of tarpaulins. Further off were the drummers, already setting up an insistent beat as the sky changed slowly from pink to indigo, and the sun set behind the drizzly clouds.

Agnes began to help Sheila wrap potatoes in foil and bury them in the ashes around the fire, endless numbers of potatoes it seemed, as the sky grew dark and more people arrived. Some friends of Sheila's arrived with a baby, and Lily immediately snatched the baby up and insisted on carrying it about.

'Uh-oh,' Sheila laughed. 'Her next enthusiasm.'

'Could be worse,' Agnes replied.

Sheila looked at her, then squeezed her hand. 'Certainly could,' she murmured.

Paz and Jenn reappeared dragging a supermarket trolley containing several cases of wine.

'Where did they get that?' Sheila said.

'I don't know about the trolley, but the wine is my contribution,' Agnes said.

'This is the Agnes equinox, is it?' Rona laughed.

'It's slumming it a bit for us,' Paz said. 'Usually we only drink champagne.'

As night fell, they lit huge candles, and Agnes saw Tom Bevan arrive with Sam, and Mike Reynolds too. Mike shook her hand.

'I gather from these two that you're a remarkable woman,' he said to her.

'No, I'm just in a privileged position,' she replied.

'I've never seen either of them so happy.'

Agnes looked across to the fire. Tom was pouring a glass of wine for Sheila, who was holding the baby. Sam and Lily were admiring each other's earrings.

'I'm sorry I had to lie to you,' Mike said.

'It was in a good cause,' Agnes smiled.

'No, but you must have thought I was a complete prat.'

'Well, not really a prat, but—'

'I'm afraid I'm the only person she's allowed to call a prat,' came a voice behind them.

Agnes turned, and smiled. 'How's the Angel Gabriel?' she said.

'No sign so far. How about you?' Bill smiled and hugged her. When she turned back, Mike had drifted to the fire where someone handed him a potato.

'Honestly,' came a female voice, 'I wish Agnes had bothered to tell me it would involve cross-country hiking, it's bloody typical . . . Sweetie, there you are, look at these shoes, ruined . . .'

'Never mind,' Nic was saying, 'it'll give you an excuse to buy some new ones.'

Athena sighed. 'But these were suede, and such a sweet shade of fuchsia, irreplaceable, darling, they're a perfect match with this jacket . . .' She kissed Agnes on each cheek, looked at Bill, then looked back at Agnes, one eyebrow almost imperceptibly raised.

'This is Bill,' Agnes smiled. 'He – um – I met him when – um—'

'Really, darling, for a nun you're just like the rest of us. Any chance of a drink?' Athena turned to Nic, who wandered off into the crowd. 'Oh, I remember,' she went on, 'you mean your baby anarchists and happy-clappy murderers? She told me all about it, you know,' she said, smiling warmly at Bill, as Nic reappeared with a couple of cups. Athena took a sip.

'Gosh,' she said, looking at her cup. She took another sip. 'I had no idea these people would know about wine.'

Bill laughed. 'Without Agnes here,' he said, 'we'd all be drinking boiled nettles.'

'That's what I thought,' Athena said.

'Or single malt whisky,' Agnes said to Bill.

Later there was just the drumming and the music, the smoke from the fires, the warmth from the dancing, the darkness of the night. Bill found Agnes again, and they sat and watched the pulsating, flickering crowd.

'Did you sort out your future?' he said to her.

'I've told my Provincial that I'm prepared to do whatever she thinks fit.'

'A big step, for you, I imagine.'

'I wrote her a letter and then I didn't post it for two days.'

'Did you apologise for being stubborn?'

'Yes. I did actually.'

'But only in the first draft,' he smiled.

Agnes looked at him. 'Have you sent the Angel Gabriel to spy on me, or did you hack into my typewriter?'

He laughed. 'Some things are obvious. So, what's to become of you?'

'What do you think of me living in a convent boarding school and teaching French?'

'I think it's most unlikely,' he said. 'But then, who are we to argue with old Gabriel?'

They both gazed across at the crowd, the dancing and the flames and the guttering candles under the trees.

'Do you think you'll be happy?' Bill said.

Agnes could see Athena and Nic sitting side by side on a tree-stump, next to Sheila and Tom. Athena, surprisingly, was holding the baby, dandling him on her knee, arranging his little hat at an angle and admiring it. She held him out to Nic to admire too, and Nic smiled, and took the baby, and then kissed her on the cheek. Athena stared into the fire, and her face through the smoke looked old. Agnes saw Nic hand the baby to Sheila, and then turn back to Athena. He took her face in both hands, and she looked at him and tried to smile. He said something to her, and she took his hands from her face and kissed him.

Agnes turned to Bill. 'Happy? Is anyone really happy?'

'Well, what then?'

'Acceptance. If I can learn that, I'll be getting somewhere.'

Much later, as the potatoes were eaten and the fire began to die down, Agnes slipped away. She left them all there, Athena and Nic and Bill and Sam and Tom and Sheila and Lily and Mike, and descended the hill as the drumming faded and the sky behind the trees grew pink with the new day.